"A haunting and passionate evocation of a strange Victorian Age twisted out of true from the one we know by dark magics and darker secrets . . . lyrical, compassionate, and complex, it should help to confirm Ian MacLeod's reputation as one of the very best writers working in the genre here at the beginning of the twenty-first century."

—Gardner Dozois

"Beautifully written, complex . . . should hold great appeal to readers who love the more sophisticated fantasy of Michael Swanwick, John Crowley, or even China Miéville."

—*Publishers Weekly* (starred review)

"The novel's industrial alternative London echoes Dickens in its rich bleakness and M. John Harrison's *Viriconium* in its inventive Gothic complexity. A gripping page-turner. A hearty read. Rising star Ian R. MacLeod offers an original political fable rivaling in ambition and execution the very best of today's new science fantasies." —Michael Moorcock

"Really, I don't know what to say. *The Light Ages* is a wonderful book, a magical book." —Gene Wolfe

"Excellent. Ian MacLeod is rapidly becoming one of the contemporary stars of the genre." —Brian W. Aldiss

continued . . .

"*The Light Ages* is simply first rate. I'm a sucker for this kind of literate, colorful, imaginative fantasy. The writing is instantly compelling. I was submerged in the setting and characters; it's escape fiction in the best sense of that phrase. It's a long book, but it was over far too quickly."

—James P. Blaylock

"Channeling Dickens by way of Coleridge, *The Light Ages'* magic derives as much from the high quality of Ian R. MacLeod's prose as any supernatural element. MacLeod has transformed London, while retaining its essential character, for a story as beautifully strange as it is emotionally affecting. Stands beside the achievements of China Miéville. *The Light Ages* is a must-read."

—Jeff VanderMeer

"MacLeod's descriptive powers are so effective that you can visualize every detail . . . MacLeod skillfully incorporates literary influences ranging from William Blake and Dickens to *1984* and the working-class novels of the 1950s—and arrives at something original. Magical, visionary, and enthralling, *The Light Ages* is award-winning stuff."

—SFX

"Dickensian, melancholy, full of smoky vistas and moments of contrasting sunshine, MacLeod's book is simply the best fantasy novel since Miéville's *Perdido*."

—Paul Di Filippo, *Science Fiction Weekly*

THE LIGHT AGES

IAN R. MacLEOD

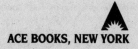

ACE BOOKS, NEW YORK

THE BERKLEY PUBLISHING GROUP
Published by the Penguin Group
Penguin Group (USA) Inc.
375 Hudson Street, New York, New York 10014, USA

Penguin Group (Canada), 10 Alcorn Avenue, Toronto, Ontario M4V 3B2, Canada
(a division of Pearson Penguin Canada Inc.)
Penguin Books Ltd., 80 Strand, London WC2R 0RL, England
Penguin Group Ireland, 25 St. Stephen's Green, Dublin 2, Ireland (a division of Penguin Books Ltd.)
Penguin Group (Australia), 250 Camberwell Road, Camberwell, Victoria 3124, Australia
(a division of Pearson Australia Group Pty. Ltd.)
Penguin Books India Pvt. Ltd., 11 Community Centre, Panchsheel Park, New Delhi—110 017, India
Penguin Group (NZ), Cnr. Airborne and Rosedale Roads, Albany, Auckland 1310, New Zealand
(a division of Pearson New Zealand Ltd.)
Penguin Books (South Africa) (Pty.) Ltd., 24 Sturdee Avenue, Rosebank, Johannesburg 2196, South
Africa

Penguin Books Ltd., Registered Offices: 80 Strand, London WC2R 0RL, England

THE LIGHT AGES

An Ace Book / published by arrangement with the author

PRINTING HISTORY
Ace hardcover edition / May 2003
Ace trade paperback edition / April 2004
Ace mass market edition / May 2005

Copyright © 2003 by Ian R. MacLeod.
Cover art by Steve Stone.
Cover design by Judith Murello.

ISBN: 0-441-01274-4

ACE
Ace Books are published by The Berkley Publishing Group,
a division of Penguin Group (USA) Inc.,
375 Hudson Street, New York, New York 10014.
ACE and the "A" design are trademarks belonging to Penguin Group (USA) Inc.

PRINTED IN THE UNITED STATES OF AMERICA

10 9 8 7 6 5 4 3 2 1

To my wonderful daughter Emily,
who helped me stand for a while on the Turning Tower.

With love.

PART ONE
GRANDMASTER

I still see her now.

I see her in the poorest parts of London. Beyond the new iron bridges which bear the trams above the ferries, where the Thames spreads her fingers through tidal mud. I see her in a place beyond even the furthest rookeries of the Easterlies, although you will not find it on any maps. Plagued with flies and dragonlice and the reek of city effluent in summer, greyed with smog and ice in winter, even the foulest factories turn their backs away.

There, beyond the hovels and the wastetips of London, I see my changeling.

I see her when I take the streets that lead away from my fine Northcentral house. I see her when I'm worried or distracted, and when the present seems frail. Past the tall Hyde houses. Past the elegant grandmistresses walking their dogs, which—thin-legged, feathered, flightlessly winged, crested like reptiles or covered in mossy clumps of rainbow fur— scarcely seem to me like dogs at all. Skirting the huge shops of Oxford Road, then the incredible trees of Westminster Great Park where prams and parasols drift like paper boats, down Cheapside where the streets grow smaller and dimmer as the sky also shrinks and dims, hazing the roofs and chimneys as evening falls. Clerkenwell and Houndsfleet. Whitechapel and Ashington. A smell of rubbish here and a smell of dogs—by now ugly and ordinary—and the sound of their barking. Not that shame or poverty could ever be said to lie here, although the contrast with the districts where my journey began is already strong. The people who live in these parts of the Easterlies are still all masters rather than guildless marts: they have the jobs that their guilds have granted them; proper furniture in their rooms.

Eventually, long after Cheapside has become Doxy Street, past where the trams reach Stepney Terminus, the muddy streets heave and the houses stick out like irregular teeth. Here in these far Easterlies, no guildsmen dare live. I peer at these people as they scurry in a landscape which seems concertinaed by giant hands, the women cowled in grubby shawls, the men clouded with beerhouse reek, the children quick and pale and subtly dangerous, wondering if this is when the change into true poverty begins.

It always seems that I choose overcast days, late afternoons, dull, hot summer evenings, midwinter Noshiftdays, for my long wanderings. Or at least that, as I step away from the bright core of the Northcentral life I have been living, is what each of these days subtly becomes. From the best districts, I pass through tiers of London smoke and shadow. I suppose that most guildsmen would give up here, if the wild impulse had ever taken them this far. I suppose, looking up at the faces, ageless and leering, that study my passage through holes in the brickwork, hearing the whispering scurry of children both ahead and behind, that I should begin to feel afraid. But *people* live here: *I* once lived here, although that was in a different Age. So I walk on and skirt the high walls of Tidesmeet where I once worked through a happy summer. The scurries of the children quieten. The gargoyle faces no longer peer. Someone dressed as I am dressed, practical and understated in a dark coat, high boots to cope with the mud, yet effortlessly conspicuous in the waxy sheen of wealth, clearly possesses money. But I wouldn't bring it here with me, would I? No—or so I imagine those ghost-grey children whisper as they congregate in alleys. And a grandguildsman, too. The repercussions that would rain down on them from the bastard police make murder and robbery seem pointless. And I must have my reasons for coming this way—or I am mad—and both thoughts will make them uneasy. I carry no swordcane, no nightstick, no obvious weapon, not even an umbrella against the rain which always seems to threaten on these overcast days, but to ambush me in that space ahead where the houses press their brows together—who knows what strange guildsman's spells I might be carrying?

Lost also in thought, lost but mostly certain, I wander unmolested through these stinking streets. There are better ways to circumnavigate the far Easterlies and reach the wastetips, although I feel that I need to acknowledge my debt to the place. There are taxi boats and smaller ferries along the main river quays at the embankment and Riverside, which will, on discreet payment of an excessive sum, bear you this way. But the trade they carry is mostly male and drunk, and flounders at midnight from the steps of clubs and guildhalls to sniff the coalsmoke air and dismiss thoughts of home and waiting wives, or even the brothels and dreamhouses, in favour of a different end to the day. Down, then, to the dank sweep of the Thames, where, black-caped and top-hatted, the grandmasters bargain and bluster before they clamber aboard the slopping ferries like tipsy bats. The cough of a motor, the touch of a haft, the whisper of a sail, then away.

It seems to me that all places of poverty are endowed with a sense of waiting, but that is especially the case here, where the houses grow yet flimsier and cease, at some indefinable point like the shifting of a dream, to be houses at all, but shanty hovels of pillaged brick, cardboard and plaster. They are like the theatre props of a play whose essential meaning, despite everything, still escapes me. And the people who live within them, those guildless people whom we call marts, lie so far down the well of fortune from the bright world I inhabit that it is a surprise when their voices come echoing back at me in choked versions of the English tongue. But here, in the grey lull of this dark daytime, I am suddenly the source of much open attention. The strangest thing is that the children, younger now, unthreatening with stark puppy-dog eyes in the bone-bleached thinness of their faces, come up to offer me *money,* of all things. It lies there in the thin clasp of their fingers. Endless pennies and pounds and farthings of it. Gleaming.

'Take it, guildmaster. A good penny in return . . .'

'Fine stuff, the best spells,' agrees a slightly older colleague, a girl with hair so mangy that her crown shines thought it, offering from her pigeon hands what looks like a heap of diamonds.

'Last you this whole new Age. Last you a lifetime . . .'

More of them gather around, sensing my hesitation, and the foul air intensifies as their eyes glitter up at me. They are dressed in bits of old curtain, barge tarpaulin, sacks. They sport jaunty grey frills of old shirts like bits of filthy sea-foam. The threat of knives and ambushes I can take, but this simple offer . . . And the money, of course, fades. Even as I take a coin from them to inspect as they watch on, uncomplaining, it feels loose, light, grainy.

I wonder now who it is that actually falls for this trick— and whether the midnight visitors are ever quite so drunk, or so desperate. Not that I don't succumb. I choose the child who has shown the intelligence to form the most valuable-seeming handful, which is not money at all, or jewels, but crumpled guild certificates, bonds and promissory notes, and I snatch at paper which feels like winter fog, and ball it in my fist and throw out in exchange all the coins I can find in my pockets, scattering still more behind me as I hurry on.

The Thames never quite seems to be the river I know where it meets the land here. It lies flat and shining as it surges past the ruined shoreline far beyond the docks; oddly clean, all things considered, yet as black—and seemingly solid—as polished jet. The ferries never venture into these currents, and they hang tiny in the pewter distance of evening. They, and the wyreglowing hills of World's End, belong to another world. By now, the children have faded. What waits ahead of me, distant from everything but this river, is a foul isthmus. Sounds are different here, and the gulls remain oddly silent as they bob and rise. Here, it would be said in a forever unwritten history, edged against the wastetips and outflows, shadowed with cuckoo-plant ivy, scratched against the sky, are the remains of the unfinished railway bridge which attempted to stride across the Thames from Ropewalk Reach in another Age. The bridge still rises from the city's rubbish in a tumbled crown. It fails only where the second span buckles beneath the river, waving its girders like a drowning insect. I move within the shadows of its ribs, clambering over slippery horns of embedded concrete and guild-scrolled bearing-sleeves of greenish brass. Here, rusted and barnacled but still faintly glowing with aethered purpose, is the crest of a maker's plate. And a sea-diver's glove. A pulley wheel. And all the endless filth that the river has washed here; tin cans and shoe soles, eels of rope and condom, speckled mosaics of tile and piping.

I begin to make my way up and along the arch which still plunges out across the river, careful not to catch my cloak between the stanchions. There are curls of mist beneath me now; faint shapes over the quick black water which suggest limbs and faces as they twine and turn amid the abutments. And the bridge itself seems to be growing, beams and girders spinning out around me. But I've been here before, and I know something of the ways in which changelings protect themselves. Although my heart is racing and my hands are slipping, I push on and soon I am squatting on a ruined bridge again, caught between nothing but the land, the river, my own desperate need.

Almost level with me now and close to where the bridge's parapet finally falls away clings an aggregation of dead metal and glass and driftwood. Further off lies all of London; the life, the ferries, the miraculous trees and the fine buildings. I clamber to the platform beyond, then duck along the wire cage of a maintenance gantry through which shards of glass and porcelain have been crammed with an intent that could be either threatening or decorative. All things considered, the air here is surprisingly pleasant. It smells mostly of rust.

The changeling who calls herself Niana dwells in the shadows at the far end of this tunnel, and always seems to be waiting for me inside her tepee-like dwelling. She stirs at my approach, and beckons me from the rags of an old wedding dress.

'Grandmaster . . .' She studies me in the glow of a bowl of plundered wyrelight as she crouches in the furthest, darkest corner. *After all, you have decided to come . . .*

Her voice, even as it sounds solely in my head, is light, ordinary, flatly accented.

I flail through damp layers of curtain, clumsily conscious of the feats of creation that have gone into this dwelling, clenched up here amid these dying girders. This tilted boarding against which I'm leaning as I catch my breath was perhaps once a cargo pallet, lashed to the heaving deck of some steamer on the Boreal Seas. And the far wall, peppered with daylight through thousands of rivetholes, was clearly part of the outer plating of a large piece of machinery. Wan daylight mingles with the wyrelight's aetherglow through the clouded eye of an old porthole, along intricate tubes of glass piping of a purpose which—barely privy as I still am to the true mysteries of the guilds—entirely escapes me. I try to imagine the struggles which must unfold on the wastetips when a particularly precious relic is heaved from the sidings by the pitbeasts: the bickering gulls, the seething dragonlice, the scampering children. All because of a broken haft; a sack of soup bones; a twitching sliver of iron; a heaped clatter of old lamps . . .

I shrug and smile at Niana, torn as I always am between wonder, curiosity, pity. There's a long cushion exploding in horsehair near to the space where she crouches. Setting strings of bottletops chiming, I lower myself onto the end that looks more likely to bear me. The iron floor curves away from me, hanging at least thirty feet above the uncurling river. And I'm squatting in a way that people of my rank are never supposed to. Still, I'm glad to be here again. With a changeling, and no matter how often or how rarely you encounter them, there's still always for me that tingling sense that today you will finally witness the unravelling of some lost, exquisite mystery.

Niana gets up now, greyly barefoot as always, and wafts around this den of hers, half child and half hag as she hums to herself and rummages out bits of things from the old teachests. She takes a chess piece, a white rook carved from stained ivory, and lifts it to her lips.

'What do you do when no one's here, Niana?'

Her chuckle cuts like the chirp of an insect. 'How many times, grandmaster, do you people need to ask such a question?'

'Until we get an answer.'

'And what answer is it that you want? Tell me, and I'll give it to you.'

'It's not unrealistic, is it,' I mutter, 'for us both to feel a mutual fascination . . . ?'

'But tell me, grandmaster. What *is* it that fascinates?' The cotton of the wedding dress sighs like sand as she moves over to me. 'Tell me, so that I can understand. Exactly what is it that you want to know? Any wish you want could be granted, grandmaster,' she says more flirtatiously. Her face is the shadow of a face, cast through glass. Her eyes are blacker than a bird's. 'Surely that's not such a difficult proposition?'

'And not that you'll be making any promises?'

'Of course. Promises are far too definite. You know the rules.'

I sigh and blink, wishing that she wouldn't treat me like this, wishing that I could feel her breath on my skin instead of this falling emptiness. Sensing my unease, perhaps even hurt by it, Niana straightens herself and leans back. Just as the priests say, there is pure darkness inside those open nostrils.

'Have you anything for me?'

'I might have, grandmaster. It depends on what you you're prepared to give.'

'Niana, you told me last time—'

'Show a little *imagination,* grandmaster. You're a wealthy man. What is it that you normally deal in?'

A difficult question. The power of my guild, I suppose. And the strength of my will, the skills of mind and body I have acquired through it. Or perhaps Niana means something more subtle. The influence, which, when you get to a rank such as mine, you unavoidably must wield. I think of summer parties, winter gatherings in the panelled rooms around polished cedarstone tables; the subtle murmur of voices, the clink of cut glass, the deep tidal surges of power and money as one trust is set against the betrayal of another.

'Come, grandmaster. Surely it's the thing about you that is most obvious. It's what draws people to you—'

'—I doubt if you mean my *looks*—'

'—so why don't we pretend we're both simply human for a moment and make the usual exchange?' Her voice continues over mine. 'Grandmaster, why don't you give me some money?'

I try not to scowl. Niana's like a child. If I gave her coins, all she'd do is add them to her trinkets, use them to buy aether, or taunt me in just the way that she seems to be taunting me now . . .

Kindly forget your preconceptions, grandmaster, she responds, although her lips are barely moving. *We're not really trolls, you know—or at least we're not monsters.*

I twist myself on the springs of this couch to demonstrate to her that my pockets are empty. But as I do so my fingers close on something chilly. Remembering, lifting it out, I watch it flower, light as fog, on my palm. The cheaply magicked promissory note that that poor girl gave me. The words and the seals sparking, fading.

You see, grandmaster?

Niana blurs into a windless grey gale as she snatches it from me. Then she floats off, holding it to her nose as if it really was a flower, inhaling as I suppose we have all done at some time or another to discover if there really is a smell of wealth, a scent of power, a perfume of money. An odour which is in fact nothing but sweat, smoke, the dullness of liquor; the same staleness you'll find lingering on your clothes after attending a ball at the grandest of mansions.

Niana absorbs whatever is left of the paper flower's fading substance. And it's growing duller in here now; the afternoon is fading, and so is Niana. The brass bowl of aether strengthens in response, throwing out more of its characteristic wyrelight as she wafts amid hanging tins and bottles and curtains. But I fear that this is still all just a refinement of whatever joke that she's playing, and worry, as I notice that the immodest rents and tears across that ancient wedding dress give glimpses of black nothing, that she'll simply keep me waiting here forever.

'I know, grandmaster, that a wide and empty space seems to stretch between us. But it's like the walk you undertook this afternoon through the Easterlies. If you follow the wrong or right roads, it's never so very far to get to the place you dream of. In fact, who truly knows where the boundary ends, or where it begins? But you've seen the ordinary people, grandmaster, that so many others of your kind choose to ignore. After all, you were once one of them. The marts in the Easterlies. You know how dim they too can become even though their flesh remains unchanged . . .' She chuckles. My skull rings with the sound. *And if you knew how you looked now, grandmaster, in that night cloak, in those night boots, with hollows for eyes, with your sagging jaw and the night odours of age and death that even now are starting to cling to you . . .*

Barely any light flows now through the clouded port-hole. But for the sea-whisper of Niana's voice, I could almost be alone. Even that old wedding dress has slipped into the spinning shadows. A waft of mist, Niana bends to inspect the contents one of her teachests. As she lifts out clattering spears of old curtain rod, clots of rag and swarf, I try to keep in check that rising sense of excitement that always comes over me at these moments.

'It was *here*, I'm sure,' she mutters prosaically.

I give an involuntary sigh. It's odd, but part of me suddenly wishes to be gone from here now, to hurry back up through the streets to my fine house on Linden Avenue, my fine grandmaster's life—but the sense remains dim, and it fades entirely as Niana drifts closer to me now, glinting, changing. She's all the creatures and wonders I dare or dare not imagine, and her smile uptilts. The fact is, I'd much rather be here—waiting for a true moment of exchange.

'Tell me, Niana, don't you miss—'

—The smell of fresh grass in spring, grandmaster. The jewelled feel of frost at Christmas. Beetles bright as brooches. Clouds changing and unchanging. Running down a hill when you can't stop from laughing. But I'm glad for my cup of stars, grandmaster. And I'm glad that you come here—you and your sort, even if I pity you all for your small requests, your little desires. Why, after everything else you

guildsmen have to go through, should you want to be taunted by trolls, changelings, half-real hags, vampires, Methuselah mermaids?

'It isn't like that. I don't want—'

What do you want, grandmaster?

'To know—'

But I've given you my gift, grandmaster, by taking what you offered. I've done everything you asked of me. Now it's your turn. To take what I have, you must also give as well.

All in all, a typically ridiculous changeling bargain. Here I sit, on this empty bridge above the speeding river as Niana shapes the air with symbols no guildsman would ever recognise. They billow silver about me. They blossom in a summer storm. And I can feel the iron around me straining and growing, this ruined bridge returning to the life it never attained in the failing last Age, forming and striding huge across the water as the whole city changes and the wastetips recede. And with it gathers the thrilling hum of an approaching engine. It comes clattering over the girders and beams, trailing clouds, sparks, and pounding, pounding.

The deep holes of Niana's eyes are upon my face as she crouches before me. She blinks once, twice. She smiles.

So tell me, grandmaster. Her fingers curl around me like smoke. *Tell me just how it was that you became human . . .*

PART TWO
ROBERT BORROWS

I

It was the biggest disappointment of my life. At the ripe age of eight, and on a typically freezing October Fiveshift-day, all of my dreams had been dashed from me. Afterwards, I stood outside the Board School railings and watched my classmates exchange shrill barks of relief and laughter amid the smoke and fog. For all of us, today had been a special day, our Day of Testing, and we all had the Mark, the stigmata—puffy on our wrists, blistered and bleeding like a cigarette burn—to prove it.

A steam tractor blared its whistle and lumbered past, the weight of its wheels wheezing the cobbles, the steamaster's face a black mask. Worrying mothers blustered through the throng, bleating out the names of their offspring. *Said you were a silly to worry, didn't I?* But my mother wasn't there—and I was glad now that she wasn't coming, because I'd avoided the embarrassment of having my head kissed and my face spit-cleaned, all for the sake of something we'd been endlessly told was nothing, normal, ordinary. The other mothers soon drew into gossip or headed back to their laundry and their children swirled into hostile clusters as they remembered the guilds and loyalties of fathers. Elbows dug, shoves and glances were exchanged.

Knowing that I would soon be swept into this myself, I turned around the railings and climbed the spoil heap at the back of the school, from where there would have been a fine view down across the graveyard and the valley if today's fog hadn't obscured it.

I rolled up my left sleeve. There it was. The scar you saw on everyone once they had reached my age, although it still had the fresh look of outrage. It was the wound which lasted a lifetime and provided ineradicable proof of my undimmed humanity. The Mark of the Elder was God's ultimate blessing, if Father Francis was to be believed. The shocked rings of inflamed skin around its edges still glittered with tiny crystals of engine ice. Of course, it would never fully heal. That was the point. There would always be a faintly glowing scab there which I could pick at and study in the dark, which I supposed would be consolation of sorts.

And I'd been looking forward to the arrival of the trollman, even though he was a harbinger of pain. First, there were the rumours of his coming. Then the police who appeared with their lists of names on leather clipboards, and the sound of their boots in our alleys, and the bang of their nightsticks on our doors. All of this, and the rumours. Deformed offspring hidden in dungeons and attics; Brownheath shepherds of sixty or more who'd somehow managed to avoid this process for their whole lives. And trolls, changelings—so many you'd expect to find them teeming around every street corner instead of lingering at the edges of your dreams. Of course, these stories came as regularly as the trollman himself, but I wasn't to know that then.

His name, disappointingly, was Tatlow—and a plain Master at that, from something which was technically known as the Gatherers' Guild. He must have travelled most of Brownheath to earn his strange living with his carpetbag and his small mahogany case of implements, flashing his official pass before settling down each night in the room of a different inn. Next morning, he'd be woken by the clatter of wagons, and would run his finger along those painstakingly acquired lists to appraise the day's work, until, as I envisioned it, his stumpy digit would settle on my own name; *Robert Borrows . . .*

'Come in, lad. What are you staring at? And shut that bloody door . . .'

I did as Master Tatlow said, clumping forward across the boards of the headmaster's study towards the desk at which he was sitting.

'And why are you shivering? It's not cold, is it?'

A fire was crackling. I could feel its heat on the side of my face.

'Name, lad? Address . . . ?'

Of course, he must know that already. Such was my faith in the wisdom of the guilds.

'Well?'

'R-obert Borrows,' I squeaked. 'Three Brickyard Row.'

'Borrows . . . Brickyard Row. Well, you'd better come around to this side of the desk, hadn't you?'

I did as the trollman said, and he swivelled around in his borrowed chair to face me. The knees of his trousers, I noticed, were bagged and shiny. His face had a similar look; creasy and glossed and worn nearly through.

'Any known deformities or strange behaviours? Have you or your family at any time to your knowledge been exposed to raw aether? Wens? Birthmarks?' I did have several small dots and moles scattered across my body that I'd have liked to have told him about, but Master Tatlow was reading from a list on grimed card, and had already moved on. He gave his nose a wipe. 'Well, go on, lad. Roll up your sleeve.'

Ridiculously, my fingers started to struggle with the button of my right cuff until a sigh from Master Tatlow stopped me. Blushing furiously, I rolled up my left sleeve. My wrist looked thin and white. A stripped twig. Master Tatlow unclipped the lid from his battered leather case and produced a small glass jar and a wad of cotton. The air filled with a bright, sharp smell as he sprinkled it.

Amazingly, he handed the wad over to me. 'Rub that on your wrist.'

As I applied the stuff to my skin, I felt the chill of destiny come upon me. It was just as I expected. There was no pain, no reddening. An even whiter patch of skin and blue vein shone.

Master Tatlow was unimpressed. 'Now drop it in the bin.'

'Isn't that . . . ?'

Misunderstanding, he attempted a smile. 'You've probably heard from your friends that Testing hurts. Don't believe any of it. It happens to everyone. It even happened to me . . .' From the same leather case, he produced another jar, smaller this time. It seemed to be empty for a moment, then it filled with silver light. I felt an odd singing in my ears, a pressure behind my eyes. This time, it truly was blazing with the characteristic wyreglow of aether; which is bright in a dimness such as that room, and throws shadows in daylight. In the silence which blossomed as he opened out a device which looked like a combination of a bracelet and horse's bridle and slipped it over my left wrist, I could hear, more plainly than ever, the pounding of Bracebridge's aether engines. SHOOM *BOOM* SHOOM *BOOM*.

The aether chalice had a screwthread which attached itself to a brass protrusion of the leather collar enclosing my wrist. Master Tatlow held my arm firm. 'Now, lad. D'you know what to say?'

We'd spent the last two shifterms rehearsing nothing else.

'The Lord God the *Elder* in all his Power has granted this *Realm* the Blessing for which I now Thank Him with all my *Heart* and will Honour with all my *Labours*. I solemnly promise that I will Honour all Guilds, especially my *own* and that of my Father and all his Fathers before him. I will not bear *Witness* against those to whom I am *Apprenticed*. I will not traffic with *Demons, Changelings, Fairies* or *Witches*. I will praise God *the* Elder and all his *Works*. I *will* Honour each Noshiftday in his Name, and . . . and I will . . . I will accept this Mark as my own Sign of the Blessing in the Infinite Love *of* the God and the Stigmata of my *Human* Soul.'

Still gripping my arm, Master Tatlow gave the aether chalice a twist.

For a moment, there was nothing. But his attention was fixed on me as it hadn't been before. I gave a surprised gasp. It felt as if I had been driven through with a frozen nail. It rocketed into my mouth in spears of blood and pain. SHOOM . . . *BOOM* . . . Then everything contracted again, and I was standing there beside the desk and level with Master Tatlow's face as, with a twist of the chalice and a brisk snap of clasps, he withdrew from my wrist the thing which had tortured me.

'You see,' he muttered. 'Wasn't so bad, was it? You're just like all the rest of us now. Ready to join your daddy's guild.'

So I strode away from Board School through an autumn fog which was rolling in quick and cold and early, pausing only in Shipley Square to glare at a verdigreed statue of the Grandmaster of Painswick, Joshua Wagstaffe, who stood in indeterminate mid-gesture just as he stood in squares across all of England. Not, I thought, that I blamed the man personally for discovering aether. Someone else would have been bound to do so even if he hadn't, wouldn't they? And, if they hadn't, where would the world be? Even the Frenchmen with their tails and the goat-eyed men of Cathay were said to have their spells, their guilds. The fog swirled around me, turning the people into ghosts, the houses and trees into suggestions of lands I would never see. When I got back to our house on Brickyard Row, I kicked open the back door and carried trails of them with me as I stomped into the kitchen.

'*There* you are . . .' My mother came briskly from the parlour bearing the vinegared rag she'd been using to clean the brassware. 'Wondered what all the noise was about.'

I dropped to the three-legged stool beside the stove and dragged off my boots. Suddenly, I was angry with her for not coming to the school gates to make a fuss of me like every other mother.

'Well? Let's see . . . ?'

I stuck my arm out for her, just as I'd done for Master Tatlow, and as I'd doubtless have to do for Beth and my father. It was a minor enough wound compared to the things I'd done to my knees and elbows, and ubiquitous amongst us guildspeople, but my mother studied the sore for longer than I'd have expected. Despite all her talk about a lot of fuss over nothing, she really did seem interested. In the light of our dull kitchen, the aether was still glowing. Finally, she straightened up, steadying herself against the cold range as she let out a long and surprising gasp, like a surfacing swimmer.

'Well, it's a big step. Now you're like all the rest of us.'

'Rest of *what*?' I squeaked.

My mother bent down again. She laid her warm blackened hands on my knees until I finally looked up at her and she gave me an unfathomable smile.

'You should be pleased, Robert. Not disappointed. It proves—'

'What?'

I was shouting, and close to tears. Normally, I'd have been a candidate for a swift smack and a long hour upstairs while I *bucked up my ideas,* but this afternoon my mother seemed to understand that my mood was deeper, and—despite all outward appearances—somehow not entirely pointless.

'Testing is part of what we all are, here in England, in Bracebridge. It shows that you're fit to be a guildsman like your father, just as it shows that I'm a guildmistress. It shows . . .' But my mother's blue eyes were slowly drawing away from me. The dull glint of the fire at my back pooled two red sparks beneath her irises. 'It shows . . .' She drew herself back a little, and rubbed at the corner of her mouth with her knuckles because her fingers were grubby with tarnish. 'It shows that you're growing.'

'And what about all the stories you've told me . . . ?'

'Those are for summer nights, Robert. And look outside—can't you see? Winter's coming.'

Then there was Noshiftday, and Father Francis stood at the door of St Wilfred's church nodding to his congregation as he passed out white sashes for us spit-dabbed children to wear. Jammed together into the front pews, we elbowed each other and examined our raw wounds. Ahead of us, clumsily executed in marble by a local craftsman, a robed and bearded statue of God the Elder, the greatest guildsman of them all, gazed down at us. And then the singing began, and I gazed up at the gilt ceiling and the dull scenes in stained glass along the walls. George endlessly slaughtered his dragon with a look of bored disdain. Saints suffered terrible tortures in the name of their guilds.

Father Francis's sermon must have been the one he gave at every Day of Testing, and his sing-song voice was familiar as a lullaby as it wafted over the pews. Then, one by one, we children were summoned to the altar. I squeezed along the bench when my time came, and managed not to catch my sash on the altar rail, but my thoughts were remote as I grasped the beaker of hymnal wine for the first time and Father Francis recited the promises of heaven. I could feel the eyes of the congregation around me, and the pounding of the earth beneath. I could see the smears that the other children's lips had left on the beaker's silver rim. I wondered what would happen if I spat it out. But I shuddered as I swallowed the tart red fluid. It was just as everyone always said: I saw a vision of heaven, where there is but one great guild and no work to perform, and where pure silver trains run through endless fields of corn whilst winged ships sail the clouds. I could easily see how regular church-attending could become addictive, but I knew even as I witnessed these scenes that they had been stirred into the alcohol of an aethered vat.

II

I was born Robert Borrows in Bracebridge, Brownheath, West Yorkshire, late one August Sixshiftday afternoon in the seventy-sixth year of the third great cycle of our Ages of Industry, the only son and second child of a lower master of the Lesser Guild of Toolmakers. Bracebridge was then a middle-sized town which lay on the banks of the River Withy. It was prosperous in its own way, and perhaps indistinguishable from many another northern factory town to the eyes of those who glimpsed it from the carriages of the expresses which swept through our station without stopping, although, at least in one respect, it was unusual. Derbyshire might have its coalfields and Lancashire might have its mills, Dudley might swarm with factories and Oxford with cape-flapping dons, but for this particular corner of England it was aether which governed our lives, and the one inescapable fact that would strike anyone who visited Bracebridge at that time was the sound, or rather the non-sound, which pervaded it. It was a sensation which passed into all of us who lived there and became part of the rhythm and the substance of our lives.

SHOOM *BOOM* SHOOM *BOOM*.

It was the sound of the aether engines.

The water wheels that had driven Bracebridge's first aether engines up on Rainharrow had long been still; their wheels and pistons had rusted, their catchpools lay empty, the shattered windows of their drive houses stared down at the factories that had sprawled in their place. Down in the valley, there was always smoke and sound and furnace glow. Inside the floors of Mawdingly & Clawtson, dervish governors spun, pulleys hissed and chains clattered. Driven down from Engine Floor three hundred feet into the earth, pristine as a jewel yet thick as a ship's mast and ten times as heavy, a great vertical axle turned, bearing force to Central Floor far below where the ears and lungs of those who laboured there were continually flayed by the deep, demented beat of the triple arms of the aether engines which they and this factory—all of Bracebridge, in one way or another—existed to serve.

Fanning out from the riven rock, the three steel and granite pistons bellowed back and forth—SHOOM *BOOM* SHOOM *BOOM*—drawing out the aether. Connected to those pistons and thin as spiderweb, skeins of engine silk carried the substance to the surface. There, the energy was dissipated in the cloudy waters of the first of many quickening pools, then stirred and filtered until the final vials were packed in lead-lined chests and borne on slow trains west and east and north but predominantly south across England, there to be put to any of ten thousand possible uses, the benefits of which, it always struck me, Bracebridge itself seemed surprisingly bereft.

Of course, it used to be said that we all took aether for granted then, but in Bracebridge it was *working* of aether that we took for granted; the slam of iron and the howl of shift sirens and the clump of men's boots and the grind of engines and soot on the washing and, beyond all that, beyond everything, the subterranean pounding of those engines. It compacted the flour in the larder and tilted the flagstones in the hall. It cracked flowerpots and crazed pottery. It shifted dust into seashore patterns and danced rainbows on the fat globules in the cream. It secretly rearranged the porcelain dogs on the mantelpiece until they crashed to the hearth. SHOOM *BOOM* SHOOM *BOOM*. We carried

the sound of those engines in our blood. Even when we left
Bracebridge, it came with us.

The house in which I lived, the third in the terrace along
Brickyard Row, with a steep drop through scratchy copses
of birch into lowtown and with many other Rows and
Backs and Ways slanting up Coney Mound behind, had
stood for most of the Third Age of Industry by the time my
parents moved in. Bracebridge then was at the height of a
new surge of expansion, and such terraces, facing each
other across yards and alleys and the corrugated roofs of
outside toilets, had been deemed the most efficient method
of housing the workers who were needed to service the new,
subterranean engines that were then being built to mine
the deep-set aether seams. Apart from my own small upper
space, there were two main rooms on each of the two
floors, although the house always seemed more complicated than that, riddled with odd corners and alcoves and
bits of cupboard and criss-crossings of chimney. The core,
from which rose most of the heat, smell and noise which
fogged my attic, was the kitchen, which was dominated in
turn by the black iron range. Above it were generally
strung clots of rag, shoes dangling by their laces, sage and
sallow, bits of fat and ham, sagging bladders of waterapples, wet coats and anything else in need of drying, whilst
the oak table glowered at it from its own darker corner; a
rival, lesser, deity.

Upstairs lay the front bedroom which my parents occupied, and my elder sister Beth's single back room. The rear
of the house was north-facing, the narrow windows ad-
mitting views only of walls and dustbins and back alleys. I
was lucky, really, with my little attic at the front. It was my
own private territory. Lives were pressed close together in
Brickyard Row. The walls were thin, their bricks porous to
smoke, smells, voices. Somewhere, there would always be
a baby crying; somewhere else, a man shouting, or a woman
crying.

Like so many other couples who lived along Coney
Mound in the compressed lower layers of the great human
pyramid of rank which still dominates England—above the

poor guildless marts but precious little else—my parents
had struggled though years of duty and routine. An old
photograph hung above the mantelpiece in the front parlour, taken on the day of their wedding. It was so blotched
by smoke and damp as to look as if they were standing underwater; and they really did both seem to be holding their
breath as they posed stiffly under the branches of a beech
tree beside St Wilfred's. But that was all a long time ago;
before Beth, before me. My father had no moustache then,
and the saucy tilt to his elbow and the way he had his hand
around my mother's waist suggested a whole life a-waiting.
My mother wore a lanternflower wreath and a dress of fine
lace which billowed to the grass in foamy waves. A truly
handsome couple, both still looking too young to be married even to my immature eyes, they had met at Mawdingly
& Clawtson, the big aether factory on Withybrook Road
around which all of Bracebridge revolved. My mother
had moved to Bracebridge from the failing family farm
out on Brownheath, and my father had followed his own
father into the Third Lower Chapter of the Lesser Toolmakers' Guild. They had crossed paths many times, if my
mother was to be believed, before they really noticed each
other, or locked eyes, in my father's dreamier version,
across the benches of the factory paintshop as he made
his way through there on some errand, and fallen instantly
in love.

Ridiculous though it is, I still prefer my father's tale. I
can still see my mother working on the fine relays amid all
the other young women in that long dim room, dipping her
brushes into the aether-laden pots, her hair drawn up and
head bowed as she traced the skeins and scrolls that would
ultimately convey a guildsman's will into some tool or engine. For my father, swinging in through the doors from
the roar of the foundry across the yard, it must have been like
stepping into a cool garden. And my mother was delicate
then, perhaps even beautiful, with her lustrous dark hair,
her soft blue eyes, her white skin and that small, elegant
body with those fine nervous hands. Aside from the use of
her family's guild connections, she had probably got her
job in the painting room because she looked as if she could

perform such an exacting task, but in fact she tended to be clumsy, making quick, brittle movements that her mind only seemed to learn about after her limbs had accomplished them. As children, Beth and I both learned to keep well away from her flying elbows. But in every sense, amid the aether drippings of her ruined brushes as the light faded into evening, my mother would have shone out.

So my parents met, they courted, they married at Midsummer, and the shifterms and the years flew by. At the time I first remember them both, they still looked far too young to be who they already were, and partly, in the stoop of their backs and the greying of my mother's hair, much too old. Bracebridge and the huge downward pressure of England's great human pyramid had wearied them both. My father was an inconstant man, prone to anger and enthusiasms, to interests and projects started and then abandoned in favour of something else. Once he found his ambition thwarted within the tight, secret structures of the Lesser Toolmakers' Guild, he wore out the energy and intelligence which had probably first attracted my mother to him. More days than not he would call in at the Bacton Arms on his way home from Mawdingly & Clawtson for a swift half which easily became several long pints, and on Tenshift and Halfshiftday and feastdays he would roll up the street, crashing into the house and swaying up the stairs, laughingly circling my mother as she lay in bed and did her best to ignore him, making jokes about what some friend for the evening had done or said before he flared into spite and finally retreated to spend the night before the stove, staring into the firegrate's glow as the alcohol seeped out of him. On ordinary nights, though, they would talk to each other as they prepared for bed in croaks and cries and calls like two keelies calling across the marshes; all those sentences married couples never finish. My father would hook his trousers by their braces across the back of his chair, then yawn and stretch and scratch himself through his vest before climbing between the sheets.

I can see them now. The oil lantern on the dresser which my father's brought up from downstairs is still glowing, its flame clawing the air. My mother is slower to get to bed, wandering about barefoot, pulling and tugging at her hair with her big silver brush, then catching her outline in the faded looking glass and staring frozen for a moment as if surprised to find herself here. My father slaps his pillow, turns over, hugs himself, muttering. My mother puts down the brush and lifts her night-gown from its hook to shrug it over herself in grey waves before wriggling from her underthings, dragging them out from beneath the hem. Finally, she hoods the lantern and climbs into bed.

There they lie, two figures half buried in the dark of their blankets and the weight of their days, people who had once held hands, taken springtime walks, sheltered laughing under bandstands from the rain. It all seems quiet now; the families are strung weary and complete along Brickyard Row, safe in their beds as the stars shine down on the roofs and a new moon rises over the backs of the houses. No dogs are barking. The yards are empty. The last train has long gone by. A dense, fizzing silence falls in snowy waves. Then, as my father grunts and sniffs and begins to snore, a deeper sound becomes apparent. And my mother lies there, flat and still, her eyes glittering from her pillow as she stares at the ceiling, the finger of her left hand rubbing the scar on the palm of the other to that endless, inescapable rhythm.

SHOOM *BOOM* SHOOM *BOOM*.

III

I suppose I was always a little different—or I told myself that I was. I cherished these inexpressible dreams. I was always looking over the rooftops, counting the stars, flying with the clouds.

So look at me now, little Robert Borrows, wandering Rainharrow with my mother on one of those rare shiftdays when we have nothing more pressing to do. I climb drifts of mining scree to squat on the topmost rise, and shred leaves and make owl calls whilst she goes in search of wild flowers. Sitting with my back propped against one of the circle of sarsens which were once placed on this hallowed spot by people like and unlike me and are now shadowed in soot and clawed by graffiti, I can see most of Brownheath spread below, rising and falling in greys and greens with bits of town and forest sprouting like bodyhair all the way to the bigger peaks of the Pennines. It can be warm here on the good days of summer, and I can see, far closer below me, the figure of my mother in her black coat and bonnet stooped amid the brambles.

Finally, she finds something and calls up to me. And I clamber down and we inspect together whatever tiny plant she's discovered clinging to this grey collier's earth, and reassure ourselves as we bend to uproot it to nestle in a scrunch of newspaper that it will better off taken home than left out here. We gave them local names which no guilded expert with his Latin books would have countenanced. But they were good enough. Heartsease and mugwort. Eyebright and tansy. On my mother's lips, they sounded like music.

So we'd take our plant home and lay it in a pot and place it on the sunniest spot on the window ledge each morning, and shift it away from the frosts at night. My mother kneaded the earth with her fingers, and watered it, and breathed encouraging words to its leaves. Then one morning, faint yet inescapable over the reek of smoke and damp and humanity, an odd scent would be in my nostrils when I awoke. And I'd stumble down through the house to find my mother preening before some tiny new bloom that the plant had stooped its stem to bear, the colours paintbox-pure in a way that nothing else ever seemed to be in Bracebridge. Not that the flowers ever lasted, but those mornings, glancing time and again at the whorls and petals, and breathing the scent which left an ache behind my eyes like first snow, had a unique character.

Once or twice, she was mistaken in what she found, and we came home with a cuckoo-plant. There were many such infestations in Bracebridge, just as there were dragonlice in its factories and kingrats in the burrows by the old barges down beside the river. It was part of the ways of our town. Of course, we children knew to inspect carefully any bramble bush we might choose to pick the berries from in case they brought nightmares, and not to brush our legs against the black-tinged nettles which erupted along the paths at the back of the aether beds, for they gave a rash which could bleed and ache for terms. Our fathers knew also to pluck out any bloodivy coming up from the drains, and the women never picked the mushrooms which grew on the rivermeads. But mistakes were easily made: a spray of simple yellow flowers, looking like big buttercups and smelling sweet and creamy, or a fine stem of foxgloves rising from the bracken, even if it was far too late in the summer. Bring them back, and the smell of their rot pervaded your house like bad cabbage and their ooze could ruin a best vase or burn your mantelpiece like acid. Still, all the fussing with newspapers and the open windows and the complaints of my father were worth it for the good days, that sense of surprise and discovery when my mother called to me from across the hill, parting the windy grass to nestle in her fingers the perfect face of a flower.

So much of everything was a mystery to me then. Board School taught me nothing beyond how to read and write, which my mother had already shown me, and the guildsmen, men like my father, kept the drudgeries and secrets of their daily work to themselves and the insides of their beer glasses. Mawdingly & Clawtson was a name, a sound, a feeling, an edifice. Industry was our purpose. Aether was our god. It was as if we were all trying to turn our eyes from something vital and lay our heads on the pounding earth, lulling ourselves into a sleep which would last a lifetime of endless duty and disappointment.

Occasionally, I would risk the attentions of the cuckoo-nettles and peer through the fences at the settling pans wherein aether was catalysed and bound with ordinary matter, which thickened to blackness on hot bright days, and blazed upwards on winter afternoons like the foundations of a heaven upturned. Sometimes, crawling into the cupboard beneath the stairs out of boredom or the need to escape, I would rummage through the old rags my mother kept there made from scraps of my father's old overalls. Within some of them, bound to the seams like the starry paths of tiny rockets, a few speckles of aether dust still clung, and shone out at me, along with the lavender scent of polish. And every autumn term, rigid as clockwork, and just after the trollman's visit, the teachers would take out a box and plonk it down on the front desk, and beckon—or drag—some pupil to the front so that he (it was almost invariably a boy) might experience the true glory of aether.

'Who discovered aether, lad?'

'The Grandmaster of Painswick, Joshua Wagstaffe, sir!'

'When did it happen?'

'Start of the very First Age of Industry, sir. By the old holy calendar, sixteen seventy-eight.'

That was the easy bit. The box itself was scarred and old and wooden and rectangular. Its lock had a sprung iron hasp which bore the look of more recent replacement, and was secured through a hoop across the front by an engraved bolt, also sprung. Small though it was, the engraving spoke of the guilds, and mystery, of work and the real adult world. Not quite letters nor pictures, although their shapes suggested writhing dancers, similar hieroglyphs could be seen on the plates of engines and the beams of bridges and even, crudely stamped, on the bricks of many a house. Guild to guild, these symbols were never quite the same, but I still always got the sense as I studied them of a single endless text which I would one day be able to read.

What those dancing figures told us all in that classroom was that the bolt was infused with the power of aether. During the process of its manufacture under the big roofs of some other northern town's factories, tiny amounts of the stuff would have been introduced into the hot metal. From there, through guild mystery after guild mystery, the metal would have been shaped, pounded and moulded into the object we saw. A functional spell had been cast over that bolt, and also over the catch and the spring which held it, and then it had been boxed and crated along with hundreds of others and borne off to end up here on Master Hinkton's desk in Class C of Bracebridge Board School.

Of course, we all thought as we froze and steamed and yawned in the perpetual schoolroom fug that we knew exactly what aether was. After all, we were the sons and daughters of guildsmen, and we lived in Bracebridge under the shadow of Rainharrow, where so much of the stuff was extracted. We could feel those engines pounding in a dull ache through the benches. But aether is like no other element, and it shuns all physical rules. It is weightless, and notoriously difficult to contain. Purified, its wyreglow fills the darkness, but spills shadows in bright light. Strangest of all, and yet most crucial to all the industries and livelihoods it helps sustain, aether responds to the will of the human spirit. A guildsman can, after the long years of apprenticeship, use aether to control whatever process is special to his guild. Without aether, the great steam engines

which power England's factories and bear the fruits of the
mill and the mine would halt, or explode under their own
pressure. Without aether, the wyreglowing telegraphs which
thread our countryside would fall silent of the messages
which telegraphers chant mind to mind to mind. Without
aether, the extravagant structures of our great cities and the
bridges which span our rivers would collapse. But with it,
we are able to make things more thinly, more cheaply, more
quickly and—it has to be admitted—often more crudely
than the harsh and inconvenient rules of simple nature
would ever allow. Boilers which would otherwise explode,
pistons which would stutter, buildings and beams and bearings which would shatter and crumble, are borne aloft
from mere physics on the aether-fuelled bubbles of guildsmen's spells. With aether, England prospers, the guilds
flourish, the shift sirens chant, the chimneys plume, the
wealthy live lives of almost inconceivable profligacy and
the rest of us struggle and squabble and labour for the
crumbs which remain. Even lands beyond our own, caught
within their own wyreglowing tendrils of aether and ridiculous myths of discovery by some other grandmaster than
ours, smoke and hammer to dreams of guilded industry
whilst the savage lands remain forever unexplored. With
aether, this world turns on the slow dark eddies of Ages beyond conflict and war. Without it—but the very thought
was impossible . . .

'Go on then.'

The ginger-haired lad standing at the front of the class
looked at the bolt, then up at the blackboard, which bore a
phonetic transcription of what he was supposed to say
whilst touching the bolt, although even these ordinary letters of the alphabet seemed now like the misspelling of an
alien language.

'Put your finger in the *middle,* idiot, or the spring'll
have the end of it off! Wouldn't be able to pick your nose
then, would you?'

Relieved titters came from all of us who weren't standing there at the front.

'Go on. Some sort of guildsman you'll be.'

At last, the lad made an effort. Or perhaps he was just

clearing his throat. Nothing happened. The ground beneath us thrummed.

'Again—and louder. Any decent guildsman worth his salt would *sing* this.'

The lad tried again. There was a loud *snap*. The clasp sprang open.

'Go on. Lift the lid. Look inside.'

Master Hinkton had his own party trick, which was to rap the lid of the box on the lad's head just as he peered in. He did it now.

'Empty, isn't it? Just like your skull . . .'

And we all laughed at that scowling fool's antics, even though we hated him.

'Look at this.'

My father rolled up his sleeve to show me the twine-tattoo of the bruise there, the sign of his aethered labour. Down the road, Matty Brady's dad who worked the big coal hoppers had one that went down his entire back as if a snake had curled up to sleep there. And there was a whole street of guildmasters down in lowtown who had bluish protrusions which emerged from their thumbs like the thorns of metal roses. No one knew quite what work they did, other than that it took place deep down in the bowels of the earth close to the pounding engines, and that they got paid well for it and didn't live long. We regarded these manifestations—the scars, the scales, the ornate bruises—which we called marks of the haft, with fear, envy, awe.

Like the cold dark beyond the moonlit glimmer of an aether pool, there was this sense of otherness waiting out-side our ordinary lives. Even more than lay-offs and lost limbs and the disciplinary procedures of the guilds, the fear was always there that an excess of aether might take hold of you and heal the Mark on your wrist. From there, your fate was terrible. You would become a troll, a changeling. Of course, the guilds would still care for you and your family as the guilds always cared for their members, but the troll-man would come in a dark green van to bear you off to Northallerton, that legendary asylum, where you would be used and tended for the rest of your life.

'They had one of them there trolls come on West Floor yesterday,' my father announced over tea one evening.

'Really . . .' My mother lost her peas from her fork. 'You shouldn't use that word.'

'What difference does it make? Anyway it was a *changeling* they thought they needed because they'd made such a mess of the beamhammer that the iron had turned brittle and they'd tried all the spells and nothing else would do. But that's pressers for you. Thing's still not working, for all I hear.'

'Did you get to see it?' I asked.

'No.' My father worked his lips around a stray bit of gristle. 'But the lads on bolt production swore it looked like a metal lizard and that the bread of their sandwiches was green afterwards.'

'Don't talk to your son like that, Frank. All that foolish superstition. And it's not *it*, Robert. They're people like everyone else.'

But they weren't—that was the whole point. Greyed flesh, lantern-eyed, hedgehog-horned, these ruined creatures of industry haunted the dead-end alleys of our childhood winter imaginings.

He's the Potato Man, Potato Man, Potato Man. He's the Potato Man, la la la la la la . . .

Because of what he was, or what we thought he might be, we children chose to torment the Potato Man above all the wandering guildless marts who tramped, begging, selling useless goods, sometimes thieving, across Brownheath. Most of them weren't trolls at all, and were disfigured by accident and birth or were simply a little mad. But the Potato Man was peculiarly odd. He dressed in hooded rags, and dragged a small wheeled cart behind him, and always seemed to arrive in Bracebridge on smoke-blue winter evenings. The first thing you heard was the shrieking of those wheels arriving with the wind down the alleys. And there he would be, a figure emerging from the swarming dusk. His face, what we saw of it as he passed the streetlights, was plainly ruined, and his hands were like badly cooked sausages, fat and weeping and burnt. Whatever he was, whatever he had been, he was plainly strange beyond all ordinary strangeness.

My mother was one of the few guildmistresses who would leave things out for these creatures on her doorstep. Old shoes, soup bones in a paper bag, stale bread, end bits of bacon. Long after I had come inside and gone up to bed, I would sometimes hear the creak of our gate and peer down from my little window at the shape which came shuffling up our short path, with that cart left abandoned in the street. Then—and quite incredibly—our door would sometimes open for the Potato Man. I would lie there in the dark, sure that I could hear the quiet murmur of my mother's voice, and a liquid growl which could only be him. But by morning the very idea that the Potato Man had ever come into our house would be gone.

On quiet evenings at home, I'd lie listening to the familiar sounds downstairs as my mother moved about the house, urging that final rasp of the drawer as she put away the family knives, the rumble of pulleys as she hauled the clotheshorse with its dripping load of washing up to the ceiling, and the wheezes and creaks that were given by the stairs as she ascended them. A pause. *Are you asleep, Robert?* Not that I ever was. Then another pause as she pondered whether to treat the steep runners up to my attic as steps or a ladder. A nimbus of candlelight would gather around the loose bun of her hair as she finally clambered up into my eaves. Hunched against the slope of the roof, our limbs pressing through the rucked coats and blankets, my mother would gather her breath.

'Long ago, there was a pretty young girl named Cinderella. She lived all alone in a big old house with her stepmother and her three ugly stepsisters—'

'So she wasn't alone, then, was she?'

'Wait, and you'll see . . .'

Night after night: all the myths and histories of England were mingled with her own and my imaginings. She'd tell me the stories of the founders of our family guild—those, at least, which women were permitted to discover. Then of

the times of the Age of Kings when there were no guilds
and nation still fought foolishly against nation, ruled by
those bad monarchs in their palaces whom we had rightly
tried and beheaded, and of stern knights wrapped in steel,
and of Arthur and mad Queen Elizabeth, and Boadicea
who fought the Romans. And once, long, long ago, before
these Ages of Industry when the magic was sucked out
of the earth, before even the Age of Kings, it seemed to me
that this whole realm must have been filled with wonder
beyond all possible dreams. Marvellous beasts rose from
the soil like steam, there were fine white palaces, and beautiful plants jewelled every hillside . . .

'So the Fairy Godmother appeared to Cinderella.'

'Was she a changeling?'

A beat of pounding silence.

'This is just a story, Robert.'

'Then tell me something true. Tell me about Goldenwhite.'

'Well . . .'

There was always both a smile and a hesitancy in my
mother's voice when she spoke about Goldenwhite up
in my attic room. Like most working-class people, she
harboured a fondness for the idea a woman of scarcely
guilded beginnings who could rise to challenge, if only
briefly, the might of the guilds. But my mother was a
guildswoman as well, and her loyalties were tugged both
ways at the thought of a creature who had been able to use
the magic as naturally as breathing, and yet who had led an
uprising which had approached the walls of London. Still,
if I held my breath for long enough and crossed all of my
fingers under the blanket and squirmed my toes in my own
youthful spell, the pleasure of telling a good story would
generally win.

'Goldenwhite—well, that wasn't her real name. But no
one knows what her real name was, or what part of England she came from, although a great many places claim
her. Even the stupid people of Flinton with their dreadful
slagheap up the road with nothing but coal in their ground
claim that she was born there—can you believe that? But
anyway. Goldenwhite was sixteen when people realised

she was a changeling, although she must have known long before that. You see, she was quite ordinary to look at, even if she was pretty, and in those days, they didn't have a Day of Testing . . .'

So Goldenwhite fled into the forests which then still covered so much of this land. There, she talked with the beasts, and she forded streams, and made the strange acquaintance of the people who would become her band of followers: changelings and madmen, the deformed and denied, marts of every shape and kind—everyone, in fact, whom the guilds and aether had damaged and dispossessed. And, drifting out through the tree-hung mists, shy at first but gaining strength and beauty from her radiance, gathered the creatures of every legend. Robin Hood and Lancelot and the Lady of the Lake; Snow White, Cinderella, Rapunzel, the Lord of Misrule and the Green Man. They were all there.

'Goldenwhite, she promised her people a kingdom, and it was both a new kingdom and an old one. In some stories, she called it Avalon, and in others they say it's Albion, although that's just another name for this country of ours. But in the best tales, the ones you hear around these parts, it's Einfell, and it's a place which lies next door to this world which Goldenwhite had somehow visited when she was young, and had brought some of its light back with her when she returned. Einfell, it glowed out of her smile, and was the reason people flocked to hear her voice and feel her gaze which was like sunlight . . .'

I willed on the procession of Goldenwhite's so-called Unholy Rebellion as her ragged army tramped south and finally looked down on the walls of London from her encampment above it on the Kite Hills.

'By then she had met Owd Jack. And Owd Jack was a changeling as well. He had torture marks on his hands— holes like wood knots—and there was a sort of blackness about him, but he seemed much like the sort of folk Goldenwhite already had with her, and she was happy to have him along. Owd Jack was her general, and the battles that she fought there and won, they were Owd Jack's doing . . .'

That was as dark and as bloody as things ever got in the

stories which my mother told me. There never was a final
battle outside the walls of London when Owd Jack betrayed Goldenwhite and brought her in chains to the men
of the guilds. In our tales, she never did burn at the stake in
Clerkenwell. Instead, it was a joyous journey, filled with
surprises and miracles, with new healings and legends
hatching at every milestone. The squirrels hopped from
tree to tree and the birds sang above Goldenwhite's lordly
procession as the forest spread endlessly before them, its
soft darkness laced with gold and shadow. Any moment
now, the next turn or that afternoon at the latest, they would
reach the place she spoke of, the place she promised,
which wasn't London at all, or even really England or Albion, but Einfell . . .

My mother sat there for a long moment as the words fell
away, the fingers of her left hand gently kneading the small
grey scar on her palm which I had sometimes noticed but
which she would never explain. The candle shifted and
glinted. The songs and the forest receded. A dog down the
street was barking, a baby was crying. The wind whispered
in the tiles, gently stirring the attic cobwebs. And deep
down, beneath everything, rising up through the bricks and
timbers of Brickyard Row, was that other sound. SHOOM
BOOM SHOOM *BOOM*.

'Tell me more.'

She kissed my forehead and laid her fingers across
my lips to silence me. Their tips flesh smelled faintly of
the hearth. 'You've had enough wonders for one night,
Robert.'

But I never had.

Then there was a Midsummer Fair down on the rivermeads, and the heat in the house on that long-awaited
summer's morning, and sitting at the kitchen table, and
studying my mother across its surface as she bustled about
in her apron, and my wondering if she really would keep
her promise to take me to see a real, live dragon. And then
we're outside in the simmering light, we're down across
the stone and liveiron bridge that gave this town its name—
and standing on the far meadow on the quiet Nineshiftday

before the Halfshiftday when the true glories of the fair will supposedly start. There are patched tents with sun-faded stripes. There are ropes of engine pipe coiled amid the cowpats like lost bits of intestine. There are shouts and sounds of hammering. There are wagons sprawled every-where. The engines that will drive the rides, small things by the standards of Bracebridge, were slumbering and clack-ing, barely smoking, unattended by their masters. There was a sense that we'd come too early, that nothing was ready. Still, an aproned man took our money as, my left hand clutching my mother's, my right a sticky ball of aniseed, we stumbled across the parched grass in search of my dragon.

A smell of shit and fireworks as we stood before a large hutch propped on bricks amid spindly thorns in the corner of the field. The creature gazed back at us through the peel-ing wooden bars from its bed of damp newspaper. One eye was sheened with a silver cataract, but the other, greenish-gold and slotted like a goat's, bore the dim light of some-thing like intelligence. It yawned as it watched us, and its jaws made a crackling, splitting sound. Its teeth were rot-ten. A storm of flies buzzed up and re-settled as the thing stretched the cramped pinions of its wings. Its flesh wasn't scaled, but grey, although patched with odd, sharp clumps of bristle.

Was *this* a dragon? I trudged home, inconsolable. Fa-ther was still out, and Beth was at school, and the house felt stale and empty even as my mother banged the door behind her. Joining in my mouth and heart with the dull bitter taste of aniseed came a distant pounding.

SHOOM *BOOM* SHOOM *BOOM*.

'Come on, Robert. It wasn't that bad, was it? At least you *saw* the dragon. Tomorrow, the day after, we'd never have got through the crowds.'

I shrugged, staring at the scars on the kitchen table. I didn't know then how such brutes were created: that, in its way, it was a fine achievement for some beastmaster to have twisted the body of a cat or pig or dog or chicken so it grew to such an extent that its origins were almost unrecognisable. But I sensed that it represented an act of pollution—that it

came from the very opposite of the fierce fires of aspiration
from which, in the time and the place called Einfell of which
Goldenwhite had sung, all such creatures of artless magic
had once dwelt.

'The world's full of surprises.' My mother leaned her
hip against my chair, she rested her elbows on the table, her
fingers tracing the greyish scar on the heel of her right
hand. 'It's just that some of them aren't . . . quite the surprise you expect them to be . . .'

And the nights rolled on through the days of autumn
when all the guildsmen of Bracebridge paraded with their
drums and their fifes, their hats and their sashes, and the
lesser guildhouses opened their doors so we children could
marvel at the jewelled books and ornate reliquaries. And
then the cold winds blew in over Coney Mound, and stripped
the leaves off the birches, and plumed the clouds above
Rainharrow. And I smiled to myself each night when my
mother clambered, half-backwards, awkward as always,
down the ladder through that trapdoor which led from my
attic, her candle guttering and fading but the dreams, the
hopes, the inexpressible words, still clinging to me. And I
wriggled my toes deeper into the coat lining that her body
had warmed, and pushed myself away from the stirrings
and the murmurings of Coney Mound and the deeper
pounding which always lay beneath it, counting off the
months and shifterms and days until I was adrift with the
moon and the stars, looking down over the smoking chimneys of all of Bracebridge and the night-time wyreglow of
its settling pans.

From there, and the edges of sleep, slight at first as grass
stirred by the wind, then gathering and shrill, the night express came sweeping through the valley. And I was there on
the footplate with the steamaster, guiding his great engine
as it swept through the meagre little station of our meagre
little town. Bracebridge—a blur of allotments, wasteheaps,
fields, yards, factories, houses—then on into the hills, the
wild barren hills with their strange lights and howlings and
cool scents of peat and heather, pouring along the tracks
with an aethereal glow. The train would glide beneath the
boughs of forests, rush through Oxford and Slough and all

the smokestack cities of the south, then clack on over great rivers and unnamed estuaries on huge arches; it would haul the reflected amber beads of its carriage windows past sandbanks and sailboats and rush-pricked marshes. It would bear me far away from Bracebridge, yet always closer to the edge of some deeper truth about my life which I always felt myself to be teetering on.

And I was sure that truth would be marvellous.

IV

'Get up, Robert!'

I shifted, stiff and cold, from the uncomfortable position in which I'd been lying. I regathered the old coats that had pooled about me, then shuffled on my elbows across to my triangular attic window.

'Come on!' The clotheshorse rumbled in the kitchen. 'It's late morning!'

It was a day at the last edge of summer. For the first time that year, the lumpy glass of my window had frosted, was scrolled over with white patterns which pulsed and reformed in my breath. I untangled my hands to touch, making circles across the pane. Swimming down below the birch trees, a distorted version of the town was clouded with gouts of smoke and steam.

'We're going out!' My mother was at the foot of the stairs now. 'You'll miss breakfast!'

Banging around to show activity, I pulled on my trews, shirt and jumper. It occurred to me that, late though the hour clearly was, my mother might still expect me to go to Board School. Today, though, was clearly uncharted territory. I could tell that just from the sound of her voice.

I studied her warily across the kitchen table as I ate my

breakfast. We had the house to ourselves, with Beth already doling out slates in her training as a teacher's assistant at Harmanthorpe and Father at work at Mawdingly & Clawtson. She was wearing a dark blue skirt and a fresh white blouse beneath her apron. Her hair was pinned up differently, or perhaps just with greater care. She shifted and arranged things with even more than her usual air of someone whose mind was on other things. As she bustled about, I noticed that she'd grown so thin recently that the sides of her apron met around her back.

'Where are we going?'

'Out.'

'Why's that?'

'You'll see.'

I slid from the chair and went to visit the privy. The sky above the yard was blank grey and the air tasted coaly and dull. I studied the torn scraps of newspaper as I sat on the freezing seat, peeling them back sheet by sheet from the nail that impaled them to the wall. The ones I liked best were the bits of headlines. TRIAL. GLORY. TRAGEDY. I could pretend they were clues to what lay ahead in my own life.

Mother was waiting for me in the hall when I finally got back inside, already dressed in her coat and boots, umbrella dangled over one arm, a gingham-covered wicker basket hooked on the other. She let out a sigh as I fiddled with my laces, then snatched my hand and drew me quickly out into the street, closing the front door with a kick of her heel.

With the children at school, the men and women at work, Brickyard Row was almost empty. Thinning threads of mist pooled around the railings and hedges, forming a dim murk over the town through which a few whiter walls and bits of new roofing gleamed like dishes in a sink. A bald grey dray nosed its feedbag. An old woman sat out in her shawl on a front step, knitting. The dwarfish local chimneysweep whistled past, his familiar a tumbling sooty shadow. Further down the road, some lesser guildsmen were building new houses from the cheap single courses of brick that were commonly used along Coney Mound, making the signs and the whispers of their trade to bind the sloppy mortar.

Even in its better areas, Bracebridge was a resolutely unglamorous place. Prone to cold winters, short summers, gales and floods and droughts, the town had grown with the guilds. The grandmasters had found ways to make money out of the flow of the River Withy, then from coal and from steam and from iron, and from the precious aether which lay beneath Rainharrow's damp and bony earth. They had re-employed the landless peasants to work in mills and factories, then changed the seven pagan-named days of old into the modern twelve-day shifterm with its full ten and a half days of labour and its little time of rest. Still, in Bracebridge they also built a new town clock, several inns, which they named after themselves and drew a healthy profit, and the large and ugly church of St Wilfred's from which the faithful emerged on Noshiftday beaming from the visions of the hymnal wine, and which the rest of us attended with irregularity and a dim sense of foreboding.

All of these sights I witnessed on that Fourshiftday morning as my mother gripped my hand and we hurried down into the town. For all my dreamy journeys speeding south on the footplates of those night trains, the purposeful bustle of Bracebridge High Street was still a source of fascination to me. The air smelled of warm bread, dung, cabbages, mud. Handcarts, carriages, wagons, steamwagons, horses, drays and endless pedestrians battled for space over the cobbles. There was a bigger dropping-whitened statue of the Grandmaster of Painswick, his raised right knee polished from the touch of many hands which still sought his blessing. And here, for those who could afford it, were more reliable means of alleviating the pains of existence. On cushioned display in a shop window reclined the speckled painstones I'd sometimes glimpsed rich and elderly guildmistresses clutching in their arthritic fingers. Permanent bliss (as I then imagined it) from nothing more than an egg of aether-treated granite, and chocolates next door, decorated with feathers like the wild natives of Thule. I'd have pulled my mother's hand to slow her down on any more ordinary day, but the purposeful set of her mouth made me simply absorb what I could, stumbling and wondering as Rainharrow gazed down on us. Here, where the

streets climbed up towards hightown, were the houses of
the better guilds, signed like inns with their coats of arms
and set behind spiked and glossy black railings. Dragged
into their shadows, I looked up just as one of the polished
doors swung open and a large man with mutton-chop whiskers, ordinary enough but for the exceptionally crisp cut of
his brown suit, stepped out. My mother glanced up at him
just as he looked down, and it seemed to me that a twinge
of recognition passed between them.

We came to the bottom of the town, with its acreages of
yard and factory. Even as the sun came out, the air thickened with tarry smoke and the dim, pushing sense of the
subterranean nearness of the aether engines. We passed
warehouses and an open yard where the pitbeasts were
kept. Mother rummaged some coal from a nearby heap and
pushed it through the bars. The scarred mole-like brutes
lifted themselves on their rusty paddles, snuffling their
snouts to take the black nuts with surprising delicacy, the
dull heat of their breath like the warmth of an oven.

We approached the railway station, where the telegraph
pylons clambered across embankments. The lines were
busy today, glowing wyreblack against the brightening sky.
Licking the coal dust from her fingers, my mother studied
a timetable she took from her coat pocket, then, seeming to
reach no particular conclusion, bustled me into a waiting
room with dark wood panels and long lines of patient,
empty benches, and an arched window giving a glimpse of
a room filled with brightness and bustle. She rapped on the
window with the handle of her umbrella. Standing level
with the counter, I gazed up at the marvellously profuse
nose-hairs of a master from the Railworkers' Guild who,
after much consulting of pages, issued us with two thick
rectangles of notched card which smelled of new ink and
smudged as I touched them; they seemed like the very
essence of far-away, even if I'd gathered that we were only
taking a local train to some barely-heard-of station.

We clanged across scrolled iron walkways. Bracebridge
station was surprisingly grand, speaking of ambitions which
the town itself had never quite fulfilled despite its profusion
of aether. We sat waiting on a bench on the far platform

whilst a few engines fussed in the goods yard. The sun
grew brighter. The pigeons cooed. The settling pans, just
beyond the first line of rooftops, glowed darkly at the edge
of the sky. The stark rails shone empty. Mother rapped
the tip of her umbrella on the rough flagstones. Tip *tap*.
Tip *tap*.

'Where are we going, anyway?'

'You'll see.'

The wires eventually hissed and the signals nodded as
our train arrived, three low wooden carriages clacking by
until the engine at the rear lay before us. It was plated red,
but small and rusty and elderly, its boiler hissing and straining, leeching a salty rime of engine ice, the crystalline growth
which aether exudes as its power is exhausted. It looked
much nearer the scrapyard than the factory—and nothing
like the sleek southbound expresses of my night-time visions. Porters hauled sacks and trolleys. The engine hic-
cupped and shuddered. We climbed aboard, settling on the
barely padded bench of an otherwise empty carriage. I gave
an inward shiver as the whistle screamed and the station
began to slide away in grunts of steam. I'd have been happy
for this journey to continue forever, to watch Bracebridge
vanish as the thorny hedges swept by, dream-like, beyond
the rippled glass, as the land rose and my mother stared out
whilst I imagined increasingly complex versions of a tale in
which she and I were fleeing some implacable foe and leaving Bracebridge for good.

The fields grew sparser. The backs of the bigger hills
reared up, topped with versions of Rainharrow's stone
crown. Scarside, then Fareden and Hallowfell. It seemed
as if our journey was just beginning—but then the track
fanned off along a single line and the train slowed as the
view from our window was blocked by a rusty sign: TAT-
TON HALT.

A cold wind whipped around my legs as we stood on the
empty platform and the train huffed on up the valley. Thin
clouds hurried over the hills. The only evidence of humanity was the whispering line of the single telegraph that
strode with the rails into the distance and the scarred remains of an old quarry.

Our feet crunched along a stone track leading east. Mother walked quickly, a brisk black figure swinging her basket and umbrella whilst I stumbled behind, unused to this big landscape where the hills barely changed their aspect. And something was different, something wasn't right. Even the ground itself seemed . . . As the grass bowed and the path became more sheltered, narrowing into a gully, the realisation that we had left the pounding of the aether engines grew within me. Here, amid huge boulders and oak and holly, the wind boomed with a distant roar and the air became warmer as green and gold branches laced overhead. It gave off an implacable sense of age and clarity— and a strange, engine-less peace. Orange, red and gold berries glittered in the bushes. We came to a clearing where willows stooped beside a river and my mother flapped out the gingham towel as we settled on the greensward to eat. I unwrapped egg sandwiches from their greaseproof parcels and breathed in their homely smell, which is of farts and kitchens, then took out the angel cakes that lay flattened in the bottom of the basket like ruined oysters, vanilla cream oozing from their sides. The river flashed. My mother watched as I ate.

We walked on beside the bank. Around a bend, still following the path that had defined our way, we came across a mossy-bricked wall. It was clearly ancient and the trees had grown around it, cloaking its lower courses with crackling drifts of leaves. There was oak and birch. There were dense masses of holly. There were late dandelions, tansy and browning nettles and wild protrusions of bramble tipped with insect-eyed blackberries. The forest shade deepened as we followed the wall's curve towards a gatehouse, twisting and ivied, and an open wrought-iron gate. The wild greensward beyond was pooled by the shadows of trees. We both hesitated. Stepping through into the grounds, there was a sense of trespass. I looked up at my mother, but her mouth was set.

We walked on, and an old house came into view. Chimneypots climbed like fingers. Roofs sagged and clambered. Diamond windows shone. The place was half-ruined, but there was such a sense of rightness, as if it had grown from the earth stone on stone and was now falling back with equal ease, that it was a long moment before I realised that it was also very odd. Like glimpsing a face in a crowd, one side beautiful, the other scarred and ugly, it remained hard for my mind to reconcile the old house's two aspects. Along the crumbling rooflines, huge runners and veins of whitish crystal flickered like soap bubbles in the sunlight. Towards the left side of the building, the stuff lumped and gathered into warty growths, drowning the eaves. Closer to, I saw that it covered many of the walls and windows in rainbow cataracts, white on the surface but winking black in its depths, and gathered in scrolls and serrate pinecone-like growths. Of course, I recognised it—this was engine ice, the same by-product of failing aether which I had noticed leeching from the boiler of the train. But I'd never seen it on anything like this scale.

We climbed the worn semicircle of steps that led to the main door and lay beyond the influence of the growth. My mother rapped on it. The air seemed to shiver, although I could hear no sound inside until the muffled beat of foot-steps came, followed by the slide of a lock. The figure standing inside could have been my mother's age, but she was smaller, wore a plain grey dress and large, round silver-rimmed glasses. She seemed almost ordinary for a moment as I stared at her, and then, with the realisation that she wasn't, the whole illusion of her humanity seemed to ripple. Although she was nothing like my imaginings, I knew instantly that she was a changeling.

'I don't know if you remember . . .' my mother began.

'Of course. Of course. Mary—Mistress Borrows! You must come in,' she said with a wrinkly smile. In many ways, she was unremarkable. She was small and old, her skin had browned and tanned, was drumheaded across her cheekbones and thinned to almost nothing over her twig-like hands. She bore little resemblance to the trolls and witches of my night-time fears and imaginings, but at the same time there was something about her which was unlike anything or anyone I'd ever seen. That *presence,* and then being so thin and brown and old. It was all of those things, and everything else I couldn't name or place, which made me sure I was witnessing something beyond the guilds, beyond my life, beyond Bracebridge.

There was a *snip*. I saw that she was holding a pair of secateurs in her thin fingers. Yes, she was plainly old, yet the way she moved as she beckoned us in across the huge and empty hall, still snipping those secateurs, you half-expected her to fly. She was wearing the kind of straw hat my mother might have worn if she hadn't had on her bonnet, from which spiderweb strands of grey hair escaped, and her ears were like anyone else's; their tips weren't even pointed. Blink once, and she seemed ordinary. Blink again, as she stepped into the deeper shadows of the hall, and she almost seemed to vanish. Mother's shoes and umbrella tapped. Shining tails of engine ice twinkled like dirty snow from the sunlight which drizzled in patches through the roof. My boots stubbed and rattled on the loose stonework. My mother and I seemed a ridiculous pair, arriving here at this strange and ancient house, unannounced but somehow not quite unexpected.

'Is everything safe, Mary? Are things all right?' The changeling's face almost frowned. 'You'll probably want to see me alone?'

'Yes. If that would be . . . Convenient.'

She nodded, smiling.

'And you're Robert, of course.' She made my name sound enchanting. 'Who else *could* you be? I'm Mistress Summerton, although your mother called me Missy when she was just about your age . . .'

But I liked Mistress Summerton better. To me, it made an intensely pretty sound, which felt pleasant on the lips and tongue. In fact, I decided, this Mistress Summerton herself was almost pretty as well, old and wizened and changed though she seemed. Her bare, thin arms were twined with muscle like the stems of old ivy, and what inner flesh there was on her left wrist seemed unblemished, but that was only as it should be. I looked around for other creatures of myth and rumour, not just along the dim spaces, but up on along the cracked and sagging ceilings as well, and on the sills of the mostly broken windows and the branches of the nearby trees which grew through them, just

in case more changelings happened to be hanging there
like bats. But she seemed to live alone here—there was a
child's skipping rope hanging in a hallway, but such oddi-
ties were to be expected. Then we reached a part of the
house into which ghostly piles of dandelion seed had penetrated. She opened a door along a passageway. The room
beyond was cluttered with flowerpots, half-dead blooms
and cuttings, seed troughs, cloudy bottles and green demijohns and what looked and smelled like a small sack of
dray manure, although, at least in the piled desk and sagging chairs, the place also gave the impression of a kind of
office. Beyond the desk, a tall half-circle of windows looked
out on an bright garden, suffusing the air with a coloured
haze. My astonishment was still growing as Mistress Summerton added to the haze by lighting a clay pipe.

'It's about . . .' my mother began, still standing, her umbrella and picnic basket jutting out from her sides. 'What I
mean is . . .'

'Annalise should be here in another moment. Then we
can begin our talk.' Mistress Summerton came over to me,
her pipe clamped within her withered lips. She studied me
from our almost equal heights. 'You've grown so finely,
Robert . . . It *is* still Robert, isn't it? You *look* a Robert
now, although not perhaps for life . . .' White smoke billowed around her. She seemed to be part of it, receding
even as she drew closer and laid a hand on my shoulder
which felt hot and light. Then she took off her glasses. Her
eyes were brown and bright. In one sense, they were the
most ordinary thing about her, but at the same time, they
were *too* bright. The pupils were large and big and glittery
as jet buttons. The whites had the gleam of wet porcelain.

Then the door opened behind me.

'Annalise! At last! And I have a job for you.'

I turned slowly, wondering, after what I had already
seen, what kind of sprite could possibly have such an af-
fected name. I was disappointed; Annalise looked, in fact,
like any other girl of about my age. She was wearing a
short-sleeved dress of grubby white cotton, and even dirt-
ier short white socks crumpled above scuffed sandals
which might have been new some summers before. Her

hair was pale blond, done up in tatters of velvet. She had a high forehead, and skin that would have been pale if it were clean, and eyes which were even greener than the sunlit grass outside. Her expression, as we regarded each other like cats forced to share each other's territory, was a scowl of disinterest. She had the look of a once-treasured doll that had been left out in the rain.

'When I say *job,* Annalise I mean a task,' Mistress Summerton was saying. 'And I hope a pleasant one. This here is Robert Borrows and I was thinking, well, I was wondering, if you two . . .' Her scratchy fingers steered me towards the door. Annalise stepped back. A moment later, we were both standing alone in the long corridor.

'Do you even *know* what this place is?' she asked eventually.

I shook my head.

Annalise stared at me with disdain. 'If you want to know, it's actually called Redhouse,' she said. 'If you're interested in facts. Which I suppose you're probably not.'

She turned and strode off. One of her sandals had a loose buckle, which jingled lightly with each step. Unable to think of anything better to do, I followed her.

'So you're a changeling as well, then?'

'What do *you* think, little Robert Borrows?' Perhaps deliberately, she was holding her arms tightly in at the sides. I couldn't see her wrist. 'Do I *look* like one?'

'I don't know. I mean no—of course you don't. But living here, in this place . . .' I was walking sideways to her as I struggled to keep up. 'Although you seem ordinary.'

'Why should *I* care what you believe?' she muttered.

My body reacted before I had time to think. I stopped, grabbed Annalise's arm, and spun her around. As I did so, the air was sheared by a thin, inaudible shriek.

'Look . . .' I was breathless as I faced her. The ruined corridor seemed suddenly endless. 'I'm like you. Nobody asked me about today, about coming here. I can either go off on my own and sit somewhere and wait for my mother, or I can stay with you. In fact, I—'

'All right . . .' I was still holding Annalise's left arm just above the wrist. My fingers tingled as, seemingly of their own accord, they let go. Beneath the grime, and but for the reddened marks made by my fingers, and to me quite incredibly, her skin was unmarked. 'But don't think I'm like you,' she added. 'Because I'm *not*.'

But Annalise was totally unique to me. And I suppose that in many ways I was almost equally strange to her; an ordinary lad from the ordinary world in which she seemed to feign disinterest. But I also felt, even then as she turned from me as she began to walk on, that our oppositenesses fitted together. That we made a kind of a pair. More and more of the crystal growth became apparent as we crossed into what would once have been the state rooms of Redhouse, although most of their roofs and the once-ornate plaster of many of the walls had fallen away. At first, there were just tiny grains of engine ice powdering the ruined floors. Then, larger, chandelier-like excrescences began to droop from the few remaining beams that spanned the ceilings.

'Lots more people used to live here,' Annalise said matter-of-factly. 'But they had to stop. They used to work aether engines here, just like in Bracebridge . . .'

So she'd heard of Bracebridge! But the questions, the marvels, were coming too quickly. We had entered a room which reached all the way up through the house to the oval dome of a huge and miraculously intact skylight. It was walled with spilled and sagging cliff faces of books, tiered with balconies. The place soared far beyond my comprehension of a library, although clearly it had once performed that function. Here, also, the two quietly warring sides of the house entwined. Darkly veined, the glowing growths of engine ice clogged the shelves, dripped down the stairways in a glittering foam that broke across the floor in frozen waves. Even the glass dome was half covered like a blinking eye. I touched some of the ice. The crystal was cool and brittle. It crumbled with a fizzing, tinkling sound.

Annalise's breath was close on my cheek.

'I like to read here,' she said.

'I like reading too, or at least—'

'—looking at the pictures, I suppose. The only problem is,' she continued before I had a chance to deny it, 'this whole library's too *old*. The books fall apart.'

I lifted a tome which lay at the top of a pile which had spilled to the floor. The pages fluttered out like snow. It seemed a sad thing; all this dying knowledge. But when I turned to Annalise, she was smiling.

'Come on! Bet you can't catch me!' She scrambled up a banister, grabbed a book from a shelf and threw it down at me. I ducked. It skidded across the tiles. The spine was ridged with crystal.

'Looking at the *pictures*! Bet you can't even *read*!' Another book whizzed past.

Half angry, half laughing, I stared to climb up after her. The wood creaked and splintered. Engine ice fizzed down. Annalise fled ahead of me, slinging more books and insults.

'Have you heard of Plato?' she shouted, tossing out a tome from the rail above me which crashed below with the thud of a brick. 'He was a person just like you, although a *lot* more intelligent. He invented aether long before the Grandmaster of Painswick, although he really just thought about it. It's the fifth element, and it just goes around in circles when all the others travel in a straight line.' Another book shot past me, spiralling down through long bars of sunlight, flapping its jewelled covers. More and more books flew by, their pages fluttering like birds, offering bright glimpses of their coloured plates. They rose and circled around me before sliding across the library's distant chequered floor. I began to throw books out myself from the shelves around me, climbing from ledge to ledge as Annalise darted ahead. Finally, we reached a truce, and lay spread-eagled and breathless on the tiles amidst the wreckage of our battle. My scratched palms and knees were dusted silver-white. The huge, eerie library glowed.

'Won't you be in trouble for all this mess?'

Annalise chuckled. 'Missy doesn't care. She's like that—she lets me do what I want.' Close to, she smelled earthy and salty; like any other child. 'Nobody minds about Redhouse now. Nobody wants it but us . . .'

Idly, I picked up the sprawled leaves of the book which lay nearest my fingers. Annalise was right, of course. It was the pictures rather than the words which then drew me. Here were ancient woodcuts from the Age of Kings, dark and swirling like the smoke of all the chimneys of Bracebridge in midwinter. Men with the heads of dogs chewed at corpses. Creatures with pendulous breasts and faces like melting lanterns flew on broomsticks through the air. The print beside it was dense, and filled with funny *f*s and *s*es. One page had a bigger illustration of what I thought at first was a flower until I saw that what I'd imagined to be the stamen was a figure writhing at a stake amid the black petals of flames.

'What's that you're looking at?' With a quick movement, Annalise snatched the book away. She studied the title on the spine. '*Compendium Maleficarum . . .* That's all *so* out of date.' With an effortless gesture, she tossed it so far across the library that it seemed to vanish into the moted air. Then she stood up, hands on hips, giving me a grey glimpse of her knickers. 'Well? Are you coming?'

I followed as she pushed open a window then dropped down into the wilderness gardens outside. Here, more of the crystal piled amid the flowerbeds in the clear afternoon air, a dense foam amid which great-headed chrysanthemums nodded and roses bloomed. Annalise grabbed a peach from the bough of a tree which was like a glittering white umbrella. Knocking the encrusted fruit against a red brick wall, cracking it open like a nut, she tossed it to me. Juice flooded my palm as I bit into it.

'You can learn all sorts of interesting things from books without having to go anywhere,' Annalise said matter-of-factly as we sat down on a lawn beside the silvered mass of a fountain. 'I mean, I could tell you more about that thingamajig place where you live—'

'—Bracebridge—'

'—from a book than you'd ever find out just by living there.'

I shrugged, plucking at the daisied grass.

'And then of course, there's all the *other* things that people get up to.' Annalise hugged her knees. 'Men and women, I mean. When they want to rub up against each other and make babies.'

'I know *all* about that. Still,' I conceded, 'you can tell me if you like.'

'Well . . .' Annalise leaned back on her elbows and studied the sky, her hair falling pale gold now, almost like the foam, her dress nearly managing to be white. She was completely unembarrassed by her subject—but at the same time, she clearly understood that what she knew was well worth telling. I supposed, watching her as she talked, that she couldn't have been totally isolated here. But, as the grass shone and the windows of the warty house glowed, as Annalise's explanation of the act of human reproduction ranged bizarrely over the complicated terrain of some language that she had taken from those books, I didn't want our shared afternoon to be anything other than totally unique.

'Then the *labia minor* . . . And thus engorging the *corpora cavernosa* . . . Whilst attaching to the *non-striated* . . .'

I listened, genuinely absorbed by the sound of these long, lovely, intricate words which spoke of rituals far more exotic than I could imagine the adults of Bracebridge—let alone my own parents—performing. Her voice was slightly breathless, high-pitched, and suffused with an odd personal accent that didn't belong to any particular time or place.

'Of course, the *zygote* . . .'

And as she talked, leaning into the sunlight beside that fountain which sparked and gushed in frozen waves, the off-white strap of her dress slipped from her shoulder. Her skin there looked almost clean and was flecked with golden hairs. Annalise had stopped talking. She looked at me for a moment, blinked, then yanked up her dress. She jumped up and walked off down the sloping garden, where lumpy balustrades gave way to a steeper drop. I scampered to catch up with her, grabbing branches, leaping from rock to root.

'It wasn't always like this,' she called as I crashed after her. 'Lots and lots of people used to live here. It was probably *much* bigger than Bracebridge . . .'

There had, indeed, once been a village beside the river down below this big house, although it was now half-drowned in engine ice, its tumourous roofs sagging or broken, the doors and windows draped, the pathways

tumbling with froth. Our feet crunched and tinkled. We
climbed to the ruins of the church, its tower fallen in a
long, crusted tail, now shining and scaled, with gravestones
leaning around it. It seemed colder and darker here; already edged with the beginnings of winter. But it would
be good, I decided with an odd prescience as Annalise
climbed over what had once been the church wall and the
backs of her legs flashed white, if Bracebridge were to
become like this one day; frozen in time, ornamented with
engine ice.

'You're not afraid, are you?' she asked me.

'No. Of course not. Why should I be?'

At the foot of a bank, close by the river, the crystal
rose in extravagant loops and claws, and the water hissed
through brittle curtains which fanned like frosted weed
from the shore. We came to the motionless waterwheel of
an old millhouse still jutting into the frozen waters of its
sluices. We climbed over ruined beams in the crackling
marsh that surrounded it, glancing up, moment by moment, at the shouldering roof, the silent wheel. But for this
strange frostfall, it was much like the old aether engines
you found up on Rainharrow. Curtains of ancient weed
fanned out, trapped within the glassy water in dense, inky
waves. The sense of the past lay heavy here. In those days
of the Second Age of Industry when this wheelhouse had
thrived, aether could still be extracted from near the earth's
surface and the engines were mostly set on open ground
like any other process of manufacturing. For eighty, perhaps ninety, years, villages such as this one had flourished
too, growing stone by stone and roof by roof, burying their
dead and raising their babies until they became too remote
to be reached by the new railways, too high to be embraced
by the canals. Then the aether started to run out. For a
while, the waterwheel would still have turned as the children of the village left to find work in the big cities of
Sheffield and Preston and the guildsmen struggled to keep
the bearings of their outdated machinery turning, using up
more and more of what aether they still extracted, leaving
less and less to sell.

We walked back up through the trees, clambering over

rustling falls of crystal then on through the village until we finally reached the glinting gardens of the big house again. Viewed from this side, standing by the frozen froth of that fountain, it seemed even more scaled and ruined. We wandered inside, skidding listlessly across floors, bonging gongs in empty hallways, knocking off stalactites of growth that dissolved with glassy sighs as the air filled with twilight. Annalise led me along eerie passageways to a large, dim room. Its windows were curtained with engine ice and what little light they admitted glittered on the only item of furniture, something so whitened and misshapen that I thought for a moment it was composed of nothing but engine ice. But the lid of the piano came up surprisingly easily when Annalise raised it and the keys inside were uncorroded.

I asked, 'Can you play?'

She answered with a scatter of notes.

'Tell me, Robert . . .' More notes. 'What's it like in Bracebridge?'

I licked my lips. Where to begin? Where to end? 'Well . . . There's the sound, the feel. I mean, the aether engines. And we live in a row of houses. There are *lots* of rows of houses . . . My mother—I mean my father, he's—'

The piano rang out again. 'What I mean is, what's it like for *you*?'

I thought for a moment. The room rippled into silence. 'It's . . .' I shrugged.

'Would you rather be here with Missy?' Her figure was dim. Scarcely there. A shadow, receding. 'Would you rather be me?'

'I don't even know what you *are*, Annalise.'

She gave a chuckle. Soft and bitter, not quite a laugh, it seemed to come from someone much older. Once again, her fingers stroked the piano. Dust sparkled up from the struck strings.

'I'm really glad I came here,' I said.

'Hmm . . .' Annalise was humming, scarcely listening.

'Now I know people like you don't just go to Northallerton.'

She closed the lid with a bang.

'I think you'd better get back to your mother.'

I scurried after Annalise down corridors and stairways. Inside Mistress Summerton's study, tobacco smoke hung in weary drapes around the plants. It seemed as if my mother and Mistress Summerton had long been sitting in silence.

'We really must be going.' My mother climbed slowly from the chair. I saw from the glistening trails that lay across her face that she'd been crying. 'You see, there's the last train . . .'

'Of course, of course . . .' Mistress Summerton stood up also, smiling with a flash of her glasses, and my mother and I were wafted from the room and back into the big main hallway where the engine ice still glimmered and sparkled through doorways with a faint inner light. I looked around for Annalise, but she had already vanished.

The two figures, my mother stooped, little Mistress Summerton as strange and alive as the house itself, regarded each other across the distance of their vastly different existences. Then, in a gesture that was rare even between people of the same family in those times of physical reserve, Mistress Summerton stepped forward and took my mother in her small brown arms. In a way, I was almost as shocked by this embrace as I was by anything I had seen on this magical Fourshiftday. And it seemed to me that the two figures merged; or rather, that Mistress Summerton encompassed them both, spreading across the hall and growing briefly vast in a beating of wings.

'There . . .' Mistress Summerton stepped back and reached to touch my mother's forehead, muttering something more, wordless words which ran high quick and clear as a guildsman's spell. Then she turned to me, fixing me with the gaze of her glasses, which filled with swirling light.

'You must take care of your mother,' she said, although her lips barely moved. *I can feel a strength in you, Robert. And hope. Keep that hope, Robert. Keep it for as long as you can . . . Will you do that for me?*

I nodded.

Mistress Summerton smiled. Her strange gaze travelled through me.

'Goodbye.'

I looked back at the house as my mother and I walked down the white driveway. The crystal growth seemed more like the honey-glow of twilight now. And above it all, the stars were forming. One, shimmering low ahead of us in the west, was a deep, dark red.

My mother grabbed my arm.

'Don't tell Beth or your father about today,' she muttered. 'You know what *he's* like . . .'

I nodded, thinking of Mistress Summerton's words.

'And take this basket—I don't see why I should have to carry it all the way!'

I carried the empty picnic basket for my mother as we hurried to catch the last train from Tatton Halt.

V

Living the hard and ordinary life we lived on Coney Mound, torn as I was between past and future wonders, my mother hardly needed to have asked me not to speak to anyone about our visit to Redhouse. Naturally, I was hungry to keep my own secret portion of this world, particularly if it lay beyond Bracebridge. So I bore my burden—along with the bright images of that day; Annalise, Mistress Summerton—in silence, although, as I wandered the town, my head was filled with questions which had previously never troubled me.

Down in Bracebridge market square, I found a patch of especially cracked and weathered old stone where the stocks had stood, and where, before that, and in the chaos of the First Age, changelings might once have been burnt before we learned how to tame and capture them. And rummaging through the town public library, sniffling over dank pages, I searched for G for Goldenwhite, U for Unholy, R for Rebellion, and C for changeling. But what *was* a changeling? All the talk of green vans and Northallerton and trolls and milk souring and babies being eaten seemed like nothing but gossip across the back fences of Coney Mound. But on a high shelf in the corner of the library so dim and dank and unvisited that the shadows seemed to give a resistance, I heaved down a tome embossed with a cross inside a letter C and flopped it open.

It could almost have been one of those books from Redhouse, but this one contained foggy photographs the colour of nicotine stains amid long columns of text. Flesh rippled and sluglike, or white and blooming. Faces cracked like peeling paint. Limbs strung with cascading cauls.

'What are ye lookin' at?'

It was Masterlibrarian Kitchum, a half-blind man of such dumb illiteracy that it was hard to imagine that his appointment hadn't been some kind of joke. Cursing, he dragged the book from me and chased me into the rain.

But there was so much I still needed to know. So, within three shifts, and on a grey Nineshiftday of irredeemable ordinariness, I set out to make my way back to Redhouse. I left home at the usual time carrying my school satchel, then doubled down and back around the edges of lowtown, trod the cabbage leaves through the failing allotments, crossed Withybrook Road and followed the railway tracks around the side of Rainharrow to the point where that lonely branch line dipped across the moors. It was past midday when, plodding on beneath dulled loops of telegraph as the wind bit into me, I took the path through the greying heather beside the old quarry. The late autumn sun was already ominously low by the time I entered the wood leading down to the clearing where my mother and I had had our picnic. Despite the new bareness of the trees, the path grew darker as I descended it, drowning in riots of thorns and holly. Wading through the undergrowth, no longer sure if I was following any kind of path, I began to panic. I was running, breathless. Then, when I was sure I was utterly lost, the wood suddenly relented and I found that I was standing again at the edge of the moor. Darkness was flooding in and the greyish path threaded back towards the empty platform of Tatton Halt. I took it at a grateful run and trotted homewards along the track, pausing only to ease the pain in my sides. The telegraphs glowed faintly above me with distant messages, and, far beyond that, the stars began to glimmer in clusters and strings. One, beckoning towards Coney Mound, was red.

Tired and afraid and disappointed, I followed the dim strings of lowtown's gaslights and the milky wyreglow of the quickening pools, and climbed the familiar streets past St Wilfred's. The cobbles were wet, each glinting with a fleck of that red star. The houses were black. The air was silent. Then I heard something screaming, and my heart chilled. It sounded as if claws were being dragged across the surface of the night. Then the noise emerged from the alley opposite me and became a dark figure. Its eyes, like the cobbles, burned with twin flecks of red light, and the air seemed to grey and shimmer around it. The night shrank and pulsed. I was sure at that moment that the devil himself had decided to walk Coney Mound, or at the very least that Owd Jack, aged and pained beyond belief and yet still living, had come to reclaim me. SHOOM *BOOM* SHOOM *BOOM*. Stretching its rags, the thing shuffled towards me. And I ran. I was leaning against the gate of our back yard and catching my breath in ragged yelps before I realised that I'd only glimpsed the Potato Man. This was, after all, the time of year for him.

'You're late.'

My sister Beth barely glanced up at me as I slumped down before the kitchen range. She thumped a dried-up meal on the table as I worked off my boots. I studied the chipped plate. A slice of shrivelled bacon. Some fibrous lumps of sea-potato, that ever-ready standby of the poor. Not even a slice of bread.

'Where's Mother?'

'She's upstairs.' Beth's look stopped any further questions. And she wasn't wearing the inky pinafore she usually wore when she'd been working at her school. Picking at my food, I tried to remember whether anything had been different about this morning other than my own preoccupation with my secret plans for the day.

'Can I go up and see her?'

Beth bit her lip. Her wide, pink-cheeked face was framed by black, glossy, carelessly cut hair. 'When you've finished eating.'

Father came in from work soon after and headed straight upstairs without bothering to wash. Hobnails thunked across the ceiling, followed by the rake of a chair, his voice raised in a question, what might or might not have been the murmur of Mother's reply.

The fire in the range spat and crackled. The sounds from the other houses of pots banging, doors opening and closing, people talking, washed in through the thin walls. Redhouse seemed further away than ever. Father came down and shook his head at the withered food Beth offered. Hunched in his chair, he lit a cigarette and stared at it until a worm of ash dropped to the floor. It was silent above us now. The evening crawled by. I went into the scullery to wash my plate, then crept up the stairs on my blistered toes, trying hard as all the usual creaks popped and clattered not to make a sound. The landing swayed in the lanternlight that came from my mother's room. Not wanting to go in now, just wanting to get to my bed in the attic and put this day behind me, I crept past the half-open door.

'Robert?'

I hesitated. The floor creaked again.

'That *is* you Robert. Come in . . .'

My mother looked ordinary enough, propped up by an extra pillow and wearing her better night-gown. Her eyes flickered to the shadows that bulked in the room's corners, then back to me.

'You look tired, Robert. That scratch on your cheek. And you *smell* different. Where have you been?'

I shrugged. 'Just the usual . . .'

Her hands lay above the blankets, thin and delicate as a bird's. The right one grasped the cloth, was slowly contracting and relaxing. SHOOM *BOOM*. The rhythmic motion stopped when she realised I was watching. A dull shudder passed through me.

'Anyway, you'd better get to bed.'

She tilted her head slightly, offering her cheek. Her skin felt brittle and hot.

My mother's new frailty became a kind of normality as Coney Mound settled into another winter. One by one, she gave up her various part-time jobs. Money became shorter and Beth, stuck with all the extra work that had fallen to her, failed her Guild of Assistant Teachers' exam. After long hours of frigid rage, Father managed to complete the necessary forms to apply for the hardship funds set up by the Toolmakers' Guild and a cheque was issued. Meagre though it was, it paid for occasional visits by that black frock-coated harbinger of death and uncertainty, a Master of the Physicians' Guild. I watched the doctor rummaging in the glimmer of his bag, bottles clinking, his steel glasses and bald head shining with the glow of his useless potions, his meaningless spells, before he applied the drainings and poultices that always left my mother iller and more fretful.

Sometimes, though, she would still be up when I got home, sitting by the parlour fire with a blanket over her legs and another over her shoulders which now seemed to rise too narrowly and too high. Occasionally, she would even be on her feet and moving about, ignoring Beth's protests as she tried to get on with some household task that she had convinced herself was being neglected. She was clumsy enough at the best of times but I remember one evening soon after the first snowfalls when I came in and found her standing at the kitchen table, trying to crack eggs into the bowl. A scatter of crushed shells lay around her and yokes and whites drooled from her fingers, glistening in the faint darkness that now always seemed to surround her as if she was receding into a dream. I stayed out late the following evening. That year, that winter, I stayed out late on many nights.

VI

Midwinter loomed. There was more snow, a glazing of icy rain, and my father took me with him to Mawdingly & Clawtson one cold December Halfshiftday. Other guildsmen with faces I dimly recognised came to join us as we walked through the coalyards and sidings, swinging their leather kit bags, crashing their boots through the refrozen slush. The back entrance into the factory was quite unlike that to the main front office, with its ceramic friezes of Providence and Mercy, where I'd sometimes been sent to collect the wages. *So this is the lad, is it? Looking after yer poor Ma, then, are yer?* The men kept asking me questions they plainly didn't want answered. *Come to be shown then, have yer, eh?* Then, as an aside. *Quiet little blighter, ain't he?*

The men who shared what was known as East Floor belonged to a variety of guilds. There were ironworkers, once known as smithies, and ferrous engineers, and platers, and ironmasters whose hands sometimes turned black and scabby, and enginewrights and finishers with missing fingers, all tangled together through processes which the foremen and the managers, themselves members of other guilds, or higher branches of the same ones, strove to control and contain. It was complicated and arcane, with hallowed meeting times, cryptic awards, spaces between walkways where one or another species could eat their lunch or hang their coats, but the overall impression which struck me as my father rolled up his sleeves and slipped the gears that would begin to turn his crude iron machine, was of an environment even more vicious and chaotic than my schoolyard. The men's voices grew loud as they chanted incantations and common curses over the rattle and whine of their machinery. They seemed both proud and contemptuous of what they did, slapping gritty oil from tins and making odd signs of control when a pulley began to slap too loosely or a strut of metal threatened to shear. The few guildless marts who swept the floors and swatted dragonlice and cleaned the swarf were spat at, tripped, flicked with grease.

My father's boss, an uppermaster named Stropcock who had a rat's pointed face and a large clip of pens bulging from the top pocket of his brown overalls, came up and said something over the noise which I guessed from the twisting of his lips was to do with showing me around. He then dragged, half threw me along grubby corridors where various lesser guilds had their offices. Forcing open a door, he tumbled me into a dim office which was stacked with half-open filing cabinets, rolled plans, greening mugs, tarnished trophies.

'So we'll be seeing a lot more of you, then, eh, laddie?' he said somewhat breathlessly.

I shrugged.

'Insolent little bastard, aren't you?'

I shrugged again.

He lit a cigarette and flicked the match over my shoulder. 'Lad like you, what makes you think that you're good enough for the Lesser Toolmakers anyway? Your father wasn't. Dead fucking lucky, I'd say he was, to get in at all.'

I just stared at him. I really wasn't that bothered by what he was saying. If I'd been cunning enough, I suppose I could have taken a swipe at him and put an end to my chances of ever joining the Lesser Toolmakers. Little men, stuck in little positions of little authority, are always the worst. He coughed up some phlegm and I wondered for a moment if he was going to spit it at me before he swallowed it back, ground out his cigarette and stalked around his desk to where an oil-stained sheet lay tented over something many-pointed. He flipped it back. Beneath lay the antlered, aetherised brass of a haft. I'd heard of such things, glimpsed them in guildhouse displays, but I'd never been this close. About a foot and a half high, grown from aethered brass, it looked more than anything like the miniature stump and boughs of a wind-eroded tree. Uppermaster Stropcock stroked the tip of one of its horn-shaped protuberances with his nicotined fingers. His eyelids flickered. For a moment, until he regathered himself, the whites rolled up.

'Know what this is?'

I nodded.

'This, sonny, is my eyes and ears. Later, when you're here good and proper, when you've backache from stooping and blisters on your hands and piles up your arse and your little head throbs from the noise, when you've seen some other lads from some other tinpot guild skulking off for an early snap, remember me. Eyes and ears, sonny, just remember. Eyes and ears. This isn't school. We aren't your pansy teachers . . .'

He stepped back. Ridiculously, it looked as if he was inviting me to touch the haft.

'It'll be the only time, laddie. So make the most of it . . .'

Slipping between Uppermaster Stropcock and the desk before he'd had the time to think better of it, I touched one of the thick brass spines. The thing felt smooth and warm and slightly greasy, like a well-used doorhandle. Then my flesh seemed to stick, to meld. And I sensed the factory pouring into me through the telegraphs and filaments that entwined it; sensed it as I had never sensed anything before. All the noise, all the work, all those lives. Mawdingly & Clawtson. SHOOM *BOOM*. That huge collision of effort which brought aether up from the ground. I was being sucked down. Through the wires, the telegraphs, the rails. The sensation was giddy and exulting. This was like my dream night-journeys. I was speeding everywhere across this realm. Hills and farms and valleys, and factories, factories, factories. Brick on brick and stone on stone, reinforced and bound and corrugated. And flesh on flesh as well. A great mountain of human endeavour. Bone grinding against bone and day against day in the endless procession of these Ages. And something else as well. Something dark beyond darkness, powerful beyond power, yet rising, rising—

The bolt of a whispered command kicked my hand away.

'That's *enough,* lad. Don't do to be greedy . . .' The oily sheet wafted down again. 'Just don't forget, eh?' He hitched up the sleeves of his jacket, unbuttoned the filthy cuff of his shirt. '—See these, eh?' Sunset-coloured bruises embroidered the insides of his palms and writhed up to the blistered navel of his stigmata. 'See, these, laddie. Marks of the haft. And don't you *ever* bloody forget them.'

My head buzzing, I followed Uppermaster Stropcock back along corridors and across a wide yard traversed by hissing pressurised pipes. Clanging up an outer stairway in his wake, I bumped into the greasy seat of his trousers when he halted halfway.

'Uppermaster Stropcock!' I heard an oddly accented voice above us exclaim. 'And how are we on this less than bright morning?'

'Fair to middling, sir.'

Stropcock backed down the stairway, forcing me with him.

'Thank you! I'm most obliged,' the voice continued. 'And who have we here?'

Stropcock shuffled back and a large man with muttonchop whiskers, a mop of reddish hair and a brown woollen suit stood regarding me.

'Just the lad of one of the workers I'm showing around.' Then he added in a loud whisper, leaning down, 'This *here,* sonny, is *Grandmaster Harrat,*' as if this personage was too important to speak his own name.

'And what do you think of our factory?' Grandmaster Harrat asked.

'It's . . .' I glanced around at the filthy buildings. 'Big.'

Uppermaster Stropcock sucked in a breath. 'He's only the Borrows lad.'

But Grandmaster Harrat laughed. 'Tell you what, Ronald. I'll take young Master Borrows from you and show him around myself.'

'But—'

'If that's *all right* with you? I mean, I take it that it *is*?' Grandmaster Harrat laid a hand on my shoulder, leading me across the yard before Uppermaster Stropcock had had a chance to reply. 'What's your first name?' he asked, in a surprisingly gentle, almost wheedling, voice.

'Robert, sir.'

'And you must call me simply Tom. It's not as though you *work* at Mawdingly & Clawtson yet, Robert, is it, or you've yet been inducted into a guild? So there's no need for formality, is there? We can just be friends . . .' The hand, which still lay on my shoulder, squeezed me gently. *Tom*—it was a ridiculous suggestion. I could never think of him as Simply Tom. He'd always be Grandmaster Harrat.

We passed through doorways into better-made corridors and rooms where the more specialised crafts were performed. Supervisors scampered around machinery to greet Grandmaster Harrat. Leaning over the workbenches, the silk buttons of his waistcoat sliding against my arm, he encouraged the guildsmen to perform some intricate portion of their duties. He spoke to the master of a familiar on west floor, who called his creature down from the spinning overhead maze of gears by pursing his lips into an inaudible whistle. The poor animal's fur was caked in oil and it was missing the tips of several of its toes. The familiar licked itself half-heartedly, then studied me with wise sad eyes set in an almost human face. It looked as lost here as I felt, far from its home in the tropic jungles of fabled Africa.

'You father works East Floor, doesn't he?' Grandmaster Harrat said after ordering me a large slab of chocolate cake in the tiled and elegant senior management canteen. 'He's a toolmaker . . . and your mother used to work in the paintshop?' I nodded as I ate, my mouth full of sponge and saliva, quite amazed that he should have heard of us Borrowses. Then I risked asking him if he didn't actually *know*

Masters Clawtson and Mawdingly. This, like most of my comments, caused him to laugh. They were both, it seemed, long dead and buried. The factory was now owned by something called shareholders, which could mean individual people, or more often as not the guilds—or the banks where the guilds kept their money. Sticking out his bottom lip like a small boy as he swirled more sugar into his tea, Grandmaster Harrat ruefully admitted that he, as a senior member of the Metallurgical Branch of the Great Guild of Savants, was on something known as the General Board, which apparently made the decisions that shaped the destiny of Clawtson & Mawdingly, although, personally speaking, it was a part of his job that he hated. Studying Grandmaster Harrat again between the silver churches of the condiments, I realised that I had seen him before; stepping out of the door of that guildhouse and looking down on my mother and I on that morning that we had hurried to the station.

I was taken to Engine Floor, where the engines that drove the aether pistons and much of the other major machinery were located, pouring out pressurised steam and motive power. We looked down as vast iron boilers throbbed and bubbled, their aetherised joints glowing in hot semidarkness with the power they controlled and contained. I stood before the largest and most ancient of these engines—*presented* was the word—whose huge, leaking iron body was lumped with barnacle-like encrustations of engine ice and rust. We looked down from the gantry where its ironmaster, who was as white and skinny as his charge was black and huge, worked stripped to the waist with braces dangling, stroking and willing his machine to bear impossible pressures.

'That engine's been here longer than any of us,' Grandmaster Harrat shouted in my ear. 'It used to have a twin, but that's another story . . .'

At the core of Engine Floor lay the axle which powered the aether engines beneath. It was even thicker and blacker and vaster than I'd imagined, and so smoothly polished and oiled that it scarcely seemed to be moving. Grandmaster Harrat led me to a gated lift, and pulled a lever that sent the earth clacking up. For a while it grew almost silent as we dropped and joists and telegraph filaments slid by. Then a sound pushed everything else aside.

SHOOM *BOOM* SHOOM *BOOM*.

The air pounded in and out of my lungs as we stepped out into a tunnel. Grandmaster Harrat wordlessly gestured the way that we should go as we stooped along a wet brick maze past the intermittent light of mesh-hooded lanterns. I caught glimpses of the grind and flash of coarse machinery. Was this foul burrow really where we obtained all that aether? Here, the air gasped, the wounded rock shuddered, the very earth twisted and groaned. Every forward step, every blink and breath, required an enormous effort. We reached a cavern of sorts. Here, on Central Floor, there was no sound but an endlessly repeated convulsion. The triple massive horizontal columns of the aether engines pounded before me on their steel and concrete beds, and Grandmaster Harrat led me beside their flashing pistons to their link with the Bracebridge earth, a great iron plug the size of a house bolted to the rockface which was called the fetter. From there, in a shadow-weave of engine silk, the engines were joined by a yard-long chrysalis of intricate metal known as the shackle. But my senses were overwhelmed. There was light and there was blackness, and I think I must have been about to faint. Probably noticing how pale I had become, Grandmaster Harrat steered me back along the almost quiet-seeming tunnels, and we waited at the lift gate as the pulley chains began to turn. I still felt ill and giddy as I looked back along those damp walls. Nubs of engine ice, I noticed, pushed out from them at intervals like the tips of pleading hands. Then the lift arrived.

Back on the surface we passed across yards and through doorways to a large high room where all the noise of the factory suddenly fell away. I stood swaying, dazed by cool semidarkness. Lines of young women sat working amid greenish wafts of aetherglow. The paintshop girls—for girls was all they mostly were, filling in the time between school and childbearing whilst their hands and eyes were good enough for this impossibly delicate work. Elbows nudged. There were giggles.

'Your mother used to work here, you know.'

I could well imagine my father swaggering towards this paintshop on some excuse of an errand—slicking back his hair and checking his reflection in a water butt before breezing through the door and setting eyes on the face of my mother, upward-lit by the wyreflame of whatever cog or valve she was then working on.

Grandmaster Harrat then took me to his own office, which looked out on the forgotten world of trees, gaslamps and drays. A fire was warming the hearth. There was a smell of sallow-wood and leather.

'So, Robert,' he said, lighting a cigar and breathing a circle of smoke, 'do you still think Mawdingly & Clawtson is big?'

I was staring around at the books and the vases and the paintings. A mermaid combed her hair on a rock.

'And what did you think of the aether engines?'

'They were . . .' What could I say? Then a thought struck me. 'The engine ice coming from the walls— doesn't that mean the aether's nearly exhausted?'

There was a pause. 'I think you should wait until you're a guildsman before you speculate on such matters, Robert. But here . . .' Placing his cigar in a cut glass ashtray, he flipped open a wooden box—beautiful to me in its simplicity— which lay on his desk. He removed a steel spindle from it and held it out, the points digging into the tips of his broad, soft fingers. The spindle had a colourless sheen and thickened at the centre. 'Engine silk, Robert. This is what your father's life on East Floor at Mawdingly & Clawtson is dedicated to—or at least, to making the machines which make the machines that finally make the engine silk. Mine as well, seeing as the Guild of Savants ensures the precise and efficient extraction of aether . . .'

Grandmaster Harrat grabbed something that couldn't be seen and trailed it out with a looping gesture. A faint glimmer of firelight laced the air.

'Go on. Touch—but be careful. That's it . . . Imagine you're stroking a cat . . .'

Light as the wind, the stuff whispered through my fingers.

'Strange, isn't it, that aether travels better along something so pure, so frail; through the fetter, to the shackle, then up through the engines and all those yards of rock to the surface of this world? And of course, there's aether in the silk itself—aether, Robert, to carry the aether—can you see it glimmering? *This* was what the Grandmaster of Painswick really laboured to produce all his life. All the rest . . .' He waved a hand, encompassing everything which lay beyond the panelled walls of his office. 'It's all just motive power, pressure. Yes, the weave of the engine silk in the shackle's the key . . .'

I nodded.

'Of course, this particular spool is useless, contaminated.' Gently, he untangled the engine silk from my fingers and wound it up again. 'A mere tradesman's sample . . .' He placed the spindle back within its box, then lifted up his cigar, ruefully studying its cold black end. 'And your father, of course. *Your* father . . .' At that moment, the familiar howl of the shift siren rippled the air. This being Halfshiftday, work on the outer floors finished at noon. 'And then there's your mother. Is she better?'

'Better? I—'

'You must send her my wishes. We all . . .' Grandmaster Harrat mused, pursing his thick lips, running a thumb down the front of his fine waistcoat, his eyes far away. 'We all wish that things could have been different. Will you tell her that for me? That we wish things could have been different?' Once more, he laid his soft hands upon my shoulder. 'You will tell her that for me, won't you?'

More snow came on Christmas Eve. Curdled clouds writhed across the valley and the men trudged home early as the chimneys blocked and the yards piled up, hunched like the negatives of ghosts against the teeming white. The shops closed, the roads and the rails became impassable. Brace-bridge found itself isolated. Even the shift sirens didn't bother to sound. The only noise, as I lay shivering that night in my freezing attic and watched my window fill up with snow, was a dense, endless hissing.

I wandered down into the kitchen on Christmas morning, stiff and cold, my fingers blue, my teeth chattering, to find the stove dead even though Father, as he always did now Mother was ill, had slept in front of it. Grunting awake, sour and angry as he struggled to get water from the frozen bucket to dose his previous evening's excesses at the Bacton Arms, he eventually set about re-lighting it whilst Beth scraped up breakfast. Still, we were all grateful for a day when we didn't have to work.

I clambered over the drifts to the bakery at the end of the road a few hours later and stood beside the dry, delicious heat of the old furnace with its smoothly bellied bricks as neighbours chatted and the younger children ran about outside and occasionally came in crying after some accident, barely recognisable beneath their crustings of snow. Collecting the roast was my usual job on feastdays and Noshiftdays, and one that I generally enjoyed; happy, for once, to share the companionship that life on Coney Mound fostered. But today I was the subject of smiles and sympathetic questions. When the family roasting pans emerged from the ovens in a glorious aroma I found that spare bits of meat, parsnip, sausage and real potato had been added to ours. I ploughed my way home through the snow, the hot tin clutched to my chest like the core of my anger.

Beth had laid a fresh cloth over the kitchen table, and put sprigs of holly and berry along the dresser. The fire was finally burning, although spitting and huffing from its night of neglect, and father was staring at yesterday's or the day before's paper, the page folded around into a neat, exact square. I counted the places Beth had laid.

'What about Mother?'

'Oh, I expect she'll . . .'

Then a sound came through the thin ceiling. A thump, followed by a dragging slide. Then a pause. Then another slide. To our shame the three of us simply gazed at each other as Mother bumped and shuffled downstairs. Finally, she emerged at the bottom, swaying, her skin grey, her face slick with sweat, her hair lank, her blue eyes blazing. Her hands seemed longer and thinner, slipping across the walls as she fought for support. 'I thought I might as well make the effort, today being today . . .' Belatedly, my father and Beth clustered around her, helping her over to the table and propping her up with pillows like a doll before the extra place that I set out for her. Her feet, I noticed, looking down as father sharpened the cedarstone-handled family knife with a flare of black-white sparks, were bare, the nails blue-black, and the Mark on her left wrist was a mere blemish. The ladle clicked as Beth served out the differently cut bits of other families' vegetables, and there was a loud hiss as father opened his bottle of ale. A thin trickle of blood oozed out from the centre of meat when he sliced into it.

'You know,' Mother said, 'I was wondering if we really
do need to get Robert a new coat when I'm *sure* that Mistress Groves told me last summer that she had a spare
one that been barely used by any of her children . . .' Her
voice was thin and quick, like the sharpening of that knife.
'I've had so much time to *think*,' she went on. 'It's surprising what comes to you . . . Remember a couple of years
ago, when I asked . . .? Not that I mean to tell you how to
live your lives . . .'

Mother hadn't eaten and her hand shook rhythmically
as she tried to drink a glass of thawed water. Then she began to cough, covering her mouth with her toad-like hands
as her fingers dangled long strings of mucus. This frail and
disgusting creature who seemed, as the light thickened into
an early dusk, to give off her own dark glow from within
webbings of skin as translucent as clouded glass, wasn't
my mother any longer, and I hated her for it. I wanted to
smash something in my rage, to kick away the table, break
furniture, to claw down the sham walls of this world.

I went outside as soon as I could. The snow looked grey
and thunderous now, heaped under the dimming sky. And
Bracebridge was deathly quiet, funeral quiet, Christmas
quiet; its edges furled and smoothed, the houses eyebrowed
like old men, the trees and bushes bowed under huge cater-
pillars of snow. I trudged on, hands stuffed into my pockets, breath steaming, unconsciously following the route
down into lowtown that my mother and I had taken those
few—those many—shifterms ago. Here was St Wilfred's,
still big and squat and ugly with its buttresses sunk into the
earth like claws, the tombstones trailing back in rows
through a heaving sea of bluish-white; orderly corpses
queuing patiently for resurrection, distinguishable only by
their dates of birth and death, membership of one or another guild. High Street was empty. Below and beyond,
down the hill where the snow banked in deeper waves beneath the white glower of Rainharrow, there was none of
the usual bustle and noise. The gate that led to the pitbeast
pens was shut and chained, and the great animals lay dim
and quiet on their beds of straw.

The main entrance of Mawdingly & Clawtson was

lightless and empty, but beyond that, down where Withy-brook Road looped north, lay another entrance which, even today, remained fouled with slush and fallen coal, shining in the lamplight, glistening in the wyreglow of the settling pans, darkly hollowed by the pristine snow. Somewhere, the balehounds began to howl. There was a pressure in my heart. My legs trembled. I could feel it now, rising up into me through the ground, through everything—SHOOM *BOOM* SHOOM *BOOM*—that dull endless thudding.

I took a different way back, sliding along the banks of the Withy beyond the yards, then climbing up through the streets at the edge of hightown where the members of the better lesser guilds and those of the ordinary guilds lived in their solid houses built of thick courses of proper brick. Through windows I glimpsed children playing in the hearthlight, families clustered around pianos. Reaching High Street, I looked up at the great guildhouses which climbed beyond snow-softened lines of railings, their windows glowing. Scarcely knowing what I was doing, squinting up at the signs until I found the house of the Great Amalgamated Guild of Savants, I pulled on a freezing copper bell chain which nearly tore the flesh from my hands.

A man with a bulbous chest furrowed his eyes at me as the lighted guildhouse laddered up into the winter sky. He was a butler; the sort of creature I knew little about.

'I've come to see someone. His name is Grandmaster Harrat.'

I could see calculations flashing across the man's face. To let this grubby little urchin in, or kick him into yonder drift?

'If you'll just wait in the hall. Wipe your feet first . . .'

Trailing muddy snow, I tramped inside and stared about me in disbelief as the butler wafted across the parquet of a hallway which glimmered with soft lights, incredible ornaments.

'Robert! And today of all days!' Grandmaster Harrat hurried through a doorway, his arms outstretched as if in an embrace. His waistcoat and his face were almost equally florid. 'What a pleasant surprise!'

'I'm sorry . . .'

'No, no, no, Robert! I'm so very pleased that you took the trouble to look in. I really enjoyed our little chat that—when *was* it?—that morning not so long ago. Time flies . . .' He steered me towards a seashell-shaped sofa. From here, I could see beyond the large doorway through which he had come into an even bigger room where many faces, thin and fat, old and young, as varied and animated as a crowd scene in a painting, were lined before a landscape of silver salvers, cut glass decanters, half-ruined arrangements of confections and flowers. One of them, I was sure before he sat back and was lost in the melee, bore the pointed, sour and unmistakable visage of Uppermaster Stropcock.

'It's a tradition that we meet up here on feastday afternoons. Guild members and a few chosen friends, although this year, the weather being what it is, there are some empty spaces. Still . . .' Grandmaster Harrat rubbed his hands. The talk in the next room door clattered like rain. 'How are things at home, Robert?'

I stared blankly at him, perched on this slippery silk sofa. After today's wanderings, this place was simply too much for me. But Grandmaster Harrat's eyebrows were still half raised in expectation of some answer to his seemingly simple question. His dewy cheeks were almost trembling. *Things at home* . . . What was I supposed to say—that my mother was becoming a changeling? A bubble of dark anguish began to form, growing as this previously unthought idea threatened to engulf me. I fought it down. My eyes stayed dry. I kept his gaze until he looked away.

'Everything's fine,' I said.

'I'm pleased to hear it, Robert. And, tell you what, you're a bright lad and I truly admire your pluck for coming here. This of all days, as well. I'd like us to meet again when I have more time. I only live on Ulmester Street. It's really just around the corner.' He stood up and rummaged in his pockets. 'Here's my card . . .'

I took the soft wedge. The ink didn't smudge. It was ornamented with the signs of his guild.

'Perhaps next shifterm—Halfshiftday afternoon. How does that sound? You and I could get to know each other—it could be our secret.'

For want of anything else to do or say, I nodded.

'And before you go, Robert. *Before* you go . . .' Grandmaster Harrat puffed out his cheeks. He stood up and walked over to a tall, flower-entwined jar painted with Cathay dragons, lifted its lid and took something round from its interior. 'Have this. It's nothing! Just chocolate. And I'll see you, yes? Just as we've said. Just as arranged . . . ?'

The butler re-emerged and I was shown from the guildhouse with a heavy sphere in one hand and Grandmaster Harrat's card in the other. I'd peeled back the gold foil and began to eat the chocolate inside before I realised that it had been marked with coastlines, rivers, mountains. But, by then, I was too hungry to care. I'd eaten the whole world and felt light-headed and sated by the time I reached Brickyard Row. Beside all the other houses, ours looked dark and empty. I kicked my way down the alley and went in though the back door, working it open with the usual push and pull. The lamp was hooded and the loose tiles clattered beneath my feet. The only light in the kitchen came from the glow of the stove. Father was half asleep beside a long row of beer bottles.

'Where the bloody hell have you been all this time?'

'Just out. Nowhere.'

'Talking like that! Don't you dare . . .' But he was too tired and drunk to be bothered to leave the warmth of his chair. I dragged off my boots and went upstairs. The night thickened as I passed my mother's room. I could hear her breathing—*Ahhh, ahh;* a rhythmic sound like a perpetual surprise—and I could sense her listening even though she hadn't called out my name. My stomach tensed as, instead of shooting past on my way to bed as I usually did, I found myself pushing back the wheezing door.

'Where have you been? I heard shouting . . .'

'Just out wandering.'

'You smell of chocolate.'

The golden wrapper still crackled in my pocket. 'Something I found.'

I stood there, looking down the length of the bed. Despite the stillness of the night, the fire was burning poorly in the grate as if the wind was against it, filling the

room with a sooty haze. Everything was too wide, too
dark, and the air stank of chamberpots, coalsmoke, rose-
water. But she'd made an effort to look her best, with
clean sheets folded around her and the pillows stacked
behind.

'I'm sorry about lunch, Robert. That I went on so—'

'You shouldn't—'

'I just wanted today to be special. I know things have
been hard for us lately. Disappointing.'

'Really. It's all right.'

'And you smell of warm rooms, too, Robert.' Her nostrils fluttered. 'And fine food, fruit, firelight, good company . . . It's almost like summer. Come here.'

I walked slowly around the bed, fighting a sense of
panic.

'You don't look in on me as often as you used to . . .'

Her pale arms snaked out and I felt the claws of her fingers caressing the back of my head. Their pressure was irresistible. I bowed down, and veils of filthy smoke seemed
to fall around me. 'You're a stranger now, Robert.' Her
voice hollowed to something less than a whisper as she
drew me in. *Don't let it end this way . . .* She stank of
sweat-sour blankets, unwashed hair—and she was hot, hot.

Letting go, beckoning me to sit down on the mattress,
she asked me about what she was starting to call *life downstairs:* how Father was managing; if I thought Beth was
coping as well as she claimed. The conversation, as we attempted to reassure each other and I stared at the pulse of
the big vein which now protruded from her temple instead
of meeting her changed eyes, was plain and predictable. I
could have filled in her words before she said them.
Mother didn't need my replies.

I picked at the sheet's loose stitching. Once-good material, probably a wedding gift, it was almost worn through
from all the times she had washed it in the zinc tub. And
Mother's fingers, I saw now, looking helplessly down at
them, were smudged black. I glanced over at the fire, at the
scuttle Beth had filled with the cheap, gritty coal we made
do with here on Coney Mound. A few lumps had fallen
across the hearth, whilst others lay flaked and scattered on

the rag mat beside the bed. I heard a scratching movement in the walls, in the corner, and glanced over, expecting a rat, or mice. But the thing which vanished into the crack beneath the wainscot was many-legged. Fattened on the madness of aether beyond the size of any ordinary insect, it had a long, glossy back: a dragonlouse.

'That day . . .' I heard myself begin.

'What day?' My mother raised the back of her hand to rub some imagined smudge from her face. 'You mean that Midsummer? Remember when it was so hot and we went down early to a fair by the rivermeads to see that poor old dragon. You were so—'

'The day this year when we went on the *train*, Mother! I saw a man coming out of one of the guildhouses on that Fourshiftday. You looked up and . . . And I met him when I was down at Mawdingly & Clawtson that Halfshiftday. His name's Grandmaster Harrat and he's in one of the great guilds. He keeps . . . Well, he asked me how you were. He seems to know you.'

My mother closed her eyes for a long moment before finally shaking her head. 'No, Robert. I have no idea who you mean.'

The fire spat a few angry sparks. Smoke drifted. My eyes began to sting.

'But couldn't we . . . ?'

'Couldn't we *what*, Robert?' She sounded distant and angry, less than ever like the person I thought I knew. 'Get the trollman to come and take me off to that ghastly asylum? Sell me as a living specimen to some guild?'

'Whatever it was,' I said, 'whatever happened, it must be down to that place. Down to Mawdingly & Clawtson. They should be made to pay. Or you could escape with Mistress Summerton and live with her and that Annalise girl. It doesn't have to be like this, does it? You could be . . .'

She sighed. I could tell that this was weary ground, long gone over, made stony and arid. 'And what about your father's job, Robert—the way he is, if we start kicking and complaining, don't you think they'll just take any excuse to be rid of him? Him without work and me stuck up here and

Beth tied, and you too young, quite frankly, Robert, to do anything other than draw stupid conclusions. How do you think *that* would be? Where do you think that that would leave us? I wish I'd never ever taken you to see Annalise and Missy at Redhouse.'

I shrugged, hurt by her sudden anger.

'Things can't be changed,' she said. 'Everything is as it is. I'm sorry, Robert. I'm just like you. We all are. We all wish it was otherwise. And I wish I'd never seen that damn shackle and that stone . . . But, please, for me, leave it alone.' There was still a rasp in her voice even as she attempted to make it softer. It was as if the foulness of this air had got into her. 'And it's so *strange* here now. I hate myself. I hate this room. Just lying here on this mattress, in this bed. So I know how you feel about me, Robert. This is . . .' She shook her head at the impossibility of finding the right word and I heard bones snapping and creaking as she did so—as if she, like everything else here, was thinly magicked, cheaply made. The rhythmic motion went on. Long before she'd ceased, I was grinding my teeth, balling my fists, clenching my sphincter, wishing she'd stop. 'And I remember when I was young, Robert. How I used to love my bed, and the dreams it brought me! I can sometimes see this valley, before the magic was stolen from its stones. Perhaps those stupid people of Flinton are right, after all. Perhaps Einfell wasn't so very far from here. I almost see it now, Robert, those fairy princes wandering through these very walls, smiling and dancing. Goldenwhite, bridesmaided by unicorns and all the fragile beasts of the air. I can still hear her terrible laughter ringing amid the trees . . .'

She cocked her head like a strange bird. She drew in a slow breath which rasped and bubbled.

'It's as if that other world is all around me, Robert. And I'm separated from it by nothing but the thinnest veil of evil air. I can smell the sunlight, almost touch . . .'

Her fingers contracted on the counterpane. They let go, tensed again, let go, tensed, in a rhythm I knew. I could see the tendons sliding beneath the near-transparent flesh like ropes.

'Yes, I loved my bed, Robert, when I was a child,' she

said eventually. 'And my dreams. It was my entire wish to stay in bed forever. Can you believe that? I never really wanted my life to start. But I was always busy, Robert, there was never enough time, always the cows or the chickens. I loved my bed as a child because I never had enough time in it. It was a big old thing, of good solid wood, a whole territory of my own with white valleys and the peaks of mountains. When I grow up, I thought, when I'm grown and tall enough, I'll be able to press my head against the board at one end and worm my feet out into the air at the other, I'll be able to claim it all. The funny thing is, I can do it now. But here in *this* bed, and only recently. Do you want to see, Robert? D'you want to see just how far I can stretch myself?'

Even as I backed out, half falling, my mother began to push away the pillows and blankets that Beth had neatly arranged. There began a cracking and popping as bones slipped and moved and her body began to elongate, the sheets spilling from her flesh like milk from a slate.

VIII

The days tumbled out; a whole new year, waiting. The pit-beasts were brought out to try to clear the rails which led south around Rainharrow and we bobble-hatted children came to watch, whooping and shouting as the great animals with their glossy grey flanks, their small eyes glimmering with ancient dark, were hauled from the yards on wooden sleds and dragged as far up the valley as the drays could bear them. The day slowly darkened and the rails, as they often did through winter shifterms in Bracebridge, remained impassably blocked with snow. But the guildsmen seemed happy—and we children, our feet insensible, tired and wild and frozen, snowballed down from the evening hills. It was the time of day when twilight and aether light reached a kind of equilibrium, when lanterns were first lit and all of Bracebridge seemed to fizz and shimmer, losing substance and seeming to hover in the fading air.

There was more snow in the days and shifts that followed, although it was never that bluish white again, but fouled and darkened by the sooty labours of our shut-off town. At school, once the pipes had been thawed and the floods were washed out and the few books it possessed were hung out to dry like weary bats, I was beginning to acquire something of a reputation for playground toughness. *Mother's a troll . . . Mother's a changer . . .* But I learned how to strike out with a wild anger which scared all but the biggest and dullest.

Thus I was buoyed up with a sort of dogged aggression when I visited Grandmaster Harrat's house—entering the foreign area of highest hightown, a place of small parks and statues and glimpses of the river, seizing the brass front knocker and striking it unhesitatingly against my dark reflection on the varnished door, although I sensed at the same time that I was risking something by doing so. But Master Harrat seemed more *himself* here than he had at Mawdingly & Clawtson, or even at his guildhouse. He lost that aura of playing a role that people who are unhappy in their work so often maintain. He chuckled, he pursed and smacked his lips, he moved quickly—wearing a dressing gown, of all things—his embroidered slippers squealing excitedly on the polished floors. The house itself was anonymous despite its obvious and well-made solidity, a lifeless place of unornamental ornaments and stuffed animals kept in glass domes, dusted by maids I never saw because they were always out for their free Halfshiftday afternoon. But my most abiding impression is of a smell. It brushed against me as I entered the hall and lingered as I spooned luxurious amounts of sugar into my tea and gorged myself on marzipan cake in the drawing room. It was partly a warm smell, coppery and smooth, and partly like the sweet rankness of decaying flowers. At first I thought it came from the gas mantles with which the house was illuminated, strange as even they were to me then. But it had a thundery oppression, a darker tang.

'Electricity!' Master Harrat exclaimed, standing up, leaving his own cake uneaten, his tea unsipped. 'It's the way of the future, Robert. You must let me show you . . .'

At the back of the house, beyond an enormous empty kitchen, he kept a workroom in a long space lit by several mossy skylights. All around us, vials and jars and lenses glinted.

'Electricity's invisible, of course—and quite harmless . . . That is, if treated as you would any volatile chemical. And not that it *is* a chemical . . .' He hovered there, looking about at his many implements as if they surprised even him. 'Gaslight is a thing of the past, Robert. It was never safe, never ideal, and the demands of the higher-guilded classes are always increasing. Yes, the future, Robert. The future . . . !'

The next part of our ritual on that and other Halfshift-day afternoons was for Grandmaster Harrat to clear a space on one of his workbenches, and then, promising that he would only take moments, muttering and tutting for hours, tying and twisting copper wires and rolling out acid-filled cauldrons, turning devices which seemed like copper-wound adaptations of my mother's wringer until the smell of his exertions mingled with all the other scents filling this long room. At the end of it all, Grandmaster Harrat would touch two ends of metal.

'Electricity, Robert,' he would wheeze. There on a work-bench, clamped within lizard-like jaws, a whisker of fila-ment would turn faint orange for a while until, with an agitated, almost aether-like spark, it died. Of course, I was used enough to my father's intermittent enthusiasms to show the requisite admiration. But Grandmaster Harrat had visions of houses, streets, towns, cities, lit by this feeble yellow glow.

'Imagine, Robert, if the trams in London were driven by electricity! Imagine if the trains which ply between our towns and the engines which drive our factories were pow-ered thus! Think how clean the air would be! Think of the purity of our rivers!'

I nodded dutifully.

'We have endlessly stuck, Robert, in these Ages of steam and industry, all these last three hundred years. Where are the new advances?'

Grandmaster Harrat was in full flight now. I barely had to shrug to keep him going.

'I'll tell you where they are, Robert—they're *here*,' he tapped his skull, 'and in workshops such as this which our guilds dare not sponsor. And why, Robert?—I'll tell you *why*. Because the guilds cannot see beyond aether. It makes things too easy for them. Why should there be progress when life is so good for those who grip the haft of power?

But the future lies ahead of us, Robert, beyond the ruins of a squandered past. Squandered on gas, Robert. Squandered on coal and steam. Squandered, above all, on the vagaries and inefficiencies of aether . . .

'Think of this land of ours—think of the way it's been shaped the best part of these last three hundred years since the Grandmaster of Painswick made his discovery. Yes, we've progressed, if progress you call it. We've learned how to harness the power of coal and gas and steam, we've learned how to turn out ten thousand versions of the same tatty object from one factory. Of course, and above all, we've learned how to use aether. Only the poorest starve, and I hear that nowadays only the weakest and most dissolute and unfortunate are sent to the workhouses. Yes, there's fresh water for most, and interior plumbing in the better houses of the few, and the worst epidemics are almost always confined to the grimmest quarters of our great cities. I could catch a train from here, and in a few hours I could be in Dudley or Bristol. I could have a message sent there by telegraph almost instantly. But I could have been standing here saying almost exactly the same things a century ago! We haven't *progressed*, Robert! Yes, there are new products, new fads, new styles and fashions—even the occasional new idea if anyone would dare to publish it—but none of it really counts as anything but more and more of the same. We in England and in the other so-called developed nations of Europe are as fossilised as the strange sea creatures you sometimes find in a lump of coal, and as stonily resistant to change. And I'll tell you why, Robert—it's because of aether. It's because of lazy engineering. When you can make something work with a coating of wyreglow and a spell, why ever worry about improving it, eh . . . ?'

Grandmaster Harrat's monologues always went along these lines. He seemed to me to be torn between hope and frustration—with frustration generally winning out. But beneath all of that, I sensed a deeper sadness. Something, I felt, had been done which couldn't be undone. Some wound, some worm, which was endlessly turning inside him. Something which related to me, to Bracebridge, to aether, and my mother.

* * *

Through that winter and into the damp early spring in the year 85 of that Third Age of Industry, my wanderings around Bracebridge grew wider. I felt as if I was claiming the place, mapping it out before I left it. I would climb over the scrolled and filthy cables of the road bridge which spanned the rail tracks as they curved south beyond the factories. The sulphurous heat of the engines blasted beneath and I would ponder as the wagons clacked by—especially aether trucks, with their straw bedding looking soft enough to break my fall—when the best moment would be to make my leap, and the places to which that leap might take me.

By then, I was missing a lot of school; a fact which the teachers were able to accept without challenge, knowing as they all did of my mother's worsening illness, and welcoming as they probably did one less sullen face at the back of class. *Mother's a troll . . . Mother's going to Northy-ton . . .* Grabbing apples and tins of polish from stalls at the Sixshiftday market and throwing them uselessly over walls, braving the blast on that shuddering bridge, smoking stolen cigarettes, facing up to the balehounds as they launched themselves at the fences, wading carelessly through the cuckoo-nettles and sweating through nights of agonised sleep—my whole life seemed filled with a sense of breaking through many small, invisible barriers. At each new turn in the street I was half expecting to find the trollman standing there; not Master Tatlow but someone terrible and tall and in a vast dark cape, as I imagined him, with his face an endless shadow. I took to carrying a knife, but the thing was blunt, cheap, unaethered, and it soon broke in my pocket. I was like one of Grandmaster Harrat's filaments; charged and ready to erupt into spitting flames.

IX

Grandmaster Harrat, in his long workroom, moved to draw the blinds back from the skylights.

'Impurities, Robert!' he said. 'Imprecision! That's what we must fight against . . . Think of lightning, Robert! I used to look out over the rooftops of Northcentral from my nursery when there was a storm and will it to strike Hallam Tower. And *marvel,* Robert . . . I used to marvel. There's no fudge, no doubt. Even then, I could see the start of a new, different Age. Perhaps one day I'll be able to explain . . .'

I watched as he leaned over one of the demijohns of acid and a droplet of sweat slid from his chin. Today, all the wires and efforts and smoking spills had failed to produce the slightest glow. But I didn't care. Shifterm by shifterm, these visits had acquired a soothing predictability, and his failures were as much a part of it as the taste of marzipan. I'd learned by now to keep well back at the crucial moments from the sparks, the burning rubber and the huge chemical-filled jars. Electricity seemed to be dangerous and volatile, and all that Grandmaster Harrat's experiments had convinced me of was that it would never work. After all, who would ever want to risk having this stuff charging through their house when they could rely on the safety of coal gas, lanterns or candles? All in all, though, I had come to look forward to these Halfshiftday afternoons as rare times of escape and tranquillity.

I could picture the scene back at home at this moment, or at any other moment lately. These last shifterms my mother had lapsed into a feverish coma, tossing and writhing, her eyes wide and white, her thin limbs stretching and aching as her jaw gaped and she struggled to breathe. Beth would be tending her now, just as she did every day and night. She braved the edgy darkness and the scuttling walls of that room. Beth would be wiping Mother's face and limbs, heating the stone bottles and seeing to the fire and smoothing the wild sheets, holding those long impossible hands that no one else could bring themselves to touch. A few nights ago, the last time I had dared to look in there, my mother had been clawing at the vanishing Mark on her left wrist. The wall above the bed, even after Beth had finished mopping it, was still thinly streaked with hieroglyphs of blood.

'I really thought we'd reached the essence this time, Robert . . .' Master Harrat's voice and the clink of bottles drifted over me. 'I really thought we'd managed it . . . Sometimes, I almost wonder if it will ever come about . . .'

He looked at me. For once, he almost seemed to expect an answer. His glossy lower lip quivered for a moment and his eyes grew grave. He had a way of looking at me like this sometimes. I'd guessed by now that I wasn't the first lad he'd brought back to his house to eat fairy cakes and watch as he fussed over his experiments. But there was more to it than that.

Grandmaster Harrat nodded to himself then, as if he'd reached some final conclusion. Without speaking he went over to a small, heavy door set in the walls between the gaslamps and spun a numbered dial. His silence in itself was unusual and I had no idea what to expect as, on a turn of oiled hinges, the room leapt with a blaze. Shadows tunnelled as he bore a tinkling tray to the desk. The vials it contained were like smaller versions of the pots that I had seen the women using in the paintshop at Mawdingly & Clawtson, but their wyreglow was much sharper; barely a

glow at all, more a shriek of light which blurred into the
other senses. The long room flared and grew dark as he
placed them down. Each vial, I saw, peering closely at his
elbow, bore a small seal.

'Aether, Robert! Of course, I have to work with it
every day to earn the pleasures of this house. I have to
pretend to the shareholders that I know enough about its
behaviour to maintain Mawdingly & Clawtson's unparal-
leled reputation for aether of the highest charm. But I
don't know, Robert. And *I* don't use it—*it* uses me. Give
me electricity and light any day—pure, simple math. But
we all must live with aether. It pervades this land. We all
dance to its tune . . . And perhaps that's always true even
though I have striven these years for the simple and un-
trammelled logic of physics and engineering . . .'

He went on like this at even longer and more breathless
length than was usual for him. To me, born in Bracebridge
to the pounding of the aether engines, the distinction he
was making between the supposed logic of electricity and
the illogic of aether was obtuse in the extreme. To me, if
anything, it was the other way around. Aether had allowed
us to tame the elements: to make iron harder, steel more re-
silient and copper more supple, to build bigger and wider
bridges, even channel messages across great distances from
the mind of one telegrapher to another. Without aether, we
would still be like the warring painted savages of Thule. I
understood, though, that I was witnessing a climactic moment in Grandmaster Harrat's many struggles with the
medium which both drew and taunted him—an experiment
in both aether and electricity which he had enacted so often in his thoughts that the actual performance of it now
had the heavy air of predictability that such matters long
brooded over can assume, as each moment clicks into the
next. Me, I simply gazed at the shining vials which he had
plainly striven for so long to avoid using in his experiments. SHOOM *BOOM* SHOOM *BOOM*. My heart was
thundering. I'd never been close to aether of anything like
this purity before, not even on my Day of Testing.

'At the end of the day, aether is simple, Robert—like
the simplest fairy tale. We make a wish, and aether gives us

what we want, although, just as in a tale, not always quite in the way that we want it. But a better engine, a sharper tool, a cheaply made boiler which can sustain pressures far beyond those it should, undeniable economic prosperity, half-mythic brutes like the balehounds and pitbeasts to do our bidding. It gives us all these things. Or now—shall we see if it works?'

Then he was busy again, snipping wires, tweezering out a fresh filament and clipping it into place between the connectors. But for a final bridge between the things he called anodes in their chemical vats—a raised copper gate which I'd grown used to watching him close with a dramatic plunge but often little other effect—the whole circuit was complete. Muttering something I couldn't catch, Grandmaster Harrat broke open one of the aether vials and squeezed the bulb of a pipette until a glowing line ascended the tube. The pipette then hovered over the space of air where the filament floated. A dazzling bead formed at the tip, a trembling fragment which broke and fell with a slow ease that had nothing to do with gravity. Every distance seemed to extend, and time with it, before the elements were joined. The aether touched the surface of the filament and seemed to vanish.

'Of course, it knows what I want from it already. The perfect circuit . . .' Grandmaster Harrat chuckled but he sounded grim. He re-sealed the vial, removed his leather glove. His hand, as it moved towards the gate of that final switch, was trembling. So was I. I'd never felt such anticipation . . . And aether of such power, purity, charm—it knew what *I* wanted too, even if I didn't. I didn't doubt that I was about to witness something thrilling and new as, with a long final exhalation, a sigh more of imminent defeat than of victory, Grandmaster Harrat closed the final bridge on the circuit he had created.

It worked.

The filament was humming, glowing.

It was a triumph.

In fact, the filament was incredibly bright, like the sun out of a clear sky when everything else seems to darken . . . I heard myself gasp as the light intensified. The whole world quivered and spun about me. The foaming rivers, the pounding factories, the shops groaning with produce, the hissing telegraphs and the endless, endless, shift-days. And for some reason, in one of those actions you understand perfectly when you perform them but lose all logic afterwards, I reached out towards that blazing light. The motion of my hand was slow and I could see the bones of my flesh through the brightness—but I wanted it more than anything.

There was an incredible flash. Then smoke, and a wild angry hissing, and a stench of burning. I fell back and saw Grandmaster Harrat's slow reaction as he attempted to catch me, the slack shape of his mouth, and heard a dull slap as my head struck the floor. But all of this seemed to be happening at a distance. I was drawing up and back. The ceiling billowed out. The air rushed up and I was looking down on Bracebridge, hovering with the stars.

Then the night began to churn. The moon swept over the sky. The trains were streaks of light. The sky blazed, light—dark—light—as the sun fled backwards. Snow flickered across the slopes of Rainharrow and the fields pulsed with the ebb of the seasons. I had no idea what was happening, other than that I seemed to be flying headlong into the past. Was this what death was like, I wondered? Then the sun climbed into the sky and settled west above the rivermeads, and a few clouds curled up into their places around it in the blue sky, their shadows lying in patches over a Bracebridge which had the busy hum of a summer morning. Little had changed in this rush of years. True, the old warehouses at the back of the Manor Hospital down Withybrook Road were still standing, and the ashpits of the brickyard still hadn't quite began their inexorable climb up Coney Mound. But it was recognisably Bracebridge. And as I felt the warm sun, and listened to the grind and clash of its engines, I began to settle down towards the town, drawing closer to the tarred and corrugated rooftops of Mawdingly & Clawtson. Suddenly yards and sooty bricks were spinning up to me, then the moss of a particular roof, until I passed silently through it and found that I was hovering in the cool glimmer of a room I instantly recognised. It was the paintshop. The scene was almost as I had witnessed it a few shifterms before with Grandmaster Harrat, but it was subtly changed in the way that time changes all things. And there was my mother, looking recognisably herself, yet younger, as she raised and dabbed her glowing brush among the workbenches.

When the door from the yard swung back I half expected to see my father stride in, but instead, and unmistakably, it was Grandmaster Harrat who entered, although he was thinner and lacked sideburns. The supervisor scampered to greet him, her large bosom wobbling. Even then, Grandmaster Harrat was plainly a personage to be reckoned with. I could tell that from the easy murmur of his request, and the tone with which it was granted. If he could perhaps borrow a couple of the paintshop girls? It was a small enough favour to ask, and he shook his head when the supervisor suggested that perhaps the particular ones he'd selected weren't the best, even if they were the prettiest. His judgement wasn't to be challenged. My mother and the blond-haired girl beside her nodded at the call of their names and put down the cogs they were working on; my mother knocking, as she did so, her pot of brushes to the floor. The supervisor raised her eyes heavenward.

I floated like a ghost in their wake as these two young guildswomen and Grandmaster Harrat left the paintshop together. They made an odd group, these two different species of human. Grandmaster Harrat in his fine clothes, my mother and her friend—whom she called Kate as they murmured to each other—in their clogs and hand-me-downs. It was plain as they walked across the yards that they could think of little to say to each other, although my mother and Kate were exchanging half-mischievous smiles. Then I heard the shift sirens and I realised as workers trooped out past them that this must be a Halfshiftday. It was an odd time to choose for a 'special', as I knew the paintshop girls called such out-of-shop work, with the yards soon emptied and only the few essential workers in Engine and Central Floors maintaining the processes of the aether engines themselves. Even within the walls of the factory the warm summer air seemed full of the promise of afternoon football and walks by the riverside. My mother and her friend Kate would be

getting time and a half for this for certain, which wasn't
something which Mawdingly & Clawtson gave out readily
to its guildmistresses.

The sirens stilled. The gates emptied. The pigeons
cooed. Cooo *Coo*. Cooo *Coo*. In an unremarkable yard
Grandmaster Harrat strode towards a whitewashed brick
wall. It was set with an iron gate, its rusty bars splattered
with old paint. My mother and Kate watched curiously as
Grandmaster Harrat lifted the padlock. He thought for a
moment, then said something which caused it to break
apart. Kate clapped her hands in delight and my mother
watched more warily as the gate squawked open. Then a
flash of flint, some fiddling with the dried-out wick of an
old lantern which flared into a dim sphere. Bricked walls
and concrete steps as they headed down and the dank air
breathed in and out to the howl and slam of the aether engines. The ways levelled out where the push of air was
strong enough to flutter the hems of the two women's
skirts. The previously neatly tiled and bricked passages
took on a different appearance. The bricks became smaller,
older, crumbling, ancient. Following the light of Grandmaster Harrat's lantern, stooping as the ceiling dipped,
Kate and my mother held hands for balance as their clogged
feet skittered on the sloping floor. There were guildsmen's
signs and graffiti on the walls. There were carvings as well,
inward swirls which reminded me of the mossy shapes on
the sarsens on top of Rainharrow. Still the pounding of the
engines grew louder.

They came to a door. The small room beyond had once
been half-tiled, although many had now fallen and crunched
beneath my mother's and Kate's clogs. Old shelves sloped
from the walls. Guild notices long obliterated by age
and damp curled amid the wreckage. It was a disappointing
place to come to after so interesting a journey; the only
item which didn't look to have been forgotten for the best
part of an Age was a rough wooden crate about a foot
square and a yard long, and even that hardly looked new.
The words CAUTION DANGEROUS LOAD were stencilled in plain red capitals on the lid. Grandmaster Harrat
took out his pocket knife and cut through the string which

had been knotted around the catch. The hinges gave a screech. The inside of the crate seemed at first to be stuffed with nothing but yellowed newspapers, but Grandmaster Harrat smiled to himself as he burrowed through it like a child at a lucky dip.

The object he found was plainly heavy. He had to hook in both of his hands to lift it out. And the pounding air seemed to quieten as it emerged—glittering, and about the size of a human head. It seemed to me that no one had spoken since they entered the room, and that even the beat of the engines grew distant as he laid the thing on the grubby floor beside the crate. For all that it was summer outside, the air seemed solid, frosty. It glittered in faint rainbow-plumes. But Grandmaster Harrat, on his knees, had the expression of a small boy at Christmas. Flurries of anticipation, joy, fear, flew across this face. The object was dazzling—wyrebright and yet black, too, in that subterranean room, flooding up towards him, mimicking and exaggerating those shifts of expression and hollowing his eyes, melting his flesh. Facets caught and glinted. It was like a huge jewel—or rather, as I then thought, knowing little of such things, it resembled a massive, glittering block of crystallised sugar. But it was the glow *inside* that strange stone which mattered. It writhed, gathered, unravelled, poured out. Shadows swept back, burning out the shapes of a crouching man and two standing women until they became raw, impersonal, emblematic. The scene, as the light began to pulse to the same rhythm which pervaded all of Bracebridge, was like some complex and everchanging guild hieroglyph. Grandmaster Harrat, Kate, my mother— they were no longer who they were but simply its acolytes, the crude mechanisms by which this thing might exercise its power. Their shadows bowed and worshipped across the blazing walls to the beat of the engines, first dark, then bright. And I was part of it, too, faint though I was. The light extended, stretching into something which was and wasn't a human form, but a silhouette gathering in smoke to reach its blackening arms towards me.

I must have screamed then. Something seemed to break and the vision began to stutter and fizz. Then, with a stench

of acid and a sharp ache in the back of my head, I was back
in Grandmaster Harrat's workroom amid the fizzing smoke
of another failed experiment. I was lying on the floor and
Grandmaster Harrat, who had put on weight and substance
over the years since whatever he had been doing with my
mother, was leaning over me. The light on his face, caught
up by the gaslight in the gleam of something spilled, was
soft and yellow and ordinary.

'Robert! Robert—can you hear me? I thought for a moment . . .' His jowls trembled. 'I thought . . .'

I sat up and felt my head and winced. A lump. Nothing
more. Grandmaster Harrat's hands were on my shoulders
as I climbed to my feet. I shook him off. The filament—the
whole experiment with electric light which lay on the
workbench—was a smoking ruin. And he was looking at
me now in that same sad and unchanging way.

'But . . .'

'What, Robert?'

But I shook my head.

I left Grandmaster Harrat's house and walked home
with my belly full and my eyes stinging, just as I did on
every other Halfshiftday.

X

Arriving home each evening at Brickyard Row, looking up at the sky as it boiled over our front gable and wishing that our house belonged to someone else, I had to force myself to go inside. I hurried past my mother's room on my way up to bed, fearing the sour reek of illness and the pulsing darkness which swirled out in triumphant eddies as the fire gasped, rocking the dim light, making monsters of us all.

Sleet drove down from the hills as winter made a final stand against the spring, peppering the windows with ice. The wind clawed at the slates; it burrowed through fissures and dragged at me with terrible fingers. Then there came an empty evening when Beth was absent from the house, Father was out drinking, and the wind suddenly ceased as if in frozen shock. The air lay almost in balance, almost at peace, as I sat at the kitchen table, raising and dropping the hood on the oil lamp so that a circle of light flooded in and out. The neighbours were out, too, as they often were now: banished by the sounds and the rumours which emanated from here. All of Bracebridge seemed hollow and empty. But the air still pulsed, drawing in and out in waves of light and darkness, tinkling the best porcelain on the dresser. SHOOM *BOOM* SHOOM *BOOM*. Then a scuffing noise made me look up and I saw something large and repulsive emerge from a narrow crack in the ceiling. It dangled as it attempted to clamber amid the joists, then dropped with a dull plop onto the table and lay there, momentarily stunned. A dragonlouse. Not a particularly large specimen by the standards of the beasts which inhabited Mawdingly & Clawtson, but I'd never seen one so close before. The bluish shield of its back was scrolled with what looked like a lumpy parody of a guildsman's seal, but the body beneath was pink and blue like the veined and near-transparent flesh of a human baby. I flipped it over as I'd seen the marts doing with their boots on East Floor. It squealed and made a thinly popping sound as I repeatedly brought the base of the lamp down on it, then let out a foul gout of ichor. I scooped the mess up with newspapers and tossed it into the fire, then moved towards the stairway.

Darkness seemed to fall in huge flakes as I ascended the stairs. SHOOM *BOOM* SHOOM *BOOM,* and the rest of the earth had stilled in a long moment of waiting as I worked back the door to Mother's room, feeling a strange resistance which was like the pressure of time itself. I realised I was holding the family carving knife. Handled with fine cedarstone, its aethered blade thinned to a sickle curve by years of Father's sharpening, it was one of those precious pieces of truly guilded workmanship that every family cherished. It felt heavy, then light, in my hand. I must have rocked back the kitchen table drawer after wiping my hands of the mess of the dragonlouse and reached in to take it, although the motion, the decision, seemed as impossible as the fact that I gripped it now.

My mother's bedroom swayed. A dull fire crackled in the grate and coal lay scattered as the bruised flames quivered. There was no heat, but my mother was crouched before it, her long, grubby night-gown pooling around her knees. I felt a pang of hope, near joy. She was up! She was on the mend! Then, sensing my presence, she twisted her long neck around towards me with a snap of joints. Gripped as a squirrel might hold a nut, a nugget of the coal was clasped in her hands. Crumbs of it clung around her lips, blackening her tongue and teeth. Her nose was flattened and her eyes were wide and deep, almost circular, glowing. Her shoulders had grown bluish spines. Around her body, a carpet of dragonlice was scurrying.

'It *is* you, isn't it, Robert?'

I sensed the struggle for recognition. The different way she now said my name.

'What are you doing here, now? Why are you bothering me?'

The membranes of ruined nostrils twitched.

'And what are you carrying?'

She stood up slowly, her bones creaking. And she was tall, tall. A few thin strands of hair adhered to the exaggerated dome of her skull. The flesh of a ribcage jutted through the open night-gown. Inside, grey-greenish organs churned and pulsed. I caught the reek of hot coal. I wanted to use the knife, but I had no idea how. And I even understood that it was what my mother would have wanted; that the worst thing that could happen would be for the creature she had become to remain alive. I raised the blade and it danced with purpose in the fire's dim flames. In that instant, I'd have done anything to put an end to this. But then the air contracted around my heart, squeezing it with winter claws. And the creature tilted its head and rolled back the aether-pouring whites of its eyes. Spreading its arms, it hunched towards me and dropped its jaw to emit a foul belch of flame.

I tumbled back and out into the landing. The thin doors of the house seemed to tear themselves open for me, driven by the same force by which I was driven until I found myself standing, doubled-over and breathless, outside and alone on the cobbles of Brickyard Row. Somewhere, a shovel raked, music played, a dog was barking. The birch trees fanned their limbs across the patch of land that sloped down beneath the stars towards lowtown and the dull grinding of the brick factory. I drew in breath after breath as the air around me shuddered and plumed. Feeling something in my hand, I realised that I still held the cedarstone-handled knife. I threw it hard over the trees and across the rooftops and the whole shimmering bowl of the valley, towards the red star which, low and in the west, was still gleaming.

* * *

A dark green van splashed up the steep way from low-town to Coney Mound next morning. It was tall-sided and drawn by two huge, shovel-faced drays. The younger children came out from their houses to run beside it and I watched from my tiny attic window as its shining panels halted on Brickyard Row. The man hunched at its reins glanced down at the children then up at rain-threatening skies. As he did so, I saw that it was Master Tatlow. His lips pursed in a whistle, checking a scrap of paper from his pocket, he climbed down. He tied up and patted his drays, then worked open the latch on our gate and knocked briskly on our front door. I heard my father's steps along the creaky passage, the characteristic nervous clearing of his throat and the sigh of the front door opening across the rush mat. The words were unclear, but the door shut, their voices rolled and shifted, and Beth's came to join with them. Despite everything, it all sounded so ordinary.

The children outside still circled the tall green van. It bore no markings of any company or guild. That in itself was unusual. Curtains, no doubt, would be twitching along Brickyard Row. Front steps and windows would be absently polished as the faces of our neighbours peered out. I began to drag on my clothes.

Come on. It's late morning.

I stopped, a sock hanging off my foot, my heart suddenly pounding. I could have sworn that I heard the rumble of the clotheshorse and my mother's voice as she called up the stairs to me from the kitchen.

We're going out. You'll miss breakfast.

I looked at the sloping walls of my attic, half expecting—longing—for that distant Fourshiftday morning at the last edge of summer when we visited the Redhouse to return. But the voices still rose from below.

The night before, huddled back in my bed after Beth had returned, I had listened to my sister's gasps as she struggled up and down the stairs with coal and sheets and buckets. The whole house, it seemed to me, stank of smoke. And I could hear as I lay there in the thin darkness the creak of bedsprings, the snap of joints, the sound—AHHH

AHHHGGH AHHH *AHHHGGH*—of something terrible breathing, and of the scratching and scurrying which now seemed to fill these walls. Here, amid my old coats and blankets, I was separated from it by nothing but plaster and lath.

I wondered as I listened to my sister's labours if she still kept a remnant of hope, or worked out of blind habit. And I wondered just how much the creature my mother had become had revealed itself to her. Tossing and writhing, I fell into a dream in which, somehow still wearing her apron, still looking as she had once looked, my mother was pinned down by chains and pipes in Mawdingly & Clawtson's Engine Floor. Then I heard Father's voice, talking in the suppressed shout which meant he'd been out drinking. And Beth was crying now, in or out of my dreams, saying that this was the end of it, that it couldn't go on. And I heard the rattle of Father's toolbox, the musical clatter of planks. The sound of hammering.

In the grey morning I descended the ladder and found that the door to my mother's bedroom was criss-crossed by lop-sidedly nailed bits of old floorboard; the kind of excessively poor workmanship of which Father would normally have been ashamed. Drawn over them, done roughly in brown paint, were protective circles, scrawls; the thin substance of his guild heritage. Tendrils of smoke writhed through the gaps. There was a sense of heat, power.

Robert? Is that you? Is that you? That you . . . ? You . . . ?

Shrinking echoes of her voice; nothing more. Barely hesitating, I stumbled downstairs. Three faces—my father, Beth, and Master Tatlow—turned towards me from the parlour as I slumped down at the bottom step.

'This here's Master Tatlow,' my father began, half rising from his chair. 'He's—'

'You think I don't know who *he* is!'

They studied me for a moment. Master Tatlow had a blood-flecked scrap of lint stuck to one of his chins where he'd cut himself shaving.

'It's always difficult. *Always* difficult.' His knees jiggled restlessly. 'I've seen cases, rich and poor, through half Yorkshire. Believe me, Master Borrows, it's for the best.

Her kind, they don't *know*. It's just the way she is—and it's no respecter of guilds, believe you me . . .'

Beth's hair, I saw, fell in greasy clumps. Her clothes looked slept-in. Father's face was grey and old and frozen.

Master Tatlow took out a fat notebook. 'Your wife, the client, I understand that she worked in the paintshop down at the big factory?'

'Yes.'

'Excuse me for asking. But it *is* helpful to know these things.'

'Of course.'

Master Tatlow slipped back an elastic band and ran his finger along a spill of pages, then nodded to himself. He licked his pencil. He made a note. 'Of course, it can happen in almost any kind of work, although I know that's no comfort to you at the moment. But from what you say, and from what I've seen in the report, it sounds to me as though this particular syndrome is more, ah, *singular* than I'd have expected from paintshop work. Could you tell me quite how the client's changes have manifested themselves?'

'Best thing is,' Father said and ran his hands back through his hair, 'you go up there and take a look yourself.'

Something stirred upstairs, dragging and banging. Master Tatlow glanced out of the window. His lips twitched. 'I wonder what's happened to the police? Promised in the telegraph they'd be here bang on nine. I've come all the way overnight with this van from our stables at Northallerton, so you'd think they could manage a few yards. So you'll excuse me for asking if I couldn't possibly have a cup of tea?'

Beth stood up to boil the kettle. Outside, splattering the parlour window, it had finally began to rain. I glanced up the stairs. At the very top, filling the landing, was horrid darkness, the reek of smoke, the sense and the sound of something waiting. Then, for a long time, until the scream of the kettle, there was only silence and the gathering sound of the rain. Father sat slumped and rigid in his chair. I could see the twitching cables of his muscles, the knotted veins and haft-marks of his workman's arms. Master Tatlow opened and closed his book, which had a gold C and cross on its front, and glanced out of the window. The spoon rattled in the saucer when Beth handed him his tea.

'Ah! Most grateful!' He sipped noisily.

'Dad? would you like one as well?'

My father shook his head.

Then Beth came over to me. 'It's what Mother would have wanted,' she said, hunching down beside me on the bottom step of the stairs. 'For someone like Master Tatlow to come when things got . . . this bad. She needs to be taken care of, and we can't do that here. *I* can't . . .'

'Mum's a troll.'

I felt her stiffen. There were sores around her mouth. 'You don't have to use words like that in this house, Robert.'

'It's *true*—but it doesn't have to be bad. Remember Goldenwhite? She drew the changed to her, made an army. She could . . .'

I looked back up at Beth. In her sleep-bleary eyes, there was no comprehension.

'I think you should go out for a while now, Robert,' she said. 'Go round to Nan Callaghan's. Knock on her door. She'll understand. She'll let you in . . .'

I barged my way out through the kitchen and splashed down the back alley. Beyond, on the street front, all of Bracebridge had dissolved in greying sheets whilst Master Tatlow's green wagon sat waiting, its windowless panels shining. The birch trees on the hill bowed and thrashed. Even the strongest, oldest member of this scrawny copse in which many generations of Coney Mound had stuck nails and scarred with their names waved like the mast of a storm-tossed ship as I climbed it.

My boots slipped on the bark as I hauled myself up, working up and along until I attained the loose territory where the marshy ground directly below me was almost lost in the rain. But I could see clearly enough across Brick-yard Row and through the window into my mother's bed-room. I don't know what I expected, but all I could make out at first was the old wardrobe, which was odd consider-ing that it should have been on the other side of the room, and was blocking the space where the door should have been. Then there came voices and plodding hoofbeats, the grinding crunch of wheels. Another wagon. It was larger and heavier than Master Tatlow's van, and several of the police who'd come with it had to climb off to help push it up the final rise to our house. They wore shining black oil-skin capes and peaked caps. As they trooped through the front gate, they looked like a mobile flock of umbrellas.

The tree creaked beneath me. I clung to whipping arm-fuls of leaves. It was hard to imagine them all standing in-side our house, squashed-up and dripping. Like a jewel glimpsed underwater through a storm, there was a stillness in that lost, familiar bedroom with its big, misplaced wardrobe, which seemed now to be at odds with everything else about this day. Then Master Tatlow re-emerged out-side, hunching through the rain to open the back of his van and haul out a weird collection of crowbars, hoops and chains. The front door closed again. The wind swept over me. When I'd regained my grip on the branches I saw that the wardrobe which blocked the door to my mother's room was quivering. Then it flew asunder in an explosion of thin wood and the bedroom, as the many uniformed figures burst in, was extinguished in their bustle. The rain seemed to thicken. I imagined strong arms lifting my mother, the dragging weight of those chains. My tree was bucking. I was starting to slip—but then I saw movement in the room again.

There was a figure, tall, swaying like smoke, rising from everything which tried to enclose it. I don't know what else; there seemed to be a thundercrack which could have been the whipping wind, perhaps genuine thunder, or the splitting wood of the sash-framed bedroom window as it began to bulge under some inward pressure. Then the panes shattered. From the height of my tree, it and I were almost level, and it seemed for a moment as if the shape which emerged on swirls of glass and white bed linen was flying right towards me. There was a momentary vision, not of some aether-changed monster, but of my mother, her smil-ing face and outstretched arms as she flew to embrace me. Then the vision faded, and the tangled shape fell, glittering sheets trailing behind from the window, to land unravelled on the stone front step with an audible *snap*.

SHOOM *BOOM* SHOOM *BOOM*.

The rain came more strongly. The shouts. The struggles to open the front door. The scurryings of the police and the somewhat calmer voice of Master Tatlow. The pale-pink runnels which snaked down our path and swirled into the gutter. The tentative prodding and lifting. The gathering arms-folded, weeping, curious, impassive neighbours. My mother's changed limbs dragging from a makeshift stretcher, and the horns which protruded from it. These are all things I saw and didn't see as I scrambled back down the tree and blundered through the rank undergrowth. A final drop, and then from here all of lowtown was spread below me in the glittering rain, with Rainharrow beyond, the stones of its peak somehow caught in a mocking fall of sunlight. The wind regathered itself, grey on grey; the foaming edges of spring breaking against the walls of winter. Then I heard another sound, an anguished howling from the valley beneath me, which was joined by another, and then another. Today being Halfshiftday, the shift sirens were going off at midday.

'Robert!' Cravat, dressing gown and cigarette holder in place, Grandmaster Harrat filled the open doorway of his house as the rain clattered around me. 'Come in! Quickly, quickly! A rotten day like this, I was worried you'd decided not to bother . . .'

I stood dripping in the hall, breathing in the flowery scent of gas mantles entwined with eau de cologne, floor-polish, pot pourri.

'Here we are!' A large white towel, Grandmaster Harrat scurrying in its wake. 'Dry yourself off . . .' Feathery warmth enfolded me. 'You look absolutely sodden. You really *should* get straight out of those things. I'm sure we could find something . . .'

But the look in my eyes made him grow silent and I waited in the parlour, still seeping rainwater as he bore in the tiered trays of cakes which the ever-absent maids had prepared. Then he sat in his usual chair and I sat on the edge of mine. The fire crackled. I caught glimpses of myself, mirrored in the glass of the streaming windows, wrapped in this white towel amid the glint of wood and brass. I surprised myself by grabbing more handfuls than ever of sweet, ludicrously decorated cakes and stuffing them into my mouth until my cheeks hurt. Then came the time to light the lamps, with the squeak of each finely knurled tap bringing a hissing intensification of the smell of gas like ruined flowers.

Other Grandmaster Harrats and Roberts seemed to stretch behind us as we walked through the house—the lost shadows of our past Halfshiftdays—and the light in the long workroom had the texture of sodden wool. But he desisted from lighting the lamps there, clattering his trays and bales of wire, and the whole place seemed emptier than usual. The desks where he usually conducted his experiments were clear. What had happened to the wires and the acids, those fireflies of electricity?

'Oh, I'm finished with all *that* for now, Robert,' he said with a forced gaiety. 'Yesterday, all of last night, I was in here labouring. But nothing seemed right . . .' He paused. 'Odd thoughts, odd problems—and real ones, obstacles that I'd never considered before—suddenly assailed me. I couldn't get any of it to work, and I finally realised why, which was the most obvious reason of any imaginable.' A smile creased his face. 'The idea, you see, Robert, is impossible. There will never be electric light—at least not in England . . . That was the message of that experiment we conducted here last Halfshiftday. All we have is aether . . .'

He trailed off, still looking at me. An inner struggle went on in his throat and jaw. Finally, he asked a question he hadn't asked me in many terms, although I'd often felt that he was on the brink of it.

'And how's your mother, these days?'

'She died this morning. She threw herself from the window when the trollman came.'

Silence fell over us with the hiss of the rain.

'Such a mess, Robert!' Grandmaster Harrat began to shift things and lay them aside. Stoppers and jars clinked, clouding the air with their variegated scents. 'But perhaps some of this will be useful to my guild. It does seem a shame to just leave it all here to gather dust . . .' He spun the dial of his safe on the wall, and took out the tinkling vials of aether. 'And what am I to do with *this,* Robert, eh? This damnable stuff which dictates our lives.' He placed the tray down on an empty bench. His shadow grew enormous, his face whitened. 'Aether is everything, Robert. Aether is *nothing* . . .'

With a sob and sweep of his hand, he dashed the tray to the floor. The precious vials shattered, their surprised contents fanning out through the shards with a syrupy thickness, exploring the dusty floor with shining fingers. How many engines would this bind and power, I wondered, as Grandmaster Harrat stood there, ridiculous in his slippered feet amid the blazing puddle, splashes of the stuff on his trousers, dribbles on his face and hands. He looked around at the room, his uplit features twisted in a sudden disgust. With a growl, he lunged out at one of the demijohns of acid which lay nearby. It rocked back and forth for a moment as if considering whether to fall. Then it did, and a smoking pool lapped from its lip to mingle with the aether. The scene grew extraordinary as Grandmaster Harrat dislodged more and more of his precious chemicals until they formed a swarming froth. Tendrils of smoke and gas writhed.

'It was a job that was given me . . .'

He began to talk without prelude, and to pace the swarming room, his feet leaving trails of wyreglow.

'But you must understand, Robert,' he said, 'it was the job I was given when I was in my first senior appointment at Mawdingly & Clawtson. A guildmaster came to see me here. He was waiting inside this house one night, standing in the hall even though the maids denied letting him in. So I knew instantly he had power. It was as if, even before the spell was made, the power of that thing was upon him. And he had a face like—a face I can't quite remember somehow, Robert, even though he was standing close to me and I could smell the rain on his fine cloak. He spoke the words of my guild, Robert, secret words of command, and I knew that he was one of the men who rule me as surely as the tides are ruled by the moon. And of course I was thrilled, excited. Of *course* I was—who wouldn't be?—even though I couldn't remember his face properly although his cloak was black and I could still smell the rain as if the storm itself had brought him . . .

'We sat and talked, Robert, and he explained in a cool voice what the problem was, and what he wanted of me, and he drew out drawings and photographs I could scarcely believe, and spread them on my table and we pinned them down with porcelain dogs. And we lit the lamps and talked, and he was polite and decent, in the way that men of such power always are. And I was happy to be trusted . . .'

Acrid smoke coiled around Grandmaster Harrat. His slippered feet crunched the glass. He was a fleshy negative; both darkness and light.

'Of course, I understood that he had no need to give his name, or even to mention which particular guild he came from. But the truth is, I was already too wrapped up in the details of how we might use the power of the chalcedony to care about the propriety of what we were doing. Even before I'd opened up the crate, I saw it all so clearly, and the design he wanted, and how Bracebridge and perhaps all of England might be changed by that glowing stone. My hands fairly danced across the blueprints. They almost drew themselves, and yet I was so proud of them. After all, what could be wrong with improving the extraction of aether? What's wrong with doing your best? Isn't that what, as guildsmen, we all owe the shareholders of Mawdingly & Clawtson? How was I to know that the engines would stop and the thing would react?'

Grandmaster Harrat's words were muffled by sobs now. His face glistened with tears and aether.

'But part of me always *knew* it was wrong, Robert. Part of me did, and the rest of me didn't. It was like a secret I kept from myself. I suppose I could have asked, I could have challenged, I could have complained. But who to? And what for? There was never any real need—and I had no idea that things would happen as they did, and then keep on coming back to us in this way for so long after . . . You *must* understand, Robert. You must forgive me . . .'

Grandmaster Harrat gave a blubbering sob and blundered towards me, a figure of flaming white. I stumbled back. I felt the touch of his hands on my chest and shoulders and ducked away. But he floundered on, tumbling through shelves. He stood for a moment amid the fog in the centre of his workroom, teetering like someone on the edge of a precipice until his slippered feet gave and he fell forward, skidding on the heels of his hands and then down onto his face and belly in shining pools of aether and acid.

He gave a gurgling sigh and struggled to get up. But already his palms were smoking, his face was melting. The rain sluiced the skylights, wyrelit and glowing as Grandmaster Harrat howled and writhed in the froth. I saw the stump of an arm glistening with flakes of aetherised glass. I saw the stripped flesh of his chest like an anatomical drawing. He was sinking, dying. His bones, white and pristine, still clawed and moved as his flesh dissolved around them.

More by touch than by sight, I stumbled to the edge of the room. Misty tendrils of light drifted up from the floor. Flakes of the aetherised glass clung to my feet. My hand, my eyes, were burning. The storm beat on. Bloody fingers slipping, I twisted on the taps of the workroom gas mantles. I tumbled into the kitchen, and up and down the stairs, falling into rooms, dragging at sheets, scattering ornaments and twisting on more gas taps. I was sobbing, groggy, half poisoned, but the darkness seemed to will me on. Finally, gasping, I saw the muddy marks in the hall that my boots had made when I entered. I dragged back the door and huge hands seemed to throw it back into its frame as I stumbled into the night.

Ulmester Street was empty, swept by rain and darkness, its curtained windows uncurious as I tumbled down towards lowtown, my clothes glimmering and acid-shredded. Then, like an intensification of the storm, came a low, deep, rumbling from behind me. I stopped and I looked back up the hill as intense light flickered over the rooftops, freezing the churning motion of the clouds. Everything that Grandmaster Harrat had stood for—the hissing gas lamps, the fires glittering in fine mirrors, the wyreglow of aether, those struggling maggots of electricity—seared my eyes in one driven surge which was followed by a crackling and roaring, and the fall of masonry.

XI

My mother's coffin gleamed. It was good wood, paid for with guild money—the same money which had paid for the stone, freshly carved amid all the others in the Lesser Tool-makers' section of Bracebridge graveyard. Father Francis made the signs of his guild as it was lowered into the wet earth and muttered of the welcome which my mother would already have been granted in heaven, where she would be free of her guildswoman's burdens and labours—free to do all of those vague and happy things amid fine houses and wheatfields which I knew that, without all the commonday tasks of everyday life, she would regard as empty and pointless.

Filled with child's boredom at this drawn-out occasion, I puffed my cheeks and looked up at the cloudy sky and down towards the lines of houses. The hymnal wine which I'd tasted today had been stale and sour. The dreams it brought were nothing more than the cold and damp and musty pages of unread Bibles. And nothing had changed. Nothing ever changed here in Bracebridge. The crooked factory chimneys still smoked. A cart clattered down Withybrook Road, rocking with empty barrels. The ground still pounded. Beth struggled with the booming wind to keep on her borrowed black hat. A few of the women, neighbours mostly, were crying, although the men's faces could have been chiselled out of stone; even now, they would not show emotion. A gaggle of children watched us across the low wall, just as I had watched other funerals, wondering what it would be like to stand here before a hole in the ground. I was still wondering.

Already, workmen were clearing the foundations of Grandmaster Harrat's house on Ulmester Street across the hill in hightown which, solid though it was, had been ruined beyond all prospect of repair by the gas explosion. From what I had heard, there was scarcely more sense of surprise at his death than at my mother's, nor any suggestion of a linkage. Domestic gas light was rare in the houses of the people of Bracebridge, and commonly viewed as so unreliable that, had Grandmaster Harrat known, he would surely have despaired of ever persuading us of the benefits of anything as strange and new as electricity. He hadn't belonged in Yorkshire. He was from London, he wasn't married, and, although I doubted if many people in Bracebridge were familiar with the word, a faint sense of the camp clung to him like the odours of eau de cologne and battery acid. Amid all of this, the fact that he invited young boys to his house on Halfshiftday afternoons would have seemed trivial, if it had been known of at all. He was dead, and that was the end of it. Perhaps he was being buried in the distant crypt of some great guild's chapel at this very moment. For all I knew. For the little I then cared.

Father Francis finished his words and people began to drift away, heading for the hall, which was really a long shed, up on Grove Street where there would be a spread of cold meats, with ginger beer for the children, sweet sherry for the women, strong brown ale for the men. I remained standing with the last of the mourners, reluctant to let this empty moment slip away. The yew trees at the far side of the graveyard stood tall and dark, like watching figures. Then one, as my gaze lingered, changed, and *became* a figure, small, and half shrouded in a broad-brimmed hat and coat. It approached, picking its way between the memorials.

'I felt that I had to come,' Mistress Summerton said, 'but I knew, especially after what happened, that I couldn't possibly be seen.'

'They've probably forgotten already,' I said. 'Or they will have by the time they've had a few drinks up at the hall.'

'You shouldn't be so cynical, Robert.'

We watched as, across the graveyard, the last of the departing mourners made their way through the church gate. None of them seemed to notice Mistress Summerton and I. Perhaps, I thought, we both look like yew trees now. We turned the opposite way, down into lowtown and the market that, today being Sixshiftday, filled the main square. We didn't speak for a long time and simply wandered amid the stalls as the awnings flapped and the sky hurried. Despite the heaviness of her coat, Mistress Summerton's feet were shod in delicate shoes which seemed scarcely more substantial that Grandmaster Harrat's slippers, although they remained far less muddy than the heavy boots and clogs that clumped around us. She wore fine long calfskin gloves and her glasses flashed in the sunlight. Dressed as she was on this grey day, no one would have guessed that she wasn't just some little old guildslady. Aether can turn both ways—I felt I understood that now as Mistress Summerton sniffed the leeks and squeezed the loaves for freshness. Just like wyrelight, it can be bright or dark. It can make fine engines and bear messages along telegraphs and stop all of England's bridges from collapsing. Or it can be the dragonlouse; the stinging, stinking, cuckoo-plant—the terrible troll which had come to occupy my mother's bedroom. It can be all of those things. Mistress Summerton took my hand and drew me on past buckets of buttons from Dudley and mountains of sugar brought here all the way from the Fortunate Isles and blotchy heaps of waterapples which came down the road from Harmanthorpe. We admired the dried bunches of sallow and lanternflowers in a corner where the stallholder, in an almost unheard-of gesture, gave her a free posy to pin on her lapel. I cherished these moments, after everything that had happened.

We walked to the river, and Mistress Summerton leaned on the rough parapet of the bridge which had given the town its name as the wind swept in around Rainharrow and in from the Pennines, booming and echoing in its arches, shivering the racing water, bearing dead leaves and branches, the scents of coal and mud. The dry petals of the posy stirred and rustled.

'I wish there was some better word,' she said, 'than sorry.'

'I don't care. It doesn't matter. Nothing matters.'

'Say what you want, Robert, but don't damage yourself by really thinking that.'

I swallowed. The wind burned my eyes. Then Mistress Summerton turned and put her arms around me. She seemed bigger as I buried myself against the leather smell of her coat. I felt warm and walled, and for a moment the day dissolved. I was floating, healed, in a different England of noonday silence, tiers of wonder, white towers . . . I stepped back, surprised to find myself still here, on this bridge with the wind and the river.

'If we could all have made this land better than it is, Robert,' she said, smiling, 'don't you think, after all these Ages, we'd have done so?' She produced her clay pipe from her pocket and I watched as she struggled to light it, turning her back to the wind in the way I'd often seen men doing on their way back from the factories, but going through match after match until she finally got the bowl glowing. The spectacle of her struggling to perform such a task left me with a twinge of disillusionment. What kind of creature was she, if she couldn't do such a simple thing? No wonder she hadn't been able to save my mother.

We crossed the bridge and walked on the far side of the river beside the half-flooded meadow. The white birds we called landgulls here in Bracebridge circled above the racing waters of the Withy.

'You know,' I said, 'I've always believed in your kind. It was Northallerton I didn't think was real. But was my mother really a changeling?'

'I don't like that word, Robert. You'll be calling *me* one next. Or a witch or a troll or a fairy.'

'But fairies don't exist—and you're here.'

She smiled, then frowned beneath those flashing lenses, brown wrinkles drawing out from the shadows and across her face. 'You know, I sometimes wonder about even that. Look at the way the buildings rise and fall here in Brace-bridge, how the tilled fields change in anticipation of the seasons—and feel that pounding! All that passion and energy and industry! My life is diffuse, Robert. The frailty of reality is always with me. It blows through my flesh. Up at Redhouse, I'm like an old dog in an empty house, growling and barking at shadows . . .'

'It must be terrible.'

'Sometimes, perhaps. But believe me, and despite everything, this is a better Age than many in which to be living. I haven't been stoned, or burnt—not yet, anyway— and I have my small freedoms . . .'

As we walked beneath the swaying trees and the Withy surged beside us, Mistress Summerton told me about her life. She'd been born, as best as she could reckon, nearly a hundred years before at the start of this Age, although she still had no knowledge of the precise circumstances. She took off her glasses then as we stood beside an old tree. In the half-light of the rivermeads, her eyes seemed brighter than ever. The soft brown irises seemed aflame, and the pupils were dark openings which went on forever. She even let me touch the flesh of her face and arms. It felt like thin leather, dry paper.

'I don't seem so odd, perhaps, now that I'm old. People who glance at me imagine I'm just antique and weathered. But when I was young, I didn't look so very different. In fact, as far as I know, I was always this way. So it must have happened before I was born, or soon after. The Gatherers' Guild has a Latin name for this condition, just as they have for every other one, and it seems that the change which happened to me is most common, although common isn't the word, amongst the charcoal makers of the forests which lie towards Wales, and which supply Dudley's fur-naces. Hardly sounds like aethered work, does it, or even guilds-work? But it is, and a spell can always twist against the person who makes it.'

'But you were just a baby.'

'So perhaps it was my mother.' She paused. 'In those days the guilds would pay good money for someone like me, someone who was new and young enough to be trained and used. I've heard that families were desperate enough to . . . *cause* an accident. But I don't know. And at least they didn't burn me on the hearth or put me out in the snows. So I suppose I should be grateful . . .'

Instead of her family and her home, Mistress Summerton's memories of her childhood were filled with the strange house in which she was raised. It was essentially a prison, and those few who passed the lane on which it lay would surely not have known. It lay, as she was to discover eventually, at the wooded outskirts of the great city of Oxford, and had been constructed for the study of changelings in an earlier Age. With bars on its windows and bolts on its doors, hidden passageways, hatches and peepholes burrowed within its walls, it had long been empty by the time Mistress Summerton arrived, and her first memories were of the smell of damp, and the dulled murmuring of hidden voices.

'I don't know if you've heard the theories, Robert. That a changed baby such as I was will begin to speak the true language of aether if it is left alone . . .'

The matrons who tended her there were starched and gloved—masked, even, for fear of some unspecified damage that she might do to them—although, as Mistress Summerton grew older, there would be whole shifterms when she barely saw anyone. Food would appear each morning at her table. Mysteriously, her bed linen would be changed. Bizarrely, to her it was the ordinary humans who seemed possessed of magic.

'But I *was* a strange and wild thing, too,' she continued, 'for what little power I have is like a kind of madness. I'm forever buffeted by the winds of the impossible—by thoughts, ideas, sensations. Little things fascinate to the point of obsession, whilst the ordinary matters of life are often dim as smoke . . .' She paused, tapping out the contents from the dead bowl of her pipe, running her twig fingers along the stained ivory. She still had off her glasses, and her eyes, as she looked at me, were like the gleam of sunlight on winter fields. '*How* can I make you understand, Robert?'

But I felt. I understood. As we walked beside the Withy, I could hear the muffled voices within the walls of that prison-house in Oxford louder than the rush of the river. At night, Mistress Summerton would gnaw the wood of her bedstead, and sit rocking on her haunches, moaning and howling. She ate with her fingers even when she had been shown repeatedly otherwise, preferred everything raw and bloody, and learned to speak the obscenities which the matrons muttered behind their masks.

It must have been a strange, impossible life. As the guildsmen studied her through their spyholes, she sensed their memories and thoughts, and felt the bells and bustle of the spired city in the bowl of the forest beyond. She sometimes heard trains sweeping north, and the shout of draymen's voices, and the rattle of carts, although she knew little of what it all meant, other than that this was real life, and she was for some odd reason separated from it. For a while, even after she had learned to speak, they persisted with silence in the hope that she might still speak some spell which was new to them. But if she spoke people's unsaid thoughts, she was beaten. If she moved something without touching it, her fingers were burned on the glass of a lamp. And she was probed and prodded as well. There was a man who sat humming whilst he bled her with leeches. There were others who presented her with cards inside envelopes, told her to read their contents, and strapped her in a chair before feathers and weights in bell jars and ordered her to move them whilst they discussed whether her powers might be increased through the removal of her sight. Having been abused for performing similar tasks spontaneously, she never knew quite what it was that they really wanted.

Mistress Summerton walked on for a while, silent, as if this was the end of her story. The stale echoes of that dreadful prison-house in Oxford faded. The trees ceased their tapping at the barred windows, and the air smelled again of soot and mud and privies and cabbagestalks. At some point, we had turned back along the bank. Beyond the bridge, Bracebridge was waiting again, grey in the greying light.

'Did you escape?' I asked.

She stopped and turned to me and pushed back her coat. She began to undo the buttons and strings of the front of her smock. It was a bizarre gesture, and I found myself backing away, my skin chilling with fear. What, after all, *was* she? Here I was, on the dark bank of this rushing river with a creature who—but then I began to see. A tattoo was emblazoned on the gnarled and flattened skin of her thin chest. A cross and C glowed out from the twilight. 'I've never escaped,' she said, and buttoned herself up again. 'England is as it is, Robert, and the guilds control me just as they control you, and your father—and your poor, poor mother. Oh, I'm free now from my daily labours after what you'd call a lifetime of service. The Gatherers' Guild don't imprison us all in places like Northallerton. In fact, they've forgotten about me down in Redhouse, and an old fool like Tatlow is hardly ever likely to find out again . . .'

Despite everything, I was still filled with questions. I pictured her returning to Redhouse today. Even after what I'd heard and seen, the place I imagined on that dull winter's afternoon was filled with joy and sunlight. And Annalise would be there. I saw her in that same dress, although it had grown cleaner, whiter . . .

'I'm afraid that Annalise has had to leave Redhouse, Robert. She's not with me any longer. She—well, she had to begin her life. Things couldn't go on as they were for her, living with an old thing like me, and in hiding. I just hope I've given her the life she wanted. Of course, I miss her, and you two obviously got on so well. Things have been difficult for her. Did she tell you anything about how her life began? And has something else happened? *What* have you learned?' Suddenly, we had stopped walking. Mistress Summerton's glasses filled with the black currents of the river. She stretched her neck forward. Her body seemed to lengthen. It began to shrivel up, change, extend. I saw, unwilled, the spectacle of Grandmaster Harrat's dying, heard the flicker and crump as his house exploded.

'What happened was—'

'No, don't *say*!' She shrunk back into herself; seemed, almost physically, to push me away. 'It's time to forget and move on. Both of us have had enough for now of terror and disappointment . . .'

Her charcoal hand brushed my shoulder and all the visions and questions seemed to drain from my mind. Mistress Summerton was right. Annalise had gone from Redhouse. My mother was dead, and so was Grandmaster Harrat. I still sensed that all of these events were somehow joined, but these mysteries seemed like nothing more than shadows from the past, and I still believed then that the future was something quite separate; to be moulded, changed. We walked the rest of the way back along the bank towards Bracebridge. Boatmen on the piers across the water paused in coiling their ropes and the tying of their windspells to watch our passage; this lad and a small, elegant woman in a long coat. Perhaps, I thought, they imagined she was my mother.

'I'll tell you more one day,' she said as we climbed the brick-paved steps beside the deserted market. 'But I, too, will have to leave Redhouse and Bracebridge soon. And you must live your own life. If you do that, perhaps our paths will cross . . .'

I watched Mistress Summerton pick her way through the market litter. She glanced back beside a shop's lit frontage and raised her hand in a final wave, then turned up a side street and dwindled into a waft of shadow. The wind was still rising, tearing at the clouds as I headed back towards Coney Mound. Slowing my steps, I gazed up at the sky. For once, even the face on the moon seemed to be smiling, but the red star in the west had vanished.

XII

My life, in the days, shifts, seasons, years that followed, remained steadfastly unremarkable. Father returned to his
work on East Floor at Mawdingly & Clawtson, and to his
drinking, whilst Beth managed to beg an assistant's job at a
school at Harmanthorpe despite twice failing her exams. I
even think that I went more regularly to Board School
again myself, and perhaps brutalised my schoolmates less,
although I have little recollection of learning anything,
or of friendships made. Life, seemingly, became normal
again, although our neighbours on either side left Brickyard Row, and Father never slept in the front bedroom
again, although the dragonlice vanished from its walls. He
kept to his chair instead, his place before the kitchen range,
growling at anything or anyone who obstructed his petty
whims as his hair greyed and he became increasingly disgusting in his ways. The bedroom remained cold and
empty, its door swollen permanently ajar on its rusted
hinges, the wrecked wardrobe still heaped in the corner.

Five years passed in this way, with little of incident to
record other than the changes that came upon my body as it
began to grow towards manhood and strain my hand-me-
down clothes. Looking at myself, fingering the down on

my belly and my chin, I sometimes remembered the distant
chime of Annalise's words in the gardens of Redhouse, and
felt amused, and disappointed, at the loss of something I
could never quite place. But I was resolute in my forgetting. My pleasures came in those days from wandering the
top of Rainharrow, tramping heedlessly and alone over the
bracken until I was exhausted, or out in the backyard chop-
ping firewood on winter evenings. I sometimes toyed with
the idea of following the tracks towards Tatton Halt. But
my footsteps always began to slow as I neared the edge of
Bracebridge. All below me lay the grey and smoking factories, and the pounding which filled my blood. I'd had
enough of broken dreams, and I knew in my heart that
Redhouse would be empty.

I was still a physical lad, filled with angry energy, unex-
pressed disappointments. Yet also at that time, long after I
should have been concentrating on guild exams, or smoking on street corners and flirting with the girls, I was still
often a knight from the Age of Kings, riding out in my
imaginings on a fine mount of silver-white into unspoilt
lands which went on forever. I was a lonely figure even in
that distant landscape, who shunned the courtly dances in
favour of paths in deep woods, craggy mountains. There,
hanging back in a stir of leaves or a drift of moonlight, I
would glimpse the one other being who still mattered to
me. My mother, a presence always receding yet never quite
gone. Once, on a whim which wouldn't have lasted if I'd
allowed myself time to think about it, I took the steam
charabanc to Flinton. All the way, jolted and sore, I kept
telling myself that the place would be nothing, just some
cheap neighbouring town famed only for its ugliness and
its coal production. Still, as I climbed down and saw its
turning wheels and slagheaps, I felt a cold wash of disappointment. This wasn't Einfell.

Other summers passed, and other winters. I heard, in the
way that you pick up these tales as you grow older, that
there had once been a Halfshiftday back in the seventies of
this Age when the unthinkable had occurred and the aether
engines of Bracebridge had stopped pounding. Several
buildings had collapsed in the aftershock, but they had

long been rebuilt. The occasion already seemed half-mythical. Not that I cared. Not that I wanted to know. There was something about this whole town, even in its rumours and dreams, which disgusted me, and although the assumption must surely have remained that I would become a toolmaker, my father was slow to take me again to Mawdingly & Clawtson. Understandably, he had become disillusioned with the scant mysteries of his lesser guild. Still the Fiveshiftday came when the task could no longer be avoided, although we both seemed to trail behind each other as we headed towards the back gates of East Floor. It was a hot summer morning. The air tasted of dust and ash and metal even before the siren blew and the machines started turning. There was no chance now of my bumping into poor Grandmaster Harrat, but I soon grew bored standing beside my father, and found myself looking down the smoking, sun-streamed aisles in the expectation that I would soon have to renew my acquaintance with the vile Stropcock. But the uppermaster who arrived was a fatter creature named Chadderton, who was amiable in the unconvincing way of people who want to be liked. Instead of that upper office with the brassy haft, Chadderton took me to the deserted works canteen and picked at his nails and flicked through timesheets. Stropcock had gone, it seemed. Not merely from East Floor, but from Mawdingly & Clawtson and Bracebridge.

Later, I was shown around the other floors and levels and depots in the company of another lad from my school who suffered from a permanent nose-drip. The paintshop seemed smaller. The girls looked more like the pouting and spotty creatures other lads of my age were flirting with than the princesses of my childhood imaginings. Everywhere else was incomprehensibly busy and noisy. I was left briefly alone in a yard after my soon-to be colleague had been sent off, his dewdrop dangling, and amid much suppressed hilarity, to find a left-handed screwdriver. I took slow breaths in the hot beating sunlight, trying hard not to believe in the life into which I seemed to be irresistibly falling. But this particular yard was familiar, and when I turned and saw a long whitewashed wall at its far

end, I understood why. It had changed slightly since my vision. The old iron gate now had a seamlessly welded chain
to complement the heavy padlock. A strange and empty
surprise dulled and then quickened my heartbeat as I
walked up to it. The arch inside had been blocked in and
the brickwork was cruder and newer than the rest of the
wall, oozing mortar like filling from a sponge. I strained to
squeeze my hand between the bars of the gate to touch it,
but it was set an inch further back than I could reach. Filled
suddenly with a sense of someone watching, I turned
around, rubbing my grazed knuckles. But there was nothing but blind black windows, broken gutters, guild graffiti,
peeling paint. SHOOM *BOOM* SHOOM *BOOM*. The
ground shuddered beneath me. Part of me wanted something else to happen, but I was mostly relieved when the
dew-drop swinging lad returned red-faced and empty-
handed from the toolroom stores.

In the shifterms which followed, I began to frequent the
iron bridge on the turn of Withybrook Road which spanned
the main railway line heading south out of Bracebridge, to
climb down across the trembling cables and buttresses until there was nothing but roaring, expectant air beneath,
and wait, and wait. Balanced thus as the trains swept by,
I already felt as if each clattering wagon was pulling me
away. I knew that I would eventually jump, and I watched
myself day by day as I went about my life with an out-
sider's curiosity, wondering when the precise moment
would come when I made that final leap, and where that
leap would take me.

It finally happened on a spring Twoshiftday night in late
March the year 90, when the rails shone clear under the
moonless stars, glinting and joining like a river. I'd been
sitting with my feet dangling over the parapet, dressed as I
was always dressed in my ragged hand-me-down clothes,
scarcely a boy now, or even a youth, but nearly a man—
whatever that meant. I had brought nothing with me, although it seemed now that I'd always known that that was
how it would have to be. The air was warm and the town
behind me had a steady, purposeful glow, stacking up roof
on roof from Coney Mound to the edgy, shifting gloom of

Rainharrow. Placing my hand on the oiled and belted stanchions, engraved, beneath their filth, with the guilded charms, I could feel the faint tremor which always came through this thinly made structure in the quiet moments between trains.

If anything, Bracebridge looked better to me than it had in years as I gazed back at it. The lights, the smoke, the chimneys; all suddenly twined together and became something else, something more, a ghost-vision, lost and blazing in the starlight. Perhaps it was that which finally drove me on as I heard the rumble of a coming train; the sense that I could stay here forever in this limbo of waiting, dreaming of lost lands, touching old stones, visiting old places. Soon, the roar of the engine filled the air as the waiting tracks shone clear. The train swept below, the hot glow of its furnace and the blurring heat of smoke followed by the first of many open aether trucks. The straw heaped around the caskets looked soft as fleece and I gauged the timeless moment of my leap from the rocking beat of the wheels against the tracks, by the pulse of my breath, and for the last time, before I released my hold and let the air take me, by the rhythm that pervaded all of Bracebridge.

SHOOM *BOOM* SHOOM *BOOM*.

Then I was flying.

PART THREE

ROBBIE

I

I lay looking up as the stars slipped through the trees, urging the train to carry me south. The wheels clanged. The truck creaked and rocked. Occasional scraps of steam blew over from the distant engine. The straw that prickled my neck was laden with a drowsy, summery smell. Within its bolts and scrolled iron bands, the rough wooden box of the aether casket looked shockingly cheap. But, staring up at it in the grey darkness, spread-eagled in the straw with my head tilted back, I fell asleep as easily as I had in years.

The air was gauzily damp when I awoke. I climbed to the edge of the truck and peered over the side at a landscape tiered with mist, dabbed with smudges of cattle. Sometimes, we passed stations, but the signs flashed by too quickly for me to read. I was already somewhere, I supposed, consulting the vague map I kept in my head, in the Midlands. The hills were lower here; shallow rises that folded into each other like green limbs. The houses, from what I could make out of the few I saw, were squatter than those I was used to, the bricks of their walls a brighter red which seeped into the mist. Some had thatched roofs pulled down over their windows. Even the trees were different, with huge oaks quite unlike the stunted versions around Bracebridge and many other bushes, some already in flower, which I couldn't name. None of this was quite familiar, yet neither was it entirely strange, and I loved each bridge and fence and puddle for not being Bracebridge.

In places on my long journey, viaducts cast breathtaking shadows from spiderwebs of iron, and the train clattered through tunnels where the swooping telegraphs shone out through noise and smoke. As the sun climbed and the rattle of points became more frequent, we entered an area of small towns. People were about now, in the fields and on the roads, in carts and gigs and wagons. I studied the aether casket more closely, the rough wood and the metal bands and fixings. I pressed my ears against it in the vague hope that I might hear some sound other than the onward rush of the rails. The casket only stood about a yard and a half high, and was about the same in depth and width. An adult man could have spanned it with his hands—probably even picked it up, for I had a dim recollection of hearing that aether itself has no weight. But I had no idea why each of the caskets had to be wadded in straw and laid in long separate trucks when it was plain that, physically, they could easily have been piled together. The greyish lumps attached to the hooped joins binding the sides of the casket, which I had imagined in the earlier darkness to be padlocks, were in fact seals made of clay. Rough handfuls had been lumped around the join, then stamped. The swirls and figures reminded me of the tiny wax ones that had been strung around Grandmaster Harrat's aether vials. Absently, I began breaking off flakes of clay with my fingernails until a bleak, sudden shock roared through me from the power of its protective spell and I cowered, feeling my bladder loosen as urine soaked my trousers. Huddled shivering in the far corner of the truck, my hands clasped around my knees, I gazed at the casket as the last of the mist cleared.

The day passed and my long journey passed with it. The landscape shifted into broader, flatter planes where the fields flashed with furrows. The scent of the air grew more luxuriant. There were huge orchards of mossy-leafed waterapple trees. Their starkly uptilted boughs, still bereft of their tumescing burdens, looked like black avenues of hafts as the sun fell through them. Tall, odd structures began to appear, with huge, sail-like arms turning against the afternoon sky. Every one was set on a raised hillock, and beside these lay sluices and pools, some of which flared with the afternoon's milky brightness whilst others cast pools of shadow like flurries of smoke. Unmistakably, these were aether settling pans, and the towers beside them could only be windmills, drawing aether from the menhirs on which they perched.

The rhythm of the train grew less regular as the rails fanned out. Evening was closing in, and the scents in the air were once again changing. Other trains clacked by, the black heads of their engines flashing over me. What was to happen when this train finally stopped? What excuse could I give when I was discovered? But the trucks lurched on, and the sky darkened; sooty blackness closing over a sky of no stars, no moon. I peered out from the truck again. All I glimpsed at first were walls, roofs, houses—scraps of a scene so dim and bleak that I almost feared that the journey had twisted in on itself and brought me back to Bracebridge. But further off, blazing at the sky's black edges, were haloes of impossible light. This, surely, had to be London. Even a bumpkin like me knew that there was no other city in all England of such challenging size, beauty, ugliness. The trucks jostled, then stopped entirely in one cataclysmic jerk. We had stopped amid a sea of gaslit rails. I ducked down when I heard the crunch of boots.

' . . . sure I *felt* something back down the trucks a few hours back. I still think we should . . .' The boots paused. I heard the pop of lips as the man spat.

'Can't check every fuckin' one, can we?' Another, shriller, voice.

They were passing right beside my truck now. I could smell sweat, tobacco.

'Could always let the fellas out, couldn't we? Let them buggers have a sniff . . .'

I risked looking out as the crunch of their boots faded down the track. The stoker was long and thin, the steamaster short and fat. The track curved slightly inwards, and I could watch their progress towards the covered wagon at the train's far end. Then, I heard a muffled baying, followed by the slide and boom of wagon doors. I scrambled through the straw to the truck's far side and half jumped, half fell, to the track, letting the impetus carry me on across the rails to the downward slope of an embankment, submitting to the will of gravity until I was scrambling through Age-old refuse and searing patches of cuckoo-nettle towards a fence as the gruff howl-bark of the released balehounds grew louder behind me. The beasts were almost at my heels as my fingers closed on rusty chains and I began to scramble up. Then I was over, and falling, until the ground hit me, and once again I was running.

The dark land rose and fell by small, difficult increments, dips transforming themselves into rises, hollows tumbling me down into mud. Slowly I became aware of lights coating the blackness ahead. The filthy ground grew firmer, whilst the air, which had been so bad at times that I could scarcely breathe, became fogged and smoky. I had entered an area of buildings of a sort, and alleys. It was a steepening maze, but by instinct, sick of the mud, still fearing the balehounds and dazed and sore from the burn of the cuckoo-nettles, I took ways that led up. Most of Bracebridge, even its poorest parts, was built of brick, but many of these buildings were of wood and wattle and daub— reinforced and remade and propped up as they started to leak and sag and tumble. The windows mainly consisted of shutters or waxed paper and the frontages leaned over each other, pressing their brows together as if in senile thought. There was an overwhelming sense of closed-in rot and damp and age.

The people were different, too—what little I saw of them. Faces floated at windows. Voices called. I felt that I was being watched, followed, that a space was constantly opening before and behind me as I stumbled up steps and waded the stinking rills of open drains. I flapped through curtains of wet washing. Once, I was sure, hands clamped on my arms. There was wild laughter. But they slipped from me as I began running again.

I finally found myself hunched and breathless in a sort

of square. The buildings which framed it were uneven, and gleamed with pinpoints of light. From them, fizzing through the night, mingling and rising, came sounds and smells of life; of voices shouting and buckets banging, of burnt fat and fried fish and bad drains. People lived here, just as they lived everywhere. Pricked by loneliness, I wandered across to where an old pump dripped on the paving. I worked the handle, and buried my face and hands in the gouts of strange-tasting water. Drenched and dizzy, I looked again at this square, and these walls ridged like broken teeth with their pale lights ebbing and flowing. Then a human-seeming shadow came towards me and rasped the paving with a boot. Something struck my shoulder. I gave a yelp. The shadow shifted. Something else hit my back. Something sharp gashed the side of my face.

'Look . . .' I croaked, spreading my arms as the massive buildings began an ancient, lumbering dance around me. 'I'm new here. Is this *London*? I don't know what—'

A bigger stone struck me.

'I was just trying to—'

And again. The boots rasped.

'Whose *water* do you think this is, citizen?'

'*What?*'

'I said, give it back . . .'

Everything blurred as another stone struck my head. Then the figure was upon me. Arms roped around my neck and a hard object, a fist or another stone, drove into my face.

I lay somewhere, my eyes gummed and crusted, something rough over me, something angular beneath. But still I faded in and out of it. A new Bracebridge loomed over me, monstrous and changed. Lights flickered at the edge of my vision as the buildings danced. Everywhere, there were voices, poundings. I was back in my attic, and my mother was raising the pulley of the clotheshorse in the kitchen. Then she was on the stairs, and up the ladder, and leaning over, shaking me, shouting as she towered through foul smoke, screaming that it was all too late . . .

Water from the same pump from which I had tried to drink, the musty taste somehow instantly recognisable, splashed over my face. I was dragged up until I was sitting. A boy—no, a thin young man—was crouching before me, a tin cup in his hand, candlelight and the blue smog of some wider space fanning behind him.

'What's your name?'

'Robert Borrows.'

He tilted his head. 'Say again, citizen?' His accent was strange.

'Robert Borrows. I'm from Bracebridge.'

'Where's that?'

'It's in Brownheath. In the north. You mean you haven't *heard* of it?'

'Should I have done? Is it something fine and special, eh? So you're Robbie, are you? I'm Saul by the way.'

I studied the face of Saul-by-the-way in this strange dim room. It was brown and angular and bony. His eyes were pale blue, alight. His clothes were tattered but had a raffish look, with hints of colour and braid picked out by the light of the candle and whatever pale but greater illumination lay behind. They were the kind of things a greatguildsman might have worn, long ago, before they were discarded.

'This is *London,* isn't it?'

He chuckled. His voice had a phlegmy rasp. 'You really are lost, aren't you, citizen? Poor bastard. Robbie from—where was it you said, Broombridge?'

I didn't bother to correct him. I didn't care what anyone called Bracebridge now. And I quite liked the sound of my new, slightly different name. *Robbie . . .*

'Why'd you hit me?'

Saul chuckled again. He reached into his pocket to extract a bent cigarette. 'Why did *you* drink the pump water? Not that it belongs to *me,* of course. Obvious to anyone that water can't belong to a single person. Comes from the sky, don't it, just like grain comes from the ground. But the way things are around the yards in this current Age, it's plain as the nose on your face that it wasn't yours to just *drink . . .*' Saul stooped over the candle in its jam jar and blew a plume of smoke as I attempted and failed to follow his reasoning. In the gleam of light, I noticed that he possessed a puckered scar on his left wrist and felt a small surge of relief. Around him, pinned in their hundreds to beams and walls and odd eruptions of furniture, were scraps of paper. 'And why come to the Easterlies in the first place?'

'I thought you said this was London?'

'Me?' He chuckled. 'I didn't say.'

'But *is* it?'

'Why don't you come and take a look?'

Saul hauled me to my feet. My head was spinning as he dragged me across the floor of a long space shaved by rafters, filled to its dim recesses by dusty wreckage, towards a huge crumbling opening in the brickwork, far bigger than any doorway.

I stood at the edge of it, swaying.

'So?' Saul asked. 'Is this what you wanted?'

All below, the sights, the sounds. And lights, lights everywhere.

II

Up in that high room that first summer, I could never get over the view. It changed moment by moment, hour by hour. The gaslight rails of Stepney Siding, the smoking mass of the Easterlies and the domes and spires of North-central beyond, the green haze of Westminster Great Park, the tall, impossibly frail lattice of Hallam Tower, the wyre-glow of its aethered brazier sweeping dark or blazing white across the London skies.

At dawn, a chorus of ships' horns, sirens and whistles started bellowing to each other across Tidesmeet. Soon, the ships out in the deeper channels where their pilots awaited the rise of the tide joined in; sound piling on sound until the air shook with it. Then the pigeons clattered up from their roosts, and the cocks started crowing, and the pigs squealing in their pens, and the seagulls began to circle as the milk trains clattered in from Kent.

I would open my eyes—and know instantly where I was, and kick back my nest of sacking, and see if Saul was awake. Then to balance on the balls of our feet close to the edge of that swarming drop and see who could piss out the furthest. Whole families would be waking as we slipped down ladders to the main stairwell, scattering cats and rats and drunken sleepers, swinging and ducking under doorways and sliding all the way down to smoke-fogged Caris Yard where that pump would already be clanging. And dogs barking, the morning rasp of vendors hawking bread, oysters and hot codlings, the cries of the newspaper boys and the rumbling carts of the costermongers. Nothing in this sunshine, in this bustle, though, could really look ugly, not even in London's notorious Easterlies. And now that summer was here, surprising numbers of trees, weeds, vines and flowers forced their way to the sun's attentions. The whole Easterlies, in those times, in that Age, and in my memory, were warm and green and verdant.

Down the hill lay Doxy Street. Along there the trams and carriages, and the cars and the carts and the drays, bore guildsmen of every kind to their daily labours in Tidesmeet Docks. Here, also, were the bars and bad hotels and the unguilded boarding houses, the pawn shops and the dealers in goods of various provenance, the dollymops who lounged in the sun each morning on steps and in doorways, their nightclothes in fascinating disarray. It was a season of prosperity, and a huge new railway bridge was going up on the muddy bank on Ropewalk Reach as London strove to extend its bounds to the marshy land south of the river. You could watch the big dredgers clawing across the shining brown waters, and hear the cry of spells as the pilings went up from their thin foundations. As the morning warmed and the work of a thousand different guilds began, the whole of the Easterlies became a clamour of voices as guildsmen struck up one chant over another. The whole of London filled with song.

This lad who called himself Saul and me citizen took me down to Smithfield on my first morning; down at the edge of the Easterlies, which seemed so different in daylight. Instead of one butcher's stall, there was row upon row of them. You could get lost in this vast square amid the white and red hanging quarters of beef and mutton. About me here were gathered an incredible mixture of London society. Mistress cooks from the big houses in Northcentral, bosoms quivering within striped blue aprons, their maids struggling with wicker baskets in their wake. Guildsmen out from their

Clerkenwell factories, each dressed in their own fashion, browsing and smoking and eating and drinking as they took their break. Quiet mistresses of the lesser guilds who'd come over on the tram from Chiswick in the Westerlies and from the gardens of the Kite Hills—women not so very unlike my mother—darkly dressed and bonneted, and moving more slowly from stall to stall, touching the squishy waterapples and the loops of dried sausage and rummaging in their purses as they debated what they could afford.

'So tell me again, just so that I can be sure I've got this right, Robbie,' Saul was saying in his strange and husky voice. 'You're from a place in Brownheath, which is in Yorkshire, called Broombridge? And you came here because you wanted to *escape*? Even though no one was actually after you?'

'I came for London.'

'*London* . . . ?' The word was muttered in amazement. It was as if, living in the Easterlies, a denizen of the sooty heap of buildings he called Caris Rookery, Saul really didn't believe that he was in London at all. 'And your father's a guildsman?'

'Yes . . . I mean . . .' I knew I had to be careful here. My head was still swollen and aching from the beating he'd given me. 'Isn't yours?'

Saul looked at me, then shook his head, although seemingly more in amazement than denial. It was already plain to me that Saul hadn't been initiated into any guild. In fact, he didn't seem to have any kind of employment, which was odd considering he was at least two years older than me and clearly managed to fend for himself.

'Perhaps you could report to your guild here, Robbie,' he said. 'Bang on the brass knocker, present yourself . . . There's *bound* to be a guildhouse. Here, believe me, there's a bloody guildhouse for everything. They'd probably even have you in. Isn't that how it works with you guildsmen—climbing over each other's backs to stop the rest of the world getting a look in?'

'It isn't *my* guild, and I don't want them,' I said, quite enjoying Saul's astonishment as we wandered on through the crowds.

'So you came for this—this city? So why are you smiling, Robbie? Why do you seem so happy? You should try it here in winter. There's no work and nothing but kingrats and lice. You should have your fun, then go back home, citizen, before the season changes. Back to your father and your mother.'

'My mother's dead.'

He shrugged. 'A few more shifterms, you'll realise eyeryone has a hard luck story . . .'

We walked on. Saul, I noticed, had a way of walking, a way of looking. A swagger of sorts, although at the same time he seemed almost to be cowering. Those red-rimmed eyes, as we ducked herbs, slipped through the steam of bubbling pots of poultice, never settled anywhere, yet seemed to take in everything. I stared and stumbled amid the smell of things roasted and things baked, spices and marinades, leaking mountains of butters and cheeses . . . And faces of different hue and aspect, too, which I'd barely glimpsed in my storybook imaginings up in Bracebridge, but here wandered real in their strange clothes, and spoke in their strange voices. Tattooed sailors who'd surely travelled the far Horns of Africa and Thule; Frenchmen—who, I was surprised to notice, didn't really have tails—even Negroes, and many other broad and swarthy men who spoke what might just have been English in impossibly strange accents. And there were bizarre fruits; things long and large and rude-looking, and things rainbow-coloured, and things strangely scented which could have been twisted by the dreams of some guildsman or borne from the far Antipodes, and perhaps both. And then there were the beasts. A dazzling red and green talking bird. Snakes swimming in tanks. Foul-looking creatures, seemingly half-lizard and half-chicken, which hissed at you from their cages, and around which there was much betting and speculation. A sad and smelly dancing bear. The whole scene, the size of everything, and the crowds and the bustle, amazed me. Bruised and light-headed from fatigue and this endless succession of new sights, I caught in one instant the mingled whiff of smoked ham and fresh bread and was ravenously hungry. Saul seemed unconcerned, his hands in his pockets and his

lips pursed and faintly whistling. Only his eyes were alert,
darting.

Then something sharp nudged my ribs. It was his elbow.

'Take this,' he hissed.

I took it.

'And this. Not *there*—shove it underneath your shirt,
you dolt. Hide it, like I'm doing . . .'

Dumbly, I followed suit. Apples and bread rolls and
the things he'd called oranges. A curl of sausage. Not
understanding—for surely they had to be priced and
weighed?

'Now *run*.'

Instantly, Saul was away, and all I could do was follow
him. Head down, I butted elbows and chests, slammed
against trestles. Baskets tumbled, shouts rang, displays of
fruit rainbowed across the paving. Ahead of me, always
just in sight, always in danger of vanishing, flapped the
grubby tail of Saul's embroidered shirt. I skidded across
cabbage leaves, scrambled over pallets. There was a brief
commotion. There were shouts and screams. But Saul spun,
and he was running again, ducking cloaks and hands. He
was quick and I was desperate to keep up with him as he
sprinted down an alley, weaving around the waterbutts, ex-
travagantly swerving and darting now for the sheer joy of
the escape, and I could hear, echoing with the clatter of our
feet, that we were both laughing.

He reached a ladder hung on the side of a building, and
we hauled ourselves up to the roof and sprawled in hilari-
ous agony on a slope of mossy tar. The London sky, cloudy
and shot through with sunlight, hung warm and damp and
smoky over the city, seemed to embrace me. Saul unloaded
the stuff he'd tucked beneath his shirt against his belly,
and I did the same, my mouth brimming with saliva.

III

England's great social pyramid climbs far higher in London, and those who struggle within its foundations are as tightly squashed as the lower strata of the earth. Turn one way, and a dank alley widens into a square, and in that square plays a snowy marble fountain. Turn another, and the pavement sinks below you to drown your boots in sewage. The likes of Saul and me, living in Caris Rookery, dwelt among thieves and pickpockets, and dollymops and seasonal workers and sailors who had lost their boats, the elderly and the mad and the infirm, and wild-eyed waifs of incredible thinness and viciousness. Here, much more than in Bracebridge, there were also the unguilded who had once been guilded—families and sometimes whole guilds which had been tossed down through the Easterlies by recession or misfortune. They seemed to me the most lost of all, those guildmistresses in their once-good clothes dragging children in torn sailor suits around the edges of the market at the end of Tenshiftdays.

But Saul and I were lucky that summer. We ranged far and wide, from Smithfield to the Halfshiftday market at Stepney to the shop displays along Cheapside and the spillages from wagons leaving the quays at Riverside, and

back down the Strand, taking risks which only the young
and the fleet-footed could have undertaken. Then down
Doxy Street to the places in the far Easterlies where we
could sell things which had fallen into our innocent hands
for, as I was starting to learn from Saul, the whole idea
of *something* belonging to *somebody* was fundamentally
wrong. But whether we owned or didn't own the food we ate
and the clothes we wore and the blankets we slept in, it was
a summer of plenty. The wealth of the whole of London
seemed to be floating down towards the Easterlies in a glittering, prismatic rain of borrowed scarves, pocketed fruit,
dropped fob watches, flighty fans and fine ebony canes.
Worst come to the worst, there was always paid work to be
had down at Tidesmeet. Saul and I spent many lazy shiftdays
working in a bondhouse by the old quays, clambering over
teachests with buckets of ink, endlessly stencilling a guild
symbol which was something like a fat-bellied three. The
teachests were piled higher than houses, and were patterned
with the beautiful ideographs of Cathay. These distant
yellow-skinned people plainly also had their own guilds, but
I soon learned from Saul that no one would care if I dribbled
ink or drew faces on the sides of those teachests—least of all
the bondsman dozing in his aromatic office. We could just as
easily squat on the roof and watch the funnels of the steam-
ers and the sails of the clippers shimmer by. All that mattered was that one morning, the master of the particular
guild which oversaw the collection of excise would attend
the bondhouse and issue the appropriate release papers.
Thanks to our stencils, the bondhouse's contents could then
be sold as if their duty had been paid. And the excise officer
would encounter a fat envelope in an unexpected place, or
the cancellation of some embarrassment or debt.

   Tidesmeet Docks were a city in themselves, which was
forever changing in its smells and substances. Every day,
there would be new arrivals of coals from Newcastle, rank
hoppers of saltpetre from the Indies, fragrant sheaves of
tobacco from the Fortunate Isles, barrels of Muscadet,
endless sacks of every kind of fruit and produce, some of
which, rotting and mouldering, brought plagues of insects
even more irritating and ugly than those which commonly

alighted on the flesh of every Londoner in those long hot shifterms. Whole markets lined the watery fingers of the old quays which had grown too small to accommodate the big steam freighters which now brought in most of the trade. There was an air of antiquity here, and the buildings along the water's edge were decorative beneath their thick layers of paint and grime. Up on the hot tiles of that bondhouse roof, eating nameless jerky encased in hard grey bread and looking down on the world as if we owned the entire place, I loved it all, although I still didn't really understand any of it. Like a magician's box unfolding in endless layers, first silvered and smoky, then delicious and filthy, then glorious and horrid, London seemed to encompass everything within its sooty bricks.

'Look at *them*,' Saul said, waving his sandwich towards some cranemen ambling beneath us. They were bare-chested underneath their leather jerkins to show off their vine marks of the haft, and so impressively muscled that they almost looked as if they could lift the loads themselves. 'Their whole lives are wasted following their bosses' instructions—and all those ridiculous signs and shouts and whispers . . .'

I shrugged. These were wealthy men by any normal standards, and, citizen or not, I was still conscious that by the standards of my Age I was nothing but a guildless mart living in a great and uncaring city. But in this, in everything, I turned to Saul for guidance.

'You see this?'

Saul had borrowed—in the changed sense that we used the word—a box of chalks which an unwary warehouseman had left too close to a window. He scratched a large white square on the tarpaper roof.

I nodded.

'Well, that's you and me. And this . . .' He drew an arrow from the square, and then a big circle beside it. 'This is all we produce.'

'Just us?'

He waved a hand, startling several gulls. 'I don't mean *just* you and me. I mean the whole great mass of the working citizens of England.'

I nodded again. I already knew that you didn't have to live in a city to be a citizen. I knew, in fact, that you didn't have to do anything beyond being born, although, like some strange food, the idea still left an odd aftertaste after I had swallowed it.

'And this—this other square here represents the high guilded.' It was a smaller square, drawn through the sticky tar. 'And this . . .' He made a marginally smaller circle. '*This* is the amount of our labour that the high guilded take from us . . .'

The squares and the circles and the arrows multiplied across the roof as the shadows of the gulls floated over them and Saul struggled to explain the complexities of the labour market. The bright heat, the blazing sky, those scraps of shade passing across my face too quick to be felt, and all of us citizens trapped below it. But I loved Saul and his muddled explanations. For my whole life, it seemed to me now, everything had been a total puzzle to me. Bracebridge. The mysteries of the guilds. The death of my mother. My father's disappointments. But here, dusted on a hot roof, fragmentary and chased by shadows, was the beginning of an answer.

On other lunchtimes, Saul would take out a pencil, peel off slivers of pale wood with a knife. With a few lines on a scrap of borrowed paper he could somehow capture the entire view which Tidesmeet spread before us. The coiled ropes and the endless spars and funnels, the cages of the cranemasters, the octagonal fortresses of the hydraulic towers which drove the lifts and hoists, the great pepperpot tower of the Dockland Exchange, all the buildings which crowded west across London like ruffled birds on a perch. He'd hold the drawing up, smile, then tear it into shreds. Nothing, after all, could really belong to anyone. Not here. Not in this Age.

'Tell me more about Brownheath. I mean, about living in the countryside. What's it really *like* . . .'

Saul somehow imagined that, because I hadn't been born in a huge city I must have spent my early life in some sweet-scented barn surrounded by amiable cows; a sunny place where life was somehow far kinder and easier than it was for the poor citizens of London. But I didn't want to disappoint him, and distance soon lent even Brownheath its own kind of charm. Saul's ambition, which he shared far more freely with me than any concrete facts about himself, was to run a farm—not, of course, that he would *own* it—and I found it easy enough to help him in his vague plans by embroidering my mother's stories of her early life with byres and haystacks and flower-strewn meadows, although for me rural life had always seemed to consist of backache and manure.

Another yellowed scrap of parchment, a resharpened pencil, and Saul's nicotined hands conjured up undulating pastures, winding rivers, avenues of stately trees; cartoon visions of a country landscape from a city dweller who was proud never to have been beyond the allotments of Finsbury Fields. His cows looked like horses in those days, and he could only do one kind of tree. But it was incredible to watch. Over the smoky dockyard clamour, you could almost hear the birds singing, smell the fresh-mown grass. He pinned the pictures he was most pleased with to the beams in our lair in the rookery. At night, as the hot wind dragged over the Easterlies, they rustled around us like the leaves of a forest.

There was a fire blazing in the Caris Yard one summer's evening, and the street musicians had combined to form a discordant band. The prim guild charities with their stalls and leaflets had long hitched their skirts and gone back to Northcentral, the soapbox prophets had returned to their chapels, and even the speakers on the Rights of Mankind had vanished in flurries of leaflets, fights and accusations. But there were always fresh arrivals; day or night, the far Easterlies seemed to exert a strange attraction to the rest of London. A braying herd of young guildsmen in caps and narrow-waisted suits from one of the marine colleges had arrived for no obvious reason other than their drunkenness.

'Bet you do!'

'Bet you *don't*.'

'Do!'

'Don't!'

I was sitting beside Saul, but for once I was no longer
the prime focus of his attention. His back was turned from
me as he engaged in this music hall call-and-response with
a girl called Maud. I was used to seeing her about. Although she was scarcely older than me, she ran, almost
single-handed, a nursery in a barn-like building which lay
on the downward side of Caris Yard, where the women of
the parish could leave their babies whilst they went to gut
herring. Maud was hardly a pretty girl—she was thin, and
her pale hair stuck out like a dry floormop even when she'd
attempted to comb and tame it with ribbons as she had tonight—but she was feisty, quick, and resolutely independent. I'd also always thought her defiantly unfeminine until
she'd turned up in this yard wearing dyed straw sandals
and started this do-ing and don't-ing with Saul.

'*You* tell her . . .'

'No it's *not*.'

'It's true, isn't it, Robbie?'

'You know what—I really don't care!'

Disappointed with both of them, I shot Maud a look of
what was probably intense hatred as I stomped away from
Caris Yard. Around the next corner, there was a bar. Anywhere in the Easterlies, and just around the next corner,
there was always a bar, although it was hard to see exactly
what was inside this one and the prevailing smell which
emanated from it was of gin, piss and vomit. But I was
flush tonight—we'd just borrowed a whole display of key-
rings—and I'd found that drink was a useful way of bringing the illusion of forgetfulness at those times when, as
even happened in that first happy summer in London, both
the present and the past seemed to conspire against me.

I sat in a dark corner, nursing a thick-rimmed tumbler
which, true to its name, wouldn't stand up on its own. The
dimly shaped citizens around me coughed and chattered in
that strange accent of which, Saul's being an oddly prim
example, I could still turn my understanding off and on at
will. Outside, somewhere, a pump kept clanking and a pig
or some other animal seemed to be screeching its death
throes. The men in these parts kept kingrats for fighting,
and one was displayed, its hood stretched out in front of

the bar's only lantern as it squealed and snapped, turning the whole room into a blood-red vision of some minor hell. A discussion about the sharpness of its teeth developed into a desultory argument, then an even more desultory fight. Sometimes, London seemed almost eerily quiet, its earth impossibly still.

'Why you sitting here alone aren't you be?'

I turned to see that the source of that tumble of vowels had sat herself down beside me.

'Finished your drink couldn't get ourselves another we?'

The girl's face was powdered an aethereal white within which her dark eyes and mouth and nostrils looked like the holes punched in a mask. Her hair was black, too, and she smelled of patchouli and a need of washing. We sat there somewhat dumbly, she with her drink and me with mine. *Got a new one, Doreen?* She gave a shrill snarl at that comment, reminding me of the kingrat. I was drinking freely, spending my keyring money so successfully that the barman lumbered over to serve us from his jug.

This Doreen had been making a furtive motion in her lap which I'd thought was a nervous habit. I now saw that she was clutching a painstone, the nearly worn-out facets gleaming dimly like grit in the bottom of a well. There was a ready market for these in the Easterlies, just as there was for everything.

'Keeps me safe in case there's trouble and the stories like you hear.' She blinked her black-rimmed eyes and offered the painstone. 'Want you to try it might as well?'

I'd never touched one before, and it felt smooth and warm and—yes—somewhat soothing. Like laying your hand on the head of a friendly dog. But the drink was better. I returned to it.

'Where is you from?'

I think I told her. My accent was probably as impenetrable to her as hers was to me, but unlike Saul who only cared about my rural fictions, she actually seemed to take an interest in my talk of moors and factories and the pounding earth. At some point, I discovered I needed to get up and piss. Wobbling outside, bumping a table and raising a scatter of yells, I leaned against the wall that seemed to be most used for my purpose. When I'd finished, I swayed around, and saw that Doreen had come as well and was just straightening her skirts.

'Walk now shall we?'

I stole glances at Doreen's white face as we swayed arm in arm past lighted windows. It was hard to gauge her age. She'd dressed herself up in a way which suggested a young woman trying to look like an old one. But whatever else she was, she was stopping me from falling over as I rambled on about changelings in crystal houses as a pink summer moon swam around the rooftops.

'Here that's like creepy is that don't to talk about things that. Like Owd Jack and he's out nights . . .'

I swayed to face her. 'Did you say Owd Jack?' We were now alone in a back alley. 'What do you know about . . .' I suppressed a liquid belch and leaned against the mossy brick for support. 'Him? Tell me—'

But Doreen had pushed against me as if to smother my questions. 'And what about this is you like?' she cooed. There was a surge of cheap velvet, gin, sweat, mothballs, and my flailing hand made contact with something soft. It was too dark in the alley for me to be able to see, but I was starting to understand.

'You want you need perhaps.'

My hand was steered down towards the portion of a woman's anatomy which I'd only ever had a chance to study in classical sculptures, and which I scarcely expected to be hairy, or wet. I was still recovering from my surprise when Doreen's hands went to work on my trouser buckle, burrowing inside to find the erection which certainly wouldn't have been there if I'd had time to think about it. The rest of the business was quickly done as Doreen parted the necessary bits of her clothes with surprising proficiency. The full London moon hung over her shoulder, riming with pink and gold the slates of the houses which fanned across the Easterlies towards Ashington in back-to-back rows. Imagining that this was what people did on such occasions, I attempted to kiss her, but my jaw was rudely knocked away. Then we were finished.

'That'll be then ninepence going rate.'

Amid everything else she was saying, I kept detecting references to money. The moon looked amused now as it hung over the chimneys and the effect of the drink was changing. I knew about dollymops—they were impossible to avoid in the Easterlies—but I'd failed until then to make any connection with what Doreen and I had been doing. Taking my puzzlement as an attempt at bargaining, a one-sided argument ensued, with Doreen shouting things at me which I didn't need to fully understand to get the gist of. Nine whole pennies was more than I had left after the drinks I'd bought, but I was happy to offer what I had left in my pockets, and to put up with the surprisingly hard punch she threw at my shoulder in a final flounce, just to be rid of her.

I wavered back towards Caris Yard, then up the ladders and stairs of the rookery. When I reached our roofspace there was no sign of Saul in his usual corner. I stood for a while at the archway, feeling lonelier than I had in all the time since I had arrived here. This was it. London. Hallam Tower, rising at it always rose, flashing misty bright. And the guildmasters sleeping in their houses. The poor in their hovels. Tidesmeet. Stepney Sidings. Dockland Exchange. The cranes. The funnels. The distant snow-white hills of World's End. The swooping, murmuring telegraphs. The greatgrandmasters, even, in their palaces. The spires of the churches, and the endless, endless factories.

Saul was uncharacteristically subdued one summer morning as we wandered the quiet markets up by Houndsfleet. It was a relief to get back to the roaring tramtracks of Doxy Street, where large guildsmen, hotly dressed in suits and hats and knotted ties, barged uncaringly past us. Then he turned without explanation into a quieter road. Here, at the furthest end of a cul-de-sac, behind stalky masses of untended privet, stood a gabled house. Taking the alley beside the dustbins, he worked open the back gate and ducked through a maze of underskirts on washing lines to enter a brown kitchen. A woman dressed in little more than a vest and bloomers was frying an extremely late breakfast.

'We're not open—' She saw Saul, let out a shriek, ran over to hug him. 'Saul Duxbury! Where have you *been*?' She studied him admiringly. 'You've *grown* so. What have you been *up* to?'

I watched as Saul and this woman patted and admired each other. Even in the unadorned state that she was in now, she was very pretty, with black wavy hair and fine white skin. I did the obvious calculation and decided that she couldn't possibly be his mother.

'I suppose you'll want to see Marm,' she said finally as my mind churned with possibilities. What was she—actress, dollymop, dancer? 'She's just upstairs. Same as ever . . .'

A stairway, a landing. The air grew thick with the smell of old and greasy carpets and stale toilet water—and, beneath that, a sharp, medicinal odour of burning. Saul knocked lightly on the door at the far end of the top flight of stairs.

'I *told* you—' a quavering voice began.

'It's me, Marm . . .' Tentatively, he stepped inside. 'Saul.'

'My darling!' A big woman in a bright dressing gown swept herself up from the window couch of a crowded room to engulf him in breathy giggles. The two of them squirmed and wrestled for a moment as I stood in the doorway. Then the woman's face, round as the moon's and almost as mottled, studied me over Saul's shoulder.

'And who's *this*?'

'This, Marm, is my friend Robbie.'

'And where did you get *him* from?' Marm released Saul and rummaged on a side table to light a cigarette then collapsed back on her sunlit couch. 'And where are you now living?'

'Robbie's from somewhere called Bracebridge, Marm. We're both up by Caris Yard.'

Ash snowed from the tip of Marm's cigarette. The sash window was half open. Outside, pigeons were cooing. Marm's eyes, I saw, as the silence persisted, were restless beneath their painted lids. Like those pigeons, her whole body was shivering slightly.

'It'll do for the summer, won't it . . . ?' Saul trailed off, standing in the rucked middle of the carpet where Marm's embrace had left him. 'I mean, the Easterlies . . .'

Another long pause ensued. I breathed more of that medicinal, burning smell as Marm ground out her cigarette in a plant pot.

'Oh, I'm sure it'll do *very* nicely. And what kind of work are you doing anyway?'

'Just around the docks . . . Collecting things. Well, you know how it is, Marm—it's money.'

Marm reached to light another quivering cigarette. 'Of course my darling there's always *money*,' she said, each word punctuated by a coil within the smoke. 'Funny old stuff, isn't it? You can say what you like about all that citizen nonsense, but we need it like the air we breathe . . .' Her eyes dulled and drooped as if in sad contemplation of this fact, then brightened as Saul began to reach into the satchel which contained the borrowed pieces we'd been hawking around the stalls all morning.

'We've brought you something . . .'

Marm was half sitting forward now and half leaning back, like someone caught in a blurry photograph between two stages of movement. Her whole body was quivering. Indeed, I thought, as she hunched forward on that sunlit couch and the pigeons chimed and the smoke and the dust played around her, there was something that was ill-defined about Marm despite all her obvious physical presence. As if you'd have to travel a long way through those folds of flesh and robe before you actually reached her real substance.

'A *gift* now, perhaps, is *always* pleasant . . . Always something to be waited for . . .' Marm was talking to herself in a breathy whisper as Saul unfolded the waxed wafers which contained a scrap of Dutch lace. 'A surprise without *asking* . . .' Marm was still talking, and her trembling had become a rocking motion as she leaned closer to inspect the contents of the paper flower which Saul had laid before her on the table. The smoke of her cigarette made agitated leaps. 'You see, your Marm loves a gift, don't she?' And there it was, a fine lace choker, beaded with tiny fragments of jet and lapis lazuli. 'Imagine all the *work,* my dearie. Those aching hours with the bobbin . . .'

Snatching it from Saul's fingers, she raised it to her

neck and fumbled with the bead clasp. 'Will you help your Marm, my darling. These things are so . . . It's a little tight. But never mind. It's the thought that counts. That's what they all say isn't it?' The thing vanished into the folds of her chin. 'And Marm's so *pleased* you're here. Yes she is. So *sweet* of you . . . Did I tell you that . . . ?' I watched as Marm drew Saul into another embrace. She was still talking, but it was hard now to make out the words as she fingered the curls on his neck.

Eventually Saul straightened and looked across at me. He coughed and smoothed back his hair.

Marm studied the end of a new cigarette. 'But I know,' she said, '*I'm* not the one you've come to see here. All the girls are still sweet on you, Saul. Always were, weren't they? So why don't you just toddle off and leave your friend with me here. What was it . . . ?' She slowly fixed me with her gaze. 'Was it *Robbie* from *Bracebridge*?'

'But, Marm, you can't—'

'*Off* you go, my darling!' Ash billowed about her. 'And you did say the lad was your best friend. So how else can he and Marm possibly get familiar . . .'

I shot Saul a despairing glance before he closed the door, then watched with a dry mouth as Marm heaved herself back to her feet.

'Of course,' she muttered as she waddled across the rugs, '*I've* heard of Bracebridge, even if *he* hasn't.' Her hands, I noticed, grew surprisingly still as she tilted the syrupy contents of a decanter into a thimble-sized tumbler on a side table. 'How could I not have, being in this business?'

I cleared my throat. 'To be honest, Marm, I'm really not sure—'

'You mean my son hasn't told you?' She tipped back the thimble, suppressed a small shudder. 'But then, looking at you, I doubt if you'd have understood . . . Not without a little demonstration.' Moving close, Marm patted my worn jerkin, running her painted nails along the seams until the stitching crackled. 'At least you don't seem to have any lice on you. You barely stink. And Saul's right—you're really not doing so very badly down in the Easterlies, although I'm sure some other people are doing worse as a result.'

She laid a hand on my shoulder. It was my turn to suppress a shudder.

'You see, Robbie, this house isn't any of the things you might imagine. We're not like the dollymops in the street, or the tarts in the pox houses . . .' She smiled. 'But then, you still hardly know what *they* are, do you? But take a tip from me and forget *love*. What we sell here is far more precious. This is a *dream*house, and we sell dreams. And the dreams come from Bracebridge, just like you do—or some of them anyway. Isn't that a sweet coincidence?' She refilled her glass thimble and sipped it. 'I'm disappointed, really, that Saul doesn't remember the name of the place, all the years he was here under its spell. But then he's been trying hard to forget, hasn't he? Neglecting his Marm, all this rubbish about people all being the same, never coming here,' she continued with a pout. 'Not that Marm doesn't like a present . . .' She worked a finger around her neck. There was a sharp snap. She dropped the lace choker to the floor. 'I'm sure this is what every hovel whore and fishwife is wearing. Pity, really, it's not quite the look of this Age . . .' She hurrumphed. 'But you still don't really know what we do here, do you? Would you like to know?'

Marm rubbed my shoulders gently, pressing me down towards a chair in the corner. It was heaped with cushions and a headrest, and bore the smell of other bodies. In a daze, I slumped back and watched as Marm busied herself. She struck a match and set its flame to a small spirit stove. Medicinal breezes wafted as she unstoppered jars and extracted their contents with fine long-handled spoons. A small retort filled with black-brown syrup soon began bubbling. Waxy, resinous, clouds filled the air; that harsh, sweet smell of burning.

'Fine in mind and body are you, my dear?' Marm asked as she fluttered about. 'Heart strong—but then of course it is.' A long needle like a hatpin glittered, and she stirred its tip in the bubbling retort, then played the glossy bead which formed under the blue spirit flame until it darkened. 'A few sweet seeds from the sun-warmed tropics. What could be more natural? And aether, too, comes from the ground. It rises and grows and flowers. But then I don't

need to tell you that, do I? You of all people, Robbie. You'll
have to tell me what it's like in Bracebridge sometime. Do
you fly about in the air like changeling sprites, where
there's so much aether?'

The pigeons cooed outside the window.

'It's simple, really. We all have *dreams,* don't we?'
Marm produced a pipe. It was long and thick-stemmed, although the bowl at the end was tiny. Then she made a sign
in whispering silk and withdrew a small inlaid box from
the cabinet. I felt a tug within me, a burning on my wrist of
my long-forgotten Mark. Even before she opened the lid
and wyredarkness wreathed out, I knew that it contained
aether.

'So you must tell me what you *want,* Robbie . . .' Marm
swirled the hatpin into the aether and then thumbed the
darkly gleaming bead into the pipe's tiny bowl. The silks
shifted as she sucked at the flame. A tiny black-white star,
the bead bubbled and ignited. She let out a jet of dark-
white smoke.

'Oh, you'd be surprised—although I, of course, never
will be—at the requests that are made here in this dreamhouse. You men never do quite want the obvious thing that
every young girl seeking a husband or a client imagines. It
never is quite *that,* although that may be part of it. But if
you have a girl you're sweet on, or one you're hoping for—
then I can give her to you in every way that you've ever
dared imagine. Or is it *money* you're after? Or the comfort
of fine things? Or something else . . .' Shadows flashed as
Marm blew out the smoke again. 'Or is it *fear* that tingles
you? A little pain to go with the pleasure? I understand the
need for that too. A little shit to flavour the banquet, some
piss in the wine . . . ?'

She puffed again.

'Open your mouth.'

There was a new tenderness in Marm's eyes as she
stooped to press her lips against mine. She tasted of wine,
cigarettes, buttery flesh, and of the sweet-bitter smoke
which came pouring into me. I felt a flowering of well-
being, a glow which continued to expand until it became so
large that the distinction between physical and mental joy

dissolved, and with it all my usual sense of self, although I remained conscious of the room, of the sparking carpet dust and the slow waves of aether-curdled smoke which wafted out of the window past the summer-intoxicated pigeons. Cooo *Coo*. Cooo *Coo*. And Marm was still with me, sharing the exquisite brush of these new senses. Suddenly, everything was laughably frail. And what *did* I want? What *did* I desire?

Easy as a ghost, I lifted from the chair and passed through the wall above the spirit flame. All the windows were open along the carpeted corridors of the dreamhouse beyond. A fresh breeze had risen up from the Thames, quenching the heat of the afternoon. Heavy-leafed ferns nodded in their pots like undersea weeds. The air pressed me on, gently insistent, as I floated on through flock walls. This was indeed a strange and complex building. Here was Saul, holding court amid the flypapers of the kitchen with the other dreamhouse mistresses who remembered him growing up as a lad here; a sweet novelty to be kissed and tickled until his growing bulk and the male croak of his voice, which would have upset the customers, forced him out into the streets.

Thistledown, I floated on, passing through a window. There was London, green and gold and floating on this warm early summer afternoon. I laughed and spiralled in the huffing updrafts of an engine house, and watched the insect traffic, the pinhead people. The rooftops grew mountainous towards Northcentral, punctuated by spires and domes and the cool recesses of courtyards, the dark flash of Hallam Tower. Here, the landscape was surprisingly green, jewelled with ponds and the intricacies of rooftop gardens, all set around the vast and jagged emerald of Westminster Great Park. I would happily have dived down to float in the wake of the striped buggies and the flecked umbrellas, or danced with the kites which floated above the lawns, but the streaming air of London still bore me upwards until the sky dimmed and I was tumbling and lost. The wind was colder up here, and I could tell from its scent, its persistence, that it was blowing me north. England was teeming below me, and I struggled against it, but the power of the aether spread its dark wings and bore me onwards.

SHOOM *BOOM* SHOOM *BOOM*.

There it lay; Bracebridge, curled once again in the lazy warmth of a summer Halfshiftday. I saw that the ashpits had still barely began their climb up Coney Mound and that the old warehouses on past the allotments were standing. I had fallen once more into the past. SHOOM *BOOM*. The rivermeads. The glinting brown river. Rainharrow's grey-green flanks, swirled by ruins and sheep paths. The grey strip of High Street. The tile and brick blur of Coney Mound. And at the centre of it all, neat in this sunlight as a map, a blueprint, a vision of this industrial world, lay Mawdingly & Clawtson. Roofs and yards. The spreading arms of tracks and depots. The black glow of the quickening pools. There was East Floor, where my father worked, and this bigger roof with its proud chimneys could only be Engine Floor, beneath which, far down on Central Floor, deep in the riven earth, the pistons still flashed and hammered even on this Halfshiftday afternoon as figures shouted and scurried across the far fields and picnic squares of blanket paved the path beside the river. SHOOM *BOOM* SHOOM *BOOM*. Then something, somehow, changed. The amazed air fell silent. The figures on the football fields halted. The river seemed to stop flowing. Even the sunlight froze. There was a rumbling, followed by a series of huge but dull detonations which rose and grew louder, drumbeat by drumbeat, pouring up into the thunderous, drifting silence which had fallen over the town. Then, in a wyrewhite torrent of gas and pressure, the roof of Central Floor exploded. Flames fountained, their light blackening in the onrush of steam and aether. There was chaos and smoke. Girders flew. Dust plumed. The darkness shivered, the sky shook, and I was tumbling back through it into nowhere, driven by the breaking air.

'You're a strange one for sure.'

I could feel a chair, a smoky rasp in my throat, as the elements of the dreamhouse room slowly gathered themselves around me. The sun was still shining, the pigeons were still cooing, I was in London, and Marm was flapping about me like a fallen kite in her bright dressing gown. My eyeballs were stinging. I felt ill and giddy.

'Don't think I've ever travelled so far with a client.' Cleaning her implements, she blew her pipe clean with a little toot. 'Or got so little out of it. Oh, here it comes . . .' With an expert movement, she grabbed a tin bucket just as I leaned forward, my stomach lurching. 'Perhaps it's the money that makes the difference,' she continued, stroking my head as I vomited. 'Perhaps you should have *paid*—not that you could afford it. But despite all the rubbish Saul talks, nothing's ever quite so good when you get it for free, is it?'

IV

Look at me now. Robbie, not Robert. Warehouse ink staining my fingers, borrowed money in my pockets, dressed in a waistcoat almost as fine as Saul's. Look at me, and look at Saul, and look at Maud, too, hopping from toe to toe in a pink skirt of surprising finery as bracelets tinkle at her wrists on this Midsummer day as we cluster around a shared cigarette by the dustbins between two Doxy Street boarding houses, watching the trams go by as we debate the wild moment for the leap which will take us to the fair in Westminster Great Park.

'It's easy for you lads—*I've* never done it. And look at these skirts!'

'Neither have I. How do we know it even works?'

'Well, it's up to you.' Saul's smile is caught in a slot of noon light. 'We can always just get *on* the tram . . .'

But that would be unthinkable. I take a long drag through wet strings of tobacco and pass it on to Maud. Of course, I have to do what Saul says, and so does Maud, although her hands shake as she puffs the cigarette, and for that alone I feel more warmly towards her. Another tram clashes by. Then it's gone, and all that's left is the sunlit bustle of Doxy Street—and that tramline; a deep, six inch-wide metal gutter, within which, rattling and gurgling, churns a wyre-bright coil of iron.

Maud goes first. She dives out through a lull in the traffic like a lacy bullet and stands astride the rail. Then, elbows tugging the corners of her skirts, she bends. Her fingers, miraculously, are still attached to her hands when she darts back to us. But they are gleaming.

'You didn't say this would be *dirty*.'

'Quick—now it's your turn Robbie.'

Dazed, I push off, dodging a cart and nearly toppling a cyclist until I'm standing astride the tramline as all Doxy Street swarms about me. I can feel the driven metal, those twisting flecks of oil and aether which hiss and clatter between the churning engine houses that punctuate the city in smoking exclamation marks. But the thing is not to think—the thing is to submit to the will of whatever it is that still drives me and to remember that Saul and Maud are watching. And then it's done, and I'm running back, tumbling dustbins, and Saul is dashing out. When I dare to lift my arms to look, I find that I still have palms and fingers instead of sobbing stubs.

'It's coming . . . !'

A tram is swaying through the Midsummer crowds, black wyreflames and white sparks spluttering beneath its belly. One, two, three carriages, all full to bursting with sweating feastday passengers, and then the last, by which time we are yelling like mad as we dodge the intervening wagons and jump at the tram's retreating rear, which is at least twice as high and grimy as I expected, and sloped without any place to grip for the very reason of this trick we are trying. But we cling on as the track tunnels beneath us, murmuring under our breath the circle of sound which we have been practising and scarcely believing all morning. My palms are holding as if glued, welded against the rivets, and my breath cannot stop the chant. We cling on, spread-eagled and singing above the turning rails as Doxy Street unwinds in shining fresh-washed pavements, the very stones flushed and steaming with all the bustle of this Midsummer, until, without any change in its direction, or halt in its flow, Doxy Street ceases to be Doxy Street at all, and becomes Cheapside, and finally Oxford Road. The signs, the buildings, the rooftops over the towering windows, the sky itself, all seem to expand and dilate in the sweetly gathering outrush of wealth. Scented with shop produce and brass polish, the Northcentral air lifts and surrounds me as I cling to the jolting back of our filthy tram. Here rise the chapels of the lesser guilds, grey-white or golden, spired and domed; antique churches pillaged from the Age of Kings and re-made with aethered statuary and bolted doors for a God who, along with all the rest of England, took the best and most obvious choice when the world changed and joined up and became a guildsman.

We jump down at Northcentral Terminus, scurrying from the tramaster's shouts until we reach sudden and amazing tracts of grass, huge sunlit eruptions of tree and water and statuary. There, we catch our breath, and Maud inspects the substantial oily stains on the front of her dress. I look about me. The greatest of all the guildhalls on Wagstaffe Mall rise beyond silver-white avenues of impossible trees in their mountain domes; coppered and silvered and glazed, winking in the sunlight over the rivers of top hats, straw boaters, piggyback children.

'Come on, Robbie—what *are* you staring at?' Saul hauled me on through the crowds. 'They're only *buildings* for God's sake! This is only a *park*. We're here to have *fun*, aren't we . . . ?'

But it was more than that. Weaving past the stalls, the spivs and the pickpockets and the scrambling lesser urchins, even on the day of the Midsummer Fair, it was the extraordinary nature of the trees in Westminster Great Park which most entranced me. In the Easterlies, just as in Bracebridge, blooms too big and lurid to be the fruit of simple good husbandry would sometimes make it to the baskets of the flower-sellers, and there was always the waterapple and the sea-potato to remind us of the guildsman's art, but here, bright and solid, were whispering, living creations of dream. Perilinden, which rose tall and silver and chattered its leaves. Cedarstone, far squatter, with its massive red trunk, which was gnarled and polished, the grain beautiful and intricate as sunset caught in the currents of a river. Firethorn, which was an ugly-spined bush up in Brownheath planted for deterrence and protection, was here a chaos of heraldic flowers. And sallow, even sallow, that common herb, became a tree of greenish-white beauty with a scent like bitter honey. As the bands of several guilds struck up brassy waves, I breathed these names like spells. Leaves red and gold, and heart-shaped to the size of trays. Trunks wound with pewter bark. Flowers like down-turned porcelain vases. I resolved to come here again—in fact, to leave the Easterlies—and wander more quietly and perhaps forever with the ghost of my mother. But the bustle of the Midsummer was pulling at me, and everywhere, there were promises of greater wonders if you stepped through a turnstile, entered a tent, touched a pretend haft; just as long as you paid, paid, paid. I sat with Saul and Maud, groaning and clapping as white rabbits vanished and reappeared amid fanfares of smoke and gong—all, so it said on the prestidigitator's sign outside the smelly tent, without the aid of a single drop of aether. It was a hot day. Passing burlesques, clowns, familiars dressed like little sailors, strange monologues and dioramas of journeys through distant lands, gazing over heads, I bought a wrap of sherbet ice and sucked it greedily. Wiping my numb lips, I looked around for Maud and Saul. I could see no sign of them. But the plan had always been that we would meet up by Prettlewell Fountains at three that afternoon. I had no watch, and no idea of where those fountains actually were, but no matter. I wasn't lost—lost wasn't something which happened when you were wandering under the astonishing trees of Westminster Great Park amid balloon-sellers, dancing familiars and spinning acrobats. Not at Midsummer. Not in London. Not when you were Robbie. This Midsummer Fair, I decided, was like London itself. By turns brash and sad, quiet and teeming, stinkingly ugly, heart-stoppingly lovely . . . And, like London, there were things more easily stumbled across than actually found.

I tried my luck shooting tin birds. I inspected the giant bones of monsters said to have been spawned in a distant Age. There were red-scaled beasts and ravening bale-hounds. There was an incredible tooting machine like a

madly enlivened forest which had been made by the
guildsmen of Saxony. I must have wandered for several
thoughtless hours, spending what money I had, letting the
crowds lead and buffet me, taking in all the horrors and
wonders and disappointments of the fair. Then I saw Annalise. She was walking alone, in her own quiet space
amid shouting groups of lads, tired families. She stopped
by a carousel ride and I caught my breath in the shadows
behind, waiting for my heart to stop pounding. She was
dressed in a light blue skirt and a puffy white blouse
which was bunched at the neck and the sleeves. She had
the shape of a woman now, and her hair, pale blond, and
coiled, ribboned, plaited, lay across her shoulders. Everything about Annalise was different, and impossibly fine,
down to the curve of eyelash which drooped and rose as
she watched the children swirling by on their painted
drays, but at the same time she hadn't changed. I'd have
been happy to stand there forever, watching Annalise
through ride after ride. But if it's possible for someone's
back, the line of a cheekbone, to convey a knowing
amusement, then that was what she managed to do. The
colours swept by, the scared and laughing children's faces,
and I became aware that Annalise had noticed me long before I had seen her.

The ride slowed. Annalise turned towards me as the
shapes unblurred.

'So it's you . . .' She paused. 'Robbie.' Those green
eyes. 'I hadn't expected to ever see you here in London.'

So many things, so quickly. *Robbie*. And *I hadn't
expected*—as if, occasionally, she had thought of me over
all these years.

'Neither had I.' My heart was still racing. 'Me—or you,
I mean.' I knew that whatever I said would come out as stupid. 'I haven't been here long. Just this summer.'

'So we're both strangers here.' Her lips grew an ironic
tilt. 'I'm almost surprised, really. I mean, that you recognised me.'

'You're not so different, really, Annalise.'

Those green eyes darkened slightly.

But it was ridiculous, really, to say that she hadn't

changed, when she so plainly had in every shape and detail apart from the one essential part of her which would never change.

'So what do you do now?'

I shrugged. Although, day by day, hour by hour, moment by moment, I was happy with my life, something about Annalise's presence made it all shrivel and fade. *I live in the Easterlies. I work the docks, forging signs on teachests. Sometimes I steal things. My best friend's mother is a dreamistress. He calls everyone citizen, and the girl he's going with has hands that are raw from boiling nappies.* And look at my own hands, Annalise. Scabbed and inked and nicotined. And I smelled—I could tell now, knew it instantly—ripe and outdoorsy, not quite unpleasant, but carrying an unmistakably Easterlies reek of coalsmoke and herring.

Annalise studied me as I stumbled through my explanation. Her fine clothes, her faint, fine scent which was sweet and unplacable, the jewels at her earlobes, the seemingly poreless flush of her skin, the presence of the assured and highly guilded; all of it breathed out at me as the carousel drays turned behind.

'And your mother died, of course, didn't she? I'm so sorry, Robbie . . .' Her green eyes darkened, lightened. A sea moon behind summer clouds. 'But you look well. You seem happy.'

'I am,' I said. 'Life's good. I'm *very* happy.'

She smiled back. 'And so am I, Robbie.' The whole fairground spun around us. We were still. Everything else was moving.

There was a pause as she withdrew her gaze. I needed no special powers to know that in another moment she would say how interesting it had been to bump into me again after all these years. If I was lucky, she might offer me her hand before she walked away.

I grabbed her bare elbow. 'Wait, Annalise. Don't go . . .'

She tensed. The fairground pipes were shrieking. The textures of our flesh seemed so different now. As my hand fell away, I noticed her left wrist. She wore a silver bracelet. Above it, raw and puckered in the sunlight and

glowing slightly wyreblack, was the Mark of a Day of
Testing which I was still sure she had never had.

'It's . . .' I shrugged. 'I'd like to know what it's like.
Whatever life you're now living.'

'Is *that* what you really want?' Her smile was returning.

I nodded, swallowed. 'More than anything.'

'All right, then, Robbie. After all, it is Midsummer . . .'
She smiled, then. We shared a smile together. It was impossible not to smile at this game we were about to play.
Whatever else we were, we were young and the world
seemed malleable. 'I'll show you.'

We walked through stepped gardens which the fair had
left unclaimed. Below us lay the pitched tents, the teeming
rides. Around us, in arbours and dangling from trellises,
grew yet more plants of strange and impossible beauty. Assailed by scents, colours, walking with Annalise, I was
moving through a different world. Ahead of us was a wide
grey roadway, and the only sounds came from the sigh of
the waiting horses. Beyond rose a cliff face of brick and
stone, a unity of matching windows and pediments. A uniformed man saluted us as the doors flashed open. Was it
this easy, I wondered, as we crossed red oceans of carpet
and a liftboy slid back a brass gate, to enter this other
world?

'How much does all of this *cost*?'

'You mustn't imagine that I live like this *always*,' Annalise said as the growl of a distant engine drew us up
through the building. There were aspidistras like small
trees and portraits hung on brass rails along the corridors
which the lift raised us to. 'Just wait here.' She halted beside one of the endless numbered doors. 'I won't be a moment. And *you* can't stay looking like that, can you? We'll
need to get you changed . . .'

A glimpse of mirrors and cedarstone, a puff of sunlight,
and the door closed. I stood uneasily, looking up and down
this long hallway. The place was hot and almost silent. Of
course, it would be a neat practical joke, for Annalise to
drag me into this labyrinth then vanish like those white
rabbits in a puff of smoke. But she soon reappeared wearing a fresh skirt and blouse, and her eyes shining damp.

Had I but known it, I had witnessed a miracle of feminine speed.

'Come on then. Let's get you sorted.' She bustled up the corridor to a lesser doorway, which was unnumbered, and layered with green baize. She ducked inside. 'Quickly, now . . .'

This great London hotel was in fact two buildings crammed into a single space; one, luxurious and languid, belonged to the guests, whilst the other was for the maids, the undermaids, the laundrygirls, the cooks, stewards, handymen, ironmasters, cleaners, shoe polishers. Even here, though, it was Midsummer-quiet, and it grew hotter than ever in these low corridors. Our shadows sped around us as we descended spiral stairways, then turned into white galleries where the air was stiff with the smell of soap and hot ironing. But even here there was no one about. The whole place was charmed, sleeping, deserted. She shoved me down another corridor to another green door.

Beyond, lustrous in the thin light, lay endless rails of clothing. They whispered and jingled on their hangings as Annalise walked between them. 'I'm just a guest here. We're never supposed to get to see all of this. But *feel* them, Robbie. Watered silk, Dutch lace, finest cambric, aethered linen, sequins, buttons of cedarstone, crystal beads from Thule and Cathay . . .' Shifting waterfalls of cloth danced before me, and Annalise danced amid them, too, smiling, turning, making mock curtsies. 'They keep it this way down here—neither hot nor cold, dark nor light— so that nothing fades . . .' She lifted handfuls to her face, inhaling deeply. 'Go on—try. This is what *wealth* smells like Robbie. This is *power*. This is *money* . . .' I took a sequinned sleeve and sniffed. But I must have made a poor choice, for there was only soured wine and sweat, stale perfume, tobacco. Behind, along other rails, men's suits were lined like soldiers. Annalise swooped one out and held it appraisingly against me, tilting her head, stroking the cloth, smoothing it across my shoulders with lovely persistence until I thought my heart would stop beating. 'No, not at all . . . Definitely not the fashion . . .' She tried another. 'We'll need a shirt for you, a tie, shoes . . .'

Annalise waltzed amid the hissing masses of evening gowns as I struggled to find my size in patent shoe, keeping up a non-stop commentary about hems and darts and braidings. She found a dress which was pale blue, a shade like the sky at early morning, and strung with pearls at the shoulder like the last stars, and tight at the waist, then spilling out like a waterfall. She looked truly glorious as she held it up to herself, her golden hair awry.

'What do you think, Robbie? Do you think some sad old dowager will ever miss this?'

We tunnelled back up through the hotel, armfuls of silk billowing and squealing. Annalise checked that the coast was clear on the floor of her room. We swept in.

'This is a guest bathroom. You can get changed in here.'

'What should I do with my—'

But already she'd pushed me into a place of gleaming spigots, white porcelain, snowdrifts of towel. Everything I touched seemed to grow dirty and the clothes I'd been wearing, my best by far, flaked and crackled as I removed them. But, much as you do in a dream, I decided to make the most of this situation, stuffing my old things into what looked like a laundry basket, discovering the knobs which caused hot and cold water to gush from the mouths of dolphins. Soon, I was wreathed in scent and steam. My naked body floated in the foamy water, deeply tanned in the places where it had been exposed to the sun, alarmingly white elsewhere, and surprisingly fully muscled. Eventually, I climbed out, and, puzzling over buttons and catches and hopping from leg to leg, pulled on my new clothes and padded down the sweltering corridor to the door of Annalise's room.

'Come in! It's unlocked . . .' Her voice was faint. Inside, I didn't find the expected bedroom, but a sunlit parlour filled with gilt chairs. I couldn't see Annalise. '*That* was quick Robbie.' Her voice drifted through a double doorway. 'You'll have to wait for me, I'm afraid . . .' I peered towards what did look like a bedroom, in that there was a bed large enough to sleep several families, and heard the faint hiss of pipes from further beyond. I sat down, then stood up, and studied my changed self in one of the mirrors. Annalise had been right in her choice—the suit definitely fitted. But every bit of it was awry. The shirt, the cuffs, the buttons. And my hair was sticking up, my face was flushed. I looked like a servant trying on his master's clothes.

As I puzzled over the bow tie, there came a knock at the door.

'Are you *in* there, Anna?' A woman's voice, strangely accented. 'Where have you *been*? Everyone's looking for you—'

The handle turned. Someone rustled in.

'Oh!' The girl's hand went up to her throat as we re-garded each other and the studs and cuffs I'd been strug-gling with patted to the floor. 'I'm so *terribly* sorry . . .' She glanced at the number on the door. 'But this *is* Anna Win-ters' room, isn't it—so what on earth . . . ?'

'It's all right, Sadie,' Annalise's voice wafted in. 'It's Robert . . . ah, Borrows. He's an old family friend.'

I offered Sadie my hand, on the offchance that this was what you did in these situations. She gave a charming curtsy in return.

'Guildmaster Borrows . . .'

'Pleased to meet you. And you must call me Robbie.' The phrases came out easily, stilted though they seemed.

'And I'm Grandmistress Sarah Passington—did I tell you that? But everyone just calls me Sadie. You must think I'm terribly rude, bursting in on you like this.'

I was enjoying this more and more. No one had ever called me guildmaster. It still sounded better than citizen. 'That was entirely my fault, Sadie. How could I have been expected?' I ventured a smile.

Sadie smiled back at me. 'It's a pleasure, Robbie, at last to meet someone who knew Anna when she was young. I feel as if I've known her all my life, but it's the first time this has ever happened. It's not as if she's secretive, but . . .'

Beyond all those doors, in the distant bathroom, Annalise—or *Anna Winters,* as it seemed she was now—was humming to herself, a soft song which went with the hiss of the pipes and the sound of the trees and the traffic, the distant stirrings of the Midsummer Fair. Warm, benign, her presence washed over Sadie and I.

'So I suppose you of all people must know what Anna's like . . .' Sadie smiled again, but more wistfully. She had dark hair done up in glossy coils, white skin, shapely black eyebrows. And she was wearing, I slowly realised now that the initial shock of her presence had faded, what was easily the most extravagant dress I had ever seen. Even by the standards of the confections I witnessed in this hotel, it was quite extraordinary. White and gold, half architecture, half wedding cake, it seemed to wash out towards me like a separate presence; yet it stopped so far below her shoulders to have caused, as my mother would have said, a traffic accident back in Bracebridge.

'You look,' I said, 'as if you're going somewhere.'

'So do you, Robbie. I mean, I take it Anna's made sure that you're coming to tonight's ball?' Her eyes travelled up and down me. 'We're always short of new men . . .'

'I would if I could manage these . . .' I lifted the end of my bow tie, one of the cufflinks.

But Sadie was in her element, fussing over me. And so was I—the tie, the room, the mirrored visions of Sadie as she leaned over me in her fine décolletage, Annalise's— *Anna's*—occasional calls and questions, this gilt and sunlit room. All of it moved and fitted together. Finally, the door to the bedroom reopened. And there was Annalise at the threshold, her hair done differently, her face in shadow and her green eyes alight, wearing that grey-blue dress which was, for all that it covered her shoulders in silk and pearls, as devastatingly simple as Sadie's was complex.

'Are we all ready?'

The hotel entrance hall was now swarming. Trunks and suitcases were being borne back and forth on trolleys by uniformed youths. Lifts pinged and opened. Outside, the lines of London's other great hotels looked frail as seashells in the pink twilight as Annalise, Sadie and I followed marble steps through illuminated gardens. Soon, I caught the scent of the river. But this wasn't the Thames which I knew downstream by Tidesmeet, or even further up at Riverside. Here, before all the outflows of the Easterlies had made their contributions, the waters still ran almost clear. Lights fanned along the embankment. A bluish moon hovered close above the river, and music blossomed from a ball-room which glowed above the waters from a pier like a great sea urchin. As if lifted by the breeze, women with bare backs, bare throats, bare arms, bare shoulders and half-bare bosoms floated into the arms of their chaperons and danced along the boards towards it.

Annalise tapped my shoulder.

'You *do* know how to dance, don't you Robbie?'

I shrugged and smiled and put out my arms. My hands closed on her back, the fabric, the pearls, and I strained against the conflicting impulses to press tighter, to pull back. I'd never have guessed that dancing, not jumping around in Caris Yard to a shrieking fiddle, but the kind of thing you saw high-born people doing in paintings, was so shockingly intimate.

'Let *go* for a minute. Watch my toes . . .' Annalise wriggled from my grasp. 'Shall we show him, Sadie . . . ?' Linking arms and turning around the benches across the embankment to demonstrate, these two beautiful women in their whispering dresses made a fine couple as they demonstrated to me how it was done; this business of dancing arm in arm and breast to breast with the moon rising across the river.

'Now you, Robbie . . . Try again . . . You put your hand here.' Sadie arranged my limbs, placing them around Annalise. 'No, a little higher . . .'

Slowly, stumbling at first like a wounded dray, I waltzed my way across the Thames towards the music of the ballroom. I danced first with Annalise, then with Sadie, and for a lovely moment I was somehow dancing with them both. Onlookers laughed and encouraged us. There were scatters of applause, shouted suggestions. They probably thought I was some dull relative from the cold and smoggy depths of the north or west dragged here by these two glittering cousins. But there was never any sense, despite my obvious clumsiness, that I didn't belong.

Pillars ascended inside the ballroom. Candelabra dripped from the ceiling. The band was playing something faster now and the beat was different, but I could have danced to anything that night. Something had clicked in me—a

ridiculous confidence, a sense of *knowing*. Annalise and I
were part of the music as we turned on the floor of the ballroom and the dresses changed colour as they swirled about
us; pink to green to blue. They pulsed like anemones in a
rockpool, and we men darted dark and sleek around them,
were drawn and repulsed until, as each melody slowed, we
were recaptured breathless and laughing within those
crinoline fronds. I was a part of it. I was part of everything.
And Annalise's eyes were shining. Her back and shoulders
beneath the silk and pearled substance of the dress she was
wearing felt slim and damp and warm. Then came a fresh
tilt to the rhythm of the music, and the dancefloor seemed
to tilt with it, and sent me spinning.

I wish I could say more about how it felt to be with Annalise that night. But there are some rare moments in life
when happiness slips past you so easily that you barely notice it, or ever believe it will end. I was entranced. It
seemed as if the great earthly pyramid beneath which I had
struggled had suddenly become aether-light. And of
course, I was in love as well. In love with the moon and the
night and all the other ridiculous things that people sing
about in songs and write of in poems out of what I had previously imagined was some stupid high-guilded literary
convention. And I was in love with Sadie, too, for the way
she laughed at my feeble jokes, and for the deep swell of
her bosom and the sweet dark scent of her perspiration as
she swept though dance after dance and pressed against
me. And I was in love with the people who joined us, and
who took to me so readily that I knew instantly that they
were my friends. These rare and intricate creatures of the
highest guilds were sleek and shy as birds, and prone just
as easily to song and laughter. They touched my rough
hands and asked me if I'd done much sailing down at
Folkestone this summer. They heard I'd come from the
north, from Yorkshire, and wondered if I knew so-and-so
who had property up there? They poured my wine for me,
sympathised at my lack of knowing anyone, and understood how strange and difficult London could be, especially in the dreadful hurly-burly of the summer season.
And then there was Annalise, Annalise who was Anna now

in her dawn-blue dress, Annalise with her shining eyes, Annalise with her red-golden hair. Every poem, every melody, every flash of starlight, was true. I believed it all. I believed in everything.

There were tables burdened with incredible food which most people were simply ignoring. I presented a plate before every tong-wielding waiter, then retreated outside to the deck which surrounded the ballroom and stuffed myself with oiled handfuls of incomprehensible flavours. Happy, full, giddy, and faintly sick, I leaned against the railing and let the night air cool my face.

'You're a bit of a mystery, aren't you, Robbie?' Sadie propped her elbows on the railing beside me. 'Coming here,' she continued, 'suddenly appearing. I wouldn't be surprised if you disappear at the end of this Midsummer night in the same way . . .' She glanced down at my feet. 'At least you're not wearing glass slippers.'

My head was swimming. I really didn't know where to begin.

'But tell me, Robbie, how exactly *do* you know Anna? She's a bit like you—bit of a mystery . . . Although I can't quite say why, seeing as I've known her all the time we've been at St Jude's. You'll have to tell me what it was like for Anna up in cold grey Brownheath, with that dreadful spinster aunt of hers.'

A strange thing happened to me as Sadie spoke those words and I stared down at the moon-glittering water. I could *see* that aunt, and the house where Anna had lived. It was nothing like Redhouse, but dark, small-windowed, rambling. There it was, set in damp woodland, beside a waterfall. The aunt was old and stooped and smelly. She roamed the creaking house, giving the young girl who had come to live with her after her parents had both died in a tragic boating accident her sour toleration. I'd been there myself, a different Robert Borrows, stepping from the carriage in my best sailor suit and looking up at the hunched grey walls. I could hear the waterfall, smell the clogged drains and dripping terraces, and see the aunt herself, her stick tapping as she crawled about in an old shawl. For all her youth and glow, there was something about Annalise that made such a

cold and loveless place entirely believable . . . As I spoke to
Sadie of sitting with Anna Winters in the green undecorated
room filled with the wardrobe stink of mothballs, the words
simply came out from me. Less of a vision than a memory,
that old dark house had the feeling of somewhere I had long
known.

'It's *really* true, then?' Sadie muttered as we spiralled
again, intricate as clockwork, across the shining dancefloor. 'All those stories Anna's told me over the years . . .'
She had an easy confidence with her body; a plump sub-
stantiality, I decided with the air of new connoisseur, so
unlike Anna's airy lightness. At some point all the lights
were turned down and every door was flung open, and I realised as we swept out into the darkness that many of the
evening gowns were threaded with aether. It was a beautiful scene as they all began to glow. I seemed to be hovering
high over everything on this starstruck night, looking down
on the ballroom which was almost invisible now in the
darkness, so that the shining, dancing shapes of the women
floated unaided above the river.

Eventually, the evening faded. Tired and footsore, I
passed people retching over the railings into the water, and
sniggering couples straddling each other in hidden alcoves.
The older and more staid contingent had already departed
for their beds, and the air inside the ballroom smelled faintly
like the sleeve of the dress I had sniffed in the hotel; of sweat
and wine, stale smoke and perfume. The band ended the final tune with ironic discord. Ribbons and spillages of wine
and squashed food and cigarette butts smeared the dancefloor. A tall, eager young man with a weak blond moustache
pumped my hand and introduced himself as Higher master-
something-or-other. He gazed at me for a couple of seconds,
blinking and puzzled, then retreated.

Sadie giggled. 'You're popular tonight, Robbie. Yet the
thing is, nobody really knows who you are. You could be a
thief, a murderer . . .'

'I can be, if that's what you want.' I suppressed a burp.
'If you really want to hear—'

'*Here* you both are.' It was Annalise, still looking entirely unwilted.

'I think Robbie here was just about to tell me all your secrets.'

'You should never believe a word anyone says when it's this far past midnight. Especially not Robbie.'

'And here was I expecting him to disappear on the first stroke of the clock.'

I gazed about me at the women fanning themselves and swinging their shoes from their toes as they rested their feet, at the men with ties awry, buttons undone. They looked ordinary now, just bodies which happened to be encased in soiled but expensive clothing which the eyesight of seamstresses had been sacrificed to make. Sadie sat down on the mezzanine at the band's abandoned piano. She plonked, semi-aimlessly, at the keys.

'Come on, Anna!' There were voices all around. 'You do this better than any of us . . .'

There was a general murmuring of assent as Anna Winters stepped to the podium and tucked in her dress. She looked puzzled at first as she studied the keys, and I wondered if she really was able to play, or if this too wasn't a part of the charade. But surely that sour aunt of hers had encouraged her to study music; I could still hear the scales she had had to practise echoing along the damp corridors. Then a chord rippled out, eerily serene, and then another; cool scatters of notes which shivered down my neck. Voices stilled. The notes seemed to hesitate and stutter, never quite becoming the melody you expected of them; always beautiful, yet pushing at the edge of confusion and silence. But of course Annalise could play—what was I thinking of? Even all those years before, she'd played for me on that frozen piano in that room in Redhouse, the recollection of which seemed to quiver and break for a moment against the vivid sense of that non-existent aunt with her house beside the waterfall.

Standing alone as the crowd of young people drifted closer around Annalise, I could feel myself receding. What secret game, anyway, had I been playing? And who *were* these people? What did I know of them, and what should I care? Of course, it was easy to envy their composure and smooth accents, but that was the very trap that Saul had

warned me about, and which the guilds laid for us all, offering these bright glimpses though guildhouse doorways
and into shop windows of a world which, of its very nature,
could never belong to more than a parasitic few who
feasted on the blood and sweat of the many. Balling my
fists, I turned across the empty dancefloor and headed outside and east along the embankment.

Morning light was already beginning to haze the horizon. The air was sharp, breezing in from the sea, more salt
than freshwater. A small ceremony was taking place as two
guildsmen, fine in the dark green apparel of the Ironmasters' Guild, exchanged their duty baton. I looked over the
railing, and saw how thin the embankment's stanchions
were; a feat of impossible engineering. Aether here was
everything. The draining of all dreams.

'Robbie, wait!'

I turned. Annalise was running out from the ballroom.
Her dress was the same colour-without-colour as the rising
mist and she seemed to have almost as little substance as
she came rustling up to me.

'I didn't want you to go without speaking.'

'Well . . .' I shrugged. 'Here I am.'

'And you *did* ask, didn't you? You really did want to
know about my life.'

'There was so much you didn't tell me, Annalise . . .
Anna. Your name for a start. About that old house. That aunt.
But I seemed to know it all anyway. Isn't that strange?'

'I have to protect myself.'

'From what?'

'The truth. A certain kind of truth, anyway. What do
you think those people in that ballroom would say, if they
knew that I was . . . ?' She paused. A dark well that I longed
to touch formed in the hollow of her throat as she swallowed. Behind me, grey in the mist, loomed London. And
the river pressed on, the heedless water laughing and
chuckling beneath us. I felt a ridiculous urge to be away
from Annalise, to get on with my life and change the world
and find my destiny. And yet my heart ached—that
anatomical condition really did exist. I thought of that day
at Redhouse, of us two children wandering its glittering

corridors. Now, I seemed to be wandering in another kind of mansion; one within which no matter how many times I negotiated the same passageways and turnings, I always remained lost.

I looked down at myself, the patent shoes, the trousers seamed with werrysilk, the buttons and fine linen of my shirt. 'And now I've lost my best old clothes back at that hotel you dragged me to . . .'

Annalise smiled, and seemed to draw fractionally closer to me through the mist without physically moving. It was like a soft fire, the warmth which seemed to come from her flesh. And she seemed so womanly in this grey light. That hollow in her neck. The down of her cheek. A seagull rose, its wings beating the first currents of morning air. Our eyes followed it as we wondered what to say next. I wondered about Saul, too, and about Maud, and the many stories of their day they would be waiting to tell me back in Caris Rookery, tales of ordinary life to which I couldn't possibly contribute. Who, after all, would ever believe me, even coming back in those ridiculous clothes? Yes, I'd risen far to be here, standing on this dawn-lit pier outside the giant sea urchin of a ballroom with a lovely woman, yet I knew enough to understand that my rising was entirely illusory.

'Annalise, have you ever thought of what happened back in Bracebridge? There was a time when the engines stopped beating. I think it might have something to do with the both of us . . .'

Both of us . . . Bracebridge . . . The words seemed to echo back at me. I'd intended them as a gift of sorts, some knowledge which might lead to the beginnings of understanding, but it was plain even as I spoke that I was making a mistake.

'I'm sorry . . .' Still, I continued. 'But I've *seen* things, Annalise. I've had—I don't know—these visions, dreams . . .'

Her whole presence, her eyes especially, seemed to shrink and darken. It was as if Annalise was pure aether, a wyreflame about to be extinguished by the sun's gathering light.

'What makes you think I come from Bracebridge, Robbie?' she hissed quietly. '*This* is my life. Here . . .'

I'd lost her entirely. Her eyes were black as that gull's, and she was breathing with animal rage. She was strange and terrible to me then, a savage creature veiled in a dress that swirled as if all that remained of the night had rushed into her. Roseate sparks played over the water as the rim of the sun lifted from the horizon, and fragments of it flashed in the corner of her eye, then trickled down. For a moment, that tear was the only thing human about her. Then, she re-gathered, re-condensed. She was a beautiful young woman in a silk ballgown.

'I'm Anna Winters. Can't you see that?'

And I realised then what the truth was—that Anna herself believed the lies she had spun about her.

'What *is* it?' I muttered, stepping back in shock, disgust. 'What *are* you?'

Moments later, I heard voices, and a cluster of figures emerged from the pillared doorway of the ballroom along the pier. Bright young things, trailing ties and collars and bottles. They were calling for her with almost desperate need.

Where's Anna . . . ?

Anna . . .

Look, can't you see . . . ?

She's there . . . !

'I've got to go.' She fished a handkerchief from some hidden pocket of her dress, and dabbed her eyes, and blew lightly at her nose, and gave me a sort of brave smile that girls of her class give which both mocked and acknowledged the situation. She looked just like her friends again, but better, more real, more beautiful. Anna. Annalise. It was I, not her, who was the stranger here. So I gave a wave and enjoyed my own small moment of mystery as I turned and walked off down the pier. All the buildings of London were still cast in fizzing shadow. But, as I headed towards them, they began to glint and catch in the morning's first light.

PART FOUR
CITIZEN

I

CLACK *BANG* CLACK *BANG*.

> ### *PHYSICAL FORCE OR MORAL FORCE?*
> *Some might argue that the debate which has long been waged between those who believe that violent upheaval is not only necessary but inevitable and those who contend that*

But contend what? From the glistening lines of watery ink, my eyes wandered across the basement printshop. Black Lucy flapped and turned, flashing her wet rollers as next shifterm's edition of the *New Dawn* was birthed. It was around six in the morning and the light was a smoggy mixture of what little of the grey spring dawn had penetrated the barred high windows and the sooty blaze of the printshop engine. CLACK *BANG* CLACK *BANG*. The sound in here was enormous and the light was worse than useless, but I still found that, balanced on a stool before a scarred workbench, I could make my best progress with an article. CLACK *BANG* CLACK *BANG*. I felt as if I was feeding Black Lucy, producing the words which Blissenhawk would typeset for her to squeeze out between her

steel and rubber plates. And from there, the damp bundles
of print would be trussed up in string, tossed on wagons,
sold, lost, confiscated, borrowed, argued over, eaten out of,
nailed in torn scraps to toilet walls and, above all, read.
There was always a special sense of purpose when a fresh
edition of the *New Dawn* was being put to bed. It was the
time when the feeling that we were close to a New Age was
most palpable; when Black Lucy, stretched to and beyond
her capabilities, was most likely to crack a platen, when
Blissenhawk most needed my help, and when the guilds,
the police or the landlord were most likely to come barging
in with fresh notices of prohibition or eviction.

Who contend that . . . The paper before me, off-white
even in the best light, seemed scarcely lighter than the trails
of my soaked-in ink. I'd ruin my eyesight doing this, as Saul
had often warned me, but at the same time, I quite liked
the fading insubstantiality of these words, and the gritty
ache behind my eyeballs which came from my work of these
early mornings. I didn't hold any great illusions about my
skill as a writer—Blissenhawk surreptitiously tidied up the
more serious crimes I committed against the English language before he printed them—and I found that it helped not
to have anything too sharp and precise staring back at me.
The words were there, they were gone, and next shifterm
there would have to be others. Beyond them, beyond the arguments and the fights and the lock-outs, beyond the calls to
arms and the bright banners and the tramp of boots and the
endless arguments in draughty meeting halls, I was sure that
a New Age was awaiting, and it was an Age which could
never be described in the pale terms of this old one.

CLACK *BANG* CLACK *BANG*.

It had been five years now since I had reached London.
Just as Saul had predicted, that first summer, the sense of
warmth and prosperity, had been an illusion. London, England, was a far harsher place. Winter had come, and the
ancient buildings of Caris Rookery turned black and wet.
Life had thinned and emptied as many of its inhabitants
headed for the workhouses or to relatives in the countryside. I grew a fever, and lost track of days and shifterms
amid the click of rainwater into tin cans and the wet flutter

of Saul's ruined drawings. Maud brought in pots of gruel whilst I muttered from my dreams about piers and hotels and strange aunts in thorny houses. Her face was distracted when I grew properly conscious; this same fever killed several babies in her nursery. But the weather finally cleared with my health. London grew colder and brighter. Icy fogs snaked out from the gutters and the waters of the Thames broke and froze into a jigsaw through which ferries, aethered braziers flaming at their prows, cut and re-cut their channels for the season's lesser trade. My stomach growled and my head swam—hunger and cold simplify even your dreams, which revolve around the hot ovens of bakeries until you awaken with frost on your face.

As much as Saul had done, Blissenhawk had saved me. That first winter, in a hall we visited more for the illusion of heat than the poster nailed to the door, he was standing on a pile of boxes over a smog of breath and pipesmoke, his raw voice carrying passion above the hecklers' snarls. For Saul, the wrongness of the world had always been obvious, but for me, still at heart a guildsman and forever puzzled at the way things were never quite how they should be, explanations chalked on a bondhouse roof would never be enough. I needed purpose, I needed structure, I needed a sense that, even though I was a mart, I could still *belong*. After his talk, Blissenhawk had rolled up his posters, scratched his curly hair, and lumbered over to offer to buy us a drink in a booming voice which, for all that he'd come from distant Lancashire, had enough of the north about it to bring in me a twinge of homesickness. He'd once been an upper guildsman, still was in the manner and the look of him. In his big, cracked-bell tones he told us of the strike he'd organised at the printing firm he'd worked for up in Preston, when all he and his fellow-workers had ever wanted was the same pay and working conditions as the panel-beaters down the road. His greasy curls quivered. The system was mad, and he'd been driven from it. Down, in fact, as far as London, but not because there was anything worth having here, but because London was the cause of most of what was bad about England, and this was thus the best place to bring it all down.

'The guildhouses. The rich. The guildhall meetings they all troop into to mutter, over fine wines that would pay to feed fifteen starving families, about how the average guildsman is fundamentally lazy . . .' Blissenhawk growled, rummaging in his beard and puffing his chest, his ink-darkened palms flurrying. 'So they sack a few poor bastards and get some others in for less. And no one argues because those that aren't in guilds are desperate to get in, and those who are are terrified they'll get chucked out of them . . .'

It wasn't so unusual in the Easterlies to hear talk like this—especially from a disenfranchised guildsman. But this was different.

'You know how long each previous Age has lasted? Best part of a hundred years. So we're due a New Age.' Even then, the way Blissenhawk said it, I could hear the capitals in that phrase. 'And it's going to be unimaginably different . . .'

CLACK *BANG* CLACK *BANG*.

Blissenhawk had the skills, and still a little of the money, needed to spread the word. And the message wasn't about injustice. The message wasn't about borrowing things and calling each other citizen and pissing from rooftops. The message was that the world could and should and would be changed. This process wasn't some vague idea, it was inevitable as the next sunrise because wise men not just in England but in the guilded nations across Europe and beyond had proved the disastrous unworkability of the present monetary system. We were standing in the darkness just before the glittering dawn. The only question remaining was exactly how this New Age would come about, and when. These were exciting times, the very end of history as we knew it, and, even though I still struggled to make sense of economic and political theory on which much of Blissenhawk's talk was founded, I was grateful to be living through them. Blissenhawk's words on that first night, and the food and the drink he plied us with, had left me feeling light-headed. And he was looking for some lads to help with the production of the newspaper he was planning— lads who could actually read and write more than their own name, which was rare enough in the Easterlies. And

Blissenhawk *believed*. He still believed, even if five years
had gone by since then and we were using another version
of Black Lucy, and working from a different basement, and
were still stuck in the 99th year of the same Third Industrial Age. But the signs were there. The signs were everywhere. Just last shifterm, and filling the *New Dawn*'s main
page, there had been the biggest strike in the history of the
Tidesmeet Docks, in which the members of not just two or
three but fifteen separate guilds had united. In the riots that
followed, four citizens had died . . .

CLACK *BANG* CLACK *BANG*.

Would contend . . . What I wanted to say, somehow, was
that the arguments weren't important. That the question of
whether you ended up hitting your foreman over the head
or joined arms with him as you marched down the street—
that none of it mattered because . . . Because the New Age
was coming anyway. But in that case, if everything was so
inevitable, why was I writing this?

'Looks like just what we need . . .' Blissenhawk leaned
over me. He smelled of solvent and linseed and the palms
of his ham-like hands were glowing. Somehow, he got hold
of enough aethered oil to keep this current version of
Black Lucy clapping and churning although, even with his
skills, it was hard work. In this hazy light, you could see
the endless letters which decades of labour and ink had tattooed through the flesh of his palms. Whole armies of
words, which we called to our bidding. 'Take a look at
this . . .' He flapped out one of the lithographic sheets
which he was now using to print the *New Dawn*'s cartoons.
He dipped a roller and wetted it. 'Pretty good, eh?' he
chuckled. All I could see was a blurred flash, but I knew it
would be some plump guildsman bending over to show his
arse whilst he leered over a cowering but gracefully drawn
guildswoman; it always was. Saul could do such things
in his sleep, and he certainly didn't need to get up at four in
the morning to make his contributions to the *New Dawn*.
But a picture could get a message across far more effectively than words, especially when so many of the inhabitants of the Easterlies had trouble reading.

CLACK *BANG* CLACK *BANG*.

'What time is it?' I shouted.

Blissenhawk scratched his beard and looked up at the barred windows. 'Must be coming up for seven. Sure I just smelled the nightsoil cart going by.'

I wiped my pen. 'I'd better leave this. I'm not getting anywhere. At least Black Lucy seems to be behaving.'

'That she is . . .' Blissenhawk wandered over to her, lovingly stroked the warm sleeve of a piston, adjusted the drip of a reservoir. I could see his lips moving although the sound was too quiet to carry. For all that his guild had cast him out, he still kept to himself the coos and phrases he used to urge his failing machine to produce one more edition.

I was almost sure there hadn't been any fog when I'd arrived in the dark at the printshop three hours earlier, but now Sheep Street, Ashington was thickly veiled. The shabby buildings floated, the traffic was a blur of shapes and sounds. A typical London fog. But I was a Londoner now, and I could tell its types and flavours as well as the Eskimo is said to distinguish a thousand kinds of snow. There were brown fogs which left you choking. There were the cold grey ones which wormed beneath your clothing. There were the fogs of hot summer afternoons that stung your eyes, and the greenish stuff which crept slyly up from the river. But this fog was white, pure as milk. It beaded the threads of my worn coat and the brass buckle of my satchel. It tasted, as I licked my lips, almost spring-pure. The fog did something to the colours, to the bricks, to the faces. Changed, both faded and intensified, they flooded out. On a workhouse wall, quick with practice, I pasted up a poster advertising this Noshiftday meeting of the People's Alliance. On another, I ripped down a rival poster put up by the New Guild Order. The factories were tooting. The trams were clacking and flashing, dark and light. Everything was new and misty and bright. On a morning such as this, it really did seem as if the New Age was already dawning. The buildings looked pale, pristine; the dreams of young architects. The children, as they scurried by towards the dripping iron gates of their school, were all laughing.

Yes, for once, the whole world seemed clear to me. I recalled Grandmaster Harrat's words about the lazy lures of working with aether, the rigid conservatism of the guilds, about England's inbuilt resistance to any kind of change which would cause the high guildsmen to adjust their grip on the haft of power, let alone risk having to lose it. And not only England. Throughout Europe, there were guilds much like our own, and there was industry, and there was aether. I had seen the produce coming in to the big wharves, borne on the same secret signs and whispers. With the spread of aether, France and Saxony and Spain—even Cathay and the Indies—had sunk just as we had into their dreams of industry, these same endless Ages, whilst beyond, through the haze of time and distance, lay lands remote, scarcely mapped and grossly underexploited; Thule and the Antipodes, the unknown heart of Africa, the frozen legend of the Ice Cradle. The world, the time, was ripe for us citizens to move out, to move on and grasp it . . .

But such thoughts couldn't last. The mist was clearing as quickly as it had arrived. Smelling of mud and dogshit, the old London arose. Guildsmen who'd been laid off by Biddle and Co., the local maker of coils and springs, were standing outside the gates in Flummary Square, wandering in their workclothes even though there had been chains across the gates for two shifterms. I moved quickly on as they hawked and spat, smacked their fists and glared at me. To them, I was just some mart who had work when they didn't. I'd grown used to such hostility. It was no use my stopping to explain that the collapse of the industrial markets was a symptom of the wrongness of society. Even Blissenhawk and the other orators who rose and fell from their soapboxes in the Easterlies on Noshiftdays would have kept their counsel here.

But at last the weather was warming. Spring was here. Soon, it would be summer. Blissenhawk had a theory that the New Age could only come in summer. Demonstrations and marches fizzled out too easily in rain, cold and darkness. I bought a copy of the *Guild Times* and studied its bland lies over breakfast in the booth of a local chophouse. Outside the window, a ragged family was dragging a cart filled with furniture. A clock fell off and shattered in an explosion of springs. They looked lost and heartbroken. But I had warm beer, cold meat, a roof and a bed to look forward to. I knew that I was lucky, and that these troubled times had mostly been kind to me.

The *New Dawn* was going well; nowadays it paid for itself and sometimes even generated a surplus. But all of that money had to be channelled back into the People's Alliance, into booking rooms and paying off the police and helping out the members who'd lost their work or been injured in brawls and demonstrations. Saul and I still earned most of our living doing the sort of drudge duties which guildsmen and their apprentices were either too proud or too lazy to perform for themselves. Over the years, there had been items which needed collection, lunchtime deliveries of jugs of beer and warm pies which we had longed to drink and eat. There had been kingrats to trap; the beasts could leap prodigiously, and seemed always to go for the fingers, genitals and eyes. There had still been occasional borrowings. The work was always hard, dangerous, foot-aching, and the London of my Bracebridge dreams receded into tramstop waits and worn shoes and weary nights in tuberculosis boarding houses. Occasionally, pricked by sentiment, I would send my father and Beth a small cheque and a telegraph to assure them that I was still alive, but I kept the details of my life secret, just as any good citizen should, especially when using the telegraphs. What kept me in London now was a different vision to the one which had brought me here, although occasionally—just as this morning, and in the gleaming roofs of tenements and warehouses, in the impossible rise of Hallam Tower, in the wyreglow of sunset—I still sometimes glimpsed it. But life went on. The years had passed for Saul and Maud and I in that surprising way that they do. We still went each Midsummer to the fair in Westminster Great Park, but I never saw Annalise there, or anywhere.

I was fortunate. I had enough time and change in my pocket to eat my breakfast, stare out of the chophouse window, and shake my head over the fantastic nonsense they still printed in the *Guild Times*. Not that my life was easy.

Not that I was remotely rich. Apart from anything else, I had no ambition to succeed in an Age which would soon be upturned, uprooted. The fog had gone entirely when I left the chophouse and the sky had settled low above the rooftops and was dimly pulsing. I shouldered my satchel and headed north and west across Doxy Street towards Houndsfleet, where I now collected rent. Money was evil stuff; the root of so much that was wrong with our society. I understood that all too well. How could I not do so, working in place of a previous rentman who'd got his brains clubbed out in an alley?

In Houndsfleet, behind terraces with house names hung above tiny porches—*Larkrise, The Willows, Freida's Farm, Greenforest*—lay the pens where London's Guild of Works kept its armies of pitbeasts, and their curious smell hung in the air. Each morning, a dire circus parade of these animals trundled past the net curtains on dray-pulled wagons. Horny and savage, uniformly blind and scarred, they dribbled trails of shining ordure through the slats of their cages across which Houndsfleet's prim residents would step as they headed off to go about the business of their many guilds. In physical terms, being a rentman was easy work for me. I hopped across flowerbeds. I ignored the shouts of aggrieved horticulturists and truanting children. I made my peace, through bribes of biscuit and the ends of my boots, with the cowardly and pompous little dogs. At least I wasn't catching kingrats. *Ah, it's you* . . . I was scarcely a face to these people, and I watched the guildsmistresses' slippers flop into back kitchens and listened for the chime of the broken-spouted teapot where they innocently kept their money. Then back again that evening for those who were out, or pretended to be. The youngest child sent to the doorway. The pause and tinkle and the rumble of drawers in search of what should, should, *should*—if only I hadn't married the bastard—be there . . .

I'd come to understand the warning signs of a forthcoming eviction. The slight extra tension in a guildsmistress's fingers before the last precious shilling was released, the sleek off-meat odour of a bubbling sheep's head when the rest of the street were tucking into chops. A glance outside along the pebbledash, work-callused hands pushed through hair, then reaching towards me, although often as not at that moment the dog would start barking, the baby crying, the kettle singing, and the dim idea of some other exchange which would put right the columns of their rentbook would remain the ghost of a possibility. These guildswomen offered their bodies like tear-stained parcels of regret, and I scarcely needed my inherent caution to refuse them. Over the years, since my near-priceless encounter with Doreen, I had learnt to take the occasional relief which I needed with cheerful efficiency from the women who openly plied their trade. Money changed hands there, too, but at least there was something straightforward—almost clean, medicinal, hygienic—about those exchanges.

After a non-existent lunch, I reached Sunrise Crescent. There were tight distinctions along these Drives, Gardens, Walks and Avenues, where members of the Copyists' Guild shared bedroom walls and dustbins with Actuarial Registrars and Lesser Certified Accountants. They all thought that they were above each other, and especially above the sorts of non-guildsmen (they couldn't bring themselves to think of me as a mart) who made his living collecting rent. So I always noticed the ones who treated me like a human being. For this reason, Master Mather, who'd lived alone at number 19 on Sunrise Crescent before his eviction last winter, had come to my attention.

Smallish, round and white, his plump face topped with a pudding-bowl fringe, and there was an innocence about Master Mather, with his reedy voice, the waddling layers of his flesh, which at first had filled me with the same impulse which his neighbours must have felt, which was to prick his jolly bubble, to press my finger and puncture those doughy folds to let out whatever happy gas he seemed to be filled with. Master Mather, who lived alone because Mistress Mather had left him long before, was a blue-overall-wearing member of the Cleaners Purifiers and Aspurgers' Guild, and he loved his work. One rainy day of the previous autumn in the 98th year of this Age, he invited me in to show me.

Soot greys and grass stains; mildews and nicotines; spillages of Béarnaise or brown perspiration rings, Master Mather filled the cramped rooms of his house with secret packages of the damaged laundry he smuggled out from Brandywood, Price and Harper, the big, gold-fronted dry cleaner along Cheapside where he plied his trade. Swallow-tailed jackets and cummerbunds and feathered boas and christening heirlooms; he could recite the life history of an item of clothing merely from the scents and textures of its folds. And as he fingered an ember-blackened strip of lace and explained the milks and soaps in which he'd simmer it, I'd realised why Mistress Mather had probably left him. Of their nature, most guildsmen were blinkered about their work, but Master Mather took his enthusiasm to the level of a happy mania. Still, sleepwalking through Houndsfleet each morning after several hours wrestling with another article for the *New Dawn,* avoiding the alleys, and returning home on sore feet each night too tired to dream, I'd come to regard my visits to Master Mather as bright islands of relief. I once even called in on Brandy-wood, Price and Harper, and pinged the polished bell. A shrug, a smirk, and he was summoned, beaming as always, happy to show around even a rent-collecting mart like me. The further back you went though the humming work-rooms of an establishment which had cleaned the vest-ments of London's archbishops for these last two Ages, the finer the clothes became. A fire-burn on a blouse so intri-cately pearled it looked like a fairy suit of armour. Ink spilled on the glowing white dress of a near-suicidal bride-to-be. I'd never thought before that the Cleaners' Guild would have much use for aether, but, with the judicious chanting of the right spell, even such ravages could be un-made. Here were open books and chalked signs I was sure I wasn't supposed to see. Singing with a tremulous sound like a cracked flute, Master Mather swirled his hands over a copper vat, coaxing eager schools of bloomers to swim up to him through the glowing fluid. His plump arms, face and chins were oddly translucent in the gloom. His was a world which could be perfected in pirouetting swarms of empty clothes. The stains were his, and he absorbed them.

As I finally walked back along Doxy Street I could even see them drifting within him, grey and pellucid as the innards of a fish.

Last Christmas, I'd received a handkerchief from Master Mather; triangled green and crimson, it felt newer than it must have done when it left the mill's presses. Touching it made my skin ache. I put it away uneasily; to him, the whole world was simply so much laundry, and the temptation was always to fling him bodily across the room into a cloud of undershirts, to yell at him and pound him with your fists, to make him understand that grubbiness was part of existence.

'Brought this home with me yesterday.'

In his dim front room, just a shifterm after, he'd produced a silk box. Someone had written on it in a child's hand, but with enough residual aether for the words to stand out like the twirl of a cigarette.

CLEAN THIS.

'Could be quite difficult, don't you think?'

As the lid creaked off, I expected a powdery waft of Brandywood, Price and Harper's air, but instead, nested unmistakably in the pure white of a dress shirt, was a moist human turd. Other boxes and presents and packages came for Master Mather from his workmates through the dark early shifterms of the New Year. Tar and piss and manure, all adorned with messages, scrawls, obscenities. I had to ball my fists as he muttered about how he'd clean them. But Master Mather's life had probably always been like this, or so I told myself as I managed to ignore the jelly-like luminosity which increasingly seemed to infuse his flesh; the nudges, the sly words, the lunchtime sandwiches strung with saliva. All he'd done by showing me these disgusting treats was to introduce me to a deeper level of the world which he'd always inhabited. But I could feel, share, their frustration. *Surely this will bloody wake him up. This will show him how things really are.* But part of me was like Master Mather, too. The limbless beggars, the dead-eyed children, the old people who quietly froze in their chairs between one rentday and the next. Then the flower-strewn parades, the great parks, the vaulting buildings. Despite the political awareness which Blissenhawk had brought me, I often couldn't make much sense of the world either. Was the money system really enough to explain what Master Mather's colleagues were doing to him? There seemed to be some dark but vital underlying counterpoint to the magical song which pervaded all of England to which I was still tone-deaf.

London fell under a deaf blanket of snow. The windows of Houndsfleet grew white beards and its children, made bolder in this changed realm, scurried after me with snowballs and insults as I headed towards Sunrise Crescent one February Threeshiftday morning. A grey pall of steam and noise rose from over the rooftops from the pens of the weather-confined pitbeasts, filling the stiff, soft air. And there was talk at *Parkrise,* number 33, that Master Mather had gone to his dustbin without leaving footprints, and at *The Spinny,* number 46, that he'd made a single line of the devil's hooves. The children showed me the evidence amid the pee-holes they'd made in his small front garden.

I banged on his door with my fist, half-hoping today that he wouldn't open it. But Master Mather peered out. His eyes were deep and red and dark. Rot-like discolorations flowered over his face and hands. I forced myself to follow him inside, where the heaps of clothes glowed brighter than ever in the snowy light which washed through the windows as, in wheezing gusts, he showed me a heavy brown carrier bag, sagging and dripping with slurry. The message on it breathed out in glowing letters—*YOU FUCKING TROLL*. To my shame, I took Master Mather's rent money that day just as I had on every other; the ten shilling note rinsed and pressed as always, the crowns and pennies polished. I hurried out through the dragging snow as the children's voices—taunting, angry, another shrill part of London's song—rang after me. I pictured some incident of inspired bullying at Brandywood, Price and Harper. Crowds of jeering faces and Master Mather's round body spread-eagled; an aether chalice spilling pure white fluid into his mouth.

The snow had thawed and the air was almost biliously warm and bright when I returned to Sunrise Crescent to collect the next shifterm's rent. Guildays were so common in this area that my first impression as I crossed the swampy football fields towards the row of houses was that one was being celebrated today. Little girls were bustling about the street inside great flags of clothing. Boys were tripping over the arms of suits. The mothers were out on their doorsteps as well, and they looked brighter than usual. One was wearing a puffy-sleeved dress of candy-stripes. Another was absently polishing a vase with a black feather boa. Ignoring my usual routine of visits, I headed straight to Master Mather's house, but sensed as I did so a guilty withdrawing, a closing of doors. I looked up at his familiar frontage, numbered but resolutely unnamed. A house, once you come to know it, needs to change little for it to appear abandoned. I rapped his door, and heard the place echo as it had never done when it had been filled with the laundry which his neighbours had now pillaged. The notice pinned to it was rubber-stamped with the cross and C of the Gatherers' Guild.

It wasn't so unusual for a tenant to be thrust out from the terraces of Houndsfleet, and the reaction amongst the neighbours—be the cause trollism, disease, bankruptcy or some arcane infringement of their guild's regulations—was almost always the same mixture of horror and relief. *He's gone, ain't he? Pity, but wasn't our fault . . . Good riddance, I say. Poor old blighter . . . Never did much wrong, did he?* And—*Suppose he'll be off to St Blate's . . .*

If Yorkshire and Brownheath had Northallerton, London had St Blate's. In every sense, it was an institution, almost as famous as Newgate or Bedlam and celebrated in the sort of bitterly lamenting musical hall songs which were sung late-on in the last drunken house, although few people ever visited it.

Number 19 Sunrise Crescent was now called *Hill House,* although it stood on no hill, and I wondered today as I banged the new brass knocker and a little boy scurried off to get his mum along the familiar but strangely empty hall if its new residents had been told about Master Mather. I certainly wasn't going to do so. And here came Mistress Williams, wiping the suds from her hands and scarcely looking at me as she gave me a damp ball of money and closed the door. I ticked my collection book and walked slowly off. After the vanished fog and that brief sense of sunny warmth, London had drifted into one of those becalmed days which seem to hang beyond time and season, when the hours extend and the traffic passes and the faces go by and street turns into endless street without anything ever changing. Summer, this coming New Age, seemed impossibly far away as my satchel bit and blistered. Although my round was less than half-done, I turned towards the estate office.

Beyond the traffic, beyond the iron bars of a counter which I was never permitted to cross, the place had the characteristic smell, part sweat, part paper, part warm metal, of well-handled money. The stuff was there in drawers, piled up in gleaming columns, bound up in rubber bands and weighed in scales like so much sugar as I tipped more of it from my satchel into the worn wooden trough.

'Hey! That's not properly sorted!' A polished-trousered guildsmen scurried out of the gloom. But I'd had enough— part of me even wished that I'd kept the money, although I knew that the prison hulks or the gallows awaited those marts who risked such a thing. I threw down the satchel and collection book for good measure, and banged my way back out through the swing door.

Left with the small freedom of an afternoon to fill, and with no particular way of earning any money, I toyed with the idea of going back along Sheep Street to Black Lucy's basement, but my article still seemed stubbornly lodged in an interminable first sentence. Contend what? And who cared? My steps, in any case, were leading me in a direction I'd long considered and put off taking. There was an odd profusion of hardware shops on this south-eastern edge of Clerkenwell, and the pans and spades and buckets hung outside them banged in the thin wind. Otherwise, the streets were quiet, and I wandered semi-aimlessly along avenues and cul-de-sacs until I saw twin weathercock turrets pricking above the chimneys. Following three sides of a blue-brick wall, I reached large iron-bound gates over-arched by soot-blackened stone which bore the dim impression of a

cross and a C. St Blate's. I pulled a bell chain and a little
door set within the larger one squeaked open. Still fully expecting, and more than half hoping, that I'd be sent away, I
began to explain to the woman who poked her plump brown
face through that I'd known, albeit remotely, a certain Master Mather. But Warderess Northover practically bundled
me in and beamed back at me as she led me down hoops of
tiled corridor, her sporran of keys bouncing. And perhaps—
a slide of gates, a slam of doors, a faint roar of voices—I'd
like to inspect their little museum? She flung back shutters
and tugged off dustsheets in a long room filled with dangling bits of iron and glass cases. Nothing was too much
trouble.

'And you *will* sign the visitors' book before you go?'

She hefted antique chains which could have lifted a
drawbridge. More ingenious were these changeling re-
straints from the Second Age, which seem—go on, feel,
master, you shouldn't just take my word for it—light as a
feather in comparison. This little silver hoop at the end,
scarcely larger than an earring, was inserted through the
client's tongue. Things of steel and leather and iron. The
propped-open pages of logbooks, foxed and splattered
with what might have been nothing more than flydirt. And
photographs, woodcuts, engravings along the walls much
like those I had once glimpsed in that book in Bracebridge
library. Ironmaster Gardler here, he was one of their most
famous clients. We gazed at the sepia image of something
like a lopsided black spider squatting amid a trellis of iron-
work. Without him, Hallam Tower would never have been
built. I turned away. I'd seen similar images—and worse—
flopping out from Black Lucy's rollers in the times when
Blissenhawk had been forced in his search for finance to
run off what he called his 'specials'; in London, in this
Age, there was a market for everything.

We crossed a gravelled courtyard. The voices were
louder here; something almost like the song of a London
morning wafted out through the barred windows of the big
building beyond. They were hoping, Warderess Northover
confided, nodding towards the dark green vans which
leaned on their shafts, that Master Mather would be making

what she called *service visits* once his changed condition
had stabilised. I nodded. I'd seen such vehicles out once or
twice in the streets although, amid all London's other traffic, they passed otherwise unnoticed. A slam of barred
gates. Up a heavy iron stairway. Through an even heavier
door. Lines of cells on either side. Once, these had been ordinary men. Now, struggling in horns and veined billows of
impossible flesh, flightlessly winged and sprouting sightless
eyes, they were angels awaiting a different resurrection. After all, changing could happen to anyone, or at least to those
guildsmen who laboured sufficiently close enough to the
real means of production to expose themselves to the dan-
gers of aether. Guildswomen, too, although there were few
enough of them here. This, after all, was what St Blate's
was for; to provide a haven, a refuge—and there was also
Northallerton in the north, which I still struggled to picture,
although I knew it would be much the same.

Here, a moth-like creature shivered and clung to the
bars; a senior ironmaster from Gloucester who'd made a
serious error in some spell he was casting. And here was a
captain pilot from the Mariners' Guild, still murmuring of
currents and latitudes as grey webbings of fin shaped themselves across his limbs and spines grew out of him. A hand,
black-clawed, many fingered, ran like a centipede along the
bars, then withdrew in a coaly flare of breath.

'They've been restless this last term. Always this way in
the spring . . .' Warderess Northover clucked and cooed and
talked to her charges. Even as I hung back, she called them
by their names and referred to their old guilds, and listened
to those who were capable of response, and even touched
their different flesh with surprising tenderness. The days
when the high society of London came in their ruffs on
Noshiftday afternoons to laugh and shriek at the trolls belonged to a different Age, and, much though I'd have liked
her to have been, Warderess Northover certainly wasn't a
monster. In fact, she was unremittingly jolly about her work,
but then sewermen were also legend for their cheerfulness,
and the corpse collectors who hauled their carts through the
Easterlies on bitter winter mornings were an endless source
of songs and jokes. That was the way of this Age.

The slam of a final door, a shivering echo of voices as her bobbing lantern bore me on. Spells and whispers and hisses. Whole families of lost names.

Is it him . . . ?
Who . . . ?
Owd Jackkkk . . . ?
Or her . . .
Goldywhite . . .
Susssh . . .
Who . . . ?
We've been waiting . . .

Echoes in the darkness. Then, through the bars, in a slide of links, loomed a pale new excrescence of London's fog. Not heat, nor stains across the bloom of fresh laundry, but something huge and white and cold ballooned towards me as, lost and uncomprehending, a single coal-black snowman's eye gazed out. I forced myself to stare back at Master Mather, but something was squeezing the breath from my lungs. *What are you doing here now, Robert?* The echo of a terrible memory came towering towards me, my mother's changed bones creaking as the membranes of ruined nostrils twitched and my hands tensed upon the handle of a cedarstone knife. *Why are you bothering me?* And she was tall, tall. I had to turn away.

'Don't worry . . .' Warderess Northover was sympathetic as I hunched gasping outside in the yard. 'It's often that way for first-time visitors. I used to try warning people, but there's no way you can, is there?' Her hand stroked my back. 'Can I get you water? I'm sure we've got something stronger back in the office.'

Straightening up, I shook my head.

'Well anyway. You *will* come again won't you? And you *must* sign that visitors' book . . .'

London life went on. Boys and men ridiculously dressed in white togas tramped and sang down Cheapside. The reeking chimneys of the factory off Sheep Street which produced McCall's Universal Balsam, which you saw dustily arrayed in the windows of almost every London apothecary, still plumed. With my rent-collecting work gone,

Blissenhawk found enough paid work for me to keep my
head above the surface. Protest, in those difficult times,
was one of the few growth industries.

There was a Fiveshiftday soon after my visit to St Blate's
in the spring of that 99th year when I went down to one of
the impromptu markets which gathered, in that inexplicable
way Londoners had, as an encampment of wagons and barrows on the tidal mudflats beyond the Easterlies. Here, past
Greenwich, blood was boiled, carcasses were pillaged, glue
was made. As I climbed out from the last tram and picked
my way around the boneheaps, I almost missed the reek of
McCall's Universal Balsam until the wind from off the rank
river began to play in my face.

I found myself a space and a scrap of sacking and laid
out the remaining copies of last shifterm's *New Dawn*, the
third page of which contained an incoherent article about
the choice between physical and moral force, on the cracked
mud. Then some pamphlets. *Freedom from the Guilds* and
The Evils of Money, but today there were no takers. Only
shaken heads, disapproving glances. Some days, people
would gather and talk and argue. But the majority of Londoners still thought people like me—agitators, disrupters,
socialists, anti-guildsmen, as they called us—were the
cause of the lock-outs and the spiralling prices rather than
their answer. I could have started buttonholing them and
talking the message, but I'd been in enough brawls. So
I weighed down my papers with stones and wandered
amid the wagons and stalls which had gathered under the
bellying sky. There were sacks and blankets for sale. Woven bits of rope and leather. Old family photographs
swimming through oceans of damp and dust and mould.
Painstones which still gave a whisper of ease. Snuff tins,
their enamel polished away. The stolen handkerchiefs
which still fluttered down from Northcentral in a poly-
chromatic rain.

I slipped into a timeless daze. I'd always liked markets,
and this one reminded me of a lost Sixshiftday in Bracebridge; wandering the stalls under similarly grey skies on
the day of my mother's funeral with Mistress Summerton
beside me, awnings flapping as the wind rustled the dried

flowers. When I looked up and saw that a small, specta-
cled woman in an old leather coat was moving unnoticed
amid the ragged crowds, I scarcely felt any sense of surprise. It seemed entirely right that she should be here, just
as she had been there on that distant day in Bracebridge,
and wrapped as ever in a scarf and gloves, that broad-
brimmed canvas hat, those glasses. It all seemed so natural
and innocuous that Mistress Summerton had almost turned
and gone from sight before I was shocked out of my
daydream.

'Wait!'

I pushed through the crowds. Perhaps I'd imagined it—
then I turned around a wagon, and there she was again, lifting the greying bits of lace which some guildswoman had
cut from her dresses and pinned to newspaper-covered
cushions.

'It *is* you!'

She turned and smiled thinly. I sensed a wariness in the
lenses of her glasses beneath the shadow of that hat, although she didn't seem in the least surprised to find me
here. And it seemed to me at first that she really hadn't
changed from the time when we had walked in a market
not so very unlike this; even to the dried flower she was
wearing on her lapel and the unmuddied lightness of her
fine-stitched boots.

'So . . . Robert . . .' Although her voice sounded frailer.
'You live in London now?'

'Do you?'

'Near enough. Just across the river, at World's End. You
don't have to look at me like that. It's true—I came here to
look for seeds . . . Then I suppose I got distracted.'

I was much taller than she was now, and she was
scarcely noticeable here in her long coat and hat. What few
glances were given us as we walked together were aimed at
me. *Fucking mart, telling us what to do . . .* And World's
End—with its ruins and white hills—meant as little to me
then as my life of deliveries and meetings probably meant
to her. It has hard to know what to say. Perhaps we'd
drifted apart. More likely, I reflected, we'd never been
close together. After all, how could we have been? The past

is like that. When it finally taps you on the shoulder, it's never the thing you thought it to be.

The tide was returning. The market vendors were departing, digging their wagons out from the mud. I rescued my papers. Mistress Summerton's gaze when she saw them was detached, amused. I followed her beyond the thinning market to the back of a ruined shed and the unlikely object which lay there.

'Is *this* yours?'

It was a small motor car. Open-topped, ebony-lacquered, steel-trimmed; a fine black jewel. Powered not by steam or coal but some vaporous and odd-smelling chemical, such objects were a common enough sight in certain districts of Northcentral, but scarcely here. She stroked its panels with her gloved hands, then lifted the handle of a wing-like door and climbed in. The engine barked into life. The machine began to move.

I shouted, 'But you never told me!'

The engine stilled. She turned towards me. 'Told you what?'

'You promised you'd explain. Remember—that last time I saw you. When we walked beside the Withy . . .'

She let out an inaudible sigh as she stroked the wheel of her little car. It was darker now. I could barely see more of her face than the flash of her glasses. *Why don't we leave the past where it belongs, Robert, and get on with the future?*

I don't know what I said next. Probably some rambled confession which started with my fall towards London and my struggles through the Easterlies with Saul to my recent visit to St Blate's and the hope for the New Age which Blissenhawk had given me. Whatever it was, Mistress Summerton let me climb beside her on the leather bench of her car as she once more set the engine thrumming. We drove off, the machine chuffing and rattling in response to the things she did to a collection of levers. I'd never been in such a vehicle and its oddness almost eclipsed her presence as we passed the backs of slaughterhouses and bumped over abandoned railtracks.

'I saw Annalise. Once. At the Midsummer Fair in the Westminster Great Park. She was—'

'I know.'

Her words cut me off. We moved on through the gathering dark.

'Are you free here?' I asked eventually.

'I told you. I was never free.'

'But the guilds, the trollmen . . .'

Her black face thinned. Through her insect glasses, she gave me a pitying glance. 'Do you think they can't be persuaded—*bribed*—just like any other guild?'

Silenced again, I directed her towards the streets of Ashington.

'This place where you live,' I said as the car finally chattered to a halt on the unlit street outside my tenement. 'World's End. I'd like to see it.'

'For that, all you need do is take the ferry.' The tone of the engine rose and I looked down at the door, wondering how it opened. There was a pause. I had a sense that this was a moment when my life was dividing. Then I was standing on Thripp Street's weedgrown paving and Mistress Summerton and her car had vanished. It was dark— and quiet, but for the screech of buffers in the nearby sidings. I hefted my papers and headed through the archway into the courtyard. Everything was territorial here. The women hung their washing in segregated lines and shrieked at the children for ruining it when they played football. I used to join in with their games—*Here, mister, knock it to me*—but over the years my returns had grown later and my risings earlier as I went to sit beside Black Lucy and worry at the never-ending threads of another article. I climbed the stairway. Physical or moral force— what, after all, was the point, the difference . . . ?

Maud was picking up toys whilst Saul sat with his feet up on the stove, sketching. The window was open but the air was pungent. All of Maud's children should already have been collected by their mothers from their evening shifts, but she still had one last infant tucked under her arm. There was no need here for the bubbling vats and the dripping washlines of the old nursery off Caris Yard, nor the space. A local cart delivered nappies fresh each morning from a laundry far less grand than Brandywood, Price and Harper, and took the soiled ones away each night. To my tired eyes, the long, narrow room, its whitewashed walls ornamented with Saul's frieze of green hills and trees, fine cattle and distant white palisades, looked welcoming and pretty. I had a small room of my own in the gabled floor above, but this, when I wasn't asleep or working, was where I spent most of my time.

'The wanderer returns . . .'

Saul stretched and yawned. He'd fleshed out in the time I'd known him. No longer the thin lad with the reedy voice, his waistcoats had grown even brighter in an affectation few other of us revolutionaries would have dared and he'd taken to smoking cheroots, although he'd kept that youthful air which people still found so appealing. His smooth cheeks creased upwards as he smiled. A narrow tube of flesh formed between his chin and top collar.

'It's not as if I ever know *when* you're coming, Robbie . . .' Maud made to put the child back down in one of the remade cots, then thought better of it and handed it to me. Maud's father had been a secret gambler who'd sold his spells to a rival guild then hanged himself rather than face disenfranchisement. Evicted, she and her mother had drifted down through the Easterlies, setting up a nursery which had thrived well enough to keep them fed and sheltered, although her mother had died after from consumption in their second winter, leaving Maud to soldier on alone. A typical story of this Age. But the baby was sweet-scented, light as hope itself, golden haired and sexless. It stared up at me with grey-blue eyes.

'By the way, Robbie. Dinner's all gone and eaten.'

I crossed to the window. The baby squalled, settled, then squalled again. Maud got the milk saucepan and handed me a warm, rubbery-smelling bottle. It rooted and pulled, its eyes turning over and closing. At least, for now, it was happy, even if its mother was out far too late to be gutting herring.

'By the way, citizen . . .' The rasp of a match. The familiar oily smell of Saul's cheroots wafted towards me. 'What time do you think we should be down at the tile factory?'

'When's that?'

'This Noshiftday—I told you only yesterday. I thought about noon. Nothing starts much earlier than that on a Noshiftday and we'll have a fresh edition of the *New Dawn* to sell by then if Black Lucy keeps behaving. Bruiser Baker should be there. And all the lads from Whitechapel. Of course, the Men of Free Will, too, unless someone's spilled to the police . . .'

I looked out of the window. Down over by the black mass of the allotments, a campfire was burning. The air shifted. The slightest hint of a breeze, which somehow bore through the tenement fug the waft of early jasmine, hawthorn, and the year's new grass. The baby smiled as it drifted into sleep, falling blissfully towards whatever it is that babies dream. Perhaps summer really was coming. Here, in Ashington, stuck between the Easterlies and the impossible reaches of Northcentral, I could make out the circling gleam of Hallam Tower, and the white hills of World's End beyond the tarnish of the river.

I said, 'I'm going somewhere else.'

II

Excited families were crowded on the Noshiftday ferry, the children banging tin trays, the mothers sitting around the wheelhouse huddling picnic baskets, the men smoking and bragging at the prow. This morning was everything it should be, clear and fine and bright, and World's End was a popular spot for day trips amongst the poorer guildsfolk; nearer than the countryside, cheaper than the fairgrounds and far less trouble than visiting relatives.

The ferry hooted as it approached the jetty. Hats and boaters streamed across the walkway. The marshy south side of the Thames had never been a populous place, and in this current Age, and since the closure of the exhibition which had signified its commencement, it had become even less so. On this warm spring day, with the leaves bursting from the trees and the postcard sellers shouting and the wind fresh in my face, World's End was London's empty cousin; the deserted room captured in a magic mirror. The distant sounds of traffic and the peal of bells carrying over the water seemed much further than a mere tuppenny ferry ride away. If I'd ever thought about the possibility of Mistress Summerton living anywhere in London, this would certainly have been the place.

The high white dunes of engine ice raised plumes of rainbows against the morning sky. My best trousers and dark blue jacket were soon coated with their gritty sparkle. World's End had been London's nearest aether source before it had been exhausted in the final flowering of the famous exhibition at the end of the last Age. Now, aether was brought in from further afield on barges and trains from places like Bracebridge, and the engine ice scraped from thousands of processes and machines was piled here with the dim intention that it might one day provide enough high ground for drainage. Here, piled in glittering mountains, was the final useless waste product of all the magic which had been pulled from the earth to service the spells of guildsmen since the First Age of Industry; the salt crusting around the eyes at the end of a dream.

I strode inland for a while with the picnic families. The road here was surprisingly wide and well-made, and still set with the weedgrown slots of dead tramlines. We made a large enough throng, but were scarcely a trickle compared to the waves of sightseers which had swept this way across the Thames almost exactly a century before. Then I turned east. Soon, after I'd clambered over a ruined turnstile, the bickering, excited voices had faded and I was alone. No one, I thought, would bother to come to the ruins here for the sake of the few panes of glass which probably still needed breaking, but as I picked my way around a livid patch of cuckoo-nettle and the main hall came into view, I gave a gasp of surprise. For a moment, the great glass edifice loomed ahead of me, glittering perfect and new as a soap bubble from every one of its many millions of panes. The World's End Exhibition of an Age before this one blazed at me through the sunlight, then sank back like a dream exhaling and I saw it for it what it was; a huge and crazily-angled collection of disarranged girders and black-starred panes.

Fallen-roofed bandstands. Signs pointing towards *The Tropic Wing, The Guildmaster's Rest, The Spa Rooms, The Perpetual Motion Machine*. Great, strange plants gone wild and to seed beyond any guildsman's control straggled upwards in leaves of every colour and shape. Then, stranger still, patches of the landscape tamed themselves into freshly turned seedbeds and green-shooted seed trays. An old ice-cream vendor's stall had been used as a compost frame. There were signs, too. *KEEP OUT* scrawled in red paint, and I felt an odd, familiar, sense of resistance. This, surely, was the place Mistress Summerton had told me about, even though her instructions had been almost impossibly vague. As I ducked under an old trellis, I found myself battling with clattering webs of tin cans. After that, I was troubled by nothing but birdsong and the scent of things growing. And there she was; Mistress Summerton neat and wizened and bare-headed, a tiny scarecrow come to life and stooped amid cloches and seedbeds.

'Robert . . .' Slowly, she straightened up, pushing her spade into the pouch of her apron as she moved towards me. 'I'm sorry about the tins. This isn't like Redhouse. There are children, gangs, in London. I have to be careful. Discreet . . .'

I met the sharp brown gaze in its withered webbing.

'But it's so quiet here.'

Mistress Summerton chuckled. 'Why do you think I chose it?' Her arm, thin and warm and faintly trembling, steered me between rows of seedlings. Beyond were flowers of shades and shapes beyond anything you would ever see in the arms of a flower girl on Doxy Street. They were like thunderheads, giving off a musky deep scent which made me want to laugh and sneeze at the same time, and their hearts were filled with wyrewhite stamens like stabs of lightning. Even this early in the season, the rows were wondrous and huge. Flowers the size of dinner plates, their leaves silver-furred, nodded in the sunlight over our heads. After all, World's End in its prime had been filled with gardens. All Mistress Summerton had done was re-turn the soil, prune and nurture the wild bushes, harvest the seedheads. Just like the huge glass ruin which lay to our left, part of this place still wanted to return to life. She plucked a black cuckoo-weed and crumpled it bare-handed. Without her glasses, in the ragged clothes she was wearing and the silvery dust of her hair, she looked strange and small and dark; a sweet distillation of the shadows which fanned between the bars of sunlight.

She led me towards a building. It was like a forester's cottage, but it was one from a storybook, with intricate pokerwork over the eaves, green bottleglass windows. It had plainly been part of the exhibition—perhaps a toy-house in which children could play, although pinned to the door now was an official-looking notice; numbered paragraphs rubber-stamped with a cross and C. It was dim inside and smelled sweetly of tobacco and garden loam. I watched as she produced a teapot and cups from the narrow shelves and sniffed various tea caddies for sweetness, then pumped up the little stove.

My mouth was dry. It was time for the obvious question. 'Do you still see Annalise?'

Mistress Summerton felt for her pipe in her pockets. 'Yes . . .' A huge puff of smoke. A long pause. In this tiny room, she dissolved, reformed. 'She sometimes visits me, although of course she has to be careful . . .' Puff. Puff. 'In fact, it wasn't so long ago that she last came. Two shifterms before last, at the edge of spring, as I remember . . .'

'I met her—'

'As you said.' More vague clouds. 'Annalise told me. In Westminster Great Park, at the Midsummer Fair . . .' Another lengthening pause. The kettle began to rattle to itself. 'Of course,' she said as she poured my tea, 'she has her own life to lead. I'm not even sure that she welcomes *my* presence here in London, any more than she would probably welcome yours, if she knew that you were still here.'

'Why on earth should I leave?'

'I hope, by the way, you like the tea. It's one of my small luxuries. Best green Cathay. Can't you almost smell those mountains, feel those distant spells?'

I sipped the hot, fragrant fluid, although the cup was so eggshell-thin that it seared my fingers. 'I've kept away from her, if that's what you mean. But why *should* I bother her? I mean—Anna Winters! She's built her whole life on pretence . . .'

'That's something she's had to do. You shouldn't blame her for it.'

'But she could have been a thousand things.'

'Could she? What would you do if you were her? Join some guild? Try to change the world? Go off and get married? Pretend to be ordinary?'

'Is Annalise really a changeling? She seems so . . .' *Beautiful? Exceptional? Ordinary?* How could I find a word to encompass what I felt? Here I was, sitting facing this wizened creature in a toy house at the far edge of London, trying to imagine that she and Annalise were somehow the same. Annalise's eyes didn't have the lost and odd and hungry fire I saw glinting at me through the pipesmoke. Her limbs weren't sticks of liquorice. Annalise had blond hair instead of these few spiderweb strands. Annalise was . . .

We're not all monsters, you know. Just because you choose to call us trolls and witches, that doesn't mean that's what we are—and just because I'm old now, and faded and ugly.

'I'm sorry.' I put down my cup, my fingers stinging, my tongue sore and blistered. 'But there are so many things I don't understand.'

'Remember, all those years before, up in Bracebridge, when we walked by the river on the day of your mother's funeral? Even then, you wanted answers . . .' The bowl of her pipe glowed. I could almost hear the onrushing Withy. 'You're the same now. What, after all, is your interest in politics but another way of attempting to explain the ways in which people behave? And I'm sorry if I didn't seem entirely pleased when you discovered me at that market. But London is a difficult place for me to be. People are prejudiced, and prejudice turns too easily to fear, and as you can see I've had to make my peace with the guilds.' She sighed. 'But the reasons you've wanted answers are probably the same ones which have made me reluctant to give them. But perhaps it would be better if we went out before you want to hear what I have to say. After all, this *is* a Noshiftday . . .'

She wrapped herself in her leather coat which hung from a hook by the door, and put on a hat, and found her glasses, and then her gloves and a scarf, although they were scarcely what the day needed. Still, the transformation was extraordinary. The person I followed through the ruined gardens was no longer the withered changeling I had seen moving through the cloches but once again an elderly guildswoman. The clothes, I finally realised, were incidental. Her disguise came from some inward effort.

She led me to her car, which she kept parked beneath a corrugated awning beside a dry boating lake. The car could have been an exhibit here too, and I could tell as she stroked the panels and touched the delicate arrangements of glass and brass that she was intensely proud of it. She did the things to its levers which caused it to quiver awake and we chuffed out into the sunshine. There was a gate to the road which the trees kept hidden. From there she took the way south, around the dazzling hills across which the day-tripping families now crawled and slid, through half-empty hamlets and past the ruins of old guildhouses, out beyond the straggling edge of London into the true countryside where the earth was no longer sanded white and cattle grazed in plain green fields.

As the road rose and fell, and as if there had scarcely been a pause in our conversation since we walked beside the river in Bracebridge, Mistress Summerton began to tell me how, after finally leaving her prison-house in Oxford, she had been put to use. The Gatherers were as secretive about their practices as any other guild, but, as well as the great edifices such as Northallerton and St Blate's, there were waystations dotted about England where the so-called lesser cases such as her could be fed and housed and employed. For many years, she remained little more than the captive of a variety of trollmen, borne from town to town and factory to factory in those green vans to be presented with incomprehensible blueprints, or told to fix the malfunction of some recalcitrant and dangerous machine.

'You were alone? You never talk about others . . .'

'Aren't we all always alone?' She gave a bitter chuckle. 'What do you want me to say? That we changelings are some great secret army, that Goldenwhite still lives deep under the boughs of some forest, and that we'll all rise up like your so-called citizens and bring about the end of this

Age?' I said nothing. She'd put it simply and better than I'd have dared to have done. Yet there was genuine anger in her voice; the same lost expectation which she perhaps had nursed through the years of her childhood.

'The guilds have always believed that there was some vital secret, some incantation or spell that my kind have always kept from them—some final song or phrase, some hidden language which would allow them to change everything about the world. They once tried to record the screams of those poor unfortunates they tortured and burned. But now all the magic has been dragged out from the ground and been stuffed into factories . . .'

We had driven into a wooded valley. The road had greened. Ancient oaks, their massive branches like the frozen limbs of dancing giants, leaned over us and the track beneath them became a grassy pathway, then not really a pathway at all, but almost a cave. The clatter of its engine stilled into birdless silence as Mistress Summerton stopped her car. From there, we wandered amid gorgeous drifts of fallen leaves. This wood was old, uncoppiced. I looked about me, studying the moss-bearded faces which emerged from the bark, urging the shade ahead to become something other than the parting of more trees.

As we walked on, and the wood remained just a wood, Mistress Summerton told me how a high guildsman of the Telegraphers' Guild had taken pity on her, and persuaded the Gatherers' Guild to pass her into his care. Working the gardens of his Devonshire house, she finally discovered the one area of knowledge in which she truly did excel, which was to make things grow. Of course, the plantsmen hated her, but she became almost a trophy, a prize. By now, in the fifties of this Age, and because wealthy guildsmen cherished her, she even accumulated a little money of her own, although it meant little to her.

We reached a bowl in the forest where the trees clustered. Mistress Summerton eased herself down in a hollow formed by their roots. The dry ground was pillowy. The clouds were thickening. The air breathed.

'I was trusted, as much as my kind ever are. People would comment on how *ordinary* I seemed, on how *reliable*

I was—all the words you would use to describe a faithful dog. And I was happy enough tending my plants, living a small and mostly anonymous life. When I was told that I would have to move again, and this time back into the world of industry, I almost fled. But I'm glad now that I didn't, for I was sent to Redhouse. Yes—Redhouse, which was still then a village, although it was no longer thriving, and the guildsmen who remained there had conceived the hopeless idea that I might be able to help them extract more of their failing reserves of aether. Of course, I couldn't. The place was already glittering, fading. But it was pretty enough, and I was happy there, even as the last guildsfolk left and the waterwheel failed and I remained. This time, the Gatherers didn't return for me. It seemed, finally, that I was free. And it was a peaceful life, to be lost and forgotten. I had long grown used to my own company, and I was already growing old. This, I decided, would be the place I would live out the rest of my life. What little power which remained in the soil helped me to keep hidden, although a few sometimes found me. Your mother was one . . .'

A damp wind stirred the reflections of the trees. The clouds turned. My mother, still a girl, living on that farm and wandering Brownheath and its hidden valleys. Finding Redhouse, glinting like a jewel in velvet, and Mistress Summerton. All those nights up in my attic room as she sat beside me, all those tales—yet this was one she had kept from me . . .

You shouldn't blame yourself for her silence, Robert. Or her. We don't live our entire lives in daylight. There are some things you never tell. 'I think your mother enjoyed my company. I certainly enjoyed hers. But then she grew as every child does, and she had to find work in that town, in Bracebridge. And she married. It was no sorrow to me—or only a small one. I was long used to my life and the lives of others drifting apart . . .'

'She had a friend, didn't she—called Kate?'

The glint of Mistress Summerton's bare eyes sharpened. 'She told you that?'

I shrugged and swallowed. Visions, long repressed, stirred. 'It was something I learned.'

'The past is better left alone,' she muttered. Slowly, her arms crawling up the trunk beside her, she stood up. 'There was an accident at that factory,' she said as we began to move on between the trees. 'Something to do with the aether pistons. One Halfshiftday, they stopped beating. There was an explosion, and several people died. Your mother had been working there at the time, right down in the bowels of the place. So had Kate.' She gave a dry click of her tongue. 'There was talk of some kind of unauthorised experiment. Of course, no one really took the blame. Not, at least, those who were truly responsible. When things go badly wrong, no one ever does . . . But for that small scar, we always thought that your mother was safe, but Kate, she was ill, she was feverish, and her husband had died in the same blast, and she was pregnant. I suppose she feared many things, and she feared above all for the child she carried. So your mother remembered me, she remembered Redhouse . . .

'I tried to heal Kate—I did my very best. I swear it. It's what people expect, isn't it, that our kind can cure ills, work miracles? But I couldn't, any more than I could help or heal your mother. And Kate had been standing right beside the pistons when they burst. By the time I saw her, her bones were turning to engine ice, her very veins were glowing. Still, at least I know more about herbs than most so-called apothecaries. And I was able to bring her some ease . . . I'm afraid Kate faded and died. But she did at least live to see the baby she had carried, and to understand how beautiful she was.'

'That was Annalise?'

Mistress Summerton was quiet for a while.

'I'm old now. But in many ways I've led a decent enough life. I've never starved. Then, out of a pointless death and the very worst of circumstances, Annalise happened. I suppose I've always been just like you, Robert. Although I didn't know it, I'd been looking for a purpose. And what better one than to give this new baby the chances I'd never experienced?'

'You knew what Annalise was?'

'Whatever the spell was to which Kate was exposed, it must have been enormous in its power. Annalise had to be a changeling, yet was perfect—and can you imagine how the guilds would treasure such a prize! So there was never any question of taking her back to Bracebridge. Tending Annalise was a long-delayed and difficult process of education for me, but at least I did have my little money, my small investments, which I discovered had grown surprisingly in the time I'd ignored them.

'So I was able to make Redhouse comfortable and secure, and to buy what was needed and take care of Annalise through the long winters and the short springs and rainy autumns of that northerly land. It's odd, but I learned more about the ways of humanity then than I had in all my years before. And I learned endlessly from Annalise. At first, I feared the guild investigators, and of course the Gatherers' Guild. All that first summer and winter, and even as I still tended Kate, I pictured dark and solitary figures—I hid from shadows, but for me, even in the wake of the tragedy of Annalise's birth, and as your mother drifted from our lives and returned to her own, those were happy times. Annalise was a constant song. Her hair changed with the seasons. It was the gold of flame in the winter and it paled with the spring to the colour of sunlight. At Midsummer it was a field of wheat. She called me Missy. And I loved her, Robert, I loved the freckles on her nose and the summer peelings of her skin. Sometimes, in the evenings when she was asleep and I wandered that frozen village and watched the shadows the starlit trees drew across the lawns, I could hardly tell I wasn't dreaming.

'And, slowly, I was able to introduce her to a little of the human world. We enjoyed ourselves in places at twilight when the crowds had departed, as the last customers on boating lakes, and late walkers along river paths, the final shoppers at markets. But Annalise always understood the need to be wary. She could feel her powers. She knew that she didn't belong to this world as any ordinary child might . . .'

'But you sent her away from Redhouse,' I said after

Mistress Summerton had remained silent for so long as we walked beneath the trees that it seemed as if the story of her and Annalise could have ended in those twilight parks they had visited, dipping lonely oars on darkening boating lakes.

'That day when you visited with your mother,' she said, 'I watched you and Annalise through the window as you sat talking beside that fountain and I realised that I was being selfish, that things could no longer continue as they were. I was keeping this child to myself—I was in danger, even, of doing through kindness the very thing about my own life which I most detested, and imprisoning her. Through that summer and autumn, as your poor mother suffered and died from the long-delayed effects of that accident, I came to understand that Annalise needed far more from life than I could ever provide, and we made plans.'

The trees parted. We'd returned to the narrow track, although the sky now was darker than the branches of the trees which stretched across it. As we reached the car, the leaves above us finally began to tremble and thud with heavy drops of rain. I helped Mistress Summerton as she dithered over the complex struts which brought up the wings of a leather roof.

'So,' I asked, as she turned the car around and drove through the rain, 'when did the tale of the aunt and the house by the waterfall come about?'

'*That*,' she said, 'was mostly Annalise's invention. But it was necessary to construct a plausible-sounding story.' Little blades swept across the front glass window, although it was almost impossible to see more than a few yards ahead as we bumped along the rutted roads. 'Of course, I was stricken to lose her, and there were many difficulties. After all the years of hiding and deception, it seemed odd to launch her into the human world on a ship of lies. But I wanted Annalise to have everything that I didn't have. A chance to be ordinary. Her other choice would be to be a freak, a specimen to be analysed, used, prodded and exploited and borne about in those dreadful green vans. You shouldn't blame her for her deception.'

'And how does Annalise feel?'

   'About the lies? Between you and me, I think she has always enjoyed them. Life, for Annalise, has always been a bit of a game. It's the thing about her that people find most attractive—and most infuriating. But the last thing I have ever wanted to do was to bring undue attention to her, especially now that she has made her own life . . . And perhaps you understand better now why I seemed reluctant to see you. And it seems to me that you probably know more about that than I do . . .'

   'And if I did?'

   'Then I hope you'd understand all the more the need to leave things alone.'

   The rain thinned and stopped as we drove on, but the mild afternoon felt thin and cold when we finally returned to World's End. The white hills were now deserted. Outside the little house, the great panes of the greenhouses seemed to rise and exhale. 'I see too little of Annalise now,' Mistress Summerton said inside as she stoked up the stove. 'Although her very presence is what brought me here to London. But in many ways this is as good a place as any to live, and I must still count myself as lucky. In what little time I have left, I suppose I've made my peace with the world. But you must be hungry . . .'

   I watched as Mistress Summerton peeled potatoes and opened tins with her thin and dithery hands. When the food was cooked, I bolted it all down from a plate balanced on my lap whilst she picked at her own tiny helping, then set it aside and lit her pipe and watched me. It all tasted good, and somehow faintly exotic, despite its plainness. Fairy food, I decided, when I finally wiped my plate, in this fairy house, in the huge, enchanted gardens of World's End, although I still somehow felt hungry.

   'Now.' Mistress Summerton stood up. Her smoky presence surrounded me. Her fingers brushed my hair. 'Perhaps you would like to see Annalise?'

Northcentral gleamed in the night air. Pallid with gaslight, built on foundations of illusion, pillars of dream, London's Grand Opera House loomed above the traffic. Carriages were spilling their high-guilded contents onto the red carpet which bled from the entranceway in a congestion of top hats and tiaras. For a moment, I thought that Mistress Summerton and I might be heading that way. But this was some great and formal guild occasion—a time for heirloom jewellery and antique sashes. Her little car juddered along a cobbled sidestreet, and she drew me out towards the narrow door set in the building's unornamented back brick wall.

A youth in a low corridor scowled at our tickets and then at us, but, with a muttered word and a glint of coins from Mistress Summerton's gloved hands, we were waved on. We climbed stairways and followed passageways until, in a widening sea-roar of light and sound, and a faint but perceptible odour of wet coats, we entered a balcony which hung almost at the very roof of the Grand Opera House's main auditorium. I leaned over the edge, and saw the balding pates and bosoms swarming in miniature beneath, the sea-twinkle of all that jewellery. I was just wondering if anyone had ever succumbed to the desire to spit from here when I sensed a small movement beside me and realised that part of the balcony was already occupied.

'So *this* is Master Borrows.' I took the hand which was offered me. 'Mistress Summerton was most anxious that I found you a ticket.' The hand felt small and cold. 'I'm Mister Snaith. How d'you do? Has Mistress Summerton not mentioned me . . . ?'

Mister Snaith smiled at me. I thought at first from his size and the odd, slurring lightness of his voice that he was a child. But his face was powder-white, his nose was long and thin, the fine lips beneath its downward curve seemed tinged with rouge, and his pink-tinged eyes were old. He wore a finely cut but somewhat tattered half-size suit in the style a master-tailor's apprentice might have produced perhaps fifty years before, and a hat of black hair which, had the intended effect worked at all, might perhaps have been called a toupee. In that he looked like anything on earth, Mister Snaith looked like an absurdly refined and anaemic boy who had been playing in his father's wardrobe these last several Ages. I suppose I must have mumbled something as I sat between him and Mistress Summerton. Then the whole auditorium darkened and the whispers subdued as the curtains swept open to reveal a gorgeously clad troupe.

There were many sights and sounds that evening, but I can't say that I paid that much attention to them. I was ignorant of the skills of the Guild of Gifts, and had little desire to be otherwise. Still, the lights were pretty. They shifted and blurred across the stage as if the music had bewitched them. And the scenes tumbled and changed from palace to tundra to woodland as the dancers danced, the actors declaimed and ranked musicians sawed at violins. All this *money,* I kept thinking, all this *effort* . . .

The curtains rose and fell. Applause clattered. There were one or two attempts at what, I had to assume from the waves of laugher which crashed below me, were humour. Two actors even put on cloth caps and attempted to ape the accents of the Easterlies. A tune would occasionally emerge from the orchestra's massed thundering, but it was soon drowned out again. I was near to sleep despite my odd surroundings when the curtains suddenly parted again on a near-empty stage.

At the centre there stood only a piano. There was a pause, some coughing and whispering. Then Annalise emerged from the side of the stage. She was wearing a long silvery-white dress and her blond hair fell down her back in a smooth grain and shone in the moted lights as she walked towards the piano with that instantly recognisable gait of hers. She seemed small and exposed. The white keys were like bared teeth, and the audience had fallen strangely quiet. Annalise didn't cast a glance their way. The impression was of someone who had wandered into an empty room and discovered, quite by accident, this fine instrument. The silence lengthened as she sat there with her hands raised, until it began to fill with restless shiftings.

I remembered our Midsummer night, and that piano in the ballroom. The first chord she now played, which rippled out to fill this huge space like a premonition, seemed similar. It was strange and abrupt and wonderful. There was no tune here that a strolling guildsman could ever whistle. The notes seemed not so much to be finding a melody as seeking silence. All in all, though, it was a short piece, and there was a long pause at the end of it whilst the audience waited to see whether this was just another confusing beat of silence, and the applause was hesitant when it finally came. Annalise stood up and bowed. The curtains closed. Gaslamps were turned up across the auditorium. I made to get up, but Mister Snaith's doll-like hand settled on my shoulder.

'May as well settle here, my dear,' he said. 'It's only the intermission . . .'

I sat through the rest of the performance in a daze, although I'm sure the second half was at least as long and elaborate as the first. My buttocks ached. I was hungry again, and thirsty. The far balconies clung to the opposite wall like golden swallows' nests.

'That was so *very* fine,' Mister Snaith murmured when the last of the applause had died down. He mopped his tiny brow with a huge and handkerchief. 'Don't you think so?'

Mistress Summerton bowed her head slightly. She looked tired, diminished. 'All quite wonderful. Although I'm a stranger to these things—'

'I *know* how provincial life was in the West Country. And then in that ghastly place in the north. Or even World's End . . .' Mister Snaith gave a soft sigh. 'But give yourself another few decades and I'm sure you'll come to appreciate the full wonders of the capital's arts. They bring such relief, I promise . . .' In the brighter light, I could see that, as well as the rouge of his lips, there were also crumblings of face powder around Mister Snaith's eyes. His skin was ivory white, and seemed hairless and poreless.

I sat between them, caught in the middle of this exchange.

'And you, Robert? I gather you're from the north?'

'Yes,' I agreed. After all I'd heard today, I hesitated to name Bracebridge. But his lashless eyes were on me. Dulled though they were, they were filled behind their make-up with the empty hunger of tremendous age. The theatre below was emptying.

'I know that Mistress Summerton doesn't approve of such things, Master Robert,' he said, 'but I have a small

gathering of fellow seekers planned for later this evening,
and quite frankly, a guildsman such as I could do with an
escort. It's only a short walk, I promise.'

Had he really said *guildsman?* I could have been mis-
hearing almost everything Mister Snaith was saying. But I
was curious.

'I'm so grateful for your company,' Mister Snaith breathed.
'I have a nice little cabsman I can trust. But he's down with
the flu. There're *still* so many germs about this late in the
season, don't you find?'

He had pulled a fur-trimmed cloak around his shoulders
and was tapping a silver-topped ebony cane. It was raining
again, and I was carrying both his surprisingly large and
heavy carpetbag and his umbrella. He was perfectly dry,
but the edge of the water was dribbling down my neck.
Mistress Summerton had driven off in that car of hers towards Chelsea Bridge, but something of her presence remained. Whatever Mister Snaith was, I didn't doubt there
were reasons why she had introduced me. He smelled like
old wardrobes; of damp and mothballs and woodworm and
lavender. Was he really a changeling, or just someone who
had been born small and white and odd? My limbs ached,
my mouth was dry. The half-remembered scenes of the
Opera House, the dragons and nymphs and the flower-like
dancers and Annalise's music, all seemed to be swirling
around us in a ghost-pageant.

'And I couldn't have a better escort, could I? I know—
oh, don't deny it!—that so many people decry what you
marts do, but anyone who has a proper understanding of
the guilds will also appreciate that you are vital to their
functioning . . .'

'Thank you,' I growled. We had entered an area of finely
laid streets and pretty churches, and then the large, square
stone-encased houses and apartments of that most expensive part of central London known as Hyde which lies between the guildhalls of Wagstaffe Mall and Westminster
Great Park. Some of these houses here looked to be almost
as big as the Grand Opera House but were so stuffed with
windows as to appear, as the rain glittered and streamed, to

be made entirely of glass. Telegraphs dripped amid the
gables—a sure sign of urban wealth. Mister Snaith steered
me behind the front facade of one of the biggest buildings,
and around it towards a tradesman's doorway. He rang the
bell and waited, his breath whistling in and out. A steward's face was glimpsed.

'There're two of you—we most certainly weren't expecting a—'

'*This* is Master Borrows of the Guild of, ah, Explorers.
He's my assistant . . .'

I kept silent as we were led up concrete stairways and
along narrow and windowless corridors. Doors creaked open.
There were whispers, giggles. The glimpsed surprised faces
of sleepy maids. Then we reached a wider passageway
which dwindled into the lamplit haze of distance. The spaces
here were so large, our footsteps so muffled, that I had to
look down at my feet to check that we were still moving. The
steward gave a final disdainful sniff and stood to one side of
a double doorway.

'Hold this for me? Much obliged . . .' Mister Snaith
briefly handed me his toy ebony cane then flipped his cloak
off his shoulders and turned it around so that the lining
showed—a flashing silk of livid oranges and greens. Humming faintly, he then rummaged in the pockets of his jacket
for his handkerchief, consulted a tiny mirror, and began,
with quick, expert motions, to smear and change the make-
up which covered his face. 'Now, Master Robert, my
cane?' He fiddled with his red cravat to make it blossom.
He twiddled with his sleeves. '*Most* grateful . . .' He then
nodded to the steward that the doors could be opened, before, in a final flourish, he removed his toupee. The transformation was complete. When we entered the huge room,
dressed in his garish cloak, tiny, bald-headed, long-featured,
dark-eyed and porcelain-white, twirling the wand of his
cane, Mister Snaith was a changed miniature wizard from
some long-lost Age.

Gas mantles leapt and murmured, were caught in myr-
iad mirrors. Whole constellations of guildpins, necklaces,
brooches, buttons, eyeglasses, cigarette ends, beads and
eyeglasses surrounded us—and there was a smell much

like that which had filled the Opera House, which was of
hot and expensive and slightly damp humanity. I gave Mister Snaith his carpetbag, which he lifted as if it were
empty, and sat down beside the door on a slippery silk
chair. The fat red sun of a large cigar winked at me. What
light there was in the room was directed towards Mister
Snaith.

'Greetings to you all, my fellow seekers after truth and
enlightenment . . .' His slight voice carried over the rustles
and whispers. '*I* am Mister Snaith. Many of you will have
heard of me. Many of you will not . . .' As he spoke, he
rolled up his left sleeve to reveal a small left wrist, which
was apparently unblemished apart from a cross and C tattoo. 'Suffice to say that I was born in another place, in another Age, and that my parents saw what I was and
abandoned me in their terror to the depths of the forest
which then covered all of this realm. I should have died in
the savage snows, but my first memory . . .' He paused, and
winced pain. 'Is of the face of a wolf. Yes, ladies, gentle-
men—' He paused again. 'I was reared by *canis lupus,* the
grey wolf, in the dark depths of a forest, and on milk and
blood and savagery. You only see me here now today because I was rescued by hunters, and brought to a church,
and shown the ways of the guilds and of our blessed Lord.'
He made the sign of the cross. 'Yet beyond that—beyond
that, there always . . .' He pressed his temples. There was
another pause. 'Lie wonders which to human eyes are un-
seeing. There are unanswerable questions beyond all the
wisdom of the guilds . . .' There was much more of this.
Phrases which seemed to make sense as you heard them,
then dissolved as quickly as reflections in the rain.

'Behold!'

Now, Mister Snaith's whole body was quivering as he
spread the sleeves of his green cloak. It seemed from
where I was sitting that he had actually started to rise from
the floor. I peered around the flickering edges of his cloak
and his carpetbag, trying to see his feet. There were gasps
from the audience. All the priest's warnings and tales must
have come back to them: that changelings have lost their
souls, that there is nothing in their hearts, or their insides.

Trails of mist then started to weep in smoky droplets from the sleeves of Mister Snaith's suit. The stuff was greenish-tinged, subtly glowing. It turned and roiled. Now, agitated gasps and murmurs started to rise from the audience. Furniture creaked. A woman tittered. But the fog still writhed, and Mister Snaith and his carpetbag were almost extinguished within it; he was a fly embedded in green amber. There was a long pause, interrupted briefly by the unmistakable splatter of someone being sick.

'I have a question.' A young man spoke from near the front. 'I have to sit my pre-semester exams in the lesser quadrant of mysteries of the Great Guild of Ironmasters this term. Quite honestly I haven't done a single spot of revision . . . And I was wondering what the questions might be.' Pause. 'Or the answers . . .'

Within the green mist, his head uptilted, Mister Snaith gave a reply, but the circuitous phrases were reminiscent of the words he had uttered earlier; all smoke and camouflage without any discernible substance. It was plain that the examiners of the Ironmasters' Guild had little to fear from Mister Snaith. He was better at answering the more general questions which followed; those about the future, and all the petty things to do with wealth and health and marriage which, it seemed, obsessed the rich at least as much as the poor. He was better, also, at advising of the state of deceased relatives, although it seemed to me that such knowledge was theologically dubious.

Eventually, the questions petered out, and Mister Snaith, amid odd thumpings and whirrings, unravelled and faded into wafts of smoke and surprisingly bandage-like appurtenances. There were smatters of applause as the lights were turned up. Doors were opened. People drifted out. As he sat down on a chair with his carpetbag plonked well beneath it, the remaining guests seemed to want to prod and squeeze him, but he took it in good heart. There were shrieks of glee when, after much bashful head-shaking, he folded back the sleeve of his shirt to show again his left wrist. But I was suspicious of that tattoo; the thickly drawn ink could have been used to disguise anything which was beneath.

I sat drained and ignored, surrounded by dozens of the tall mirrors. In my best trousers. In my dark blue jacket. In the worn-down heels of my shoes. As if such things mattered, but here—there was no mistaking it—they did. I looked almost as out of place as Mister Snaith. I noticed that I had succeeded in tearing the back of my jacket, probably on Mistress Summerton's webs of tin cans. Somehow, I managed to look both flashy and scruffy. Everything the other men here wore was black and white—and the women, the women . . .

'Hello, Master Robert Borrows . . .' One of them came towards me from the many angles of several mirrors. She had dark hair, bowed lips, arched and humorous eyebrows. 'You've barely changed. But you don't even remember me, do you?'

There were diamonds at her neck and ears. Her eyes, too, had a diamonded, feverish glint. Yes, of course I remembered. How could I ever forget? Annalise's friend, from that Midsummer night when we'd danced across the pier. Grandmistress Sadie Passington.

'Of course I do, Sadie. You haven't changed either.'

'What a sweet thing to say.' In her dress and manner, in her scent and the sound of her voice, Sadie was still almost beautiful, and certainly pretty, but there was a hint of tension around her eyes, and at the corners of her mouth. Not quite lines, exactly—she was still too young—but a sense of the flesh hardening.

She waited for a servant to find a chair on which she could perch.

'You know,' she said as she settled herself, 'I still remember that season. It was one of the best. *The* best, probably, seeing as we all went our separate ways a bit afterwards. You especially. You were hardly there, but you seemed to be such a part of it . . .' Her eyes travelled up and down me with a frankness I'd rarely seen in a woman, least of all one who claimed to be a guildmistress. 'You fitted in so well.'

'I probably misled you a little about who I was . . .'

She gave a shrug, showing off her fine bosom. 'I don't think you ever really said that much about who and what you were, Robbie. You just tagged along with Anna Winters.'

The name hung between us. Our gaze met, but it was unfocused.

'Did you see her this evening?' I asked. 'Were you at the Grand Opera House?'

'Who wasn't? I'm not sure what people made of that tune of hers, though . . .'

'I liked it.'

'Well, so did I . . .'

We talked for a while longer as the room emptied. Sadie had also studied at the Academy of the Guild of Gifts after leaving St Jude's, although she made light of it. Such things as work were, for her, not to be taken seriously.

'And what about you, Master Robert? What are you doing?'

'I'm . . . involved in publishing. We have a radical newspaper.'

'Publishing a newspaper!' She clapped her hands. 'How thrilling! And you must move in the most interesting circles, to bump into, ah—Mister Snaith here.'

'As a matter of fact, I only met him today.'

But Sadie studied me, her eyes glittering. 'But what a *life* you must lead.' Apart from a few servants and Mister Snaith, she and I were the only other people left in the room. 'Now, where *is* it!' Sadie began to ruffle inside her bead purse. 'There's this big do next termend. Some saint's day or other, although of course it's all in aid of charity . . .' She paused and looked up at me. 'Do you know Saltfleetby? It's down from Folkestone . . .' A card appeared between Sadie's coral-painted fingertips. 'Here we are. All the information you'll ever need. And I *very* much want you to come. Think of it as a personal invitation. And as a favour to me, even if you *are* a radical and think I'm shallow and stupid and fey.' Sadie gave me another of her direct, appraising, looks. 'I want you to promise.'

The paper was vellum, thick as a bedsheet. The last card I'd taken from anyone which had looked remotely like this had been from Grandmaster Harrat.

The Pleasure of Your Company
is Requested
Walcote House
Marine Drive
Saltfleetby
April 24th–25th 99
RSVP

'So you will come, won't you?
'Will Anna Winters be there?
'Of course she will.'

III

Clutching my cardboard suitcase, I dodged across the main road outside Saltfleetby station. The trams here were odd devices, open-sided and with striped blue and red awnings. They posted their destinations in chalk, and chuffed and rattled on dead rails. Even the carts and drays looked different here, and the tropic palms I'd seen on postcards in London pawnshops flapped like mad umbrellas in the wind. I stumbled past flowerbeds and white shelters, down steps where the path blazed and my feet slid and sank as if in a dream. And there it was. Blue over green over grey over blue. For the first time in my life. The open sea.

I drank a pot of tea in a café along the seafront, and studied today's *Guild Times*. At long last, a major strike had been reported in its pages, albeit with gross inaccuracy. It had been over the introduction of a cut in pay for the steamasters who maintained the engine houses which drove London's trams. For a whole three days, the tram-tracks had stood silent and the song of London had changed. The strike had been broken by the expedient of offering the steamasters a small rise on their old wages if they went back to work for longer hours, and by firing and expelling those who didn't. As always, divide and rule. Once again, the trams were running back in London, but those three days had been a glimpse of something better and I almost regretted leaving London, if only for a couple of days.

But what time to arrive at Walcote House? And how to get there? The café waitress gave me vague directions and I headed west along the shining sand, past the squat live-iron pier and the families with their hired deckchairs and windbreaks. The men, barefoot, their cheeks holiday-unshaven, struggled with their newspapers. The children paddled in the foam. The beach grew quieter as I walked on and the coastline rose in cliffs of wedding-cake white. The morning sun turned hotter. Here, where the tide mirrored the towers of the increasingly extraordinary dwellings which peered over the cliff face, there were no whelk vendors or donkey droppings. The sand was white. The sky was blazing. Sweating, squinting, I climbed the steps to Marine Drive. The sea below seemed lost and distant. The houses vanished behind their walls. Footsore, I continued walking. Walcote House—I'd pictured it on the seafront, tall and wide; an elegant boarding house. But the trams didn't run this far out from Saltfleetby and the passage of each private carriage was a separate event, signalled by a lacquered flash and the slow appearance of darkened windows.

Summer really had arrived at last. It was hot up here, and noonday quiet. Looking back along the shimmering road, I saw the glint of another carriage. It gained on me with slow ease, then drew to a halt just ahead at the roadside. The creatures which pulled it were too fine to be called merely horses. Their white coats were the same shade as the sand and seafoam. Their breathing made an edgy whistling, punctuated by snorts and the creak of harnesses as they rolled their ruby eyes. A liveried carriage-man clicked his tongue and ran his gloved hand across their flanks, then, nodding in reply to a voice which came from inside the carriage, opened its door for me.

'Well, Master Robert,' a female voice came from inside. 'Aren't you getting in?'

After the brilliance of the day, all I could see at first, shining out like a porcelain mask dropped into the depths of a well, was Grandmistress Sarah Passington's face. I sat down opposite her, as, with a queasy motion, the carriage rolled on.

'You really should have told me. I could have got you a lift . . . You didn't come on that *train,* did you? Stuffed with malodorous day-trippers?' Everything that I had done to get to Saltfleetby surprised her. 'And what are you coming *as* for tomorrow's ball? What secrets have you got tucked in that—that case of yours . . . ?'

The carriage interior was large enough to accommodate six people but Sadie's dress took up more than half. It was blue-grey, touched with green. There was lace at the hem and around the dark scoop of her bosom. It shimmered and rustled with the rocking of the carriage.

'Ever been to Saltfleetby before?'

'I've never even been to the seaside.'

'The sea*side*! Robbie, you're *such* an innocent. I bet I've done every single thing you've never done. And that you've done every thing I haven't.'

'We both live, eat, breathe . . .'

She smiled. 'Well, we'll have to see about that, won't we?'

The angle of the sun changed. We were passing through gardens, then beside a lake. Beams of sunlight moved across the leather. One caught on Sadie's sleeve, then the velvet choker which surrounded her neck, which had the same sheen as the pelts of the fine horses.

'I *so* envy you, coming here to Walcote for the first time . . .'

The place which came into view certainly wasn't a house. In fact, it was so large that there was an odd, extended impression as the carriage clopped and rocked towards it that we were getting no closer. Walcote House was white, with fluted pillars, and extended two arms like a giant marble crab to embrace a fountain considerably bigger than London's Grand Opera House which frothed and sparkled at the centre of the oval drive.

'Here we are,' trilled Sadie. 'Home!'

I lost track of her as her luggage, trunks which had the polish and substance of coffins, was lifted from the carriage and borne up the steps. Not that it mattered. The guildsmen and women who served here were used to receiving guests. *This way, Master* . . . Light though it was, my case was carried for me, and I was asked twice if I had any others. *And do mind the step* . . . I was ushered across a huge hall and up stairways and along corridors. There were flowers everywhere, giant blooms in vases and growing in pots and billowing across the walls in plaster and tapestry. There were refreshments on trays. Today truly was the start of something grand at Walcote House.

I was left in a sunlit room filled with the scent of new-laundered towels and sheets; my own personal suite. Sipping the fizzy wine which I discovered on my dresser, I prepared myself a bath. Easing myself into the scented water, I could feel years dissolving as easily as the fragrant salts which fizzed around my flesh. I was older, it was true. There was a dark flat chevron of hair now on my chest, and a white scar on my left arm where I had been slashed in a territorial brawl with the sellers of the *Socialist Nation*. But as I gazed at the stained-glass diamonds which poured through the steam from the window, I was back in that London hotel, with Sadie and with Annalise, preparing for the dancing which would soon begin on the pier . . .

Wrapped in towels, I opened windows to let out the steam. I was at the opposite side of Walcote House to the frontage, and several stories up. The gardens fanned in shaded avenues of metallic-shaded perilinden trees along which many figures were strolling. I flopped my case onto my four-poster bed. It looked far smaller and cheaper now than when I had bought it at a hardware shop. My father had had such a thing, I remembered now, which he kept for his rare trips to the Toolmakers' Academy in York. The scent of London inside it hung in the air for a moment until it was threaded away by coloured breezes. I'd packed a new jacket, plain black after my experience of the shiftend before, along with my two best pairs of trousers, three shirts, several collars of various styles and a re-heeled pair of shoes. Now, it didn't seem like much. On that near and distant Midsummer, Annalise had found me fresh clothes of the finest styling. Had I been expecting that, too, just as I was expecting her?

Dressed in my best trousers and new jacket, I set out to explore Walcote House. This clearly wasn't a hotel. Nothing was properly marked or numbered, although there were clues I began to notice. Every segment of corridor had its own colour scheme. Pale blue, green, many shades of red and pink. Everything matched. Even the flowers and the fruit laid in bowls. But the main public rooms, the vast hall through which I had entered, even my bedroom, remained elusive. I was lost in that particularly infuriating way which involves passing the same places time and again. There was a painting of a classical-seeming landscape which I grew to hate. Back in the Easterlies, I'd have easily re-found my way from glimpsed spires, the different stenches and changing customs of the street . . .

Finally, when I was certain that I was heading in a completely pointless direction, I found myself walking along a carpet which was so thick as to retain the footprints of someone with the same stride and shoe-size as me who had passed lately. I made a fresh impression beside them; it was the same. Following my footprints like a child through snow, I came to a door which looked promisingly like mine. I was about try it when Sadie came bustling around the turn in the corridor bearing an expression which changed a little too rapidly when she saw me.

'Master *Robert!* I'm glad they've found you a nice room.' Her hair was pinned up in silver combs. Her face was differently made.

'I think this room is mine. But how do you tell?'

She chuckled. 'Oh, I'm sure it is. Every door on this wing is made from the wood of a different tree. It used to be a passion of one of the past greatgrandmasters.' She laid her hand on the swirling surface, more like marble than grain. 'I think this one grows in Thule.' Then she said something, a sound like which, odd though it was from her lips, I recognised as a simple guildsman's chant. Although she hadn't touched it, the brass handle turned, the door swung open.

'*You* did that?'

'I'm absolutely full of useless knowledge.' Sadie was ahead of me into my room. 'It's the *useful* stuff you'll have

to go elsewhere for.' From a pocket near her waist she produced a steel case and a lighter. She wafted the smoke towards the windows like someone shooing birds. 'I've been
dying for a fag. It's something Daddy's dead against. Says
it's unladylike and ugly . . .'

She offered me one. Smiling it away, closing my cardboard case and moving it from sight, I sat down on the
edge of my bed and studied Sadie as she bustled around the
room. I wondered if they really always lived like this—
these rich, high-guilded people; clouded in restless smoke,
sunlight, mystery. This place, I had to remind myself,
was the very heart of all that was wrong with England.
This strawberry wallpaper, that marquetry cabinet. All useless extravagance, laboured over by the masses.

'So—who exactly owns this place?'

'*Owns?*' She caught her cigarette in the corner of her
mouth as she turned to look at me and the powder around
her eyes flaked in a sudden harshness of the light. After all,
I thought, we are simply human. And there was something
about Grandmistress Sarah Passington, some knowledge
and sadness, which I didn't understand. Surely, I thought,
these people owed it to the millions they exploited to at
least be happy. She ground out her cigarette in the pot-
pourri. 'I've never really thought of people actually *owning*
Walcote.' She waved away the smoke and thought for a
moment, her head bowed. 'There *has* to be *someone,*
doesn't there? And I suppose you might say that that someone is Daddy, seeing as Walcote is entailed through the
Guild of Telegraphers.'

'Doesn't that mean that your father's—'

'—he's the greatgrandmaster.' Sadie flashed another of
those looks of hers; full of meanings and contradictions.
'He's in charge of the entire guild. Or thinks he is.'

Silence fell between us.

'We used to have marvellous games of hide-and-seek
here,' Sadie said eventually. 'Although there's a sad story
of a lad a generation or so ago. They only found him years
later, mummified like an old apple in some cupboard.
That's servants for you . . . But everyone's so *changed* now.
The children I was with, they're all grown up.'

'Does Anna Winters come here much?'

'Not back in the hide-and-seek days. Although, later . . .' A puzzled look crossed Sadie's face. 'I can almost see her wandering these corridors in tinkly old sandals.' She shook her head. 'But Anna was probably never like that. Somebody so poised and elegant. Do tell me, Robbie. What was she *really* like back then?'

'I think we notice things differently when we're children.'

'Hmmm. And that old house by the waterfall. Her poor dead parents. That dreadful aunt.' Sadie picked up a silver-backed hairbrush which lay on the gleaming dressing table. 'I remember the first day when Anna came to school at St Jude's as if out of nowhere. There's always one in every year. Someone with whom you know you can't possibly compete. No matter what you wear, no matter what you do or who you are, there's always . . . Anna. And she took me as her friend. That was the marvellous thing. Anna chose me as her friend even though I'm clumsy, wealthy Sadie Passington, halfway good at many things but never particularly good at any of them, trailing this whole bloody guild and all these houses around behind me like a huge lead weight . . . Every night, she let me brush her hair.' Still carrying the silver-backed brush, Sadie went to the window. 'When Anna's around, everything's always brighter, darker, different . . . Oh, *you* must have your stories about her too, Robbie . . . *Do* have a cigarette . . .'

I took one from her case. It tasted like the feathers of some perfumed bird. And I did have my stories; the memories of Anna Winters were waiting as if they had always been there. The mint smell of decay and bluebells in the sloping woods of that old aunt's garden. Me, and Anna Winters. Anna Winters, and me. The two of us exploring the wet-leafed valley and the game we played of racing sticks under a bridge, urging them on until the gong called us back for lunch in that sere house beside the waterfall . . .

Sadie sat down on the bed beside me, rocking its springs. This, I thought, as Sadie leaned against me, the light from her necklace shuddering sparks with each heartbeat, is a better vision of the past than the truth of Redhouse and

Bracebridge and that dreadful accident. I decided Mistress Summerton was right; I'd judged Anna too harshly.

Sadie showed me Walcote House. From the east wing, through state rooms far bigger than the inside of Great Aldgate Station to narrow stairways which contained the inner workings of this great palace, which was at least as complex as the largest factory. Then a balcony which looked down into the steaming crater of the main kitchens. Whole farms serviced Walcote House, set downwind at the edges of the estate, hidden from view by hills which had been raised for that purpose. There was even an underground system of rails. There were telegraphs and tunnels, and honeycomb ducts to provide a clean flow of whatever temperature of air the climate outside was failing to provide. And yet all the while, as she showed me this and this and *this,* Sadie kept pressing me for stories of my life. It made an odd counterpoint.

'So. What does it mean, to be a radical? Would you have me fire Lessermaster Johnson over there who picks up fallen petals in the orangery, just because he's old now and doesn't do anything productive?'

'Real production means making something that people need, Sadie.'

'And isn't any of this?'

It was a genuine problem—what to do with guildspeople such as the thousands who serviced Walcote House, although I'd never heard it discussed at any of the People's Alliance meeting. They would certainly need to be retrained, re-educated. And this whole place, too, would have to be stripped, emptied; with its big rooms and huge sleeping capacity, it might make a useful citizen's academy. All these ornaments and paintings could be shipped to a museum. But it seemed a harsh truth to tell Sadie, and I guessed that she knew far more than her cleverly misguided questions revealed. Of all the many things that she was, Grandmistress Sadie Passington most certainly wasn't stupid.

'And don't you have lots of secret signs and codes just like the guilds, you revolutionaries?'

'We're nothing like the guilds, Sadie. That's the whole point.'

We were standing in a plush and windowless corridor. It was a dead end, and the willow-green walls looked almost conspicuously ordinary.

'But *we* could exchange secrets, Master Robert. How about that?'

I opened my mouth to assure her that true knowledge was priceless, then closed it again as Sadie started loosening the pearls which held the low frontage of her dress together. Disappointingly, she ceased unbuttoning when only the upper curves of her breasts were revealed. She drew out the rest of the necklace I'd been admiring earlier. The strung jewels were fat as teardrops, dark-hearted and glinting.

'Daddy has given me one for every year I've lived. I wish there were fewer of them. And I'm due another one— oh, much too soon . . .'

'What are they?'

'Have you heard of whisperjewels—they're a bit like touching a haft, only more portable and useful. You saw what I did with your door. That's quite simple really, just another way of opening the thing without all the faff of having to turn the handle. But take *this* and have a try . . .' The whisperjewel felt warm as a hen's egg as Sadie clasped my hand around it. I still had no real idea what the thing was, other than that it was something which probably involved a lot of money and aether, but as my fingers closed, I heard something chime in my head.

'What was that?'

She chuckled. 'The whisperjewel's telling you its secret. Now . . .' Sadie bustled me over to the blank green wall which blocked the end of the corridor. 'You have to chant that spell yourself.'

I closed my hand around the whisperjewel again. The sound I heard would have been impossible to transcribe using the ordinary letters of the alphabet. Sadie laughed out loud when, with a sound that was a cross between a starving chick and a broken hinge, I attempted to imitate it.

'No. It's more like this . . .'

She laid her hand on the green wall beside which we were standing, and made a clicking, musical sound. When she had finished, I realised that the previously featureless wall beside us had changed, and that a door, which looked as solid and well made as any other, had appeared in it. Sadie gave a little bow, her dress still askew, and the door swung open to reveal an upwards-spiralling staircase.

'This leads to the Turning Tower,' she explained as we began to ascend it.

This circular turret was the highest point of Walcote House. From its parapet we could look down on all the rooftops' leaded complexities and out across the greened and blued landscapes of its grounds. So much land, so much sky and sea, so much air . . . Heights never normally bothered me, but this one was dizzying. Doves circled the rooftops, looking like scraps of Walcote House's white stonework come to life. I felt as if I could walk across the sun's rays which hung around the Turning Tower. In the centre of the tower, gleaming in the sunlight, stood a golden haft.

'Does the tower turn, then?' I asked.

'What a lovely idea! No, no. Not in any physical sense anyway.'

I walked closer to the haft. I'd seen such objects, through which guildsmen of various kinds communed with their charges, in my wanderings around the Easterlies, although all of them had been smaller than this, and none had quite this gleam, this power, this polish. It writhed upwards like a solid flame from the brass—or perhaps gold— collar of its base and reared, at its triple-horned peak, far above my height like a black rent in the summer sky.

'What does it do?'

Sadie shrugged. 'It's a telegrapher's haft. Just like all the ones you see in the back room of every telegraph office. Or almost. They come in different levels of power and access, and this one's a prime, like the one you'll find at the very top of the Dockland Exchange in London, and in a few other special places.'

I walked around the object. It both shone in the sunlight and seemed to absorb it. It cast no shadow.

'It's mainly for show,' Sadie said. 'Hardly anyone's allowed up here.'

I took a step closer. The landscape seemed to recede. The air whispered around me. Even on this Halfshiftday afternoon, England's telegraphs were busy. I could feel them all now, the endless chorus of orders and bills of lading and invoices and proclamations of birth and death and bankruptcy, humming along the wires from town to town.

'But I wouldn't touch it,' Sadie said sharply. My hand fell away. 'Daddy's made me do that once or twice just at the lesser haft of some minor local exchange I've had to visit. Even those ones always make me feel sick and giddy.'

I stepped back. The air stilled. The sunlight of the Turning Tower settled once more around me.

'And I suppose we should get a move on before someone notices us up here. The afternoon's almost gone and I'll have to get changed before dinner.'

'You look fine.'

She flounced down from the Turning Tower. 'There's so much more onus on us girls to put on a show. But the dinner tonight's no big thing. You could go straight down as you are and no one will mind. There's barely a hundred attending . . .' The door behind us closed, and vanished. 'No, *you* go that way. Straight down the stairs, then ahead. The servants will direct you. You can't miss it . . .'

A glint of silk, and Sadie had already disappeared down the corridor. Rubbing my temples, feeling the beginnings of a headache, I plodded in the direction she had indicated. Straight down and ahead. But there seemed to be many landings in this part of Walcote House. The statues clustered around me. I was lost. Then I saw someone striding along the white-pillared corridor. He swung his arms. His shoes clipped purposefully. I waited for him.

'You don't seem quite at home . . . ?' His hair was a little too black for someone of his age, and cut a little longer than was the custom. But he was tall and possessed the sort of fine features that don't easily fade.

'I was trying to find my dinner . . .'

That hadn't come out quite the way I'd intended—but

the black-haired guildsman smiled his understanding. Laying a hand on my shoulder, he steered me left a few paces, then pointed me ahead. I was soon in Walcote House's huge but elusive main hallway, following the guests who were heading into one of the state rooms. Glasses chimed. People stood framed by tasselled mirrors as they threw back their heads in laughter or waved to friends. At the furthest end of the room, which was even bigger than the entrance hall, open doors gave glimpses through the twilight of a structure which I might have described as a tent, were it not for its size and grandeur. I was ravenously hungry, but the food at this strange standing-up dinner was oddly small: wafery discs topped with single shrimps; solitary lumps of mouldy-looking cheese. Still, I grabbed what was going from the passing silver trays. Realising I was thirsty too, I downed several glasses of the same light and fizzy wine which I'd drunk a bottle of in my bedroom, until, hearing the sound of a piano in a far corner, I went in search of it. Sadie had been right about the need to change her dress. Elaborate though it was, it scarcely compared with these visions, which reminded me of meringues. I was still feeling hungry—and thirsty. I'd have got better food than these scraps at any chophouse in the Easterlies—and good beer, too, although I was getting a taste for this fizzy stuff.

The piano player turned out to be a youngish man with heavy-lidded eyes and thinning blond hair which fell in a lock across his forehead. The piano was long and high—like a wooden yacht, with its uptilted sail—but the sounds he produced from it were tentative. Nevertheless, an admiring group had gathered around him to listen, and I, with little idea of what else I was supposed to do, did the same. The men nodded thoughtfully. The women fluttered their fans. It was as if they and the music were infused with a subtle beat which I, standing here beside them, stretched and reflected in the piano's polished outlines, couldn't quite catch. And they fitted here, these people. Into their bodies, their faces, their clothes. I took another passing glass and swigged it. Suppressing a burp, I noticed that a cluster of young men had turned towards me.

One of them offered me a hand, and said a name I didn't quite catch. Another followed in his wake. I caught the flash of impossibly white teeth. Then another. Their flesh was as full and soft as Sadie's. *Upperhighergreatandseniorgrandmasterofthisandthisandthis* . . . Even as I smiled and nodded back at them, their identities remained a blur.

'*D'youhaveacard?*'

'What?'

A slower smile. 'Do you have a card?'

I'd made sure to transfer the invitation Sadie had given me to this jacket—just in case someone should ask to see it. 'I've got it somewhere . . .' I fished around in my pockets. 'Here it is.' The man took and inspected it, his face a studied blank. He passed it on to a friend. Someone nearby made a choking sound. The music—little more than a child's one-handed plinking, really—continued. They were all still smiling. But whatever card it was I was supposed to have, it was plain that I didn't have it. My invitation was flicked by a manicured thumbnail, then handed back to me. 'Useful, I'm sure. Tells you where you are for a start, doesn't it?' *Tellsyouwhereyouareforastart, doesn'tit?* It took me a moment to decipher the slurring words. The suppressed guffaws of his companions rose, subsided.

'And from whom did you get this?' another asked. 'Your ticket to the show?'

Back in the Easterlies, you didn't have to understand a joke to thump someone for it. But that wasn't an option here. 'I was invited by Sadie Passington,' I said. I'd expected more hilarity, but at least Sadie's name gave them pause for a moment. 'I was with her this afternoon,' I continued. 'She showed me—'

OneofSadiesdiscoveries. The phrase was whispered again. I paused, losing whatever I'd been trying to say. *OneofSadiesdiscoveries.* This was like some new guild, some new language. And the smiles were knowing, insidious. The music, I noticed, had stopped now. I balled my fist around my empty glass. My skin tingled.

I flinched as a hand settled on my shoulder.

'Tell you what—Master Robert, isn't it? Trifle hot in here, don't you think?' The heavy-lidded face of the man who had previously been playing the piano leaned close to me in a breath of hair oil. 'I could show you some of the grounds. Atmosphere's a *lot* less stuffy . . .' I heard a final departing whisper, a hiss of syllables, then we were walking out onto the terrace under the evening sky.

'Sorry about that.' The man sat down on a lichened wall beside a tumble of roses. Long, low sunlight glinted through his thinning hair. 'Known them for years. They're like—what would you describe it as? When something new and interesting suddenly appears?'

'Flies around a heap of shit?'

He chuckled once, then louder. 'I'll have to remember that! Me, I'm just a journeyman here—as you are, I'd guess. I'll play for my supper, and I'll be grateful for it when it comes.'

'Haven't we had supper already?'

'Oh no.' He nodded towards the huge tent which could have housed several circuses. 'Supper's over there. That was just *hors-d'oeuvres*. But you should call it dinner, really, rather than supper, Robert.'

'Thanks. I'll try to remember. I—ah . . .'

He smiled. 'Haven't told you who I am, have I? You'll think I'm as ignorant as the rest of them.' He offered me a soft hand to shake. 'Highermaster George Swalecliffe. I'm in the Guild of Architects, nominally at least, not that I ever get to build anything. So I have to bide my time with these people and play the piano when I'd much rather be out supervising foundations. What did you think of it, by the way? My little composition?' Finally, he let go.

'You mean that noise on the piano?'

His blue-grey eyes had brightened. Now they subsided again.

'I wouldn't take too much notice of what I think, highermaster,' I said. 'I really don't belong here.'

'Oh, just call me George. And you should never dismiss your own opinions, Robert. They're always important. Please.' He patted the stone wall. 'Sit by me. You must be the revolutionary Sadie's been telling us so much about. Even if I hadn't known who you were, I've been looking forward to meeting you—if you see what I mean. We've got so much in common. After all . . .' He clicked his fingers to draw over a waiter bearing more wine glasses. 'We're both socialists.'

I drank my wine, and stared into its bubbles. Not for the first time in Walcote House, I was at a loss for words. 'Do you know Sadie well?'

'Everybody knows Sadie. As to how *well*—you should be warned that sweet Sadie does have a habit of bringing people to Walcote and—ah—rather dumping them. She doesn't mean it intentionally. She's brimming with good will. But then something else comes along, and she gets distracted . . .'

'I think I know what you mean.'

Highermaster George smiled. He nodded towards the great building which rose behind us in white piles of stone columns and buttresses like a beautiful skeleton, the final pinnacle of the tower raising its bony finger into the dusk. 'Halls and secret passageways, eh? They say this palace uses up more aether than all London on a busy Oneshift-day. And all of it wasted for party tricks on the few thousand of us who draw our money and power from the great guilds—or the lack of both, in my case. Such a waste. I'd love the day to come when Sadie shows round crowds of shopgirls and crossing sweepers, and offers them souvenirs afterwards. There could be a teashop where that gazebo is over there. They could play football on the lawns, use statues as goalposts . . . Sleep in the staterooms for a penny a go. Still, we socialists can have our dreams . . .'

Other guests were drifting down the tiered steps onto the lawns. I could hear the bonging of a gong, but there was no sense of hurry. Everywhere, amid the evening bird-song, the whisper of the trees and the distant splash of the fountains, I could hear the same long sibilant voices, incanting that smiling, whispered song of the single Great Guild of the Wealthy. Highermaster George pointed out Sadie's mother. She was a small creature, her wizened face almost as painted-on as Mister Snaith's. And here were a couple in late middle age. Small and ordinary though they were, there was something about them which kept my eye. The man had shifty, rat-like features, and the woman on his arm could almost have been his fatter twin. Our gaze met, and there was a brief *something* before he looked away.

'Who's that over there?'

'Oh—they're the Bowdly-Smarts . . .' Highermaster George clicked his tongue. 'But they're pretty odious, believe me. New money always is. Ah! Now here's someone . . .'

There was a general stirring, a turning of heads like flowers lifting to the sun. Yet the man who stepped out barely seemed to notice their regard. He was wearing the same plain but well cut suit he'd had on earlier when he'd shown me the way. It was a fine piece of tailoring, but no finer than many of the others, and set off by nothing more than a red tie and a plain unruffled shirt. His too-black hair hung loose to his collar, and parted and fell in a heavy fringe across his broad brow. The effect was casual. Almost as if he didn't care about his looks—almost, but not quite.

'*That's* the greatgrandmaster?'

'Of course.'

A sea of people formed and parted about him as he crossed the patio. The men touched their flies, their guild-pins. The women's fans and bosoms fluttered. And here in his wake was his daughter, Grandmistress Sadie Passington, who looked marvellous in a cream dress. Our eyes caught for a moment. She smiled mischievously.

'That's our signal as well.' Highermaster George got up.

I stood up beside him. But something held me back as the guests dwindled along the terraces.

'What is it, old chap?'

As if in a shared thought, we both turned towards the house, which was now a ship of light, hanging over the transparent greys of the terraces and gardens. The gong had ceased. The birds were no longer singing. Anna Winters stepped alone through the open doors and into the twilight.

'Oh, Anna! Wait . . .'

She paused and turned at the sound of Highermaster George's voice.

'You're so late . . .' He took a breath as he rushed over. 'You've almost missed everything.'

'Oh, I don't think so,' she murmured. She gazed for a long time at Highermaster George before she glanced at me.

'I seem to have lost all my manners this evening, Anna. This is Master Robert, ah—it *is* Borrows, isn't it? I don't think you mentioned your guild. But we've been having a most interesting talk.'

'We've met before.'

'You *have?* Well that's—'

Annalise turned to face me. The lights of the Walcote House were behind her. Her features were in shadow and her hair was like the light itself.

'What are you doing here, Robert?'

Her voice was soft, gently enquiring. Yet her anger was like a force against my chest. And visiting Missy at World's End—and what were you doing *there* also, Robert? *Why can't you leave my life alone?*

There was a long pause. Slowly, I became conscious that Highermaster George was still standing between us. He cleared his throat.

'Well . . .' He offered her the crook of his elbow. 'If you'll perhaps allow me to lead the way?'

I followed them across the lawns to the marquee. Inside, in the trapped heat, there were more drinks and trays and servants. *And could Sir perhaps indicate . . . ? Or would Sir prefer . . . ?* This particular *Sir* was at a complete loss, but Highermaster George untangled himself from Anna to help me find a place, and then sat by me under the lamplit grandeur. Anna Winters was several tables away.

Anthony Passington, Greatgrandmaster Exultant of the Great Guild of Telegraphers, arrived to applause at the raised top table where Sadie and her mother, the painted prune, were already seated. Then everyone stood, and Canon Vilbert intoned a prayer, which, like some tedious guild anthem, seemed just about to round itself to conclusion when it gained fresh wind. After all, there was so much you had to thank God for if you lived like this. For a long time, I kept my head bowed and my hands pressed together. Then I risked raising my eyes and saw that everyone else was staring into the upper reaches of the marquee.

It was an interesting revelation to me that the people of the
Great Guild of Wealth didn't lower their eyes but looked
straight up at God when they prayed to him. After all, they
were almost equals.

Anna Winters, what little I could see of her across two
tables and through the massive foliage of the flower display
in front of me, was standing like the rest. Further down
my long table were the Bowdly-Smarts. George was right.
They did seem odious and ugly. The man had a rat's pointed
face. He and his florid wife seemed wrong inside their
clothes, whilst everyone else here fitted everything as
tightly as a bud . . . The canon's voice ascended to another
convulsion of adjectives, paused, and then droned on again.
Anna, I saw, peering around a huge centrepiece of flowers
to get a clearer view of her, was still gazing up into the air.
If I tilted my neck and squinted slightly, her face became
one of the flowers in the arrangement, although more perfect. Anna Winters—Annalise—as a flower. Something I
could grasp, pluck, control. But everything about her, even
her face, her pale simple beauty laid amid the blurring
petals—seemed withdrawn from me. The air shimmered
for a moment. She was barely there. A space in my eyes.

My head fizzed with wine and hope. That cursed vase of
flowers. I don't know if I let out a small groan, but I sensed
with the final *amen* that Highermaster George and several
of the other surrounding guests had glanced towards me.
People were sitting down now. Servants were presenting
the first course to the diners at the top table. I remained
standing a moment longer in the hope that I might get a
clearer sight of Anna. But the flowers were still obstructing
me. Casually, I leaned forward to brush a fern out of the
way. But as my arm reached across the table I saw that my
fingers had become like smoke, were near-invisible. I let
out a yelp and the vase of flowers, although I was sure that
I hadn't yet touched it, exploded in a spray of glass and
stalks. Then I was sinking, or the table was rising, water
was pattering everywhere, and the white cloth was sliding
back.

Faces clustered as I lay surrounded by cutlery on the
floor, but only Highermaster George registered any concern

about my well-being. The rest of them, as I swayed upwards protesting that I hadn't even touched the vase whilst the table was mopped and cleaned and rearranged by servants, regarded me with vivid distaste. A new and even larger arrangement of flowers was then plonked on the table before me, even more effectively obscuring my view of Anna. *One-ofSadiesdiscoveries*. The whisper drifted with the clink of serving tongs. There were nods and smiles. The flowers pulsed like faces; the faces were like flowers, like Mistress Summerton's hothouse blooms—Missy, whom I should never have visited. One of Sadie's discoveries. Of course. That was me.

So began one of the worst nights of my life. Social embarrassment may seem as nothing compared to mortal grief, the dull terrors of poverty, the agonies of physical pain. But being laughed at, being made to seem foolish— that is something which is unbearable even for the dogs on the street. The first course consisted of the eggs of quails, which I, distracted in my sopping clothes, attempted to scoop the meat from with the end of one of the many spoons. Looking up as I detected a resurgence of sniggers, I saw that the other guests were prying off their shells with their fingers and eating them whole. After that, and dropping my offending spoon and bending down to pick it up instead of leaving it for the maid, Highermaster George did his best to anticipate my problems with discreetly murmured instructions. But by then it was too late. I could tell, as each new dish arrived, that the people on my and several of the surrounding tables were far more interested in how I was going to tackle it than in eating anything themselves.

Salad should always be eaten from a side plate. There are some dishes which you may consume with your fingers like a savage, and others which you must dissect with your knife. It is also inadvisable to drink large amounts of wine on an empty stomach before you commence eating, and even more so to attempt to stifle your crushing sense of stupidity by continuing to drink through your meal. Above all, it is probably best to ignore comments which are not intended for your ears, nor to ask loudly for them to be repeated, and applaud sarcastically when, after a long pause and an exchange of glances, something else is said in their place.

Staggering outside as the courses continued and my stomach started to roil, falling over flowerbeds under a grin of moon, the laughter streamed with my tears as I spat out large amounts of what I'd eaten. What *was* I doing here in any case? I'd thought, to the extent that I'd properly thought about it at all, that it would be a chance to witness a rare species—the disgustingly rich—in their endangered habitat before they vanished entirely, and, of course, to see Anna. But it had never occurred to me that I'd stand out like a monkey at a wedding. After all, hadn't I managed well enough on that Midsummer? It had been the same people. The same suits. The same faces. Even now, sniggering and whispering from the darkness, they processed around me. But, back then, I'd floated above the waters of that ballroom. Even the food had been no problem to me and I'd danced like a dervish to every tune . . .

There was a whispered discussion behind me. The perilinden trees tinkled and swayed. A white shirt bobbed like a lantern, another drifted away.

'You're not quite at your *best* at the moment, are you, old chap?'

I recognised Highermaster George's voice, the soft pressure of his hands.

One of several Walcote Houses loomed into view. There were servants like dark folds of paper, windows and lights and corridors, conversations about the whereabouts of my room. Apart from the bilious tilt of the ceiling, I felt almost painfully sober, but these people seemed deaf to my protests. And I knew now that the walls would dissolve if I blundered into them, that you could find yourself elsewhere and yet still be here, that the carpets could tilt, the floors turn to seas.

'Here we are . . .' A door of marbled wood loomed. 'Think we should get you to bed old chap . . .'

'I'm fine! *Fine* . . .' I struggled as George tried to remove my jacket from me. '*You* were there weren't you? On that pier, at Midsummer?'

'You mean by the embankment? There *was* something that used to go on there, now that you mention . . .'

I flopped on the bed. My shoes were prised from my feet. My socks came with them.

'But there are so many balls and dances. It's difficult to remember the details of every one. Especially if it was a few years ago.'

I willed the bed to stop turning, the room to cease cavorting.

'Still, you look as if you'll be all right. I've put a glass of water on the bedside table.' His shadow moved towards the door.

'Annalise.'

The shadow paused. 'What?'

'Annalise Winters.'

'Annalise . . .' He chuckled. 'And I'd always thought Anna was her full name.'

'Well it isn't.'

'Right.' His face blurred and reformed. 'She's a good friend.'

'I knew her when she was . . . Much younger . . .'

'Oh really?' Was that a tightness I heard in his voice? Something harsher? Protective? But there were too many Georges, and I was starting to feel sick again—and disgusted, and empty. Where Anna Winters should have been, all those treasured memories, there was nothing now.

'She can make herself disappear behind a vase of flowers, you know,' I told him. 'And I know her well. Even if she says I'm nothing. Just ask Sadie.'

'Oh, I believe you.' George's face retreated. The gaslights flickered down. I heard the whisper of the door across the carpet. 'And I think you'll be fine now 'til morning.'

'And that vase.'

'Yes?'

'I didn't touch it. My hands were invisible and it just exploded. Anna did that as well.'

Highermaster George chuckled as he closed the door. 'Now *that* would be quite a trick . . .'

* * *

Blazing shadows. The clatter of silverware and porcelain.
The people moving in this bright room are like tropic
birds; shockingly iridescent. The windows are painful
slashes, the curtains waterfalls of blood. I managed to still
my hands sufficiently to pour myself a cup of coffee. I
lifted the heavy silver lid of one of the tureens. Steamy visions of maggoty rice poured up at me. No, definitely not
food. The voices, the whispers, were more subdued this
morning. I was the only one properly dressed in my only
remaining trousers and jacket, whilst everyone else was
wearing silken extravagances which I supposed might be
called morning coats. I was almost invisible again and I decided I might as well stay that way. Even on a Noshiftday,
there must be trains to take me back to London, and I had
only a few minutes' worth of packing. I could walk straight
out through those doors and along Marine Drive. By late
afternoon, evening the latest, I could be back with Saul,
Maud, Blissenhawk, Black Lucy.

Two more dazzlingly attired figures emerged into the
breakfast room, the man with a gold chain the size of a
dock-mooring around his neck, the woman wearing fairy
slippers. The Bowdly-Smarts looked as out of place and
ugly as they had yesterday, and Grandmistress Bowdly-
Smart was proclaiming in a loud voice, waving her wrists
in a slide of bangles. Her vowels slid around most of England. I could almost enjoy the raised eyebrows, the whispers, now that they weren't directed at me.

Grandmaster Bowdly-Smart glanced over at me as
I stared at him. Then he turned his back and began to
heap out kedgeree. It was him rather than his wife that I
recognised—I was sure of that now—but it was the sound
of Grandmistress Bowdly-Smart's voice which finally did
it for me. She was telling a supposed friend, who was doing her best to disentangle herself, about some or other
gathering of *fellow seekers*. Her excitement grew so intense in doing so that all the padding with which she had
attempted to encase her voice fell away. I knew then. I was
sure of it. I'd heard such voices a million times, shouting
to each other over the fences up and down Coney Mound

as they all beat their rugs on Twoshiftday. Grandmistress
Bowdly-Smart was from Bracebridge, and her rat-faced
husband, as he moved away with a final backward glance
to consume his mountainous breakfast—he was Uppermaster Stropcock, who had leered down at me in that tiny
office at Mawdingly & Clawtson, and told me I wasn't
good enough for the Lesser Toolmakers, and let me touch
his puny haft. *Eyes and ears, sonny.* Even the widow's
peak of his hair, although now there was somewhat less of
it and it had greyed, was the same. I was sure of it. All that
was missing was his clip of pens and a fag end dangling
from his lip.

Uppermaster Stropcock and his wife. Here at Walcote
House, and stinking rich, and calling themselves Bowdly-
Smart. This was even odder than my presence here. What
had they done to manage this seemingly magical trick?
Whatever it was, I had the advantage. Stropcock must have
slapped and intimidated so many potential apprentices that
he didn't recognise me. I poured myself another cup of
coffee and felt my hands grow more steady. I decided that I
would stay on here for the rest of the celebrations after all.

The white walls of the seaward side of Walcote House rose
above sheer white cliffs, from white sands. The cliffs curled
east away from Saltfleetby and then on towards Folkestone
like a protective arm. Below them, in waters clearer and
bluer than the sky, sailboats hung, fish darted, bright weeds
waved. Weightless swimmers were beckoning as I took the
long steps down.

'It's Master *Robbb-bert* . . . !'

Sadie, as under-dressed this morning in a blue-striped
costume as she had been over-dressed the night before,
surged out from the sea towards me. Jaunty in her bathing
cap, touching me with fish-wet hands, she told me she had
seen little of what had happened last night, but had heard
everything. Laughing, she sent out spray. That huge vase
going over!

'You must come and join us in the water, Robbie!'

But I shook my head. I couldn't swim—the Withy or the
Thames never held much attraction once you knew what

poured into them—and I had a headache. So I sat down on the crystal beach and watched the bathers.

Highermaster George flopped down by me. His limbs were thin in his striped swimsuit, licked like sunlight with golden fur. He laughed away my attempts at an apology for last night. Such performances were seemingly a matter for congratulation. Why, he'd once been ill over a pile of everyone's coats in someone's house and had dined out on the tale for the rest of the season . . . We fell into silence. Sails drifted past in the heat, their reflections upturned. The bathers swam out to a diving platform and basked like seals. With an apologetic backward glance, George joined them. These swimmers had the restless energy of children. They laughed and played in the water. They crashed through the spray. There were servants, black figures patrolling the edges of the sands, stooping like wading birds to offer iced trays. Sadie returned to me, her hair clinging to her shoulders.

'Oh, I know how you must feel. Try this. It's a guaranteed pick-me up. My own special recipe.'

A crystal glass the same no-colour of the ocean, and as cold and salty and deep. But I really did feel better after it—or at least different. And I became conscious as I sat in the sun of a figure further off at the edge of the headland, walking at the lip of the waves. Grey knee-length shorts, a tucked-in white blouse, hands in pockets, long hair and bare calves. The bathers were still laughing, splashing, arguing over the rules of some complicated game. No one else had noticed Anna Winters. The heat shimmered, dissolving her for a moment like the wind puffing out a flame. I got up. Moving quickly across this dry white sand was like running in a dream. It took me an Age to reach her.

'D' you know what all this stuff is made of, Robbie?' she asked without turning her head, still gazing out at the sea. 'Classroom chalk. All of it. Isn't that strange?'

I looked down at the blurred sand as I caught my breath. It was obvious now that she'd said it. 'Why,' I gasped, 'wouldn't you talk to me last night?'

'Aren't we talking now?'

Shaking my head, I felt Sadie's potion swimming

within my skull. 'But you seemed so annoyed that I'd come here. And that thing you did to me last night, with the vase, the drink . . .'

'You think you need *help* to behave like a clumsy drunk!'

'I'd thought we were friends.'

'You mean like you are with Sadie, or with George?'

'They're just people I happen to have met.' I waved my hands. 'At the end of the day, the people here are just like people everywhere else. In fact, they're much worse because they just live and eat and drink and do nothing. I know that now, Anna. It's probably the only thing I do know about them.'

'I do wish you hadn't come, Robbie. But at least you're calling me Anna.'

'And you really want me to leave?'

'No. Not now. You're here, aren't you? And perhaps I was too harsh on you yesterday . . .'

Annalise stuffed her hands deeper inside her pockets. Her hair slid over her shoulders, the sunlight chasing up and down it with the pulse of the waves. A larger wave came rolling in, clear as glass, changing the angle of her legs. I felt my trousers go sodden to my knees.

'I know it's not your fault,' she said as she started walking away from the bathers and towards a turn in the headland, her lovely head stooped in that way of hers, her face in profile against the sparkling water. 'I don't blame you for what you've done—or for your life. It's nothing to do with your being a radical and a mart and not some wealthy Northcentral guildsman, as I know you're probably thinking. These people are no better than you are, Robbie. I understand that as well. But you shouldn't imagine that they're worse than you either.'

'You know I saw Mistress Summerton?'

'Of course I know.'

'And you know what she told me?'

'I can imagine. That tale of hers and all those terrible things back in Brownheath and the death of my poor mother and how Missy saved me and raised me and did everything and that it's really her money that still keeps me going. It must have taken most of the day, until you got up in that box in the Opera House to gawk down at me.'

'It's been part of my life, too, Anna—the things that happened. My mother was a friend of your mother's. She died as well. It just took longer.'

'I'm sorry. I know all of these things. But they're in the past, aren't they? We're adults. We've made our own choices. That's why we're walking here now.'

We walked on, in the bright sunlight, beside the waves. Not so long ago, Anna, I thought, I'd probably have agreed with every word you said about the past being gone and finished. But not now. 'I can't help feeling,' I said carefully, 'that, after all we've shared without even knowing, we might be able to help each other . . .'

Annalise blinked slowly. Her eyelashes were as blond as her hair.

'You think you know what I am, don't you? That's the place from where your problem comes. It was a pity, really, that I let you find me at the fair. Yes, it was fun at the time, but it was also a mistake . . .' She shot me a look colder than the waves. 'And now you come trailing after me with half-understood secrets.'

'You're different, Anna. How can you deny that?'

'I don't. But everyone's different in their own different way.'

'That's just a riddle. You're—'

'What?' She threw up her head, the sunlight thinning her limbs. 'You mean, I'm like Missy? Or—who *is* that dreadful creature? Mister Snaith? Believe me, Robbie, you really don't know! They're not me!' She waved her hands as if she was banishing something and the sea flashed dark through them. Then she stopped and turned. She held out her wrist. Of course, the Mark was there now. Its scab glinted on the pale inner curve of her wrist like a ruby.

'*This* is me.'

I opened my mouth, but it filled only with the dull burrowing ache which I always felt in the presence of Anna, Annalise—whoever or whatever she wasn't or was. That ache was growing even now as the wind picked up and drew a slash of hair across her face; it continued growing when I had thought it could grow no more and had already consumed me. But her lucent flesh; the very substance of Annalise. I could have studied it forever. Her veins were so fine I could see the living pulse within them like a darting blue fish. She let out a sigh and stamped her bare right foot in the waves and yanked her arm away from me.

'You really are hopeless, Robbie!'

'But you could be so many things. You could have been anything! So why this?'

She turned and continued walking. Up ahead, the cliffs were divided by a steep vee. A pathway led up from the beach beside the stream which cascaded down from it, winding from side to side on neat little wooden bridges as we followed the ferny shadows. It was a chine, moist and cool and dark even on this hot morning.

'Unlike you,' she was saying as she walked briskly ahead and the water fell beneath us and pooled and fell again, 'I don't see that there's anything wrong with simply being happy. And then in making happier the lives of the people who surround you. Your problem is that you imagine happiness is too easy, that it's some cheap illusion to be scorned in favour of . . .' Searching for the words, she glanced back at me. 'Whatever it is that you want to bring down on us all, Robbie.'

Vegetation dripped. Mist rose. A rainbow hung in a shaft of sunlight. I half expected each turn to reveal the house of that imaginary aunt.

'But it's been a struggle sometimes, that I'll have to admit. And I suppose I *am* different, or I could be if I let things get through to me. When I enter a room, I can feel people's thoughts like the roar of this water. When I pass a haft, a building, a machine, I have to close my mind to it or else its spell comes tumbling into me. If I were to blur my eyes, if I were to open my ears and forget myself and let it all in, the whole world would overwhelm me. It's like a madness. And I'm lost then. I'm like those poor creatures you hear about. The ones far worse than Missy whom they keep in St Blate's. So why on earth should I want that? It's a door which I've always striven to push shut.'

'But you have power—'

'—don't talk to me about power!' she snapped. 'I want my life as it is. I still want to be Anna Winters. I want to be happy and ordinary . . .' We had neared the top of the cliff. The path was levelling out. Ahead of us was a gate. Predictably, beyond that, and seeing as we'd walked less than a mile, lay some part of Walcote's huge gardens. You could still see the house's many rooftops from here, and the high white spire of the Turning Tower. 'If you want power, Robbie,' she muttered, 'you should look over there.'

The stream which fed the chine fanned out. There were ponds and water-gardens. Huge fish, golden-armoured, ancient-eyed, nosed our reflections. With every new turn and surprise, I tried to imagine how this urn or archway or that stretch of lawn might be put to better use in the coming New Age, but it was becoming difficult. This whole place had been designed to overwhelm.

'And I'm still waiting for you to tell me,' Anna opened the gate which led back down into the chine, 'what's wrong with being happy . . .'

'Nothing. If that's what you really are.'

We descended the winding paths back through the chine. The air down on the shore was midday hot. My feet dragged. My headache was returning.

'Have you met Grandmaster and Grandmistress Bowdly-Smart?'

Anna shook her head. 'Who are they?'

'They're here as guests. I thought they might—well, that doesn't matter . . .'

We were drawing closer to the bathers again. They were still splashing, floating, playing.

Look! Is that Anna!

Yes, yes!

All the usual excited cries.

'Everyone here seems to think the world of you,' I said aimlessly.

Momentarily, Anna's footsteps slowed and she nodded, seemingly pleased. If she has a weakness, I thought, it's that she likes being liked. That's why she puts up with me— that's why she puts up with everything. Wet and ridiculous in their skimpy clothing, the bathers were rushing our way. I

hung back and watched as they clustered around Anna, curious to see the exact nature of the trick she was performing.
But in this different world she'd created, which was suddenly as real as the noontime heat, Anna radiated nothing
more than happiness, and the guileless mystery of being
what she was, which is something few of us can manage.

I sat down on the sand. The game the bathers had long
been trying to play took shape now that Anna was here to
urge them on, quietly directing from the edge of the waves,
although, like me, she didn't swim. Her friends suddenly
looked graceful as mermaids as they swam and dived and
chased each other. Finally, the morning had to end and,
wrapped in towels, dropping soggy bits of swimsuit which
the stooping servants collected for them, they performed
the extraordinary dance of getting changed. Sadie, ruffled
and damp in an expensive daydress, sat down beside me.

'Makes a difference, our Anna, doesn't she? Always
has.'

Anna was talking to Highermaster George now. She'd
taken off her sandals, although she'd managed to walk with
me beside the waves without getting them wet, and dangled
them by their straps. When she bent down to put them back
on, I saw George's hand trace the line of her back. My
heart dropped, and then started pounding, as I watched him
and Anna head up the steps towards the house.

'Hey, you all!' A plummy-voiced shout. A young
guildsman—one of last night's gathering around the piano—
was standing over a rockpool, water trickling from his hands.
He was holding something tiny and alive. 'Look what I've
just found!' He gave a barking laugh. 'It's another of Sadie's
discoveries!'

Throughout the rest of the day, Walcote House continued
awakening. There was an archery competition. Folk dances
were performed on the lawns by charmingly dressed children of the local guilds. There were raffles and treasure
hunts. In a brass and leather library there were crisply
ironed copies of today's *Guild Times,* which was filled with
more strikes and lockouts, although the *Times* called them
insurrections and *necessary precautions.* But from here,

with the smell of sunlight on old hide, none of it, not even London itself, seemed real.

Back in my room, I lay on my four-poster bed and stroked the fine wood and rubbed at the dragging pain in my temples. Framed on the wall was a list of the charities this shiftend was supposed to benefit. *The Distressed Guildswoman's Fund, The Society for the Restitution of Chimneysweeps, The Manx Home for Old Horses, Emily's Waifs and Strays*—even *St Blate's Hospice and Asylum;* it covered every imaginable kind of misfortune. And out on the lawns, guests were buying raffle tickets, attempting impossible tasks for a wager or slipping rolled ten-pound notes into silver boxes. After their efforts, it was hard to believe that anyone could ever suffer from poverty, disease . . .

I prowled the corridors. Lunch had passed without any clear signal for food, and the breakfast rooms were empty. There were wandering groups of guests on the lawns, playful or quiet or conspiratory. *One of Sadies discoveries.* But I had no idea where Sadie was—or Highermaster George and Annalise, although it was hard for me now not to picture the two of them together. There were lakes beyond the lawns, glades, walks enough for a thousand lovers. And there was nothing in Westminster Great Park to compare to these trees. Fire aspen and perilinden. Sallow and cedarstone. Their leaves chimed and rustled above me, their shadows made tapestries, their scents and colours carried on a hectic breeze. But I was sick of wonders, and I felt nauseous and hungry. Eventually, I found some cakes to eat at a charity stall, although the woman who served me gave a disappointed chirp when I only paid the sixpence she asked for.

Evening came. The lawns quietened. It was the time for the guests to change. After my performance last night, the prospect of an even bigger occasion sounded ominous. I decided to ignore the trays of drinks. But what was I going *as*? I'd heard that question several times today, but I had no idea what it meant. Still nursing my headache as Walcote House grew louder and brighter, I headed towards the long shadows of the hedges.

'All you ever do is bloody nag . . .'

'You said I looked marvellous ten minutes ago.'

The voices came from beyond the hedge. Imagining they were alone in these gardens, Grandmaster and Grandmistress Bowdly-Smart had dropped all southern pretence from their vowels. I kept pace with them on the far side of the hedge. Like all long-married couples, the Bowdly-Smarts could keep an argument running indefinitely. I felt almost nostalgic—it had been a long time since I'd heard such phrases through the thin walls on Brickyard Row. I scurried ahead to a gap in the hedge and rounded it as the Bowdly-Smarts came into view, although they were still too deep in their argument to notice me. In fact, I wasn't entirely sure that it *was* the Bowdly-Smarts—let alone the Stropcocks. The two figures walking the shadowed side of the path which lay between the trimmed hedges could have stepped out of the Age of Kings. He wore a crown, an ermine cloak. She had a wimple on her head, and was carrying the long train of a red dress. Only their tart, bitter voices remained.

'Then, bugger me if you don't . . .'

I cleared my throat. They looked up, stiffened, headed on towards me in silence.

'Charming weather, don't you think?' Grandmistress Bowdly-Smart's other voice was back. They were planning to head straight past me until I got in their way.

'I'm Master Robert.' Between the crown and a small fake goatee beard, Grandmaster Bowdly-Smart still had that same hard, appraising look in his eyes as he studied my offered hand in the moment before he took it. 'I'm sorry if I seemed to stare at you this morning,' I said as his rings dug into me, 'I thought I recognised you, but I was wrong. You know how it is sometimes.'

'Bet you get to see a lot of faces in your line of work,' he growled, wiping his hand on his ermine. 'Whatever that is.' He plainly recognised me as well, in the sense of knowing that I didn't belong here.

I glanced at his wife. She was wearing an excited expression. 'I *know* what it is . . .' Her hand shot out to grab my wrist. 'You were *there,* weren't you? How silly of us

both not to realise! That little gathering of seekers at Tamsen House.'

I gazed at her. 'Tamsen House?'

'Oh—you know! On Linden Avenue. With Mister
Snaith!'

'Ah . . . Yes, I was.' After all, Grandmistress Sadie Passington had been there. So why not Grandmistress Bowdly-
Smart as well?

She beamed at me. 'My darling husband here, he
doesn't understand. Everything has to be business.'

'I think we should get going,' Grandmaster Bowdly-
Smart put in through his wife's twitterings.

'You will accompany us, won't you, Master Robert?'
Grandmistress Bowdly-Smart twittered. 'I think it's time
for the wishfish.'

'The . . . ?'

But the Bowdly-Smarts were already striding off, he in
his kingly cloak, she in her wimple. Was it possible to shift
so completely from one identity to another? But in a white
courtyard, beneath a pink evening sky, clusters of other
guests at least as strangely dressed as the Bowdly-Smarts
were now drifting. There were middle-aged pirates and angels, plump tropic savages, classical scholars with laurel
leaves stuck on their balding heads. The centre of attention
was circular marble fishpond beside which a tall guildsman
was handing out crystal cups. Peering into the pond, I
saw small fish darting. One of the guests, a red-faced de-
mon, chased his cup through the waters, inspected its contents to be sure that it contained a fish, then gulped it down.
A few moments later, one of the pirates did the same. The
Bowdly-Smarts were next. In Bracebridge, this would have
been a story too wild to be believed. But an odd thing happened as Master Bowdly-Smart worked his stringy throat.
His beard somehow became less fake. The fine clothes and
crown made a better fit on him. Even his features, although
still noticeably ratlike, were indefinably changed. And his
wife looked almost graceful too, in fact—yes—*queenly*
now that she had drunk her wishfish as well. Even her accent had improved. One of the pirates was now performing
a convincingly athletic jig as he left the courtyard to the

tooting of his shipmate's pipe. Dressed as I was in my scruffy black jacket, I decided to give this a try.

I slipped a cup beneath the chill surface of the water. The fish were translucent, but seemed eager to be caught. One was in my cup as I raised it; its tiny gills pumping, an aether-bright stripe along its back. The water had no scent, and no obvious taste. But I felt something slick and living slide over my tongue. I glanced around. The Bowdly-Smarts had drifted away and the pirates had been replaced by a troop of elderly ballerinas. Back outside in the grounds, tall mirrors within which the guests could inspect themselves dangled flashing from the trees. I saw a dark-suited form emerging from the twilight. But he seemed taller, older, far darker and more powerful than me. Something in my stomach jittered. It took an effort of will for me to approach the mirror. Not Robbie, no; nor Robert or Master Borrows, nor quite any of the other versions of me. The evening air stirred, turning the mirrors, silvering the trees. That dark jacket, the lean cut of my body, that gaze, which was somehow both merciless and knowing. My hands touched my sharp cuffs and brushed the planes of my face, which were smooth and warm as aethered metal, although it had been hours since I had shaved.

Whatareyoucomingas? The whispers, the gleeful surprises, fluttered amongst the hedges. But I knew now what I was—it was as clear as the threads of music which twined around the ballerinas as they arabesqued and pirouetted between feverishly scented avenues of roses. I was the incarnation of everything these people feared and tried to ignore in the hope that it would go away. I was the spectre of the New Age.

'That's perfect! You do really look threatening, like a real revolutionary. I knew you wouldn't disappoint me.' Sadie came flouncing out of the twilight in a dress of cobweb greys. 'Well . . .' I caught her scent as she stood close to me. 'Do you like me?'

I touched her arm. I could feel the fine dusting of down. 'What are you?'

She gave a semi-mocking curtsey. 'You'll have to guess . . .' Her hair, bunched in luminous folds and tresses by the same tiny red bows which held her dress, seemed almost blond tonight. Her flesh was paler, too. ' . . . still no idea?' It was plain as Sadie rose and her eyes blazed that she, too, had drunk a wishfish. 'Well. Maybe it'll come to you.'

We headed with the other guests towards the ballroom and the sound of music. The wishfish, Sadie explained, lasted only a few hours. But the stories she could tell! Hence those ballerinas, and—see—the little bald grey man over there who's snatched a fiddle from the orchestra and is cavorting around with it. Dear Greatmaster Porrett does love his stupid tunes. Can't hold a note normally, but whenever there's masquerade, old Porrett spends the whole night scampering with a wishfish inside him, bowlegged, elbows sawing, as the music pours out . . .

In the candlelit haze of the chandeliers, the ballroom was like some great ocean. Breezes stirred, there were bright islands, dark swirls, twinkling lights.

'It's now that I wonder if this is ever worth it,' murmured the shepherd who came to stand beside us.

'Oh, don't say that, Daddy!' Sadie gave him a playful push. 'Do you know Master Robert Borrows, by the way?'

The greatgrandmaster smiled at me slowly. He waved his crook. 'I think we met yesterday in the corridors. I hope you enjoy tonight. I can't promise, by the way, that there'll be many other occasions on this scale. It would be far better if we were to simply advance the cost of all this straight to the charities. I'm sure you've heard how difficult things are becoming. And yet here we are, fiddling and dancing . . .'

'You really are such a pessimist, Daddy!'

I noticed as Sadie and her father talked that all of the people around us were also listening. It was an impressive performance—and the greatgrandmaster truly was a handsome man, who could dress up in a brown smock and banter with his daughter about the state of the realm without seeming ridiculous. But after a while, their chatter became repetitive and I left them to it, wondering as I wandered off and everyone else gathered closer to them just how I would remember this shiftend—as the dream it now seemed, or as a real part of my life—and then deciding that I could at least afford to drink a little wine. The wishfish had finally banished my headache. And here was Highermaster George dressed in nothing but an expensive suit, and seemingly as himself.

'I hope,' I said, 'that you don't expect me to guess what you are . . .'

He jumped at the sound of my voice. 'Oh, it's *you*, Robert.' His eyes seemed odd, unfocused. 'Well, *you* certainly look the part and no mistake.'

'Do I?'

He gave a dissatisfied shrug. 'Not that I've come as anything.'

'You haven't tried the wishfish?'

His eyes trailed away through the dancers. 'I'd have to be as stupid as the rest of them, to believe in such fripperies.'

But there was something about his eyes, his mouth, the sheen of sweat.

'Tell me, Robert . . .' He licked his lips. 'Last night, when I helped you find your room—what you said about Anna.'

'What did I say?'

'Oh—just the way you laughed at the thought of her being Anna Winters, as if that was all some fine joke which only you and she shared. You must have laughed a great deal with her. You know . . .' His voice trailed off. 'When you were both young.'

'It wasn't exactly—'

'And she *is* such fun to be around,' he continued. 'She's quick and charming and all the things I wish I was. Yet she never quite seems to laugh in an ordinary way.' His brow furrowed. A trickle of sweat wavered across his cheek. 'And I was wondering if, knowing Anna as you did or do, you might know the sort of thing that, well . . . Tickled her.'

I stared at him.

'Not *physically,* I mean. Although you may have done that as well.' His expression grew more pained. 'I'm really just asking you, Robert, what you think might make Anna laugh.'

I stared back at George, remembering the glide of his hand across her back on the beach that morning. And now he was expecting me to help him. But what *would* make Anna laugh—break that strange and lovely composure? I could picture her now, leaning against me as we shared that all-too-human gift. The brush of her face. The scent of her hair.

'There you are Anna! You were just talking about you.'

'And what were you saying? Nothing but good, I hope?'

'I don't think there's anything *bad* about you, is there?'

The edges of her mouth twitched at this silly compliment. She knew what we had been saying; of course she knew. A threaded silver bangle weighed her bare left arm. Her dress was silvery too, bustled and flared, extravagant by the standards of anything I'd seen her wearing since that Midsummer night on the pier. It caught the light and blended with her hair. Anna Winters had come simply as herself again tonight. She needed no wishfish.

'Perhaps, if you'll excuse us . . .' George offered me an apologetic glance and Anna the crook of his arm. 'You might care to dance?'

Anna nodded. Her green eyes glittered. She made a perfect gesture to brush back the fall of her hair, and I watched as the music drew her and George away. All around me now, the dancers swirled. The floor of the ballroom was sprung; even walking, the rhythm of the music tried to carry my steps, but it was no use my dancing tonight. I was a socialist, a revolutionary—the very opposite of everything that these people stood for. Drinking a wishfish might grant me many things, but the ability to move my feet in accordance to these changing, tricky beats . . . That was not to be expected.

The dancers turned. Sadie and her father were putting on a good show, their faces set and grinning. The greatgrandmaster's gaze, both bland and intense, swept the room beyond his daughter's shoulder. It scarcely registered me, but then it settled on Grandmaster Bowdly-Smart who was standing not far away, and some other expression, something I couldn't quite gauge, some dark pang of worry, seemed to writhe up towards the surface in the moment before it vanished, and the music moved on, taking him and Sadie with it. Outside, beyond the great doors, there were more dancers out in the starlight, although I'd lost track by now of Highermaster George and Anna Winters. And the mirrors here caught the stars, as did the stilled waters of the fountains. Slowly, the music changed. Soft palls of smoke and powder seeped out from the ballroom. The ivy which covered a nearby wall was fruiting, and the fruits glowed pale white; moonivy, like so many frail paper lanterns, and the trees which hung their branches beyond had a misty aethereal glow. It would never really be dark here. It could never become night.

Where a long terrace projected above the path along which I was walking, a couple were entwined and leaning across the balustrade. The woman's hair and dress were grey now, and the darker tones of the man's suit paled and merged. They didn't move as they pressed their faces together and Highermaster George's hand cradled Anna's back. In fact, they were so still as I gazed up at them from the shadows that they could have been statues. My heart seemed to be made of stone, too. Feeling absolutely nothing, I walked on through the preternatural night, and re-entered Walcote House through a small doorway. It was quiet here, far from the thrum of the distant ballroom. Occasionally, there were servants. I stopped one and announced that my name was Bowdly-Smart, and that I'd lost my room.

By now, I had some rudimentary grasp of the house's layout, or at least of some of the floors of its east wing. The Bowdly-Smarts were staying on the level below me, around a further couple of turns. The corridors here, I couldn't help noticing, were higher and wider than my own. The carpets were patterned with leaves and flowers, the archways were carved in the form of trees which sprouted in goldleaf across the ceilings. I found the Bowdly-Smarts' doorway, but the handle held uselessly in its sleeve. For lack of any better idea, I attempted to murmur the phrase Sadie had used to open my own door. I didn't hold out any serious hopes, but tonight the wishfish was in me. There was a beat of silence, then I felt, heard, something within the lock engage. The door swung open.

The Bowdly-Smarts' suite—I still couldn't really think of them as the Stropcocks—was much larger and more impressive than my own. They had a private balcony giving a view of the sea, twin four-poster double beds—and their bathroom made mine look like a closet. I turned up a gaslamp. Everything was floral, coloured in vividly unnatural lime greens, strawberry reds, lemon yellows. I was more attuned to the ways of Walcote House now and I wondered if this gaudy over-statement was intended as a subtle dig. The air smelled faintly sour, and there were signs of recent occupancy. One of the bed covers was rucked, with scraps of wimple and broken bits of tiara scattered across it. I was touching the fallen jewels when I heard a splash in the bathroom. I froze—for I'd already checked that I was alone . . .

I pushed back the door. Empty convolutions of tile and porcelain. Yet the muffled splashing continued. And the sour smell was stronger in here, too. It came, I decided, from beneath the seat of the one of the two toilets. Slowly, I raised it. A wishfish was flapping in the bowl as it died amid flecks of vomit. Clearly, it had rebelled against the near-impossible labour of making Grandmistress Bowdly-Smart seem queenly. My own gorge started to rise in sympathy. I swallowed hard and flushed. Back in the bedroom, though, there was still much to admire about the Bowdly-Smarts' trunks and cases. How long were they staying here? Shirts, slips and dresses sluiced through my fingers. From Bracebridge—to this. On top of the bureau, beside the sand and ink, Mistress Bowdly-Smart was in the throes of writing a letter. It was filled with empty exclamations.

I slid open the empty drawers of the bureau. These pieces of carpentry were intricately worked, and many had catches which would cause a hidden drawer to spring open. I felt around underneath. There. On oiled runners, a shallow drawer slid out. Rolling around inside it were what I took at first to be boiled sweets. But they were too large, and the one I lifted felt too heavy. I unravelled its screw of paper and spilled it cautiously into an ashtray. A softly glittering stone, holed like a necklace bead in the middle, and marked with a glowing hieroglyph. I'd seen smaller versions of such things strung in abacus lines in the offices of cashiers and storekeepers. I had an idea that they were called numberbeads, and were used in the storage of records and accounts. But I'd never touched one before, and had little idea what to expect. A dim, half-made landscape of figures came and retreated before my eyes; a numinous sea of budgets and balances, manifests and invoices. I unwrapped another of the numberbeads, and felt the names of ships—*Saucy Lass, Dawn Maid, Blessed Damozel*. I was blown on the ghost breezes of bills of lading and import duty. What guild exactly did Bowdly-Smart belong to? It plainly had something to do with trade. Another numberbead, and I saw the laddering timetables of goods trains, arrivals at Stepney Sidings, the capacities of Tidesmeet's quays and warehouses. The information was dizzying, hard to retain. Another numberbead detailed goods, and distant ports of departure, Africa and Thule. I caught the scents of raw cotton, dried fruits, salt meats, skins and teas.

Carefully re-wrapping the numberbeads, I placed them back in their hidden drawer, then extracted a sheet of paper from the scented pad on which Grandmistress Bowdly-Smart had been writing and tried to note down what I could remember. Already, the figures were receding like memories in a dream. But the name of a ship, the *Blessed Damozel*, that at least was something. Balling the paper in my pocket, I left the Bowdly-Smarts' suite. Everything was quiet in this part of Walcote House. A clock chimed midnight, but that was far too early for any glass-slippered princesses to rush home. Back in the ballroom the scenes had grown more boisterous. Flocks of young men and women were wheeling and shrieking in their stupid costumes. The wishfish ballerinas looked like pink rag dolls now, oozing stuffing as they lounged and smoked in a corner. The pirates had turned into tramps. I glanced at an arrangement of flowers. Huge dark velvet petals were dancing to and fro, and I saw that their crystal bowl was filled with a sour froth of undigested bits of food within which, tugging at the stalks, several wishfish were slowly expiring. Needing fresh air, I went outside.

The stars were still blissfully bright, casting their feathery

shadows, black on grey on grey. Greatmaster Porrett staggered past, his borrowed violin still cradled in his arms. As
he brushed its strings with his bow, it gave an agonised
shriek. The upper terrace where Anna and George had
stood was now empty. I touched the cold stone where she
had leaned. The perilinden trees shifted faintly, their leaves
tinkling in the breeze like silver change.

   Away from the smell of vomit and the dying wishfish,
the dark-bright gardens expanded. Looking back, Walcote
House was hazy, scarcely there. I let the paths lead me.
The way Sadie spoke, you could carry on forever through
these grounds, perhaps reach London without seeing a single object which wasn't expensive and beautiful and of no
practical use. This realm of the rich truly was another England, threaded deep within our own, yet totally invisible
until you stepped through the right door, found the right
key, the right spell, the right bank account. The tall white
trees parted. Another house lay ahead. My heart paused.
Just how far had I come? It was a greyly beautiful structure, propped on the spreading arms of a pale sea-froth of
rococo masonry, smaller than Walcote House, but still
huge. Slowly, I passed into the vast shadow of its door.
Starlight fell from barred windows on heaps of gold; fresh
straw, and the air had a pungent, cleanly sweet smell. As
my eyes grew accustomed to the shadowswept darkness, I
made out the flanks of great beasts. One snorted, its hooves
thundering the walls of a stall. Another thrust its head out
and down towards me, snorting a warm gale. I reached to
stroke its muzzle. Even in this light, the creature was totally white. It was like the horses which had pulled Sadie's
carriage, but much bigger and even more beautiful, and
from the centre of its forehead, far too high for me to reach
and spiralling like a glistening candystick, projected a ta-
pering horn. The unicorn sighed and nudged me.

   Most of the great animals were sleeping. Some were
grey—or jet black. Some, I could have sworn, had wings,
and golden hooves, and eyes like blazing lanterns. In my
dreams, and perhaps in their own, I was clinging to their
manes as landscapes fled far beneath me. I wandered on
through the barred light, and saw, in the far end of one of

the long stable avenues, a place where brighter flecks of starlight had fallen. It had a redder glint, which grew and faded until I caught the unmistakable scent of Sadie's cigarettes, the rustle of silk and muslin.

'*There* you are. Somehow I thought you'd find me.' Her voice was slurred. She offered me a cigarette from her case. 'So.' Her lighter flared. 'How's it going back at the house?'

I took a drag. 'I'm not really the person to ask. You know what they call me back there—*Oneof Sadiesdiscoveries . . .*'

'One of . . . ?' But for once, I'd done a good impression of the way these people spoke. She could hardly pretend not to understand me. '*That* old joke. Here's a tip, Master Robert. You should never believe the things that people say out of the corners of their mouths.'

'I'm not exactly the first, though, am I?' My gesture made a comet of my cigarette. 'You've dragged other people here to Walcote House. People like me.'

I felt the pressure of her hand on my shoulder. 'There's no one like *you,* Robert. Look at yourself—how could there be? Oh no no no.' She fell back against the stall. 'I know you think I'm being glib. But I'm not being glib at all. You *are* different. And I don't say that to everyone . . . Well, I do, actually. But what I mean is that this time I really mean it.' She stifled a burp. 'And here's another tip. You should believe people far more when they make a mess of what they're trying to say. Just like I did then.'

'I still don't understand why you brought me here.'

'Haven't you enjoyed yourself?'

'It's been . . . interesting.'

She gave a soft chuckle, and drew on her cigarette. 'You'd do it all differently, wouldn't you, if you were me?'

'Of course I would.'

'And so would I. If I had the chance—d'you know what I'm going to say next?'

'That it's not easy being rich.'

'Bang on the money! But we both know life's not simple or easy, don't we? We wouldn't be standing here talking in the dark like idiots if it was. We're young enough still, both of us—we should be dancing and getting tiddled while we can.'

She lit a fresh cigarette from the one she'd been smoking. Sparks sprayed as she squashed out the stub. 'This has always been my hidey-hole. No one can smell my little vice this far away from the house. Not even Daddy.'

'You're afraid of him?'

'Aren't you?'

'I don't belong to any guild—why should I be?'

'Haven't you heard, darling?' Sadie leaned forward, pouted, then fell back against the stable door again. 'We're all in the guilds these days . . .' She made a cooing, clicking sound in the back of her throat. In response, the creature in the stall behind us moved forward. It was immense. The blood-heat of its body warmed the air.

'He's mine,' she murmured. 'Daddy gave him to me on one of my birthdays when he wasn't handing out whisper-jewels.' Her hand swept the giant flanks. 'Beautiful, aren't you, Starlight?' The unicorn's coat was mostly black, but flecked with silver like the veins in fine dark marble. His horn was the same.

'Is there anything you *don't* have, Sadie?'

'Star's the only thing that's really mine. Aren't you, darling?' Her voice was muffled by his mane.

There was a long pause, filled only by the unicorn's breathing. I knew little of the making of these creatures, other than that they took a lot of aether, and had to be re-made generation on generation for the delectation of the rich because they were sterile. I glanced back along Starlight's massive flank; there were no wings.

'I take him out hunting here in the winter. Don't like the summer heat, do you, Star? And the beastmaster who made you said you were *too* beautiful, *too* big . . . But can you imagine anything more delicate?' She kissed his pelt. Her hand passed and re-passed across the pillar of his neck.

'Does that horn have any use?'

'Why, Robbie . . .' Sadie disentangled herself from her unicorn. She lit another cigarette. Red and silver sparks caught in her pale hair. Drunk and tousled though she was, she looked different here tonight, and quite beautiful. I reminded myself that she, too, had swallowed a wishfish. I still hadn't worked out what it was that she'd come as, but it had filled her tonight with something that wasn't Sadie. 'And I thought you were a dreamer like me.'

'Dreams are just dreams.'

'I know you don't believe that, otherwise you and your kind wouldn't be publishing those horrible grubby newspapers which are always going on about destroying the guilds.'

With a raise of his magnificent head, a rumbling sigh, Starlight backed into the shadows.

'Have you heard of the Bowdly-Smarts?' I asked.

'The woman with the terrible voice? Wasn't she at the thingy with the sad old changeling at Tamsen House? Of course, we didn't speak. I spend a lot of my life avoiding the likes of her.'

'And her husband?'

She shrugged.

'You don't know what he does?'

'Why don't you ask him? He's here, isn't he? Of course, I do know they're *terribly* rich.'

From Sadie, such a comment was an insult. No one she knew was supposed to be *rich* in that obvious and shameful sense.

'Why do you ask, Robbie? Is this another of your mysteries?'

'I don't have any mysteries.'

'Well, you still haven't given me the low-down on Anna.'

'You know Anna Winters far better than I do, Sadie.' I paused. 'Although you'd probably find out more if you asked Highermaster George.'

'*Him?*' She chuckled. 'Master Bohemian Revolt? You don't *think,* do you . . . ?'

'I saw them kissing on a terrace just a few hours ago . . .'

Sadie surprised me by flouncing off between the stalls. She stopped in the huge atrium, her dress rustling, her shoulders shaking.

'One last tip, Robbie,' she sniffed. 'The high guilded also have feelings.' She fished for a handkerchief amid the dress's folds. 'Oh, it's not *you*. And it's certainly not Anna and George. It's just—well . . .' She gazed out at the trees beyond the archway; still ribboned and made up to be whatever she was, her hair bleached or powdered, her whole body had somehow thinned and paled. 'You can come here to Walcote, then you can go away and get back to plotting to destroy us all. And I bet you've got somebody waiting for you back in London—somebody sweet and uncomplicated.'

I said nothing.

'But I haven't pressed you about your personal life, have I? And I'm not asking now. I don't want your secrets. Days like this are *so* disposable—I've already thrown thousands of them away.' She stamped a slippered foot. 'I mean, look at me! Another few years, and I'll be like Mama, shaving my eyebrows and painting them on again.'

'You're young, Sadie.'

'You saw those creatures in the ballroom! The debutantes are like little girls to me now, tottering around the playroom in their mothers' old gowns and heels. I can remember when that was *me,* and now it's gone. Even Anna's found somebody. And I—I'm going to have to get married.'

'Well, that's . . .' This obviously wasn't the usual cause for congratulation. 'I mean, who's the—'

'It's Greatmaster Porrett. And, before you try to be polite—yes, I do mean that withered old man with the stupid violin. His previous wife died a couple of years ago trying to give birth to a child, poor thing. So now it's my turn.'

'You make it sound like you have no choice.'

'Of course I don't! I'm Grandmistress Passington, daughter of the greatgrandmaster and all that kind of thing. I've always been groomed to get married to someone who will strengthen the Telegraphers' Guild, although I must say I had rather hoped he would be a little more presentable than Porrett. Still, he's a sweet old sort in his way. Used to sit me on his lap when I was a little girl and stuff me with chocolate-coated peppermints . . .'

'I'm sorry.'

'Perhaps now you'll believe me. There's more to being rich than judging vegetable contests and waving at snotty-nosed children on guildays. But then I suppose it really all probably boils down to doing your duty. I don't know the full details, but basically we Telegraphers need the money, and Greatmaster Porrett's guild, which is the something or other of thingy and involves chemicals, has it.' She gave a smile. 'After all, times are hard. Doesn't sound so very complicated, does it, if I put it that way?' She laid a hand on my arm. Her fingers brushed my face. They bore the scent of tears and wine, sweat and cigarettes. 'But let's forget that now . . .'

I let her lean against me. She felt warm, substantial, real. I sniffed the crown of her hair. For a moment, I was back dancing with her and Anna on that Midsummer evening. And then I was here, and Sadie was still pressing against me. 'Oh, I wish it was winter,' she murmured. 'Even if I'll have to get married, I can at least ride Starlight . . .' She sighed against my chest. The ribbons in her pale blond hair tickled my nose. My hands, unwilled, strayed across her shoulders. There were ribbons there as well, holding the top of her dress. 'You must come at Christmas. Everything's so different at Walcote in the hunt season. The snow. The blood. The cold.'

'What do you hunt, Sadie?'

'Dragons.'

I traced the tight, slick ribbon at her shoulder. All the wonders of Walcote House could pass though me now. All that mattered was this knot with which my fingers struggled. Then something gave. The ribbons parted, and she pulled away. Her right breast was fully bared and she seemed curiously complete and entirely beautiful as she stood there, and yet somehow not quite Sadie. This was nothing like the economic exchanges in the back rooms of by-the-hour hotels. The moment, as I raised my hand to stroke her flesh and her nipple tautened, was charged as some secret guilded ritual. Then, with a laugh, a turn, Sadie ran out of the stables.

'Come on, Master Robert!' A voice in the trees, already fading. 'You'll have to catch me!'

The trees hung heavy, draining the stars as I blundered between them. A stone nymph reared up. Tied around its finger, trailing like a long drop of blood, was a red ribbon.

There were faint sounds, night murmurings. I reached a clearing. In the centre rose a sundial, its shadow strewn with the fading glow of the stars. Tied to its apex was another ribbon. I sensed laughter not far off. Thorns thrashed my face. Another ribbon dripped from the bough of a tree, stirring as my breath heaved. I plunged on. It was no longer quite dark now, but filling with the light of pre-dawn in waves of glittering grey. The sky, the forest, were shifting in thickening mist. Then there was a strange, salt, sweet-sickly smell as the way sloped rapidly down and the trees fell away.

'Where are you?'

There was a roaring in my ears, and the ground was soft, and giving. I looked down and saw foam-flecked sand.

Here.

Everything was suffused in hints and glimmers. And there she was, standing naked in the waves. I understood now, from the paleness of her skin, from the fineness of her features, from the power of the wishfish, exactly who Sadie had come as. She was Anna Winters, Annalise, clothed in a gauze of golden-grey and rising like a goddess from the foggy sea. Needy and breathless, I waded towards her.

'Well, Master Robert? Was I worth the chase?'

But the voice was still Sadie's, and the wet hair was peroxide. I blundered into her, still half expecting dreams, smoke, but finding instead the chill reality of her flesh as she shivered and we embraced. The tide surged around us. Her knowing fingers unbuttoned me. We kissed. I wanted her now, but the waves were too strong and it was difficult to keep standing. We fell into the freezing foam and dragged ourselves to the sand, where I pulled off the remains of my sodden clothing. We made love. Sadie had her little moment. I, eventually, the wet sand rubbing my knees, had mine. I fell back. A bigger wave crashed over us. We looked at each other, and laughed, and got to our feet.

'I think that was worth it,' Sadie said as she crouched to wash the sand from her buttocks. The mist was thinning now as quickly as it had come. Her dress was strewn a little further up the tide, billowing and glinting like a huge jellyfish.

She looked different now, and matter-of factly human, with snakes of hair and seaweed stuck to her blue-mottled flesh. 'You took your time, and that counts for a lot to us girls. It's a rare thing, believe me . . .'

I smiled to listen to Sadie as she chattered on. I knew I was a considerate lover in the way that she meant, although the dollymops on Doxy Street complained if you spent too long between their thighs. I always enjoyed more these brief moments afterwards—and Sadie looked no different to those working girls now, talking to me and washing herself in much the same matter-of-fact way, with her nipples blued and her belly creased and orange-peel-like corrugations showing on her thighs. Perhaps it was true after all. Perhaps, underneath it all, people really were the same.

'Why are you looking at me like that?' She peeled a wet hank of hair back from her cheek. 'Have I still got a starfish stuck to my back or something?'

I kissed her cold forehead. 'You're lovely as you are. You don't need to pretend to be anything.'

'Well . . .' But for once, it was Sadie who was lost for words.

The horizon was a trembling lip of light.

I went in search of my clothes.

IV

'Morning, citizen!'

It was the Oneshiftday after my return from Saltfleetby when I first heard this greeting—unforced, unironic, not said in the emphatic tones which members of the People's Alliance used it—called out workman to workman across the street. I walked on, my bag and my worries lightened, whistling a tune I couldn't place, towards Black Lucy and Blissenhawk and all the empty columns of this shift's *New Dawn*. Perhaps this really would be the summer when the Third Age of Industry would end. No one quite knew how such changes came about, for the turnings were spaced at least a century apart, and the histories were vague. As a child, I'd imagined that greatguildsmen would look out of the windows, sniff the morning air, and decide that England needed a fresh coat of paint . . . I knew that the First Age of Industry had started with the execution of the last king, the second with some massive and complex re-organisation of the guilds, and that the start of the third had been signalled by the triumphant exhibition at World's End. But how? Why? Even in the pages of the *Guild Times,* let alone those of the *New Dawn,* there was no consensus.

'Morning, citizen!'

The buildings quivered. The Thames shrank and exhaled. It was a summer of visions and portents. A real hermit took up residence on Hermit's Hill and started proclaiming the end, not just of the Age, but of time itself. Church attendances went up and the dark seemed denser when you passed the tall open doorways, scented with a new variety of hymnal wine. A tree in the courtyard of one of the great guildhalls which hadn't budded for five centuries fulfilled some old prophecy and came into leaf. Almost all the citizens of the Easterlies seemed to have signed a huge petition calling for change known as the Twelve Demands. Dry thunder rattled over the Kite Hills. The evenings smelled close and foetid and muddy, and the gaslights simply added to the yellow swell of heat. The days were so hot now that people took to sleeping through them and coming out at night, and many of the shops remained open, and everyone was spending. Prices had increased so much recently that, in an odd kind of way, the value of money suddenly seemed less important. The masthead of the latest edition of the *New Dawn* said *4 Pence, or Something Useful in Exchange,* and Saul and I often returned home with shrivelled marrows and bent cigarettes.

'So . . .' Saul lit a cheroot and waved away the match as we sat outside one evening in a bar which had tumbled into Doxy Street. 'When are you going to tell us all about that shiftend of yours down by the seaside?'

'There really isn't much to tell. The people are much like the ones you see here, only with more money and worse accents. They're . . .' I thought about Walcote House—the soft carpets and high ceilings and dissolving walls. Just the other day in the *Guild Times,* I'd noticed an announcement of the marriage of Grandmistress Sarah Elizabeth Sophina York Passington to Greatmaster Ademus Isumbard Porrett of the General Guild of Distemperers, which would take place at Walcote House on something called the Feast of St Steven. Innocence, really was the overriding impression I'd taken back with me from Walcote House to London. Those people were like children and they would still be dancing, laughing, clinking crystal glasses, when the mob came to beat down their doors . . .

'Go on—and there must be an article in all of it some-where. Better than that weird thing you wrote last shift about Goldenwhite and the Unholy Rebellion. I mean—who believes in fairy stories?'

'All I was saying was that she was a leader of the people in her own way, too. It was a revolt, wasn't it? And it did. happen. She led her people. She was defeated at Clerken-well.'

Saul chuckled. 'Have you *been* to Clerkenwell?'

Of course I had—we both had, many times. But I'd never found what I'd been looking for, mainly because I still didn't know what it was. A statue, a monument? I or-dered another beer. Posters flapped on the walls in the hot night breeze; exhortations to come to gatherings and meet-ings long gone—if, indeed, they had ever taken place at all. Old scraps of the *New Dawn* or one of the dozens of other similar Easterlies papers bowled merrily along the gutters.

'Have you heard about the fruitworkers of Kent?' Saul was saying. 'They've formed a collective. They make their own decisions. The signs are there'll be a record harvest, and then they'll be able to share the profits and re-invest. It's a halfway house, I know, to true shared ownership, but I thought we might join them soon as this Age has changed. Not too many acres, of course. Just enough for me and Maud and the little 'un . . .'

I was thinking of the Stropcocks—the Bowdly-Smarts—whose sour faces still seemed real to me in this glowing city now that Walcote Manor had receded. '*What* did you just say?'

Saul chuckled. 'Thought you weren't with me there for a moment, Robbie. Maud's expecting a baby . . . I'm going to be a daddy!' He shot out a laugh, shook his head.

I went to a Workers Fair one afternoon that summer up on the Kite Hills. All the vast and hazy city lay spread below. Spires and towers. Hallam's slow blink. And there really were kites on these hills—coloured flotillas which caught and bobbed on the hot wind and tugged at the puppetstring people below. One, the size of a small shed, but silken, shimmering, crimson, was temporarily grounded, and had gathered a cluster of onlookers.

'Used to have one like that myself. Well, perhaps not quite so big . . .'

I turned to see Highermaster George.

'It was the most complicated thing I ever did, Robbie, getting that thing in the air. It was aethered, of course. Just like this one—see those strings.'

The kite roared up. We and the land seemed to drop away.

'So,' he said, squinting as the sun flared on his freckled scalp, 'I suppose you're here to sell the *New Dawn*?'

I nodded, and George bought one of the copies I had under my arm, then surprised and flattered me by revealing that he'd already read it, including my own rambling piece. He did his best, he said, to keep abreast of what he called *the debate*. A little further down the hill, where the kites' shadows danced in the air which rose off London like the heat from an oven, a straggle of marquees and awnings was basking. It was called a *Craft Fair for the New Age* and George was seemingly one of its leading lights. There were *Free Displays* and *Still Life Dances, Educational Talks* and *Exhibitions of Goods of the Highest Quality Not Produced by Any of the Guilds*. Contradictions abounded, although George's tone was apologetic as he took me along the stalls. Concave cakes, dubious pottery done in a bread oven, lumpen carvings, knitted dolls and poker-work frames. We sat for a while on folding chairs in the headache heat of a tent and listened to a seemingly endless debate about how the calendar might soon be changed. Even God himself in the old versions of the Bible had only been expected to labour seven days—so why not go back to that system, and work for five and a half days, then rest on the other one and a half? Or even just work the five . . .

'I know we've got a long way to go yet. Doesn't compare to your years of hard work with that paper. But we're experimenting with dyes, fresh processes . . .'

George drew me away, still apologising, still explaining. The Kite Hills, he told me, had once been called the Parliament Hills after a group of rebels led by a man named

Fawkes who had gathered here after trying to blow up the long-dead assembly which had once existed beside the Thames. Of course, the guilds had suppressed the name—the idea of a parliament, a real one in which properly elected representatives might control the way we lived, was far too dangerous.

'And Goldenwhite—she gathered her army here as well, didn't she?'

'Hmmm . . .' George smiled vaguely. 'Just as you say in that *most* interesting article. Although I do wonder if the reference isn't derived from Queen Boadicea.'

'Who?'

'It's all just history now, isn't it? That's the most marvellous thing about these times!'

George gestured towards the grey haze. He had plans and detailed designs for new garden suburbs. Neat, pretty and hygienic rows of individual cottages where families and groups of workers could live, ruled by nobody but themselves and the fair exchange of their produce and skills. Village greens near the heart of London. I realised, as George and I talked and we wandered, that we weren't perhaps so very far apart in our hopes after all.

'How's Anna?'

'She'd be here today if she wasn't doing something to help Sadie with her wedding.'

'You mean . . . ?'

'Oh, yes, Anna's quite a supporter of the need for change. She signed the Twelve Demands just like all the rest of us. Well, I mean apart from Sadie, of course—and *she* really couldn't, now, could she?'

We walked on across the hot hills. I was bemused and irritated to think that Anna and her jaunty chums were all leaping upon the bandwagon of change. What could they possibly know, or believe? But at least I got the impression from the remote, admiring and puzzled way George still talked about Anna that things had gone little further between the two of them than that kiss I had witnessed at Walcote House. In fact, even that was hard to believe now. I could, after all, have been mistaken. If Anna and George were what my mother would have called an item, they were a strange one. But then, Anna was always Anna. That was the whole point . . .

Whilst George and I wandered the blazing Kite Hills on that hot afternoon, her presence seemed to stay with us. I thought of her here, in a long summer dress and a summer smile and plain girlish sandals not so unlike the ones she had once worn at Redhouse. I could picture the glint of sunlight on the soft down of her bare arms. The bathing pools today were predictably popular, and George and I, unenthusiastic swimmers both, were happy to sit in the watery shade of the trees beside the Men's Pool as male bodies of every shape and size and haftmark sluiced in democratic confusion. He told me about his father, and his failures in the Architects' Guild, which had stemmed from a belief that the workmen of the lesser guilds would do a better job if they were better paid. George had inherited that same belief and developed it in this new climate of change. He'd never make an orator any more than I would—he was too quiet, too deferential—but as his eyes watched the play of sunlight on those pale and hairy bodies, he spoke passionately of his belief in the need for change.

'And the *nobility* of the workman, Robert. Look at them!' He shook his head; wondering, amazed. 'The beautiful nobility of the common working man . . .'

Something scratched at my window one night. It could have been a bird, a stone, but the noise was somehow more specific. It was as if someone had called out my name. I lay there, feeling the pressure of the night welling up from the tenement beneath me in coughs and groans. The grimy glass was wedged far open; a tiny target. I unpeeled myself from my sheets and leaned out. Sadie was clutching the whisperjewels at her throat in the dark yard below. She smiled and waved.

I pulled on a few clothes and headed down the dark hot gullet of the stairs. Sadie stood by the dry water butts in a long coat of silver fur. It shivered about her as if it was still alive as she brushed her lips against mine in a kiss which was too quick to decipher.

'It's an informal engagement present from Isumbard,' she explained about the coat as we sat in a hired cab and she lit a cigarette. 'I'm promised it'll be as warm in winter as it is cool now. Oh, I know it's ridiculous! And don't ask me what animal was killed to make it . . .'

'I saw you in the papers—'

'Bloody awful, that photograph wasn't it? My nostrils look like bloody railway tunnels. Tonight I felt I had to get out. Just away from Northcentral.'

The sweating bricks of Ashington clopped by. I could feel the heat of the horse wafting back over us, jostling with the presence of all the other bodies which had filled this carriage.

'We had to do this promenade along Wagstaffe Mall. And all the people were supposed to wave. Not that many turned up, though, but someone threw a lump of paving at me. Look . . .' She slid back the collar of her coat to show me her shoulder. There was a surprisingly large and angry-looking bruise. 'They didn't report *that* in the *Guild Times,* of course . . .' She reopened her bag to light another cigarette, then realised she already had one going. 'Filthy habit. I have to bribe the maid to go out and get them for me. She'd be in almost as much trouble as me if she got found out. Every time I have one of these things I tell myself that it's the last . . .' She sighed out a blissful, guilty, plume.

The streets of the Easterlies were quiet tonight, and strangely wyredark. Wondering if Sadie had any idea of the risk she was taking, I told her about the coming Midsummer, and how it was exactly a hundred years since the opening of the Exhibition at World's End which had signalled the start of this Third Age. It was so obvious that this should be the time when this Age should turn again that the only surprise was how long it had taken anyone to think of it. Then there were the Twelve Demands. Rumour had it that two had already been semi-officially conceded, and that the guilds had negotiated with the new workers' councils over the details of several more. The Age was collapsing like a paper fist, and it really did seem that the great gathering which was now being planned in Westminster

Great Park on the coming Midsummer Day would bring about its spontaneous demise. The occasion would be bright, joyous, uplifting. So many things were planned. The united brass bands of many guilds. Mass marches of apprentices. Makers of the previously obscure Arthropod Branch of the Beastmasters' Guild were even planning to release a new kind of butterfly. But there were always the few, the greedy rabble, who would give anything, revolution included, a bad name. And Sadie and her kind, with their huge houses—

'I know,' she sighed, 'we're bloated parasites sucking the very lifeblood out of the tired and over-exploited workers whom we treat little better than the bondsmen of the Fortunate Isles. And we should all disappear from the face of the earth forever. I'm really not sure if we'd be any better off at Saltfleetby, or our little cottage by the Lakes . . .' She counted off some of her many residences until she ran out of fingers. 'That is . . .' She studied the end of her cigarette before tossing it from the carriage in a bounce of sparks. 'If you seriously expect anything to *happen*. Oh, I know George is all for some better Age, and Anna now as well, so it's become almost *de rigueur* . . .'

The beetle-black gleam of Northcentral rose over the Easterlies. There was no sign of Hallam Tower. It was if as if tonight it had absorbed itself in a vast single dark and timeless pulse as Sadie talked of an upturned world, where even she, too, might think of joining in with the marching banners.

'But anyway, I really have to stay in London. There's so much to sort out. I never realised how complex it is, to get married. I mean, I can't even settle on my choice of *bridesmaids*—apart from Anna. There are so many people just waiting to feel upset . . .'

Marriage wasn't really the right word. I was reminded, as Sadie talked of ceremonies and valedictions, of the occasions early in my time in London when I'd watched the great iron freighters being tugged in to their berths at Tidesmeet. It was a slow dance, ponderously elegant, a great meshing of powers. Even now, in this Age's twilight, the guilds were circling each other in bellows of money and might.

'It's all to do with paint, Robbie . . .'

Apparently, the spars of the big telegraph pylons you saw striding everywhere across the country were seriously rusted. The solution, in the typical make-do-and-mend pattern of the guilds which even I had come to recognise, was to team up with Greatmaster Porrett's Guild of Distemperers, which had access to aethered technologies which could not only delay rust, but undo it—replace the damage of neglected decades with new growths of fresh steel. Part of that teaming up was Sadie.

'You won't believe the ceremonies! And the ridiculously unflattering clothes and hats I've had to wear! I've even had to swear allegiance to Isumbard's grubby little guild. Part of me, the Telegraphers' Guildmistress that I am, rebels against it. But Mummy just sighs and mutters about duty, and Daddy's not ever there. But, I mean, we've even had to hand over some of our chalcedonies . . .'

'What are they?'

'Oh, they're just these big crystals. About so large . . .' She illustrated with a twirl of her cigarette and the shape she made in the dark was a spell, a vision of the heavy crystal which I had once glimpsed Grandmaster Harrat holding, his face lit with wyreglow and awe. 'They're like, I don't know—bigger versions of these whisperjewels.'

'Or painstones, or numberbeads?'

'Oh, yes, that's right. Those things accountants waste their lives fingering. But chalcedonies are *much* bigger and more powerful. It's where the great guilds store their spells . . .'

I fell into silence. This, I supposed, was the time when I should ask Sadie to speak to the man she called Daddy about the entirely reasonable nature of the Twelve Demands. Who else would ever get such a chance? But I sensed the futility of the conversation even before I began it; not just Sadie's powerlessness, but the greatgrandmaster's as well. The guilds existed above and beyond the people who served them, even those at the highest level. I tried to picture the greatgrandmaster from my brief glimpses of him at Walcote House. All I saw was an ordinary man, with his hair unconvincingly dyed, a smile he put on his face like a mask, and the shade of something bigger and deeper and darker behind, which both was and wasn't him, and which was beyond power and reason. For the first time, a cold rush of worry passed over me about what might really happen in London on this coming Midsummer.

'Penny for them. Here.'

To be companionable, I smoked one of Sadie's cigarettes.

'You know, Robbie. I almost hope you're right. I hope it does all come tumbling down and I can go and work somewhere as a milkmaid and get varicose veins. But it won't happen. It won't . . .'

'But you'll be careful these next few days, won't you?'

'As long as you promise as well.'

Then we talked, as we could always talk, of Anna. We both agreed, from the perspectives of our vastly different knowledge of her, that the link, the association, whatever the thing was, between her and Highermaster George had little to do with what might ordinarily be thought of as love, or at least the physical kind. They were both too—too *something*—Anna especially, we assured ourselves, but George as well . . . The carriage had moved out from the Easterlies, crossed Doxy Street, meandered west. I really had no idea where we were heading until we stopped with a jolt beside a kind of ruined dock.

The drawn-back waters of the Thames beyond were bright against the darkness, winding in islets through the grey cratered mud . . . But I *knew* this place, although the entrance which had once been festooned with bunting was now chained and gated, and no light now came from the sea-urchin dome of the ballroom.

'I do so love empty places . . .' Sadie raised the heavy links which held the gate. I caught the gleam of her whisperjewel necklace as her breath made an impossible cloud of frost and the padlock fell away. 'Of course, it's quite disastrously unsafe . . .'

The arrowing boards swayed drunkenly, rising and tipping like a stormy wooden sea. Next winter when the Thames rose and froze again, a heavy tide in the spring, and all that was left here would be borne away.

'What went wrong?'

'I think it was just money. Too much expense and not enough profit. What an *Age* this is, Robbie! Remember when you and I danced here with Anna? But everything seems long ago now. Help me across this little bit, will you?'

Teetering like tightrope walkers across the remaining solid boards, we reached the ballroom itself, where the doors hung off their hinges and the black floor inside was scrawled with dust, bird-droppings, the wreckage of crashed chandeliers. We stumbled around for a few moments, breathless, almost laughing as we pretended to dance until some sense that the building was watching made us stop. The slope outside was so steep that we had to grip hard to the railings as we explored the walkways. But then Sadie leaned against them and pulled me to her and I felt the chill brush of her coat against my face. My hand slipped inside the furs and her breathing grew windy in my mouth as I found her breast, the spidery sharpness of that whisperjewel chain. The warm hardness of the charms sang in my ears as I stroked them and glimpsed again the tunnelling corridors of Walcote House. Then suddenly, the whole structure of the ballroom gave a shuddering, agonised creak, and we pulled away, shivering in the heat.

'I think we should be going.'

'No! Listen . . .' Sadie tucked her hair back behind her ear. 'Shssuh. Can't you hear?'

Then I heard it. The dim beat of the music like an undersea bell. The sigh and rise and exultation. The scented rustle of summer nights. The ballroom remembered; of course it remembered. Its ghosts danced around us in twirling gowns. *Come on, Robbie, you can dance, can't you?* And I could. Then the structure gave another protracted, agonised groan and the night air collapsed around us.

'Thank you for being the gentleman that you are back there and not taking, ah, *full* advantage of me,' Sadie murmured as she smoked and the carriage rocked me back towards Ashington. 'Not that I would have minded, but things have changed since that nice time we had in the spring at Walcote. It's all to do with this damn wedding. The ceremonies and spells . . .' She gave me a smile. Sad and unfathomable. 'You see, I'm a virgin again.'

V

A hot wind was blowing on Midsummer Eve just as it had been blowing all the night before. No one had slept, and the tin roof was trying to lift off the old concrete-floored workshop where the morning's meeting took place. *Shoom Boom* as Blissenhawk and spokesmen for the various groups with whom we had formed a wary bond stood on precariously raised packing cases above the objections and the rants and the points of order. Doubtless there were other meetings taking place in empty warehouses and factories across the Easterlies in which tomorrow's activities were being planned. The wind was flying in from the south, hot and strong as the searing African deserts from which it surely came. It carried with it the rooftop roar of a hundred other cities where, in France, across the Lowlands and the lands of Saxony, there were sure to be similar eruptions of change.

It really was the most extraordinary day. The sun was invisible, but the sky was white, ablaze, and sparkling drifts of sand pecked at my face as Saul and I carried the crate which contained our portion of the Twelve Demands back towards the relative safety of Black Lucy's basement. At the corner of Sheep Street, a dislodged door came bouncing down the road. When we dropped the crate to avoid it, several hundred sheets snowstormed into the air. We stood there laughing to watch them fly over the rooftops into the white skies, wiping the tears and grit from our faces.

Back at the tenement, we agreed that Maud, with her sore belly and bad ankles, should stay back in Ashington tomorrow and take care of Black Lucy. Then I set off alone to explore what I fully believed would be the last day of this Age. There was already a holiday air about the Easterlies on this Midsummer Eve. Roads, in preparation for tomorrow's street parties, were being argumentatively closed. Pub signs flapped. Children skipped and sang in the glittering wind. Down at the ferryport, none of the usual crossings were running, but a citizen, his breath reeking of spirits, was happy to lend me his small boat. We dragged it across the dried mud. I dipped my oars and pushed off, and gave him a cheery wave. When I'd finally fought against the surprisingly strong current and the pressure of the wind and hauled the boat up the far dry bank, World's End still seemed to be receding. I wiped my face, I dusted myself down, and a layer of sparkling powder almost instantly re-adhered to me. The tops of the hills of engine ice plumed. Everything was glittering, mirror-coated, changed as the hot wind picked up the crests of these white dunes and flung them across London.

The great hall of the exhibition was invisible today as anything but a pale skeleton and the wild gardens were ransacked by the wind. Struggling on, battered by trellises strung with swinging, clanging, sharp-edged tin cans, I finally reached canes and cloches and beds of biliously bright flowers. A thin black line of smoke stretched at right angles from the chimney of Mistress Summerton's toy house, but there was no response when I banged on the door with its fading, fluttering notice. I tried the handle and the wind almost pushed me inside where the smell of pipe tobacco hung in the air, and that earthy aroma of potting sheds which I would always associate with her. Ducking, peering, calling out her name, I was amused to find a broomstick propped in the room's far corner. I gave it a few experimental waves, although it had plainly only been used for simple domestic purposes. Beyond the main room there was a small inside privy and up the stairs, where the gables narrowed, was her bedroom. It was austere. I'd expected—I don't know what I'd expected—but the eyelet window seemed to take out more light than it gave from the howling storm and the bed was brown as a forest shadow. Pillows made from stuffed sacks. The deep scent of leaves. Did she really sleep up here? Did she *ever* sleep? And here was that long leather coat which she often wore, hanging in the near-dark like a discarded skin as the fire spat and leapt. And there were those glasses, set down on an old orange box at the bedside. Perhaps she really did need them to read—

'Come looking, have you?'

I spun around. 'I was just—'

'I can see what you were *just* doing.' Mistress Summerton stood there.

'I'm sorry.' The little room seemed to whirl around me. 'I should have waited outside.'

'In this weather? I do understand—who wouldn't be curious? But I sometimes get lads, unwanted visitors—' She made a gesture. 'As you can probably imagine, they trouble me . . .'

I followed her back down the stairs. She began pumping up the stove, then warming the water in the kettle.

'You know what's happening tomorrow?'

She gave a dry chuckle and stirred the pot. 'Of course. It's Midsummer.' She looked far older than I remembered as she gave me the steaming toy cup and saucer. Still hatless, her skull was visible beneath her wispy grey hair and her skin was stretched and gaunt; a withered skeleton. I sipped the scalding liquid as she watched me with her strange bright eyes. The wind boomed. My wicker chair creaked.

'The thing is,' I said, 'there's much talk that this whole Age will end tomorrow. Not because the guilds will it, but because the people do. And you know how it all began here with this exhibition. So what I was thinking, what I'm saying is, that things might happen here tomorrow, and it might not be entirely safe for you to stay.'

'*Entirely* safe, eh? I don't think my life's ever been that . . .'

'But you know what I mean.'

'I'm not going anywhere tomorrow,' she sniffed. 'There'll be a lot of my plants to rescue once this weather has settled, apart from anything else. One of my cold frames has already blown clean away.' Outside, the wind gave an extra-loud howl. Despite the heat, the vision through her window was white and wintry. 'So I think I'll stay here, if you don't mind, Robert, changing Age or no changing Age.' Her laugh was like snapping branches. 'But, yes. I suppose I do know what you mean, and I'm touched that you thought of me when there are so many other things you could be doing.' She stood up, finding her pipe and sucking on the dead dottle. 'But I too have to work. I have to sell my precious blooms. Why, otherwise, do you think the Gatherers' Guild permits me to live even here, in this abandoned place? You have no idea, for example, just how much it costs me to keep Annalise or Anna whatever she now calls herself in the manner in which she's become accustomed. Although I suppose that you probably *do* have an idea by now, seeing as you've been hanging around in the same kind of company . . .' She banged a few tins in search of tobacco. 'I used to have savings, you know. But not any longer. They've all vanished even without my spending them. I don't know what's happened to money . . .'

When my tea was finished I followed her outside into her gardens. She was in a mood I'd never seen her in before.

'Look at this place.' The combed beds were flattened, madly waving. 'All my work. All my efforts . . .'

'It's still beautiful.'

'You're going to tell me next I should be proud.'

'Aren't you?'

'It isn't *mine* to be proud of, is it?' She was still bareheaded and wearing a sacking apron which snickered about her. 'Nothing is.'

'Have you met Anna's friend, Highermaster George Swalecliffe?'

'How could Anna share me with someone with a name like that? Still, I suppose he might just think I was that dreadful supposed aunt of hers, if *she* wasn't supposed to be dead already.'

'George's a kind and decent man. He's not like the rest of them.'

'And Anna *is*?'

I shook my head. Her eyes were rheumy, brown as a dog's, I thought—or tried not. 'Anna's unique. And George sees something of that in her. And he, too, sees the need for change. He has a deep sympathy for the downtrodden . . .'

Another bitter laugh. 'Well, perhaps he *should* come and meet me.'

We came to an avenue of roses. The bushes bowed and scratched in the moaning wind. 'All this talk of change,' she said, 'and what difference would any of it make to me?' From one of her pockets, she produced what looked to be the same pair of secateurs which she'd been carrying when she opened the door at Redhouse to my mother. I watched as she grasped the swaying branches and began to snip—this alien creature with hands like twigs, her clothes whipping and smoking about her to reveal a blurring glint of that cross and C on her tiny chest.

'You should forget about me, Robert, no matter what happens tomorrow. And you should try to let go of Anna, too, or whatever it is of her that you're holding on to. She could have been many things—she could perhaps have even been the creature of wonder that you wish for and which I'm so plainly not. But she isn't.'

Briefly, the wind died. In a sudden, ragged flash of sunlight, the river, London, the great falling structure of World's End, the white hills, swarmed into view.

'Look at this place . . .' She gestured with her secateurs. 'You can see who this world belongs to, and it's certainly not my kind, revolution or no revolution. In that house in Oxford, when I was young and I knew no better, I used to dream that there were many others just like me waiting in the world beyond. Like me—but infinitely more powerful. One day, tomorrow, I was sure, the gates would swing open, and I would tumble out, and the world would be more of everything than I had ever imagined. The trees, the very clouds, would shape themselves to the winds of my favour.'

And people would bow down before me—I believed that, too, even as I raved and gnawed . . .

'But all I've ever seen of my supposed kind is creatures like poor Mister Snaith who cavort and dress up for you humans like tame apes, and the sad monstrosities in places like St Blate's who don't even know their own names. Still, I suppose we all need our stories . . .' A click of secateurs. 'Have this.' She gave me a rose; it was deep red, velvet-petalled. 'And promise me you'll be careful tomorrow . . .'

I wished her goodbye and pinned the flower in my but-tonhole. The wind shrieked through the empty panes of World's End, driving my little boat back towards the north bank. The Thames was skinned with the same sparkling dust of engine ice which twirled over the rooftops and threw incredible shadows like coloured rugs and turned the people into strange herlequins. I caught my breath on the viaduct over Stepney Sidings. The tracks and yards below were silent and empty; it might have already been Mid-summer Day. I thought of the time when I had stood on a much smaller bridge, gauging the moment when I might leap. And here I was now, on the eve of the change which I had spent much of my adult life working towards, and still thinking about jumping onto the backs of trains.

Then the wind shrilled and the long grey-black furnace of a big express bellowed beneath me, its wagons clattering point over point into the sidings. They were smart, blue-liveried. When the doors were slid back and ramps put out a whinnying herd of horses, huge, black, and almost as beautiful as Sadie's unicorns, emerged. It seemed like a day for strange sights.

The fountains in Westminster Great Park clattered in wet rainbows across the paving. The perilinden trees tossed their leaves. The revolving doors of the foyers of the big hotels spun emptily. The buildings grew somewhat smaller when I reached Kingsmeet at the edge of the Westerlies, al-though they still remained grand. Only the numbered bellpulls and the slight wildness of their front gardens betrayed the fact that these apartments were distant relatives of Easterlies tenements. But social distinctions, I knew, were stacked as tightly here as they were anywhere in England. Here—along streets where the windows gave glimpses of rooms filled with too much furniture, or too little—lived the not-quite wealthy, those who were on the rise, or on the fall. The nearly-rich of Kingsmeet clung to Northcentral's coattails and sometimes even visited its mansions, arriving in hired carriages at least as grand as those their hosts owned, and returning home later on foot, for the sake of economy. Here, too, in top rooms amid unfortunate confluences of plumbing, lived the artists and intellectuals who had enlivened many a greatguildmistress's afternoon salon. Here, in a small bed-sitting-room on Stoneleigh Road, and at a rent which would have bought you half of Thripp Tenements for a year, lived Anna Winters, guildmistress of no particular guild. And nearby, around the corner and past a bicycle shop, also lived Highermaster George Swalecliffe.

I gazed up at the pebbledash frontage and the third-floor window of Anna's room. I'd come this far before, but today was a time to move on—a time for change. Still, I had no idea what I would do, what I would say to her, as I pulled open the green wooden gate and tugged at the bellpull beside her name. One of the front door's loose blue panes rattled in the grainy wind. Then the door drew back and a neighbour peered at me. She had a once-expensive shawl draped around her neck, slippers with holes in their toes.

'You're not that guildsman . . . ?'

'What guildsman?'

'Oh . . .' She waved it away. 'Just someone or other who's been asking after Anna. She's not in, anyway. You could try the institute around the corner, I suppose . . .'

The institute was a cheap extension to an ugly church. Posters for cancelled amateur recitals and whist drives flapped on the front notice board and it was stiflingly hot and dark inside. For while I could scarcely see, but I finally discerned that placards were being hammered and painted. And George was everywhere, encouraging and supervising an odd mixture of guild widows, retired highermasters, their sibilant-voiced daughters and sons. He gave me a delighted near-hug when he saw me and instantly set me about sanding the splintered edges from a stack of plywood squares. I gazed about me through the busy gloom, searching for Anna. I still didn't know whether to feel encouraged or dispirited to think that these people, who raised their little fingers when they drank tea even when it came from chipped enamel mugs, should also want England to change. What New Age could we possibly share? George's vision of hand-dyed fabrics, well-made dressers, folk dances on the village green? But there she was, in a corner by the rudimentary stage, working at stitching together the strips of the coloured banner which flowed across her lap. Even in this dowdy place, with the doors banging in the wind and people tripping over each other in their hurry to seem busy, a different light fell on her from the wire-threaded window at her back. Remote, cool, heraldic. The needle dipped and rose. The thread gleamed, and it and her hair were the same colour as the gold in the cloth. My heart ached pleasurably as I smoothed the rough wood. I could have stayed doing this charmingly pointless task, and watching her, for a whole Age. This, I thought, is the real Anna Winters. She's the face you glimpse on a rushing train. She's the voice you hear from a room next door but never meet. She's all of those mysterious things, yet even when you stand close by her, or gaze from beside the rattling dustbins at the window of her room, the mystery remains.

She looked over, pulled an exasperated face, then beckoned me over.

'Will you help me with this, Robbie?'

The cloth of the woven banner was fine but slippery. It floated up in the hot drafts which tunnelled across the hall every time someone opened the doors.

'Hold this while I knot it . . .'

The design was complex and hard to make out amid the folds.

'This material's so difficult to work, even now I've almost finished it.'

'*You* made all of this?'

She gave a small nod which was both mocking and
knowing. *Of course I did, Robbie.* After all, she was Anna
Winters, who could turn her hand to anything, from playing the piano to dancing to this, yet never chose to make a
special show of any of it. Outside, the gritty afternoon billowed on. But she and I were the centre beyond the storm.
Stillness radiated across the marvellous cloth from Anna's
graceful hands.

'You've been with Missy, haven't you?'

I looked at her a little more warily. 'How can you tell?'

'That flower.' Her fingers brushed my lapel, and I saw
that Mistress Summerton's rose was dusted with a
sparkling dew of engine ice. 'But I'm glad you went to see
her today. She's lonely over there, although I know she'd
hate me for saying it. And I should go more often. I feel
guilty for not doing so.' She lowered her voice as George
breezed over to see how we were doing. 'But you'll understand it's hard.'

Cradled in the quiet light, Anna worked on. The cloth
slipped through my fingers. The needle rose and fell.

'I think I do,' I said eventually.

'Do what?' She looked up at me, small silver earrings
swinging on their threads from the lobes of her ear.

'Understand why you live as you do.'

She smiled, nodded, continued working. Anna Winters,
who was here simply because this was what people of
her kind in Kingsmeet were doing today, and because she
wanted to be supportive towards her friend George and,
perhaps, even towards me and all the rest of us citizens
who had struggled so hard for change across the Easterlies.
Not that she believed in this New Age, and not that she
didn't. She was Anna Winters, and she thrived on how people felt, and on making them happy, just as she was doing
now for me. The needle sank and rose. The banner unravelled across her lap, waterfalling in beautiful pools, and the
motion of its making was so soothing that I felt as if I was
being put together, mended, made whole.

'What do you think will happen?' I asked.

She paused in her sewing. 'I don't know.' She looked up
at me. Her green eyes dimmed, then brightened. *All this*

*talk of change, and what difference would any of it make
for me?* Mistress Summerton's words came back to me.
But Anna looked entirely wonderful, serene and cool. 'Do
you?'

I shook my head. 'Look, Anna—'

'You're going to tell me to be careful, aren't you? That's
what everyone seems to be saying today.'

I smiled.

'But it's you I worry about,' she said. 'And George over
there. And all the people like you and him, which seems to
mean most of London at the moment. Hopes are such brittle things, and they can hurt you when they break.' The needle gave a final dip. She took the thread and tugged at it
with her teeth. It made a sharp momentary indentation in
her lower lip which I longed to smooth away. 'Now.' She
stood up. The cloth rustled about her. 'It's time. Take this
end for me, will you?'

The cloth spread out from Anna and I as we walked
away from each other across that little Kingsmeet hall.
There was scattered applause and firework oohs and ahhs
as we unfolded the great long night-blue banner with its
patches of russet colour and its gold and silver threadings.
It shimmered and fluttered in the drafts like those kites on
the Kite Hills, ready to take flight into this New Age. I'd
expected it to form some picture or slogan, but Anna's banner fluttered in gold and abstract swirls. Look at it one way,
and you saw a comet-crossed night sky. Look at it another,
and there were the folds of distant mountains, the spells of
some arcane guild, the faces of children. The teasing, glittering colours invited you to see whatever you wanted to
see in them. I realised that, from her own unique stand-
point, Anna had cleverly captured the very heart and spirit
of this coming Midsummer Day.

I left a little later and walked back through London. The
sun was lower. The winds swirled black and orange and
pounded against the walls of the yards. Something would
happen tomorrow. That was true now beyond certainty. But
how? And what? A trickle of sweat chilled my back. I was
just off Doxy Street by now, and close to Ashington, and
walking beside a bow-fronted row of poulterers and cheese

merchants. They were shut now, probably had been all day, and the street was empty of all life and traffic. For once, in London, I was entirely alone. The shadows were climbing out from under the eaves as the sun sunk deeper in its veils. They stretched smoky fingers to tug at my clothes and retreated in crazed shrieks of glee. As I took a short cut along a side alley, I had to resist the stupid urge to look back, or to flee. The wind had tipped over the dustbins and was banging them about, flinging their contents into filthy heaps. I was picking my way over them when I sensed that something had followed me into this alley. I spun around to face it, and I saw, with an odd sense of triumph, that a figure really was standing behind me amid the spilled tins of rancid fat. It was a guildsman. Darkly dressed. Darkly cloaked. He wore no hat or hood, but his face was hard to make out although I knew that his eyes were upon me, and that they were amused, and knowing, and predatory. He stood there in the hot shadow darkness of that stinking alley, radiating the sick, draining complacency of knowing everything that I would never know.

'Who are you?' I tried to yell, although it came out as a whisper. 'What do you want?' I stumbled back around the tumbling, clanging dustbins towards him, careless, despite my fear, of anything beyond the need to know. 'Why are you doing this? Just tell me. Just . . .'

Then the wind gave an even mightier surge and my feet slipped in the spillages of rotting cardboard. When I regained my balance, my hands scrabbling along the walls, all that was left of my dark guildsman was a twirl of engine ice and London rubbish.

VI

Get up, Robert! It's late morning.

My eyes prickled open to absorb the stained ceiling of my tenement room. This was Midsummer Day, and the wind had drawn back and it had rained in the night, puttering restlessly through my dreams. Saul was singing on the floor below as he washed at his basin and Maud sounded bright and cheery for once as she lumbered about with her growing belly. At long last, her sickness was fading. She was blooming into pregnancy, and eating enough for twins, as Saul cheerily said.

Outside, the engine ice of World's End's hills had become a coat of varnish in the night's rain. The whole world seemed almost impossibly stark and clear. On Sheep Street, we joined up with Blissenhawk and left Maud to tend Black Lucy in preparation for the last ever edition of the *New Dawn*. Then, arm in arm, gathering ranks, we headed west. By the time we'd passed out of Ashington the crowd was so big that it welled up like a river over the edges of Doxy Street. Rumour was rife, sweeping us back, pushing us forward. The Twelve Demands had already been conceded! The money system had been changed! The dollymops were with us, in their gladdest of rags. So were

the Undertakers, in their black top hats. And the Lesser
Beastmasters, with their familiars on their shoulders;
miniature furry citizens, chirping and waving tiny flags.

I'd never known such a walk to Northcentral. Hallam
Tower flashed as always, a beckoning black star. We surged
from Cheapside and along Wagstaffe Mall where the greatest of all the great guildhalls rose in terraces of pink Ital-
ianate stone. But the Goddess of Mercy who surmounted
the final spire of the Gearworkers' Halls had somehow acquired a hat and a scarf. Even she was a citizen today, and
the sunlight was spinning around her, rising with the cries
of guildsmen of every kind and glinting on the vast dome
of the Miners' Chapel, where the catacombs were said to
be made of carved and polished coal. But this wasn't a time
for the suppositions of old. Those high gates, these studded
wooden doors, they would soon all be flung open. This was
the Midsummer to end all Midsummers. This was the end
of the Third Age.

There was to be no fair this Midsummer in Westminster
Great Park. As the crowds teemed in from all parts of London, there were the first flurries of disappointment. After
all, once the guildgates had opened and the Twelve Demands had been accepted and the Age had officially been
changed, what was to be done with the rest of the day? But
the perilinden trees, now that you thought of it, made for
fine climbing with their knobbed silver bark and their
leaves which tinkled like glass as you crawled amongst
them. And all those incredible flowerbeds, the lanternflowers and the moonivy—they were good for the picking,
come to think of it. Guildmistresses from Whitechapel paraded with garish topknots of petal and leaf, dancing and
kissing strangers, tipsy on nothing but the wild peculiarity
of the day. Those crashing fountains, they were for bathing
in! Of course they were—and always should have been.
Naked children and many who were old enough to know
better were soon cavorting amongst the spouting dolphins.

There were banners everywhere. Placards. Flags of
guild association. I searched for Anna's glittering blue-
gold creation, but Saul had grabbed my sleeve. It was time
to gather with Blissenhawk near the gates of the Guild of

Works where all the huge crates of our petition would be presented. It was noon. The bells and clocks began to blast. Bronze figures emerged from their clockwork doors high on guildhouse towers. The Twelve Demands for twelve o'clock. It fitted perfectly. Everywhere, now, there was a regathered purpose in the crowd.

The sound of all the clocks and bells rang clear in the magic air across all of London. The striking of a New Age, golden as this sunlight. The crowd drew back from the silver-tipped railings and gates of the Guild of Works as a wave does in the moment before it beats the shore, then drove forward again. The soot-weeping building beyond the gravelled paving and the elongated statues wasn't the most graceful of the great guildhalls, but it was certainly one of the biggest. I was near the front of the crowd as the last beat of noon faded and every soul in England, it seemed, waited for something to happen.

When it did, it came from behind us, and we heard it first as a surprised, delighted sea-roar rippling out from some distant spot as we all craned our necks to see exactly what was happening there. Nothing at first. Then a ripple of colour over the flags and banners and the white trees. The colours swelled up, filling a corner of the sky. They were varied, changing, impossibly beautiful. It seemed as if Anna's banner had grown and had taken flight, but it was a long moment before those of us at the front of the crowd were able to work out what this spreading rainbow really was. When we did, we joined in the cheering and laughed as the new creation of the long-neglected Arthropod Branch of the Guild of Beastmasters plumed into the air. Butterflies, just as promised, and they were huge and blue and red-golden. And in the instant of their release, in that glorious upward sigh of colour, this unique Midsummer Day had at last acquired a name. In the history books, in the songs which mothers sung over cribs, on plaques which we were sure would soon appear on the very paving on which we now stood, this would forever be Butterfly Day.

The creatures fanned out across London with a soft fluttering. The blue sky returned. The cheering ceased and joy settled back on our lips, and with it came a renewed anticipation. We looked once more towards the great gates of the Guild of Works as, in the quiet first minute of that first afternoon, the thing which we had long dreamed of, but which some nagging corner of our minds had always felt to be impossible, finally happened. With a screech and a shudder, a flash of bronze and the grinding of some hidden mechanism, the guildgates began to open. The crowds were silenced, awed. Apart from the cries of babies and querulous questions of children, apart from the hiss and clatter of the fountains and the soft tinkle of the perilinden trees back across Westminster Great Park, a deep stillness reigned. On this moment of Butterfly Day, cheering would have been wrong. We wanted to know. We wanted to see. When there was a sound, it came from within the guildgates, and from behind the wings of the great, squat building. It was the clop of hooves.

In a flash of helmets and breastplates, a nod of crimson plumes, they emerged; the cavalrymen, astride hundreds of the beautiful black horses I had glimpsed yesterday at Stepney Sidings. The two streams which came from either side of the guildhouse merged and jingled through the gates and spread out in a double line on the far side of the railings. Once more, silence reigned. I could see what would happen now. A captain with an especially large red and white plume to his helmet was already dismounting. Now, he would come forward, and, in the face of this threat of force, a delegation of citizens would soon be formed. They would go forward and the guildgates would close on them and the rest of us would be left waiting. There, inside that huge, jumbled building, there would be discussions and compromise. There would no longer be Twelve Demands, or ten or eight or six. And the old Age would continue. Still, even I had to concede that it was a brave act by that captain of the cavalry, to dismount and walk alone towards the vast line of us citizens. Even with his plume, the swing of the sheathed sword, he looked small and almost insignificant.

'Is there anyone . . .' He paused. 'I only ask that—'

It was at that moment that the first rock was launched at him from the crowd.

* * *

Much happened after that on Butterfly Day, but most of it was blood, storm, confusion. Those who were there to witness it perhaps knew less than the many others who later claimed to have been. The severed limbs. The pounding hooves. The savage balehounds. Or that brave captain, stuck down and engulfed by the mob. But for me, in the enormous push of the crowd, my main concern was not to be trampled. I didn't resist when I was pushed back towards Prettlewell Fountains; there, at least, there might be something solid to hold on to instead of this treacherous pavement. I'd lost all sight of Saul, Blissenhawk and anyone else I knew. Then I heard a voice I recognised. It was Highermaster George, and he was atop Prettlewell Fountains. He'd clambered up from the seething mass of bodies which had surged over the marble lip into its waters and stood high above the frothing mermaids. Dripping around him like strands of vivid blood as he shouted and waved were the torn and leaking remains of Anna's banner.

'Citizens!' He balanced on the marble dome at the apex of the fountain. 'Citizens!' He almost slipped. 'We mustn't give up hope . . .' But the rest of what he said was drowned out by the clatter of the fountain, and by a chorus of voices. *He's one of them . . . He's not us . . .* The unfortunate thing about George's voice, beyond its resonant upper-classedness, was that it sounded remarkably like that of the cavalry captain who had walked towards the crowd a few minutes earlier. And red dye streamed from Anna's banner across the marble. He looked as if he was drenched in the blood of the innocent. Highermaster George gazed down on us, and smiled in that knowing, faintly patronising way of the high guilded as he flipped back a wet lock of his thinning hair. *Get him . . . The bastard . . . Let's . . .* Figures started to scramble up the wet statuary towards him. He slipped, tumbled, disappeared.

WHERE'S GEORGE!!!!!!!!!!!!!!!!!!!

A voice screamed out as I tried to wade through the fountain. I turned, but the crowd was surging in the pools and there was no one I could see. Then the voice came again like the rush of my own desperate anxiety as I slipped and the foul, foot-jostling waters came up to swallow me. My head went under. I was stamped on. When I finally pulled myself up, gasping and spitting, a woman's face loomed up beneath the churning surface, grey as the pool's fine marble, her eyes wide and her blue lips threading a thin scarf of blood and vomit. I didn't see any of the supposed many who were killed by the cavalrymen's swords or the balehounds' jaws on Butterfly Day, but I saw several who were drowned in those dreadful fountains. Choking, I struggled on through the pluming water in the direction in which George had vanished. I was surrounded no longer by individual people, but by whatever it was that people become when chaos overtakes a crowd.

WHERE'S GEORGE!!!!!!!!!!!!!!!!!!

The voice roared at me, chill with fear. The jostling bodies around me seemed to sense it too. They shrank back and stumbled over me and stabbed at my ribs as they attempted to retreat. *WHERE'S GEORGE!!!!* Then I saw that it was Anna, pushing through the crowds. But it wasn't the Anna of yesterday in that little hall, or of any other day. She was as drenched as I was, and the same spilling dye that had leaked over George had ruined whatever clothes she was wearing, and her hair was black and lank and redflowing. But in this maddened, bellowing crowd, there was more which was strange about her. It was the burning power of her eyes, which were painful to look into, and the roar of her voice inside my skull, which, even in this awful place, sent others staggering away. This both was and wasn't Anna Winters, and she was terrible to behold.

WHERE'S!!!!!!!!!!!!!!!!!!! Then she saw me and a little of the normality of ordinary recognition crossed the white flame of her face. 'Robbie—you've got to help me find George. You've *GOT* to . . .'

She grasped my hand with hers. It was colder than the marble, bleaker than that drowning face. But in that moment, I was more afraid of her than of anything that I had witnessed on that terrible day. In my horror, I think I might even have tried to push her away. And the crowd was still powerful, pouring back around me. *'PLEASE . . . !'* Anna's fingers weakened on me as, in the moment of my repulsion, I was swept away.

Butterfly Day; the name was perfectly chosen. Something bright and frail, which rises with the sun and only lives a few hours. I saw one of the creatures stuck to a shopfront as I wandered past the shattered facades of Oxford Road, shouting for George, for Anna, for Saul and Blissenhawk, searching for any face I could recognise. It was still fluttering, but its wings were adhered to a smear of hair and blood. And I could still hear the balehounds, the distant rattle of hooves, the slide and crash of glass. A huge grinning bear loped up to me and I shrank back, but it was only an old woman carrying a rug she'd looted. *Fuck off, citizen,* she scowled. This was Butterfly Day, and the shops might have been emptied, but the guildgates had held and no concessions had been made. This old Third Age would continue. Nothing would ever change.

Buildings were burning. Their smoke hung low in the air. A sort of night came, although the sky remained bright and hot. Wherever he had gone, whatever had happened to him, there was no sign of Highermaster George. I made my way back towards the Easterlies some time after midnight with the many walking wounded, the dangerous mobs of children, the weeping grown men. Fires were burning here as well, and the prominent smell was of burning rubber. I passed a balehound, captured and crucified on a lamppost, in Cheapside. I saw a severed hand lying in the gutter just past Tidesmeet. Some poor unfortunate was being beaten up by a crowd at the edge of Houndsfleet, and I walked on and did nothing. That same grey, greasy pall of defeat had settled over everything, but, apart from the smoke, Ashington remained unchanged; there was still even Midsummer bunting. There was no sign of Saul or Maud at our tenements, and no sign of Blissenhawk either, so I wandered down to Sheep Street where poor Maud, for all I knew, might still be waiting with Black Lucy for news that the Age had changed.

The door to our printing room hung at an odd angle. I

froze, but then heard with relief the sound of Saul's voice. But inside, down in the grey light and the filling smoke, the basement was almost unrecognisable. The stink of spilled solvents. Dripping scrawls of aetherised ink on the walls and ceiling.

'Saul? Saul? Are you all right?'

'I'm fine, Robbie. It's not me . . .'

I scrambled through the mess, and saw the dim outline of his face behind what remained of Black Lucy. Maud was beside him, balled up and whimpering with her hands stuffed between her legs. She cowered and gave a small scream when she saw me.

'It's all right.' Saul stroked her hair. 'It's just Robbie.'

VII

Maud survived, but her baby didn't. So did Highermaster George, although I didn't learn what had happened to him on Butterfly Day until some time later. The tired old Third Age limped on, stale and angry and arthritic, and many pointless proclamations were made. After the long early summer of hope and preparation, autumn came in early that year. It crept into London like a foul old dog, unsanitary and dank-smelling, clotted with mud and blood, long-dead hopes, the filth of disease.

Physical force or moral force? There was no point now in argument. The idea of a benign change to society was the frail, hot dream of a summer night, lost with the chilled sweat and pain of this new, aching daylight. We moved what little remained of our printing works to a shed behind a slaughterhouse, but this time we no longer called our paper the *New Dawn*. In fact, it had no consistent name and was scarcely a paper at all, but a blotchy and irregularly issued series of single-sheet rants, calls to arms, instructions as to how the common domestic materials and the implements available to almost any guildsman could be made into weapons. Paraffin in bottles with a rag in the top. The sharpened spike of a stair-rail. Simple spells which would

unravel the workings of a machine. Saul was more than
happy to supply the illustrations. We moved from our
rooms at the top of Thripp Tenements to smaller lodgings
nearby, not so much out of fear as because Maud, with the
pains she was still having, was no longer capable of running a nursery, and there was little business now in Ashington in any case; the women all stayed at home. This time
Saul didn't bother to decorate the lead-green walls with
friezes of the countryside. He was out much of the time, on
business neither I nor Maud knew of.

Once I'd learned that George was safe I put my interest
in him and Anna and all the prim Westerlies aside. I
remembered that ridiculous gesture of his at Prettlewell
Fountains—a call to arms to make better tapestries and
hand-turned chairs. No wonder, with that accent, he'd been
set on by the common guildsmen he pretended to admire.
And he'd escaped as well—that, too, was typical of his
kind. And Anna, Annalise, Anna Winters, whoever and
whatever she was—that glimpse of her I'd has as she
screamed into my head through the roar of the crowd was of
something alien, impossible, strange. This was an entirely
false Age, and she was part of its falseness. As for Sadie,
her guild, her father the greatgrandmaster, their huge
houses, that ridiculous marriage, I'd fallen out of their spell.
They were all in their way responsible for those black
horses, the flashing sabres, the screams and the drowned
faces. She even wrote to me once or twice but I scarcely
read the contents of the ridiculously long telegraphs only
she could have afforded to send. They were filled with all
the exclamations and underlinings I'd come to expect from
her kind, the same glib protestations of shock and innocence.

The thousands of posters of the Twelve Demands
slipped from the walls and rotted in the gutters. But over
the streets and houses, the telegraphs still burned with bilious light. This Age was like a dying patient who grows
brighter and wilder and more active even as life fades. The
power, the skeleton, whatever it was which kept this country functioning, was peeking terribly through the thinning
flesh which had once covered it, but it was as ugly and

powerful as ever. More than anything, I came to hate money. Money seemed, in its presence, in its absence, to be at the core of whatever was to blame with the wrongness of this Age. Guildsmistresses could grow so thin that the sides of their aprons met at their backs and die from terrible trollisms, but still the terror of poverty and the uncaring privilege of wealth remained. I thought again of those laddering figures of accounts which I had glimpsed within those numberbeads at Walcote House. Something was wrong, something about this continuing Age was so hollow that I yearned to push my fist through it, but still it held, held, held.

Tidesmeet Docks had become a dangerous place to make even innocent-sounding enquiries about directions to this or that berth. For the few who were prepared to break the rules of their guilds, there was more money than ever to be made. Ships came and went in the night. Whole cargoes vanished. Bodies of the betrayed floated in the stagnant waters. Frauds such as the one which Saul and I had innocently helped commit on that bondhouse full of teachests really did seem to belong to another Age. And the *Blessed Damozel* lay in an abandoned wasteland of river sludge. She was nothing more than a hulk. Only the nameplate on the stern, still faintly aethered, glowing black, and the green-hung spars of her rotting sails, spoke of the fine vessel she had once been. Then there was Grandmaster Bowdly-Smart himself, whose face I glimpsed through the rain in a grand personal carriage, and who lived, I discovered, just north of Oxford Road and conveniently close to Westminster Great Park, where the blood had been washed from the paths and turf had been relaid so that the likes of his wife, in a huge hat and an improbable outfit, could exercise her extraordinary little dog beside the chatter of Prettlewell Fountains whilst a maid followed behind with a scoop.

What had they *done*? What *was* it? Their house was a blue-tiled mansion called Fredericksville on Fitzroy Street, which was in fact one of those ornate Northcentral squares which are centred around the railings of a small private garden which no one but the gardeners who tend it ever

bother to enter. I stood at night beneath its dripping trees
and watched the Bowdly-Smarts' comings and goings. I'd
never studied the lives of such people before, and the thing
which astonished me most was just how many others were
required to service their needs. Clothed in wealth, in money,
the high guilded grow huge and greedy in their needs.
Barrow-loading butchers and bakers and milkmen, and the
produce of several grocerers straight from Covent Garden
were required long before dawn. Then came the laundry
and service maids who lived out, and all the variously
suited suppliers of endless different kinds of goods and
services, most of which I couldn't even guess at. All day,
they came and went, came and went. It was as if—although
the Bowdly-Smarts had no children, no family, and lived,
but for that ridiculous dog and all their servants, entirely
alone—their lives would collapse if some new morsel
wasn't brought to feed their back door every quarter of an
hour between dawn and sunset. The plateglass windows on
Oxford Road might have been broken in the tides of disaffected guildsmen, but for the Bowdly-Smarts, whatever
and whoever they were, life could never have been sweeter.

I watched Grandmaster Bowdly-Smart as he stood each
morning outside his front door, sniffing the air as if it were
fine wine even when there was stinking fog. I followed his
carriage as he set about his business and visited the offices
of this or that trading company and took meals in restau-
rants of the kind which didn't advertise their food. In
Tidesmeet, he concluded deals beside the wind-whipped
waters of quays, and shook the vine-bruised hands of the
cranemen and exchanged jokes with the porters. They were
wary and evasive when I spoke to them afterwards, but I
found out that he was nominally a member of the Guild of
Reevers and Factors, an organisation which, for all the fine
turrets of its guildhouse, was essentially a shopfront from
which the newly rich could buy the status they craved. His
real skill was clearly buying and selling, but the truth of
what he bought and sold remained irritatingly out of reach.
I spoke to some of Fredericksville's servants in a squat pub
where their kind gathered, but all I discovered was that his
first name was Ronald, and hers was Hermione. I even

risked adding to the bodies which floated in the flooded dry docks by breaking into the offices of quaymen. But all I found were account sheets and more numberbeads; laddering figures, money and money and more money. I was no nearer to knowing exactly what Grandmaster Bowdly-Smart was, beyond the obvious fact that he was simply one of that new breed, the self-made businessman, which had come to flourish at the end of this Age. I even began to doubt my own memory and wonder whether I wasn't in the grip of some odd obsession, and whether Grandmaster Bowdly-Smart had ever really been Uppermaster Stropcock from Bracebridge in the first place.

Unemployed guildsmen gathered at lit braziers on freezing street corners and shouted through the fog as I made my familiar way one evening around Westminster Great Park towards Fitzroy Street and the bare and dripping trees of that private garden. Tonight, the lights from Fredericksville's windows outshone its neighbours and several carriages were drawn up outside, beside which the drivers stood smoking. I stood, too, in my freezing hiding place, and waited. Several hours later the front door finally opened. The women who emerged into the coloured light squawked and fluttered and were dressed in hats and furs. This had plainly been quite a gathering, and Madame Bowdly-Smart's foghorn voice carried as she shouted her goodbyes. The front door almost closed, then opened again, and a last small guest scuttled out, peeping nervously both ways before heading off on foot out of the square, lugging an improbably large carpetbag. Unmistakably, it was Mister Snaith.

I had to shout before he noticed me beyond Oxford Road, and then he cringed against a boarded-up shopfront, sheltering his face in the crook of his arm.

'Oh! It's you . . . Master Robert!'

His shoulders uncringed. He wiped a dewdrop from his long, odd nose.

'What happened to that cabsman?'

'He's still unreliable. Can't just be the flu, can it?'

I took Mister Snaith's carpetbag and carried it for him as we walked on.

'You've been inside that house? With the Bowdly-Smarts?'

He nodded. 'She's a promising customer. What I mean is, she has a group of friends who, um . . .'

'Fellow seekers?'

'Exactly. It's this way here. Foul night isn't it? I do so welcome your presence . . .'

I'd expected us to turn out from Northcentral—perhaps into the Easterlies or to the old wooden buildings which still squatted by Riverside—but instead we then turned left along Linden Avenue, right into the opulent heart of Hyde. Hallam Tower was close here, dissolving into the night clouds. Then, around another turn, the scene grew more familiar. Even Northcentral needed its sewers and gasometers—all the more so, considering the amounts of everything which were consumed here—as well as an engine house to drive the local tramtracks, which was still thumping and smoking, and quite recognisable despite the attempt that had been made to make it look like a Grecian temple. Beside it was a soot-encrusted warehouse. The arch of the main doorway had been half blocked with cruder and more recent bricking.

Mister Snaith fiddled for some time with his keys. Inside, it was somewhat quieter, although the pounding of the engine house remained as he lit a lamp and led me up a series of rough wooden stairs and along corridors lined with boxes and sheeted furniture. This, he explained, was where the guildspeople of Northcentral kept all the things they couldn't fit in their houses. A smell which I had noticed coming off him was far stronger here. It was essentially dusty, but overlaid with woodpolish and stale mothballs. He reached a crossroads of four-poster bedsteads and led me to door pinned with a browned and illegible notice.

'Most obliged. You'll be staying for a while, I hope . . . ?'

The walls of Mister Snaith's dwelling in the depths of this warehouse consisted of piled packing cases and the furniture was opulent and old and ugly—unwanted fitments which, he explained, had never been collected at the expiry of their storage contracts. I sneezed from the dust.

'Now this medal.' He gave me a lump of brass. 'It was presented to me on St Barnabus's day by Greatgrandmaster Penfold, who was then generally reckoned to be the second most prominent guildsman in the realm . . .' Then a silver plaque, and a daguerreotype in an otherwise empty book, and a guild medal in an ornate worn velvet box. The dates went back to the start of this Age. *Thump, thump, thump* . . . The engine house outside must go on all night, providing the power which was needed to bear the last of Northcentral's errant occupants back to their huge houses. 'This was painted by Guildsman Phenix. It's me, of course . . .' Mister Snaith sighed. His tiny fingers stroked a trace of cobweb from the miniature frame. 'You're familiar with his work? He was the greatest portraitist of his day. Dead now, of course . . .' The colours might once have been luminous, but the paint was darkened and crazed. Mister Snaith; standing one-legged in a fake-storybook landscape, dressed in green like a elf, toupee-less, and smiling.

'How long have you lived here?'

'Not so long *here*. Perhaps only twenty years. I don't have to pay rent, and the Gatherers' Guild has provided me with all the necessary permissory notes. They say my presence helps keep the vandals away. Of course, I've always lived in the city. But Northcentral's not what it used to be.' He shivered. His toupee slid askew on his head.

'People like the Bowdly-Smarts live here now, don't they?'

Mister Snaith rustled and gleamed. 'Grandmistress Bowdly-Smart may not be the most ah, *cultured* client I've ever had, but needs must, as they say.' A faint green phosphorescence of the kind you might find on bad meat leaked from his sleeves.

'That bag of yours,' I said eventually. 'It must be heavy. And, if that cabsman's still letting you down, I was thinking . . .'

'Oh, but I'd *never* expected . . .'

I put down Mister Snaith's carpetbag on the iridescent carpet. 'We met at Walcote House in the summer, grandmistress. Do you remember?'

'Of *course* we did!'

The Bowdly-Smarts' hallway was glittery and dense. I was reminded of Grandmaster Harrat's long-vanished townhouse back in Bracebridge—but this place was at least twice the size, and stuffed with six times the contents. There was a different odour as well; ripe and damp and fierce and unmistakable, the reek of dog.

'Of course, Ronald's not here to see you tonight.' She gave a protracted sigh and patted her strings of jade and pearl necklace. 'Out on business, don't you know. This is *such* a difficult Age.'

Then the other guests began to arrive. Pushing aside maids as she charged through her hallway to greet them, Grandmistress Bowdly-Smart gasped and fluttered her hands whilst Mister Snaith, his carpetbag and I trooped into a long room which was stuffed with more ornaments and artefacts than a well-stocked shop. Figures and figurines and statues and vases, paintings and silhouettes and daguerreotypes, weird relics of other cultures, screen prints and paintings, frame piled upon mirror with rug and lionskin clambering over tapestry and tasselled throw; it looked as if all of the efforts of the recent Age had risen up in one huge tidal wave to beach themselves here. The dusting, the polishing, the rinsing and waxing, simply didn't bear thinking about. And the guildswomen who had gathered here this winter's evening, perched on the edges of stools and chairs, were as ornate as their surroundings. Unlike Grandmistress Bowdly-Smart, who had favoured crimson tonight as strongly as she had at other times favoured lime green or canary yellow, most were dressed in iridescent versions of black, like the ornaments of polished coal and jet and iron which surrounded them, and picked out in black pearls and night-sparkling diamonds. They rustled and cawed at Mister Snaith's entrance. The dog which was the cause of the smell which hung even stronger in this room like an incipient headache was a thing named Trixie, which one or other of the grandmistresses would occasionally scoop up and make cooing, kissing noises into its squashed-up face. Trixie's fur was pink and turquoise. He had little claws, and a crest along his spine. Less a dog, in fact, than one of the

Cathay dragons which guarded the mantelpiece come to life; another tribute to the powers of aethered industry.

The conversation, to begin with, was loud and quick and animated, although Mistress Bowdly-Smart's vowels didn't stand out here as strongly as they had at Walcote House. I caught traces of Bristol and the West Country from the other guests, and Preston, even the Easterlies. People *did* rise from humble beginnings in England, difficult though I still found that to believe, and I wondered now if the Bowdly-Smarts' ascent wasn't the simple result of hard work and good luck, and if this whole weird enterprise into which I'd dragged myself wasn't merely an expression of my own stupid envy. At close hand, the life that Mistress Bowdly-Smart had spun for herself was even more complex than I had imagined. There were photographs and miniature portraits on side tables of mutton-chopped high guildsmen whom she claimed to be close relatives. If Mistress Bowdly-Smart, previously Stropcock, was to be believed, she and her husband had, if anything, descended from far greater heights to end up living here in Fitzroy Street. It was clever—to twist the past so far around that even I, who knew the truth of it, found myself lost and wondering in this over-crowded room.

The other guests cast me nibbling glances as they sipped their tea and talked of the evening ahead. A fire raged in the hearth, but a chill fog of anticipation slowly began to gather over the gilt and crystal. Mister Snaith looked weirdly at home. Ever the professional, he shuffled about in his reversed green and orange cloak with his toupee off, his pointed face at almost the same height as those of the seated chattering guildmistresses. He flashed the tattooed patch on his powdered left wrist, then snatched it quickly away. He laid his bird-fingers on the hands of each of them, and made soft murmurings close to their ears. Whatever it was he said to each of them, they all seemed changed by it. Perhaps, I thought, some final mystery really would be revealed tonight just as he always seemed to promise, although, knowing what I now did, I very much doubted it.

'Well? Shall we begin?'

The maids extinguished the lanterns, and we fellow seekers sat at an empty circular table at the far end of the darkened room, away from the glow of the fire which pulsed
and glimmered across the glass and metalwork, turning the
whole place into a strange, exotic cave. Mister Snaith sat
alone at the furthest, darkest end; he was so small on his
chair that little more than his head, disembodied, dimly reflected, seemed to hover above its polished surface. The rest
of us held hands, which was an odd sensation in itself, to
feel the nails and rings tensing, the surges of sweat and chill.
I had come here as colluder and sceptic, but the atmosphere
in that coalescing darkness was earnest.

As Mister Snaith's breathing grew ragged, the questions
were of young Master Owen, who'd fallen under the ice
whilst skating twenty years before, and of baby Clark, who
had lived for six short happy hours. A whispering chorus of
lost suitors and dead children, the missing and the stillborn,
gathered around these grieving women as they sat around
that table with Mister Snaith. I'm not sure quite how he managed on his own when I, or that long-lost cabsman, wasn't
with him, but, even though I understood some of his trick-
eries, a chill fell upon me and I felt myself thinking of my
own losses, and poor Maud, and especially of my mother. I'd
placed the carpetbag on the precise spot he'd instructed just
beneath the table where he could reach it with his tiny foot.
But the cottony stuff which emerged, the tinsel and the phos-
phorus and the rubber balls you squeezed to make sounds,
even the vague words which he spoke in many cracked and
croaking voices—I understood now that all of these things
were incidental to the real purpose of such gatherings as this.
These guildswomen hardly needed Mister Snaith. His tricks
and preposterous claims were incidental. They made their
own magic, and it came from the loss in their hearts and the
want of not knowing; it came from the cheek unkissed and
the thing not done or said, or said once and regretted forever.

'He'll never leave London, will he?' Maud had her best
hat crammed down on her head as she stood outside our
latest tenement. Wiry, mist-beaded spills of her hair stuck
out from all sides of it like tangles of spiderweb. She gave

me a bright, frail smile. 'All these years of big talk, those
stupid drawings. And look where we still are . . .'

'These relatives of yours—are you still sure?'

'Can't be any worse than this, can it? I suppose they're
guilty about those years ago when they should have helped
my mother.'

Then her carriage arrived, although it was really just a
wagon pulled by an elderly dray, and Saul emerged from
wherever it was that he'd been pretending to keep busy at
and helped Maud stack the few belongings she was taking
with her.

'No, no. Just wait there! Leave it all to me.'

'I'm not an invalid, Saul. God knows, I've lifted enough
heavy things in my life.'

But Saul, as ever, was struggling to be the gentleman.
He'd even dusted off one of his best waistcoats.

'And you'll write as soon as you get there? I mean,
Kent's not so very far?'

But Kent might as well have been on the other side of
the moon on that day. Some distant relatives of Maud's had
a farm there, and had written to say they needed help.
Maud was taking a risk by going there, but then, as she'd
said to Saul often enough in the quiet that had fallen between them now that they'd stopped arguing, she was taking an even bigger one by staying on in London—and,
after all, she was sick of the place.

The same faces as ever, the old women, the scabby,
furtive children, the distracted mothers who now mostly
took care of their own babies, came out into Thripp Street
to watch Maud's departure. Some of them were crying,
but that made it easier for me not to, and for Saul to put on
a brave face. But for the mist, Maud's features were dry
and distracted as well as she kissed Saul and hugged me. In
her mind, I thought as the driver cracked his whip and we
watched the tarpaulined rear of the carriage jostle off and
disappear into the grey, she left us long ago, on Butterfly
Day.

I received a message from Highermaster George a term or
so later. It was written in a flowing hand on expensive

paper, and contained all the usual *if you don't minds* and *most exceptionally gratefuls* that his kind have drummed into them at school, although the tone was somehow desperate.

I'd never been to the top of Hallam Tower before. I was a true Londoner by now, and such places were for visitors, although, as the lift clacked me up from the cold and smoke of a London morning into almost-sunlight and the turning, irresistible sweep of the lantern's wyreglow, the view was certainly well worth the sixpence I'd paid at the turnstile. I'd got there slightly early, but I was even more certain that something was wrong when I wandered the iron gantries with the morning's first sightseers and found that the perpetually considerate George hadn't arrived before me.

'Robbie, Robbie . . .' Flushed and apologetic, he appeared a couple of liftloads later, wearing a bobble hat with a hole in it. His coat had seen better days as well. Frayed and with hanging bits of lining, it was almost like the one I was wearing, now that I kept the few decent things I had for my trips out with Mister Snaith.

'Well . . .' We studied each other and smiled in mutual acknowledgement that, like our coats, we had both seen finer days, and winters, than this one.

Irresistibly, though, we talked of politics, just as we had done in the summer on the Kite Hills, although so much had changed since then. It was common wisdom in the Easterlies that the failure of Butterfly Day had come about in large part as a result of the treacherous connivance of the middle guilded of the Westerlies, who had diluted the Twelve Demands in cottony compromise and irrelevant talk about changing the calendar. In a way, in my fondness for George, and my longing for Anna, in the blithely stupid way I had allowed myself to become one of Sadie's discoveries, I was a textbook example of the case. But I shared with George a nostalgia for a better kind of future, and deep doubts about whether it would ever be achieved.

The black glittering prisms of Guildmaster Hallam's great lantern flashed and turned on the oiled runners of their gantry just a dozen yards above our heads. The object must have weighed many tons but it moved with nothing

more than a dull swishing like the wingbeats of a huge
bird, supported on the thousands of tons of steel girder
which had been erected almost eighty years before with the
help of the changed Ironmaster Gardler and the Gatherers'
Guild. A dark tunnel swept into the sky above us and all
of London, through the patchy mist, the pale sunlight,
changed and reformed beneath. At times such as this, all
I felt was the impenetrable power and solidity of this
never-ending Age. It was the same when I visited the
Bowdly-Smarts, where the master of the house, to show his
disapproval of such shenanigans as communing with
changelings, was always out on business, and Fredericksville's bewildering rooms, on the occasions I briefly
excused myself and crept about them, were filled with
nothing but expensive junk.

There were strikes again in the Easterlies, and there had
been trials and hangings at Newgate. Blissenhawk had
taken to wearing an old military tunic and calling himself
major. Rough bands of raggedly armed guildsmen paraded
behind him up and down on Sheep Street whilst Saul was
more secretive than ever about what he did. A literally
feverish atmosphere gripped the whole city; there was an
epidemic of the same bronchial ailment as had gripped me
during my first London winter. This time, people had less
food in their bellies, and less hope in their hearts, with
which to fight it. But from up here on Hallam Tower the
golden dome of the Miners' Chapel still glowed, and the
paths of Westminster Great Park loomed and receded beautifully in the tiers of chilly mist. And the people down
there, with their bright hats and the strange dogs, were like
spilled buttons, or those strands you got sprinkled on your
ice-cream at long-lost Midsummer Fairs.

'This ridiculous structure . . .' George slapped the iron
handrail and wiped the fog from his stubble. 'All this metal
and money. What's the point of it, eh . . . ?'

He balanced on the tips of his boots, his red-rimmed
gaze following the thin linkage of girder to girder all the
way down through the mist. From here, with the effect of
perspective and the fog's changing greys, we seemed to be
hanging on almost nothing. But it surprised me, as he

stretched so far over that people glanced towards him and
I found myself taking a step closer, that George of all
people, a guilded architect looking down over brash Northcentral, should find the extravagance of Hallam Tower particularly hard to understand. For me, its purpose was as
blazingly obvious as its light. The rest of these other spires
and crenellations were scarcely visible from the Easterlies.
So what better demonstration of guilded power could there
be than to have this great, frail structure, endlessly flashing
through the rooftop smog?

'Anyway . . .' Somewhat to my relief, George leaned
back. 'I just wanted to show you something. No, it's not
here . . .'

We trundled back down in the lift and I walked with
George around the edges of Westminster Great Park where
the fountains splashed and frothed as if they were endlessly trying to wash themselves of the blood of Butterfly
Day.

'I was so glad to hear that you were safe,' I ventured. 'I
was worried that you'd—'

'It's around here.' He turned quickly ahead of me along
a tall, narrow passage between the halls of the Dockers'
Union and the enormous walls of the Apothecaries' fragrant gardens. Beyond was a sort of square, although the
paving was weedgrown and the place looked scarcely visited. It was faced by a building with brownish-grey twin
towers. You would have said the thing was big in its own
right but for the fact that it was dwarfed in height, size and
extravagance by the sides and backs of all the buildings
which shadowed it.

'Marvellous, isn't it?' George stood there, breathing
hard as he looked up, a smile quivering on his face.

In fact, it looked squat and ill-proportioned; an old, fat
lady wearing too many clothes.

'It's a church—an abbey. This whole area of Westminster's named after it. It's where we used to bury our kings.
Perhaps that's why they left the place standing, and didn't
doll it up with fancy new aethered stonework and give it
to one of the guilds—they were frightened of upsetting
the ghosts. And this bit of ground where we're standing.

This is where England used to have its parliament. Remember—I told you when we were on the Kite Hills? Of course, *that* was razed . . .'

He strode up to the abbey's big doors and rattled their chains. They boomed emptily. There didn't seem any obvious way of parting them and George plainly lacked Sadie's knack with such things.

'All this,' he gestured upwards. 'Made without a trace of aether.' He sniffed and rubbed his eyes as a flake of rotting stone fell into them. 'They were great, great men, the builders of this place, yet no one even knows their names. And later, in the fading Age of Kings, half London was razed by a terrible fire, and a new capital was planned. Fine, straight boulevards and tall, neat elegant buildings instead of all this bluster and confusion. Some of them were even built, but of course the guilds changed and possessed them. Did you know that there's a dome *beneath* the dome of the Great Hall of the Steamasters? You can still even get inside it if you can find the hidden stairs and stand beneath the pure, simple engineering of great beams of solid timber. Of course, it's been ruined on the outside by endless layers of extra gilt and coloured stone, but it's still there beneath all the pointless extravagance—that fine and beautiful building. Pure and clean, a hymn to God instead of aether and Mammon. And *that* is how my buildings will be, in their own lesser fashion. Pure and rational and straightforward. I know you think it's money, but for me, aether's at the root of so much that's wrong with this Age. And what we need, what we all really need and thirst after, is a sign, a symbol, a gesture, to make that plain to everyone. The very opposite of Hallam Tower, don't you think?'

As I tried to imagine what the opposite of Hallam Tower could possibly look like, I found myself thinking instead of George balancing atop that fountain on Butterfly Day and shouting down to the crowds. 'I hope you're not going to do something . . .' I was searching for the word. 'Brave— or foolhardy.'

'Ha!' He slapped a pillar. 'You mean like that poor cavalry captain? Surely you know me better than that by now, Robbie. After all, I've Anna to take care of me, haven't I?

Did you hear, by the way, that it was she who kindly rescued me on Butterfly Day?'

. I glanced at him as we walked back across the uneven
paving. I knew him well enough to understand that this was
something other than male resentment. But *which* Anna
had rescued him, anyway? Was it the Anna of the church
hall, or the one I'd seen at Prettlewell Fountains—transformed, her eyes darkly ablaze?

'Oh, I know that you and I both think the same about
Anna,' he continued. 'That she's quite marvellous and
beautiful and all that kind of thing. But she's an odd sort as
well, isn't she? And that room of hers in Kingsmeet—did
you know there's hardly anything in it? A prison cell might
be more welcoming. It's almost as if Anna disappears and
ceases existing when there's no one to watch her and . . .
well, *feel* for her as, let's face it, you and I both do.'

'You have to remember that she's an orphan, George,' I
said carefully. 'Contrary to all outward appearances, her
life hasn't been that easy.'

He chewed his lip and nodded. 'I even thought briefly
this summer that she and I might be—well, all of the ordinary things that a man and a woman are supposed to be to
each other. But that didn't work. Oh, don't look at me like
that, Robbie. I've always known we were rivals of a sort.
You could see that even back at Walcote, the first time I
ever mentioned her name.' He barked out a laugh as the
dark old abbey receded. 'But you've no need to be *jealous,*
for God's sake. I'm a useless suitor. Always have been and
probably always will be. It was nothing to do with her. It
was all entirely my fault. Forget about political enlightenment and the power of the masses and the essential beautiful honesty of your average working guildsman.' He gave a
sniff as we walked out from the quiet square and the proud
buildings of Wagstaffe Mall coloured the mist with their
aethered buttresses. He wiped a long dewdrop from his
nose. I thought it was simply the cold that was affecting
him, or one of the germs which were rife, but as I looked at
him again, I saw that he was crying. We stood outside a
souvenir shop not far from the looming base of Hallam

Tower. Shoulders hunched, George pretended to inspect the carousels of postcard stands outside as he wept.

'What is it, George?' I asked, laying a hand on his shoulder. The traffic roared and receded. He tried to shrug it away. 'What happened on Butterfly Day?'

He turned to me. His eyes were so wide and wet that I could see myself reflected in them. And I realised as we stood there that he and I were not alike at all, despite all our mutual assurances to the contrary. We might be wearing similarly ragged coats, but George, to his bones and to his soul, was sensitive and high guilded and complicatedly educated. He could never do anything without worrying about its consequences. He'd probably not even stamped on ants as a child. And I, in my jumbled accent, my stubbled chin, my roughness of manner and black, uneven nails, in the smell of cheap lodgings, of damp and smoked herring which came off me, was the ghostly image of the men who had assaulted him on Butterfly Day.

'Look—'

But George gave a stifled sob. He turned and ran away.

VIII

London whitened and blackened and froze. The telegraphs creaked and strained. Some even snapped and flailed across the pavements in a stream of disconnected voices, their messages hissing and billowing with the breath of the wondering crowds.

'But they *believed* last shifterm, didn't they, Master Robert?' I was carrying Mister Snaith's bag for him through the night streets of Northcentral towards our next appointment with the Bowdly-Smarts. 'You saw the reaction . . .'

He'd become less circumspect now about what he called his small deceits. The phosphorescent stuff he used could be purchased at the same apothecaries which supplied the bandages, and wafted all the better for the addition of some taper smoke. The fragrances of heaven were available at any perfumerer's. The knocks and bangings, the rising and turning of a table, could be made by clever use of the knees. Often enough, the seekers were so eager to be convinced that they produced effects themselves. I'd even been to one or two other houses with Mister Snaith, and witnessed scenes which were much the same. The only part of his patter which he seemed to enjoy varying was the part about his origins. After first hearing that he'd been reared by wolves, I'd since been told that his powers had been revealed when he started flying about the room on his Day of Testing, that he'd been a wizard in the Age of Kings, that he was the secret lovechild of a great guildsman.

'Don't you sometimes feel as if you're laughing at them?'

He considered for a moment. 'Believe me, Master Robert, the laughter comes the other way. I'm accepted as an eccentric sight, and the Gatherers' Guild permits me to live here with them in Northcentral—but only just, and then only because I provide a welcome bit of eccentricity for the high guilded and perhaps scare the robbers off from stealing their old furniture. So don't tell *me* about laughing at others. I hear it often enough at my back, and read that dreadful graffiti, and feel their stares and the chants of their children and the pelt of their stones . . .'

'But where did you come from really? That story you told last evening . . .' He'd claimed to have been twisted into his present state when he tried to commit suicide by drinking aether when he was jilted by a lover.

'I'm old, Robert. My memory's fading. Are you denying me the right to have a life?'

'Of course not. I was just—'

'But I'll tell you one thing. London's not the city it used to be. It's more dangerous. I'm not even sure I should stay. Oh, I do so *miss* the old days. I performed for Greatgrandmaster Penfold, you know, who was generally reckoned to be the second most prominent guildsman in England, and certainly the wittiest.'

We moved on through the submarine fog. The occasional carriage passed by, hooves and wheels muffled to near silence, lanterns glowing like deep-sea portholes.

'Grandmistress Bowdly-Smart . . .'

'What of her?'

'She's not who she claims to be.'

'Well, *there's* a surprise.'

'The fact is, I used to know her husband back in Yorkshire, when I was a child. They had a different name. They didn't even belong to the same guild, and they certainly weren't wealthy. I'm convinced . . .' But I still didn't know what I was convinced of. 'I was wondering if you could give me a little extra time on my own tonight to take a proper look around their house?'

'What? So you can poke about even more than you have been doing?'

'If you choose to put it like that. But I'm not a thief.'

'You're not, are you? But you're one of the sort who'd love to reduce these nice residences to ghastly tenements, fill the gardens with pigs and chickens. Have us all pretending we're exactly the same.'

'It's not about that either.'

'No . . .' He looked fearsome as he peered up at me from the evening's clouded depths; the powdered white dwarf of some peculiar collective nightmare which only London could possibly have dreamed. He sighed. 'And there is something *wrong* about that house, and about the Bowdly-Smarts. You don't need to be me to feel that. Somewhere, there's a darkness. I sometimes feel it watching me. I've always avoided communing with whoever and whatever it is that Grandmistress Bowdly-Smart claims to want to reach, because I know that she doesn't really want it. Does that sound odd to you?'

The grandmistresses were already waiting in Fredericksville's parlour in their black fineries, sipping sweet sherry. We bowed, shook hands, exchanged pleasantries, ate cakes. Then, it was time; Trixie was evicted, the cups were laid aside, Mister Snaith reversed his cloak and straightened his toupee. I'd thought he'd forgotten our bargain, but he paused just as the lamps were being darkened and I'd placed his carpetbag beneath his chair.

'Tonight, Master Robert will remain outside our circle as an independent observer. With so much deceit in these matters, I'm sure you all understand . . .'

With a rustle of approval, the grandmistresses settled in their chairs.

'We come here in search of the truth . . .' his frail voice began. I waited near the door until the pattern of breathing around the dim table had changed, then eased it open and slipped out into the dark hall. Trixie came trotting up to

me, but a shove of my boot shooed him away. How long
did I have? Mister Snaith's communions with the spirits
had the timelessness of any good theatrical performance—
and that power seemed to follow me even as I picked my
way around the aspidistras towards the stairs. Fredericksville had a breathing, waiting feel. I glanced back at
the front door. What if Grandmaster Bowdly-Smart should
return early from his guild club, that little actress he was
keeping, or whatever else was detaining him? He certainly
wasn't someone to be underestimated. Guildsmen had
ended up floating face down in the docks for less than this,
yet still I climbed the stairway and the questioning, agitated voices from the parlour followed me.

Paintings too dark to be made out, windows into the
night, leaned down at me. The top landing was further than
I'd gone before. It swept both ways around the broad swell
of the stairs. Fredericksville was worse than Walcote
House. At least there, there had been light and space. Here,
I was terrified, especially after a near-collision with a huge
porcelain elephant, of causing an enormous crash which
would summon far more than the dead.

The air smelled differently in this part of the house; less
strongly of Trixie. Gaslight. Polish. Pot-pourri. Of lives
scarcely lived in rooms seldom visited by anyone but the
dusting maids. The sense of it filled my mouth with a heavy
ache. *Impurities, Robert! Electricity . . . !* For a moment,
Grandmaster Harrat's hopeful, wavering voice boomed out
at me. I could smell the acids of his experiments. Taste the
marzipan of his cakes. The doors along the corridor gave
easily. I was hoping to find some sort of office. Grandmaster Bowdly-Smart seemed to waft on nothing but dubious deals, quayside meetings, the stale air of abandoned
ships and empty warehouses; waves of pure money. Even
more of those numberbeads would have been something—
this time, I'd simply pocket them, and damn the consequences. There'd always be another cabsman for Mister
Snaith, whilst Saul or Blissenhawk would be able to steer
me towards a disaffected member of the appropriate guild
who could decipher such things.

I tried door after door. White tundras of unslept sheets

whilst thousands slept under railway embankments. Peering through the curtains, I could just make out the line of waiting carriages, the soft glow of the drivers' cigarettes. Beyond that, the fenced garden where I had often stood was an inky seepage of trees. But it seemed for a moment that someone was standing there even now. I drew back, setting a Staffordshire figure rocking. There was nothing but mist when I looked out again.

A door around the corner seemed momentarily to be locked. I was almost disappointed when, at a slight shove from my shoulder, it finally gave. The first thing I noticed about the room beyond was that it was light, and then that it was dark again. The maids hadn't drawn the curtains here and the window looked south towards Hallam Tower's circling blaze. I blinked and waited for the light to come again. Somehow, I could still hear the unmistakable honk of Grandmistress Bowdly-Smart's voice from the parlour. I couldn't make out the words, but her tone was both hopeful and pleading; she sounded more than ever like an uppermistress from the terraces of Coney Mound. The light returned. The room was a nursery, filled with plushly expensive furniture and toys. All the animals of creation were queuing to board an ark. A rocking horse gleamed on glossy black aethered runners in the bay window. The mere breath of my passage set it swaying. The room had none of the odours of childhood which I knew from Maud's nurseries. The whole place was more like a shop display. After all, the Bowdly-Smarts had no children—not here, or even in Bracebridge—that I knew of. I slid open a big chest of drawers. Each level was filled with expensive baby clothes. Some were still inside their wrapping. All were stiff and new. But the air which escaped from the bottom drawer was ancient and frail. A tattered collection of browning baby things appeared in the next white flood of Hallam Tower. They were simply made, repeatedly repaired. I touched them, strangely moved, and heard, at that moment, the wail of Grandmistress Bowdly-Smart's voice from the room deep beneath me.

Hallam Tower receded. The darkness drew back, scented with old talcum and kitchen bleach. A chill went over me. I was sure, at that moment, that I heard a baby crying. I slid the drawer back. When the light of Hallam Tower next swept across the frieze of dancing elephants, it did so with an audible swish, a push of memory. Even when I closed the door and slipped back along the corridor's fresh darkness, the sense remained. *Sooh Booooo*. The air hissed and exhaled. At the furthest end of this corridor was a smaller door. I touched it with wondering fingers. It pulsed like something living, and the handle turned for me.

Beyond was a narrow upwards-leading stairway. The room at the top had slant walls which pushed into the roofspace and was piled with the wreckage of old furniture. The pale, continuing flash of Hallam Tower wafted through a skylight to stir the cobwebs and glint on splintery wood, a rusted iron bedframe. We had had a washing plunger exactly like this one in our house on Brickyard Row. Here, even, beneath a sheeting of dust and more cobwebs, was a guild certificate honouring some minor success in the production of engine silk. It was granted by the Third Lower Chapter of the Lesser Toolmakers' Guild, stamped with the seal of Mawdingly & Clawtson, and had been awarded to Uppermaster Ronald Stropcock. I peeled off the back of the frame and pushed the document into my pocket. Proof, at last, of something I'd long known, but the attic air remained tremulous, expectant. There was a longer box in the furthest corner which looked as old as everything else here, and was even more roughly made. But it seemed too big to belong in a Coney Mound terrace. And there was something—a tug of memory which joined with the shuddering pull of the darkness. *Soooh Booooo*.

CAUTION DANGEROUS LOAD. Those stencilled words amid the old washstands and cracked mirrors—and the vision I'd had long ago at Grandmaster Harrat's; he and my mother and another woman called Kate clustered around this same rough wooden casket in the depths of Mawdingly & Clawtson. SHOOM *BOOM*. The pulse of it beat with the circling of Hallam Tower and the hammering of my heart as the casket lid shuddered open. Inside were crisped, ancient newspapers, yet the light which had dimmed that subterranean room where my mother had once stood was scarcely there when I lifted the strange object out; a roughly cut lump of crystal about the size of a human head. I knew now that such things were called chalcedonies, and that the guilds used them to store their major spells. But this one was faint; the wyrelight at its core was scarcely beating. Its power had exhaled long ago. SHOOM *BOOM* SHOOM *BOOM,* then silence, and I was back in London, in that dusty attic.

I laid the chalcedony back amid its newspapers. I closed the casket lid. I floated across the landings and halls. Still totally absorbed, unthinking, I reopened the door into the Bowdly-Smarts' parlour, but inside there was light and commotion. Mistress Bowdly-Smart was howling and sobbing and Trixie was barking, whilst Mister Snaith still sat at the far table, the contents of his carpetbag still spilling out around him. Mistress Bowdly-Smart, her face streaming, let out another howl.

'I left Freddie crying,' she wailed in a broad Brownheath accent. 'It's *good* for babies to be left, ain't it? That's what every mother'll tell you, and that's what my Ronald insisted. Spoil him, Hermione, he said, and he'll grow up like a selfish little sewer rat, but let the little blighter fend, and you'll raise yourself a fine upperguildsman. Oh, we were so bloody happy! But you *do* leave them once in a while, don't you, for their own benefit, even if they've had a wee bit of a fever—otherwise, just like Ronald says, they grow up greedy and expecting it all on a plate . . . It wasn't a big house we had then, you understand. Just the two rooms up and down, the way things mostly are in Brownheath. But me and my Ronald was happy then, and I had my own sweet baby. No matter where I was in the house, and if it wasn't for the sound of them damn engines, you could hear him breathing. But sometimes, I left him crying for the sake of his own good . . .'

A baby was still crying in some other room in some other house, but the sound was faint, and dulled by a distant pounding which only I and Uppermistress Stropcock would ever have recognised. Then even that faded, and there was a long pause. The other guildmistresses looked pale and shocked by the transformation which had come over their hostess. This was what was not what was supposed to happen. But, at the same time, I could tell that Mistress Bowdly-Smart's tearful admission of a past quite different to that which she claimed was scarcely a surprise to them. They were used to brushing bits of their lives under the carpet. The silver cutlery which was really thin plate. The infidelities of their husbands. Their eyes turned instead, in anger and in blame, towards Mister Snaith. All the hope and wonder had gone from his audience, and the whispered words which were now exchanged over the cakestands were harsh. Hateful creatures like him, *it*—well, they were inhuman, mad, ungodly and alien. They would have been burned in a better, more sensible Age, and any God-fearing guildswoman would be happy to warm their hands on the blaze. At the very least, he should be locked up with all the other monsters in St Blate's. In their crackling black dresses, with their hats pulled down over their set and angry faces and rigid hairdos, these fellow seekers reminded me now not so much of birds but of beetles as they scuttled for their shawls and coats.

The front door slammed as they started departing. Then it opened again.

'Some odd commotion up around Strand,' Grandmaster Bowdly-Smart's flat voice boomed in the hall, 'But what's happened here? What's going on?' Still wearing his silk-lined coat, his wing collar, his red cashmere scarf, he burst into the parlour.

'What *is* it, Hermione?'

More mascara and powder than seemed possible had spread across his wife's face. 'We should never have left Bracebridge,' she whimpered. 'We were *happy* there, least until little Freddie died. We should have stayed and looked after his grave. And *you*, Ronald—always promising something better. Sniffing around for something, finding bad things out. That guildsman—and look where it's got us! And you've been with that tart this evening . . .'

'Hermione—how could you think . . . ?' He cradled her wet face in his arms whilst the remaining guildmistresses made their excuses. He glared about for the source of his wife's anguish—at me, and then at Mister Snaith. He stalked across the long parlour, pushing low tables and cakestands out of the way. Cups flew. The glass front of a big cabinet cascaded in a glittering wave.

'You fucking troll! I'll pluck your sodding wings...' He hauled back the table behind which Mister Snaith was cowering. His feet snagged on the carpetbag. 'And just what the hell *is* this? And this...? All *this*...!' Bandages, rubber balls and tapers flew out. 'You cheap little fraud! You're not even...' Mister Snaith, still wearing the coloured side of his cloak, made no attempt to resist as Stropcock threw him against the wall. His toupee went flying. His sleeves jetted tiny plumes of tinsel and smoke. For a moment, Stropcock stood over him, his breath hissing. Perhaps even he was waiting for some sign, some twist of magic. But Mister Snaith just cowered. With a roar, Stropcock grabbed him and wrapped both hands around his throat.

I tried to wrestle Stropcock off. But he was a strong man—and determined—until I jabbed him in the face. With a renewed roar, Stropcock threw Mister Snaith aside and turned towards me. In another moment, as I slipped backwards across a spillage of milk, Stropcock was on top of me, his knees driving hard into my ribs and pushing the breath out of me whilst his hands encircled my throat. I always had been a poor fighter in London brawls, and he had weight and experience on his side.

'What makes you think...? Little bastard like you...'

Uppermaster Stropcock was muttering the same insults he'd used all those years before in his office. And he really hadn't changed. Age had been good to him—he'd scarcely even lost any more hair. The only thing which had receded into the past, I thought, as my arms flailed and my sight began to blur and redden, was that brown overall with its clip of pens. Then, something other than anger contorted Stropcock's features. His eyes widened. His narrow lips half-shaped a name and, in the shock of doing so, his fingers weakened momentarily on my throat.

I skittered away from him, gasping.

'*You...!*' He aimed a shaking finger. 'You're that

jumped-up bastard's son from East Floor.' He attempted another lunge at me, but I threw a chair in his way. Whilst he was rubbing his shins and cursing, I hauled Mister Snaith out from the corner, pushed my way past the watching maids and fled Fredericksville.

'That was all most, most unfortunate . . .' Mister Snaith was muttering. His cloak was half one way and half the other. His toupee was missing. There was an angry scratch across his powdered cheek.

'I'll get you a new carpetbag,' I said. 'It was all my fault. I'll replace everything.'

'No,' he sighed. 'It always happens eventually, in one way or another. People tire of me. Next Noshiftday, they'll all be back in church, telling the priest how foolish they've been. I just hope they don't report me to the Gatherers' Guild. Well . . .' He stopped. We'd already reached the turn between the grand buildings which led to his warehouse.

'Will you—?'

'Oh. I'll be fine. After all, and not so very long ago, I *did* perform . . .'

The little changeling walked away towards the clamour of Northcentral's engine house, still muttering about the good, great old days when he'd been respected, feted. A sharp wind was stirring over the houses, tearing the fog into stripes of black. Glimmers of the stars and fragments of the moon were showing overhead.

But Stropcock had been right about the traffic; it had backed up both ways along Guild Parade. Somewhere, something was happening, but I had no desire to investigate. The pulse of that chalcedony stone, faint though it was, still roared out at me. Rubbing at my bruised throat as the cabs streamed and steamed, I took a short cut towards the Easterlies along the series of interlinking sidestreets behind Goldsmiths' Hall. After the noise and bustle around Westminster, they were dark and empty. Even the streetlights, to save gas or through some oversight, were unlit. Then I heard the thud of hooves, the heavy creak of some big carriage. My blood chilled as it pulled out of the darkness and stopped beside me.

'Where *have* you been?' Sadie's voice, and her face framed in silver fur, floated out. 'Get in, get in—quickly! Are you all right, Robbie? You look as if you've seen a ghost . . .'

The driver had calls and cries which made the late evening traffic of Northcentral part for a grandmistress's carriage.

'It's George,' Sadie said. 'He keeps mentioning your name—we thought you might be someone he might actually listen to.'

'What is it? What about Anna?'

She sighed and lit a cigarette. She had several extra rings, now, I noticed, on her fingers. 'Poor Anna seems to be the last person he seems to want to listen to at the moment. He's been saying the most odd things.'

The modestly named Advocates' Chapel, in fact an enormous church, had been standing at a crossroads on the Strand for an Age and a half. As a separate guild, the Advocates no longer existed, having been swallowed by the Notaries' Guild, and the chapel's large but dumpy spire had long been a useless landmark, largely unnoticed by the traffic which smoked around it. But tonight, it was the centre of much attention. Theatre-goers and revellers spilled across the roads, smiling, pointing up as the fog thinned and the spire glowed. The general impression amongst the crowds as Sadie and I bundled through them was that they were witnessing some odd guild ceremony.

The chapel's main doors looked as if they had been prised open, and George was inside amid many lanterns and much dust and smoke. Anna was there as well, and she was pleading with him, although George looked through her and through Sadie and I as well as we rushed towards him across the rubbled floor. He was stripped to the waist, ribboned with sweat and dust. In his left hand he had a rolled-up plan. In his right he was waving a crowbar.

'Ah—*Robert* . . .' George seemed to notice me on second glance 'London's a bog—did you know that? This whole building's afloat on nothing but the swill of some old drains . . . This thing's probably hollow.' He struck a pillar with the crowbar. Flakes of stone flew. 'What time is it, by the way?'

'Close to midnight—but what are you doing?'

'Midnight?' He gave the pillar a push. The thing was six feet in diameter. 'I'd hoped it would be quieter outside by now. We'll have to stop the traffic—clear people back. I really don't mind the involvement of the police.'

'He's talking about singing the chapel down,' Sadie said. 'Whatever that means.'

'You've *got* to speak to him, Robbie,' Anna added, her face wide and white. 'He's stolen the spells for this building from his guild academy. He keeps saying something about the opposite of Hallam Tower.'

'Got to go up top again,' George announced, waving his crowbar like a dandy with a cane. 'Why don't you come with me, Robbie? I can show you just what I mean . . .'

The tower's spiral stairway went up and up. George paused halfway on a gantry and waited for me, absently rapping the great single bell. Dust and plaster rained down on me. The air boomed. The Advocates' Chapel's main spell, he explained, scampering ahead of me again, wasn't just bound into the foundations. It wove all the way up to the spire and through the walls and around the buttresses in aethered strips of engraved copper. Once that was unbound, the entire building would become as frail as paper. But the weight of the stones still seemed impossibly solid as I peered down from the tower's high balcony at the turning lights of the Strand. Guildhalls. Theatres. Glowing tramlines and telegraphs bound up in a vast cat's-cradle which I thought, for a dizzying moment, might catch us as we fell.

'There's Anna!' he shouted. 'She's outside!' She was easily recognisable in a red beret, standing beside the silver of Sadie's coat amid the angels in the graveyard. She looked up, her face a small white heart. George had roped lanterns around the spire to illuminate it. The night wind licked over us and London shimmered and yellowed as he showed me the verdigrised copperplate engravings which were bolted to each side of the four compass-facing pediments. I traced their swirls and felt a thrill of something heavy, musty. 'Now—just listen . . .' George spoke slowly, his voice wavering up and down a long semitone. There was a gritty rumble beneath us, like a millstone turning. 'Now . . .' He grabbed the crowbar he'd leaned against the parapet just as my fingers were snaking towards it. 'We'd better get back down . . .'

To unbind the spell which sustained this ugly old building, to unlock its buttresses and foundations as a guildsman might twist open a seal, it was necessary to know the entire charm which had bound it, and which existed in its entirety, so George claimed, within the scrolled lines of the drawing he'd stolen from the libraries of his guild. But that wasn't enough. Copper strips were buried in the rubble beneath the Portland stone facing, and the strengthening chants which long dead workmen had infused into them had to be exposed. He hefted his crowbar. A winged white marble memorial unpeeled and shattered across the aisles. George's forehead was cut. His thin body was smeared and shining.

'This place isn't safe!' I shouted. 'Why don't you do what Anna asks and go outside?'

'Ha! Anna!' The dank building gave a groan. 'She's always right about everything, isn't she? And I don't suppose I *have* been myself lately. It must have been something I've eaten. Clams it was, I think . . .' He spat dust from his mouth. 'God, I can still taste the foul things. Like salt and some sort of rotting weed.' The traffic was hooting outside. A police bell was ringing. 'Maybe they were cuckoo-clams—can you have such a thing? God knows we sluice enough aether and filth into the Thames.'

He drew me to the apex of the church, the point beneath the centre of the tower, which tunnelled up above us now like a crystal grotto as engine ice began to seep out of the stone. He swept the glittering dust away from the key-plate which bound all the other spells and lay embedded in the paving. It was circular, and the points and ornamentations were pooled with vivid enamels which rippled in the light of George's lantern. When he touched his fingers to them, the colours were already wet. He smeared them across his face and started chanting. The phrases were convoluted and ragged. Some wooden part of the tower must have caught light from the heat of one of the many lanterns, for wafts of smoke were beginning to trail around us.

'You've done *enough*!' I yelled.

George turned to me. 'This is just the beginning.' He spat and coughed. 'Didn't I tell you England needs a sign—the very opposite of Hallam Tower?'

He was empty-handed now and I grabbed his shoulders in an attempt to drag him outside, but he threw me off with an easy shrug, tossing me back across the aisles. His strength, pouring into him as the power drained from the church, was prodigious.

'People have noticed you, George. They'll believe and understand—isn't that what you wanted?'

'Tell that to the cavalry captain!' He wiped his mouth with his paint-smeared hands. 'Tell that to all the rest of the people who died and suffered on Butterfly Day. But you're right, Robbie—this isn't safe. You should go out . . .' Then he raised a hand. An expression of puzzlement, bizarre in its ordinariness, crossed the paint-smeared mask of his face. 'But wait—just one moment. I've been meaning to ask you something. It's about Anna . . .' A blistering wave of heat and plaster dust swept over us as an archway collapsed. 'Fact is, I'm not sure that she's entirely who she claims to be. Those parents of hers—there aren't any proper records. Odd, isn't it?' He shook his head. 'You're the only person who remembers her as a child. I've been to her room in Kingsmeet—oh, I know it was *most* unguildsmanly of me . . . Nearly burnt myself on the tiny vial she keeps on the dresser. Why on earth should Anna need acid, and a pipette? And when she rescued me on Butterfly Day—it wasn't really Anna at all. You *do* understand me, don't you? You of all people. You do realise that it's not just—' He licked the dust from his lips. '—those damn clams I ate . . .'

'George—Robbie!'

Anna emerged from the dust and flames.

'There you are Anna! Just in time as always.'

'Look,' she began. 'Whatever happened to you, George, it wasn't—'

'Can't you see?' He spread his arms. '*This* is what England needs.' He turned slowly. 'This church. *Me* . . .' The bell was ringing out now as the spire creaked and swayed above our heads. I glanced at Anna; it wasn't just George who was mad to be here now; we all were. Then, in a sudden splitting of wood followed by a rending of stone, the bell dropped towards us through the tower roof.

It would have been hard for anyone to describe exactly what happened next. Even for those outside, and for Sadie who was standing just at the chapel's doorway, there was disbelief and confusion. But the spire of the Advocates' Chapel began slowly to collapse in on itself, puffing out, its flaming weathercock descending through the sparkling night. And the bell thundered as it fell. Then its sound changed. To those outside, it gave one last almighty *clang* which rang out far across London. For a moment, many swore that the spire actually seemed to regather itself and rise back upwards in a trail of sparks.

To me, standing beneath that collapsing central tower, that final sound from the bell was something I felt rather than heard; a peal richer and deeper than mere aethered bronze. Even George was thrown back by its blast. Then Anna was standing on the key-plate, her arms raised as the rainbow colours of the engravings blurred around her. Briefly, the entire church stilled. The flames were swirls of polished copper, and the falling bell hung just above us, its clapper frozen in mid-swing, trapped in the solid air. Then there was a gush and a rush and we were all running, driven back and out by the bellowing dust and stonework as the spire finished its collapse.

The crowd outside cheered, backed away, surged forward, then universally started coughing in the quicklime clouds from which Anna and George and I somehow emerged. The newspaper men, alerted by George's rambling letters, were waiting. Flashtrays puffed as they clustered around him. Then the police arrived. But they were surprisingly gentle. In other situations this would have been time for the nightstick and the boot, but they knew a high-guilded person when they saw one, even when he was stripped to the waist and smeared with dust and paint. It could have been George's finest moment, and he did make an oddly impressive figure. But he spoilt it all by struggling and shouting after a young blond-haired woman standing nearby in the crowd.

'What *is* it, Anna! For God's sake, *why* did you save me? It was the same on Butterfly Day! Why don't you leave me alone . . . !' Half-handcuffed, slippery with sweat, he lunged. '*What* are you . . . !' He shook his head and spat. His eyes blazed. 'You should be in St Blate's! Hey, someone grab her! Take her arm—the left one—get her to show you her wrist, the one she drops acid on! Troll! Changeling! Witch . . . !'

But Anna had already slipped back through the crowds, vanishing in that way she was always so good at, and the firemen had set to work. Those jetting arches from their hoses, the crashing sighs as further walls collapsed, the drifting dust, the continuing flames, the spreading snakes of fluid—all of it added to a dream-like sense of aftermath. Sadie was talking quietly to a senior police officer. He nodded, listened, and his eyes widened slightly at the mention of some name or connection, but George was still hauled away.

'Well, *there* you are, Robbie,' she said after the police vans had departed. 'Pity I couldn't get poor George unarrested. But I suppose that wouldn't have been what he wanted.'

I shook my head. I felt lost and drained.

'I explained to that officer that the balance of his mind had been upset,' she continued. 'And I told him that no one else was involved, which I suppose is near enough to the truth, when you come to think about it.' She laughed, shook her head. 'Near to truth is about as close as life ever gets, isn't it? I mean with you—with Anna.'

I said nothing.

'No wonder poor George's been behaving oddly. And that tower, that bell. I saw enough just then, from where I was standing—but a lot of other things make sense to me now. Little things, over the years. Things you notice and forget about, or put down to the magic of the day. And you as well. You could never dance, could you? You can't even use a knife and fork the right way . . .'

'You think Anna ever had any choice?'

'No.' Sadie eyes were reddened, and glittering. 'Of course she didn't. But she could have told me, couldn't she? God!' She looked up at the sky. '*Me* of all people, her closest friend. I should have known! All these years! All these *bloody* years! I've been so stupid! And now I suppose I'm going to have to look somewhere else for a chief fucking bridesmaid . . .'

I watched her walk away towards her fine black carriage.

IX

MAD ARCHITECT BRINGS DOWN CHURCH. The papers were full of George's deeds in the morning. The vendors were shouting his name over the clatter of the trams, and shopkeepers were brushing up glass from the night's minor disturbances. But the London sky was as heavy and smoke-laden as ever; the city, as I walked through Northcentral and across glorious Westminster Great Park towards Kingsmeet, hadn't changed.

The same guildswoman who'd sent me around the corner to the institute by the church on the eve of Butterfly Day was coming out of the pebbledash apartments on Stoneleigh Road as I approached them. With a vague nod, she let me in, and then I was ascending the stairs through the smell of last night's cooking and the sound of someone practising scales, badly, on a poorly tuned piano. Anna's room, as I'd known for many terms, was the third on the left on the second floor. My heart felt light, then heavy, as I raised my hand to knock on the browned paint.

'Come in, Robbie,' she said, just before I did so.

Anna was sitting on her bed beside a large, scuffed leather suitcase in that famously empty room of hers although, compared to what I had just come from in Ashington, it didn't look especially bleak. There was a small dresser. A sink and a hob. A wardrobe from which all the clothes had been removed and laid in the case.

'I don't know how you stand the sound of that piano,' I said.

'*That's* one thing I certainly won't be missing.' She gave an Anna almost-laugh. She was wearing a grey woollen cardigan. The sleeves were a little long and she'd turned them up, although her wrists remained covered. Her face was composed, but her hair, for once, looked as if it could do with a brush.

'You really are planning to leave?'

'After last night, I don't think it's a question of planning or not planning. Here—' She waved a letter she had scrunched in her hand. 'You might as well read this.'

I took it to the window. The cheap yellowish paper, unevenly typewritten, had holes punched through the full stops. The heading, rubber stamped, was of the West London Sub-Office Gatherers' Guild. It could have just been a reminder about a library book; it mentioned *discrepancies* and *minor irregularities*. And would she mind calling in at their offices, at her suitable convenience? At least it wasn't from St Blate's.

'Doesn't sound very urgent,' I said.

'I like that question mark—as if I could just say no and carry on with my life. But you know what these organisations are like. The more apologetic they get, the more you know they've got their claws into you.' Guessing she didn't want the letter back, I laid it down on the otherwise empty dresser beside a mark where a small spillage had blistered the varnish. 'Oh, it's not because of last night! Even the Gatherers' Guild isn't that quick. No, they've been sniffing around me for ages. There's one particular character named Spearjohn—he's called here several times but I've always managed to be out, or at least to pretend to be. He's not outside there now, is he?' I shook my head. There was nobody in the street now but a child playing hula-hoop. 'But after what George shouted, and what Sadie saw and what everyone else heard, they won't give up, will they?'

'George won't betray you, Anna—not once he's come to his senses. And I don't think Sadie—'

'It's not *them* I'm concerned about. It's the whispers, the rumours. Oh, *Anna*—she was always a bit strange. You saw how the people drew back when George started shouting . . .'

I sat down on the far side of her case. That piano was still stumbling up and down the scales. I thought for a moment, in a flash so brilliant that it made me blink, of that day in Redhouse, the magical notes she had drawn from engine-ice-encrusted machine. 'I'm so sorry, Anna . . .'

She gave a small snort through her nose. She didn't want my pity. Even like this, even today, as her eyes travelled away from mine and along the gap between the thin carpet and the dusty wainscot, there was still that green fire.

'I understand better now. All the things that Missy told me but said she hoped I would never have to learn. How it's always been for my kind. For anyone . . . changed. You try to live an ordinary life. Perhaps you even start off believing that everyone is the same, or that how you are makes no difference. But little things happen. With Sadie, back at St Jude's, there was an incident—a near-accident. She was acting the fool when we were practising archery in that way she used to when she got struck right in the shoulder. There was quite a lot of blood, but I think I stopped something worse happening. She looked at me oddly for a while after that. And then she forgot, or she thought she did. But these things pile up. Sadie's started looking at me in the same way again. I mean—look at poor George. What did *I* do to him?'

'He's got himself all over the newspapers this morning.'

'Has he? Good for him. That was exactly what he wanted, wasn't it?'

'I think he wanted the world to change.'

'Well. Don't we all?'

'The tone of the press isn't so bad. Even the *Guild Times*. It's as if everyone in London can understand how he felt—his frustration. There'll be a proper trial at Newgate, in public. Not a soul got hurt when the chapel fell, and the place was abandoned, so what can they possibly do to him? Chuck him out of a guild he despises . . . ?'

Anna's eyes flickered back to me. 'What happened here?' She reached to touch my throat.

I swallowed, and felt a renewed ache where Stropcock's fingers had dug into me. I could feel the past, in Anna's eyes, in the memory of that strange crystal, welling up between us like the faintly mothballed air of her suitcase. 'You know of a couple called Bowdly-Smart?'

She thought, then nodded.

'I was at a meeting, a sort of séance, at their house yesterday evening before Sadie found me. I was there with— with Mister Snaith. You know who he is as well, I suppose?'

'I know what he is.' Her gaze didn't change. 'Or what he claims to be. But, Robbie, why on earth . . . ?'

As we sat there in that small room with her case between us, I explained to Anna about my recognising the Stropcocks at Walcote House. It was a tangled tale, with glimpses, confusions, memories, dead ends. Before I knew it, I was talking about my mother, and about Bracebridge, and Halfshiftday visits to Grandmaster Harrat's house— things I'd told no one, not even Mistress Summerton, which led me step by step, fall by fall, and vision by vision, all the way back to that chalcedony I'd discovered in Stropcock's attic.

Finally, not so much finished as worn out, I lapsed into silence. Even that piano had stopped its endless plonking.

'So . . .' Anna said finally. 'You're going back to Bracebridge?'

I hadn't even thought, but I nodded. After all that had happened, it was the only thing to do which seemed to make any sense. 'And what about you, Anna?'

'Perhaps I might come as well . . .'

The next afternoon, Anna and I took the ferry to World's End. It was raining heavily. The hills of engine ice guttered in rainbowed pools. The tin cans rattled their warnings. The late heavy plants bowed their stems.

'It's happened, hasn't it?' Mistress Summerton sighed,

small and dark and weary, as we stood in her clattering porch and I unshook our umbrella, 'That guildsman with the chapel who's in all the papers—I thought I knew the name . . .' She and Anna hugged, and I thought as I watched them of the strong wings of comfort which had once beaten around my mother in Redhouse, and how much Mistress Summerton had diminished since then. Finally, she drew back and busied herself with her pipe, which quickly added to the room's steamy fug and dulled yet more of the light from the streaming windows.

'I suppose you'd better tell me . . .'

Mistress Summerton remained oddly absorbed in little tasks as Anna spoke of Highermaster George and the Advocates' Chapel and the letter from the Gatherers' Guild. After the pipe, there was the ritual of the finding the tea, filling the kettle, lighting up the stove, the clink of spoons . . .

'I'm sure it's not as bad as you imagine, Anna,' she said eventually. 'That highermaster—you know how the guilds always take care of their own. Even that grandmistress will come around and remain loyal to you, if she's the friend you say she is. Of course, I know it's dreadful. You may have to change your address and a little of the story of the life you've been living. But it's not the end.'

'You never warned me, Missy,' Anna said, 'that it would be like this.'

'I never warned you because I didn't *know*.' One moment, she was like a bundle of old sticks. Then a flash of those dark-bright eyes. 'I still don't. And I knew that you would never listen in any case . . .'

The teacups were offered. The little roof creaked and ticked.

I cleared my throat. 'Anna and I—we've decided to go back to Bracebridge. There are things . . . Things I've found out, here in London. It's all to do with what happened to my mother, and what you told me—'

'The fact is, Missy,' Anna said, putting down her cup, 'that I'm sick of these years of deceit and evasion. I even hung around outside the local offices of the Gatherers' Guild a few days ago—wondering what would happen if I simply walked in.'

'Please, don't do *that*.' Mistress Summerton waved her thin head. 'Look at you, Anna. Do you think you could be here as you are now, dressed in that smart suit, those nice shoes, and still talking about taking some trip on a train with Robert here, if everything was as ruined as you pretend? I'm sorry for all that's happened, and I'll do all that I can to help you. But now you want to start digging up the past. Is that the best you can do, after all I've sacrificed for you?'

'But that's the *point*. These are just *clothes*, Missy!' Anna's eyes searched the room. 'What difference does anything make unless I can get to the bottom of what I am?'

'I gave you a chance to live an ordinary life. I don't think any of our kind has ever had a better one, and you still have it unless you choose to throw it away. You're remarkable, Anna. Remarkable in every way. Look at you—you're beautiful, perfect. But how can you believe that there's some special mystery that you and Robert can unearth that will make sense of your life? There *is* no answer to the world, Anna. There never was. The further you go along that road, the more you'll be disappointed, and the more you'll put yourself in danger. Whatever it is about Bracebridge that Robert thinks he's found about your poor mothers, it's *bound* to be dangerous if it's anywhere near to the truth. People died there, people suffered. And you're both young and alive. Isn't that enough? If you go there you'll be no safer than you are here, and probably much less so. I can help you to hide from the Gatherers' Guild, Anna—I can help you rebuild what you've lost, and I can give you what's left of my money. But I can't do anything if you insist on blundering into the past like this. You think the guilds will relish having their old secrets upturned, you think this Stropcock character is harmless?' Then she turned towards me through the swirls of her pipe. 'That day at the market, I should never have let you notice me. I've just sent you off searching for things you'll never find.'

'I was searching anyway.'

'But never . . .' Her eyes flickered towards Anna as a wet gust of wind shook her little house. 'For what you think.'

PART FIVE
ANNA BORROWS

I

There had been a time, not long before, when the trains ran in and out of London as smoothly as the interlinked mechanisms of a single vast machine. Now, as Anna and I bumped our cases along the platform of Great Aldgate Station, you simply had to ask, and hope, and wait. The timetables had been superseded by chalked blackboard notices, which were smudged beyond understanding, and Bracebridge was too small a town to merit a twinge of recognition on the faces of guards. The only trains which had ever gone directly there were the long, slow wagons of aether caskets which arrived at Stepney Sidings.

Anna noticed the name *Oxford* first, and we hurried to a platform and squeezed down a crowded second class aisle. As we stood at the window and the carriages crawled out through London and finally began to pick up speed, I told her more about the Stropcocks—about the numberbeads, the empty warehouses, the *Blessed Damozel*. Even these last few days, I'd gone back to watch their house from my space beneath the trees. But the servants and supplies still came and went. Nothing, outwardly, had changed.

'Why didn't you confront him—as soon as you were sure who he really was?'

I shook my head. Now didn't seem like the time to mention the men who'd come to Blissenhawk just yesterday, asking after someone who matched my description. The landscape greened. Fat cattle in their pens, cornstooks and flashing tunnels: these were the tracks which had borne me here. We reached Oxford before midday, where there was talk of a train that afternoon travelling in the direction of Brownheath. But there were several hours to kill, and Anna had been here once, so she could play the guide to this city which was so different to London that it scarcely seemed to me like a city at all. The stones glowed with winter sunlight. The great colleges, each sponsored by their guilds, rose around quadrangles in spires and ivy. It seemed like one endless guilday as the bells shook the frail blue air. The women marched openly here to demand change. EQUAL RIGHTS FOR GUILDMISTRESSES. They looked so proud in their boaters that you could forgive them for forgetting about us marts. *Here, sister, come and join us . . . !* Anna did, for a few steps, swinging her arms to the drum's beat. If everyone could live like this, I thought, catching our reflection in the polished windows of the bookshops and the gold of Anna's hair, there would scarcely be any need for a New Age. No wonder poor George—who was in the papers here as well, although they called him *ex-Balliol man*—had found London hard to accept. I'd have happily played the tourist, wandering beneath bridges and tossing our sandwiches to the ducks, but there was a place Anna wanted to see, and it lay outside the city where the buildings thinned across the half-frozen earth. One last house lay out amid chicken coops where the first copses of forest spread their arms. It seemed like the last house in Oxford, and it was up for sale.

The place looked much smaller than I'd imagined. Its walls were lower. Its gables and chimneys were hunched and mean. The only gate was locked.

'Wait! Master, Mistress!'

The land agent almost fell off his bicycle in his hurry to reach us. He bowed and presented his card.

Mistress Summerton's prison-house had been through many changes of use and occupancy, but the rooms, with their few random scraps of furniture, looked far bleaker than they would have done if they had been entirely empty. How many years, I wondered as the agent chattered about potential for improvement, had it been since she had clawed at these walls? The best part of a human lifetime. Perhaps Anna was wrong, and this wasn't even the place. But I as inspected the windows I found the rusted marks of old bars and the remains of heavy shutters. The panelled walls, when I rapped them, sounded hollow.

'That's a most unique aspect of this property. Almost every room has a space around it—probably for insulation. It means that they could all be enlarged. Of course, you could re-use most of the panelling. Everything's sound. All you'd need is a good carpenter. We at Adcocks have strong links with the local guild . . .'

Oxford had already sunk into the smoky well of evening as Anna and I walked back down towards it, but its spires rose and gleamed with the last of the sun. Our train was already waiting at the station.

We reached Yorkshire in the racing dark. Stations flashed by with glimpses of windows, milk churns. A ruddy-faced old woman came swaying down the carriage, the shoulders of her coat shining with dirt. She sat down beside us and began talking in a way that no Londoner would have ever done as the telegraphs blurred white trails in the darkness. Then the train stopped and the guard came shouting that this was Bracebridge, Bracebridge, Bracebridge . . .

As the smoke of the train faded, Anna and I carried our cases over the iron footbridge my mother and I had once crossed on our way to Tatton Halt. It was dark in the yard outside the stationhouse where the coal was kept and timber was stored, near to the pens of the sleeping pitbeasts. It wasn't much past ten in the evening, but this was Nineshiftday—the tired end of the long slog towards next payday, and the Lamb and Flag was scarcely lit.

'Don't you want to go to your father's?' Anna asked.

I shook my head. 'I'd rather wait until morning.'

'So—where do we stay? Isn't that a hotel up there . . . ?'

It was—or rather an inn; the Lord Hill, which was the.

closest Bracebridge possessed to such an establishment.
My mother had had to steel herself the few times she'd
been in there, although, dim against the grainy hills, the
building had shrunk in the time I'd been away. I took a
breath. My heart was pounding. All of this was too sudden,
too quick.

SHOOOM *BOOOM* SHOOOOM *BOOM*.

I laughed out loud.

'What is it, Robbie?'

'That noise!'

'You mean you've only just *noticed*?' As Anna shook
her head in amazement, I led her on up the streets towards
the smaller shops at the bottom of Coney Mound, with
cards strung in their windows. Mongrel puppies were for
sale—or had once been. A cot—scarcely used—told its
own story. Anna blew on the glass and wiped the mist with
her sleeve, peering forward in the dim gaslight. And there
it was. SMALL HOUSE FOR RENT FULLY FURNISHED
SUIT YOUNG GUILDSCOUPLE NO PETS NO MARTS.
The sign looked almost recent.

Past Reckoning Hall, past the removals yard. The address of the keyholder was at the east of Coney Mound,
looking right over the river-swept bowl of the valley. She
studied us in the light of her front door, smoothing her
hands across the greyed front of her apron.

'Thought I heard the night train stopping. Doesn't happen much these days.' Mistress Nutall had the brisk
getting-on-with-it manner of many a Bracebridge widow.
'So you're after the house? Master—Mistress—is it . . . ?'

'Borrows,' Anna said before I'd had time to think.
'We're just up from London. You know how things are.'
Without my noticing, she'd slipped the silver ring she'd
been wearing to her left hand. 'My husband here—
Robert—he has connections with the town.'

'*Connections?*' Mistress Nutall studied me. She was
younger than I'd first thought—I could see her, or her sister, crowded in a straining pinafore at the Board School
girls' entrance—or I perhaps I was getting older. 'You'll be
of the Toolmakers', won't you?'

I nodded, too astonished by all these revelations to look surprised.

Clogs slapping, heels showing white through the holes of her stockings, Mistress Nutall led us through the cold dark towards 23 Tuttsbury Rise; an end-of-terrace, although it was hard to make much out of it this far from the road's solitary lamp. A small hall with the parlour one way, front and back kitchen the other. Plenty of coal in the coalshed, although it might be a bit damp. There were tapers and firelighters and matches, and lime in the privy. Mistress Nutall would bring us milk as well, and a nub of bread and a cup of sugar. Anna and I were waited on ridiculously that night by Mistress Nutall and her neighbours. The house was lit and warmed. The lanterns were replenished. The front bedroom double bed was made. Borrows, Borrows—yes, they knew the name, and Anna, she looked pale and I seemed peaky. Tea so hot and strong you could stand your spoon up in it, that was the trick. We were fussed and flustered over. We were treated like high guildspeople.

Finally, we were alone in the house with the crackle of the fire and the beating of the engines and the empty sound of the wind outside pouring over the pines and birches which sloped down from this side of Coney Mound in a loose cliff which, on lost summer days with the brown Withy sweeping beneath, we children had climbed. SHOOOM *BOOOM* SHOOOOM *BOOM,* and Anna, Anna Borrows, was sitting opposite me in this Bracebridge parlour, her hair ridiculously aglow and the small, familiar furniture pulsing and receding as the firelight and the memories beat over me.

'We're here,' she said. 'So what do we do now?'

'We'll see . . .'

I puffed out the lanterns, settled the fire in its grate. Through the wall, in coughs and scrapes, I could hear our neighbours doing the same. The arrangement of the stairs in this house was different to my own on Brickyard Row a few streets away. These led up from the hall, with a turn halfway over the larder. Anna bore the lantern first with the railings sweeping behind her across old wallpaper and the paler spaces where family pictures had once hung. There was no doubt, in my mind at least, about which of us was going to sleep in what Mistress Nutall had called the master bedroom, where the newly aired blankets were so drum tight that Anna's case, when she tossed it down, almost jumped off again.

'We must make a convincing enough couple . . .' In small gestures of hers I'd never seen, Anna ran her hands down her sides and pulled clips from her hair.

'People would never think otherwise of us, Anna. Not here . . .' I watched in the bevelled mirror; the way she pushed back her hair again as it fell more loosely when she bent to open her case.

'You really want me to have this room?'

'Someone's got to have it, Anna. They'll be looking for the lights—our shadows.'

'I thought you just said . . . ?'

I shrugged. How could I explain all the things I knew about these people, this town?

She began to hang out blouses on the rattling hangers in the wardrobe.

'The room next door'll be cold. I'd say try to light the fire, Robbie, but didn't Mistress Nutall mention that it smoked?'

'Perhaps I'd be better off downstairs.'

She took out a bigger, longer dress—something which would have been virtually ordinary in London but which opened itself here in dark folds like the petals of one of Mistress Summerton's roses. She smoothed it against herself, then smiled at me over it. I went back into the lower part of the house, where only the fire and the stove were now glowing. SHOOOM *BOOM* SHOOOOM *BOOM*. I heard Anna moving about upstairs. Someone in the house next door was still coughing, and probably would be all night. Here on Coney Mound, you grew used to such things. I went outside through the bitter night to the privy, knowing my way through the dark all the way to the feel of the latch, and wondered as I stood there and the air rose up at me what Anna had thought of this sour place when she used it.

I closed all the doors. I gave the kitchen stove a final rake. I ascended the stairs. Outside her room, Anna had left the spare sheets and blankets Mistress Nutall given us in a tidy pile. I took them into the back bedroom. The darkness rose and fell. I could taste smoke in my mouth. SHOOOM *BOOOM* SHOOOOM *BOOM*. BLESS THIS HOUSE in needlepoint, homely stains across the mattress. But there was something about this room which I couldn't bear. I went back down the stairs with my blankets and punched the cushions on the settee. The curtains didn't quite meet, and wavered in the wind. The cushions, cold, and faintly damp, sagged and dug under my back. But it would do.

II

I was woken in the morning by the sound of someone banging on the front door. Still mostly dressed, I stumbled blearily through the hall where a female shape dimmed the frosted glass. It somehow didn't look like Mistress Nutall. The wind had blown up the cliff from the river all night and the door was stuck frozen in its frame. When it burst open in a flurry of ice and light, I saw my mother standing on the step.

'I can't stay just now,' she said. 'But, Robert, you could at least have *said* you were coming . . .'

It was my sister Beth; word of my arrival had spread quickly on Coney Mound. She wouldn't come in—Board School down in the valley was depending on her, and even as we stood there and thought about hugging each other and decided that the moment had already gone, the big sirens at Mawdingly & Clawtson started howling. Beth now wore the enamel badge of the Schoolmistresses' Guild on her navy coat, but it seemed a little bit late to congratulate her on finally passing her exams. And I was *married*? I nodded even more awkwardly as I felt what I had previously thought to be Anna's small but necessary deceit beginning to grow a life of its own. *Some guildmistress she must be,* Beth's look said, *to let her master be up in his braces at this late hour without any sign of breakfast.* We stood there for a few moments longer as the wind whipped over us and Beth's resemblance to my mother came and went with every beat of the aether engines.

'Aye, well, the Borrows lad—don't you remember him? Mother took bad. *Really* bad, if you get my drift. But that's all old history. Old Frank's still around, of course. Sister looks after him and teaches my daughter's little Alf. Then, puff! Turns up one night again with a wife and everything. Pretty little thing—but seems a bit vague. Staying at the house on Tuttsbury Rise that used to be Mother Ricketts'. Been down south, and you know the way it is down *there.* Now he's come back here, tail near enough between his legs. Oh, yes, he's been inducted. Toolmaker, just like his dad. Always do, don't they? My lad was just the same and look at him now. Oh, no—hasn't done any proper guildswork in years, by the look of him. Not a haftmark on his lily-whites. Can't even say the pulley-twisting spell for toffee, is my guess. Still, Maureen says we should be kind. He took a chance and it didn't work out, and now he's back here in Bracebridge. It's in the blood, ain't it . . . ?'

The Tenshiftday market was in progress when I left Anna and went down the hill into lowtown that first morning. The town hall clock had acquired a new face. Rainharrow gleamed with snow. People I didn't know smiled at me, and those that did—old schoolmates, ex-apprentices grown pompous and jowly in their minor rank, and women who had once known my mother or scolded me for dirtying their washing with a football—came up to say hello. Happy and uncurious, they were genuinely pleased to see me. By returning to Bracebridge with little more than a wife and two suitcases and the dim hope of work in my father's old factory, I had done them the favour of confirming that there was nothing out there which their town couldn't offer. Their accents were extraordinary—it was almost like my early days in London—but, like spells in a dream, I found that I could understand them easily.

Bracebridge was surprisingly prosperous. It wasn't just

that new town hall clock. Several of the buildings had new red roofs, and the market was bustling. Even the guild-mistresses of Coney Mound were out buying fresh groceries, whilst my mother had most often waited until the bargains of the afternoon. The town, in the shock of my first full immersion in it, looked more cramped than I remembered, but also newer—a brightly painted toy version of itself. Yet the whole north of England, in the pages of the *New Dawn* and many another paper, was supposedly in ferment . . .

Just like any diligent schoolchild, I began my researches into Bracebridge's past in the town's public library. The place looked brighter and cleaner than I remembered, but otherwise little had changed. A few elderly guildsmen were pretending to study the news in the sunlit dust as they pulled at their nose hairs. I wondered as I studied their faces if I shouldn't have gone straight to see my father back on Brickyard Row. But Beth standing at the door had been enough of a shock for one morning. So I bought myself a pencil and a cheap notepad, and moved back through the sleepy shelves into the past which this crystalline present seemed to hold and mirror so perfectly; back towards *something,* although I still didn't know quite what. SHOOOM *BOOM* SHOOOOM *BOOM*. This was better than Black Lucy in Blissenhawk's cellar. For the first time since Butterfly Day, I felt a genuine urge to write.

All the windows were open and the rugs were hanging out in the yard and smoking with dust when I returned to our house that lunchtime. The women along Tuttsbury Rise had all taken pity on Anna, who had no proper boots, poor soul, not a single workcoat or apron, and struggled to boil a kettle on an ordinary coal stove. But Anna was nothing if not adaptable and she greeted me with her hair tied back and her cheeks reddened. She looked entirely beautiful, did this new Mistress Borrows, as we settled down at the scrubbed kitchen table to the bread I had brought and the dried sausage she'd been given by Mistress Martin at number 14.

We finally called on my father at seven o'clock that night, after we were sure that Beth would have returned from Board School and had a proper chance to warn him.

It was no distance at all from Tuttsbury Rise to Brickyard
Row and my hand was on the gate and pushing it slightly
up and to the side in the way it needed before I'd fully realised. Then Beth was at the door again and I saw with a
pang that she'd dressed up for us as she took in Anna, in
her far better clothes with the lights of the town shaped
from the darkness behind her. There was a fire lit in the
front parlour and lemon cakes were laid on the cornflower
plate of which my mother had been so proud, although
they had lost the gloss of their icing in the time they'd been
waiting. Some men puff out and bloom as they get older,
but my father had greyed and shrunk. He almost bowed at
Anna. The porcelain trembled as Beth poured out the tea.

'You've not done so badly, lad . . .' He stopped himself
tipping his drink into his saucer. 'Eh?'

'We received the cheques,' Beth added. She was sitting
beside Anna, who was trying hard not to look queenly. The
only chair left in the room was the one that had pride of
place in the small bay of the window, which we reserved
for guests. My father had given up guildswork on East
Floor several years before. He worked now most nights and
some lunchtimes at the Bacton Arms, helping to clear up
the left-overs, although from Beth's expression I guessed
that that mostly involved him drinking them.

'And you've been inducted?'

'It was down in London.'

'And you're looking for work?' My father's neck looked
scrawny and abraded in the collar and the tie I knew he detested wearing. 'And this is your Mistress . . . ?'

So the conversation went round, and the cakes sat uneaten, and the ground pounded. SHOOOM *BOOM*. It continued that way on Noshiftday, when he and Beth insisted
we come around for lunch, which was the usual grisly back
end of beef frazzled in the oven up the road.

'So? You're from the south . . . ?'

Anna nodded and chewed hard at a lump of beef which
she'd unadvisedly gone for first, then made her second
mistake in trying to help it down with a greyish-green segment of last season's sea-potato. She gazed at father's and
my beers, which she wasn't supposed to like. I suppressed

a smile. I'd never realised before that the rules of eating in Bracebridge were almost as complicated as they were in Walcote House.

'Yes,' she said eventually. 'But I have some relatives in Flinton.'

'Hmmm. Flinton.' My father nodded as if that explained everything. Anna's Flinton connection was news to me as well, but the place was perfectly chosen. Near enough across Brownheath to account for her loose ties with the area, but far enough away, in view of the long-standing mutual animosity between the towns, to put off any further enquiries.

My father tilted his head to me. 'And I gather you've been busy down at the library?'

I nodded. Pages of old newspapers and guild announcements crackling open like seedpods into the sneezing, sparkling air. It was the ordinary things—especially the photos, the bland lists of names, births and deaths and marriages and inductions and awards and disciplinary procedures—which pulled most strongly at me. Then there was the annual Toolmakers' tug of war held on summer's guildays between the masters and the uppermasters. My father was there back in year 57, standing frozen for the photograph on the sunlit rivermeads, grinning for the camera through the browns of age. His shirtsleeved arm was looped around a fellow guildsman, who was also just a master then, and wore a fringe instead of the greased back widow's peak which so amplified the smallness and pointedness of his features.

'I'm just curious,' I said. 'I came across a name just yesterday which I was sure I remembered. Stropcock—wasn't he your Uppermaster?'

'Never should have got the job,' my father said more vehemently and quickly than I'd have expected. 'He was a mean sort of bastard.'

'Father . . .' Beth said warningly.

'He's not here in Bracebridge now, though, is he?' I persisted.

My father snorted. 'Shouldn't think so. Got promoted again, didn't he?'

'I thought I heard someone mention his name once . . .' I slowed, grateful for the lump of sinew I was having to chew. 'When I was down in London.'

My father snorted and wiped his moustache. Stropcock in London was just taking it a little too far. 'Furthest he ever got, as far as I heard, was Preston.'

'The past's gone, isn't it?' Beth added, giving me a look which suggested it had better stay that way. But from here I could see the turn of the stairs which led up to my mother's old bedroom. SHOOOOM *BOOM*. There was something odd here, something adrift, something tingling in my blood, grinding at my bones. It was as if Anna and I had stepped off at a place which nearly was but wasn't quite Bracebridge.

'Books, the library . . .' My father worked his mouth and hooked a fingernail inside a molar and spat out a piece of gristle into the serviette Beth had laid out for him. 'And I never thought you were brainy.'

'Down in London,' I said, 'I worked for a newspaper. I wrote articles.'

'What was the paper called?' Beth asked.

'The *New Dawn*.'

They both returned to their food. 'One of *them* papers was it?' Father muttered eventually. 'Used to have one like that up here. A lad touting it for tuppence, if you please, 'til he got the shit beaten out of him.'

Beth put down her knife. 'Father!'

'Well, it's true. Telling us guildsmen that we're wasting our lives working hard and bringing home a decent packet.'

'Working men in London are often the same . . .' I began, then managed to stop myself.

'And all them marches. What the hell was that about *butterflies*? Why, there's even some guildsman barmy and disrespectful enough to bring down one of God's own good churches—'

'That's *enough,* Father,' Beth put in. 'I'm sure we don't want to spoil our Noshiftday meal with men's talk of politics, do we, Anna?' She smiled semi-sweetly at Anna. Then there was suet pudding.

'I've found some old things of yours,' Beth said when

we'd finished eating and Anna had quite properly ignored
Beth's protests and started stacking the plates in the sink.
'You might as well take a look at them. It's just up the
stairs.'

I followed my sister up the narrow rise.

'It's just stuff.' She gestured towards the small pile of
old schoolbooks and other objects which she'd laid out on
the landing floor. 'But of course, you left without taking
anything. We thought you were dead. Then cards started
coming. Eventually, cheques as well—but I've thanked you
for those already, haven't I, so I don't suppose I need to
thank you again. Even then, we weren't really sure if you
were still living, especially after all we've heard about
London recently.'

To Beth, to the people of Bracebridge, London in this
last year had become a place of blood and flame.

'I could have sent you a card or two back,' she continued. 'Like last year when Father and I went to Skegness.
We're not country mice up here. We do travel as well. But
we never had your address, did we?'

'I had too many.'

The brooch she was wearing, the twist in her mouth as
she looked at me, were both my mother's.

'I'm sorry, Beth.'

'For yourself?'

'No. For us both . . .'

We stood there for a moment. The air beat around us.

'I didn't see you at church this morning.'

'It's not something Anna and I do.'

'Ah!' She nodded as if it all made sense now. 'And do
you remember what the word *ikey* means?'

I had to think. Anna, downstairs, was talking to my father, clinking plates, rocking open drawers.

'It means stuck up, Robert Borrows, and there's not
much of a worse thing you can say about someone here,
other than perhaps that they like delving into the past. The
people here in Bracebridge are *nice*. You know how nice
they are. They might go to Skegness these days, but they
won't understand you coming here with that pretty wife of
yours on what seems like an odd kind of holiday. I should

get some work, if I were you, Robert Borrows, if you really do plan to stay here . . .' Beth stomped down the stairs.

Schoolbooks. Ink blots, fingermarks and stains. *Five Useful Verbs. What I Did Yesterday.* We couldn't have written about what we did on our holidays then; the people on Coney Mound hadn't been able to afford such things in the way that they seemingly could now, against every other trend of this Age. Plonked on top of my few old things was a glass snowstorm bubble which contained a corroded miniature of Hallam Tower. Half the water had evaporated. Instead of aether for the lantern, there was a tiny lump of glass. I'd never seen it before in my life. I gave it a shake, watched the greenish water slop, and smiled. This, if George had really wanted it, was the very opposite of Hallam Tower. Beneath, heavy and curling with damp, were a few children's storybooks. *Now, Goldenwhite* . . . And there she was, still wandering the forest depths, through the blooms of damp and age. I recognised the story as one which my mother had told me, although in memory there had been no book; the words always seemed to spin fresh-minted from her head. And Flinton—hadn't she once said that that was where you might once have found Einfell? Grey houses under grey slagheaps—and now Anna came from there as well.

I stood up, dusting my trousers, and climbed the ladder which led to my old space in the attic; weighed down with lumber and age, the trapdoor wouldn't budge. But here behind me was my mother's room. Bed, a different wardrobe, chair and fireplace. I could see that Beth had made one or two attempts to reclaim the place—a vase here, a lace doily there—but its terrible essence remained. SHOOM *BOOM. D'you want to see just how far I can stretch myself* . . . A few lumps of coal, oddly glinting, lay in the cold grate. They were like jet, and greenish—a scatter of jewels, peacock-tinted with jade. This bedroom was like an old scene, freshly painted. My feet crunched slightly as I crossed the floor. I worked open one of the empty drawers. Beth had placed balls of lavender inside each, tied up in squares of old linen, but they gave off no scent, and felt cold and hard and heavy. I undid one of the ribbons. Inside was a solid glittering lump; the florets of lavender were encased in engine ice. And fanning across the walls was more of a watery glitter which I had taken at first for damp or frost, but crumbled to my touch and left my fingertips glittering.

SHOOM *BOOM* SHOOOOM *BOOM*.

I was conscious, as I left the room and descended the stairs and faced their stares, that Beth and my father would have heard me moving about their little house. It was time for us to leave.

III

I came back from the library on Twoshiftday morning to find Anna sitting with the *Guild Times* spread before her on the kitchen table. Highermaster George Swalecliffe was on the front page. These first days, she'd seemingly been happy to busy herself with the rituals of domesticity. She had aprons now, and the blacking for the stove had worked its way under her fingernails. She'd experimented with cooking ham and cabbage, bleaching teatowels, drying herbs—failing and succeeding in equal measure under the guidance of the other women of the street who vied with each other over the best way to do each thing. Cautiously, step by step, Anna was travelling back towards the lost life of the parents she'd never known. But George's name, the reports of the trial which had began yesterday, had jolted her back to London.

Bits of the bun she'd taken to wearing had come loose over her face and there was a burn across her thumb from yesterday's bread-making, which had resulted in a black lump of far greater solidity than the aethered bricks from which Bracebridge was made. She'd rolled back the sleeves of her fraying and greying blouse and her stigmata looked like a wet ruby; raw and inflamed. I turned the paper around, reading it as I ate. George had made a long statement in court, which even this newspaper summarised. They called him *the deranged architect* but his views about the wrongness of the Age were somehow allowed to seep through. Tame though it seemed after the columns of the *New Dawn*, it was extraordinary to read of such things even being hinted at in the *Guild Times*. Something was plainly happening—I almost wished I was back in London—but to me it all seemed forced and wrong. I suspected that the guilds were using George to concoct a version of the Twelve Demands so watered down that even they might pretend to accede to them.

Anna remained preoccupied as we walked the afternoon streets and alleys of Coney Mound.

'I feel so responsible for what happened to George,' she said eventually. 'It wasn't just recently. It's—what is it that men say about women?'

'That you led him on?'

With Anna, that was a wild guess. But she nodded. 'We've known each other for years, and I think what first attracted us was the fact that neither of us was part of the crowd . . .' She chuckled. Her face was half hidden by the upturned collar of her herringbone coat, which glittered with her breath. 'And the fact that we weren't attracted to each other, if you see what I mean. It was an odd sort of courtship. I suppose we were like people trying to dance, watching what others did but never understanding. It was never what we *were*. The only time we ever kissed was that time when you saw us—at Walcote . . .'

We were walking beside the small shops where we'd found the advertisement for our house. The sky was solid blue. The cold, even in this sunlight, was brutal. Apart from the white gleam of Rainharrow, the snow had held back on Brownheath, but you could feel the weight of it longing to fall like silent thunder.

'His dream of some better Age was never mine, either, much though I enjoyed sharing it. And then there was Butterfly Day. When I found him—when I'm supposed to have rescued him—the men who'd caught him just seemed to run off when I shouted his name. I think they were almost as ashamed as George was about what they were doing to him. But perhaps just my knowing was hard enough for him. Anyway, George was bleeding and crying, and I took him back to Kingsmeet. The noble working man—he couldn't blame them, so he blamed himself, and perhaps he blamed me . . .'

'He took me up Hallam Tower just before. I should have seen it coming as well, Anna.'

'Perhaps I should have told him what I was—*am*. Sadie as well—perhaps that would have made the difference. I mean, *you* know, Robbie, and you're still here. *You've* never betrayed me . . .'

We had walked on past the houses, unthinkingly pacing together to the rhythm of the engines, towards the rise of St Wilfred's. The graveyard was winter-bleak. But there was the stone, set above my mother's grave. The guilds were good at paying for such useless things. Still, I was moved to see it here amid all the others as I had never been when I was younger. We wandered up through the dead grass to another stone. AETHERMASTER EDWARD DURRY 46–75. Anna's father, who'd been only five years older than I was now when he'd died on the day the engines stopped beating. Amongst the many papers and remnants of that time which I'd now collected, I'd found a photograph of him and his wife Kate in an old guild yearbook as they headed towards some dance. Caught in flashlight, they made a handsome couple, him especially—almost bursting out of his best suit with a grin which was broad and unashamed. Anna looked even more like him, I'd decided, than she did her mother. But she was alive, and as she leaned forward and touched the stone beneath which he was buried, I could smell the scent of her hair through the cold air, like fresh straw and almonds.

'I used to come to Bracebridge sometimes with Missy— on days like this, just as the chimneys of the houses started smoking,' Anna said as we wandered further up the hill amid the long shadows of the monuments. 'We had to go shopping for soap and flour like everyone else, although I know you find that the hardest thing to believe about us . . .' Her eyes gleamed. She swallowed. 'Missy even offered to

take me here, but I dragged her away through the twilight. I
didn't *want* to know then, Robbie, about my mother, my father, about anything to do with this place. All I felt was this
lost . . .' She sniffed and looked up at the paling sky. The
muscles in her jaw quivered. '*Rage*. That was probably why
I was so awkward with you when you came with your
mother that summer to Redhouse. I knew you were part of a
past I didn't care about, a life that had been taken from me
by some accident in this stupid town . . .'

The sun was settling beyond Rainharrow. The last
gleams of its rays poured incredibly to illuminate the
rooftops of Coney Mound in shades of gold and brown. I
thought for a moment, just as we closed the churchyard
gate, that there was a figure standing amid the far yews, but
with another glance the darkness had settled. It had gone.

Past the wall where the young lads smoked and the gig-
gling girls trailed past on summer evenings, at the better end
of Coney Mound which was almost lowtown, to a house
where the front was unlit, but the chimney was smoking, and
the faint lights of the kitchen glowed into the parlour with
glints of glass and porcelain. Anna pushed her chin down
into her coat and let out a long, cold breath. 12 Park Road,
with a decent bit of back lawn where you might actually
grow something. This was where her parents had lived.

SHOOOM *BOOM*. The day the engines stopped—the day
that Anna's and my life had changed before we were even
born into them—was a vague absence, a stillness, in the interminable library records, distinguishable by some meetings cancelled and football matches postponed, repairs to
the damaged town hall, a few new buildings commemo-
rated a year or so later to replace those which had inexpli-
cably vanished. Beth was right—people hated digging into
the past here almost as much as they detested people who
were *ikey*. My few more direct enquiries about those times,
even when I forced myself to stay late in the Bacton Arms
and knock back slippery pints of Coxly's, were met with
blank stares or dark hostility. Anna, in her quieter way, did
far better.

By asking the neighbours, she found the Stropcocks'

old house, which wasn't so far away from that of her parents on Park Road, a thin but double-fronted grace-and-favour dwelling which the Toolmakers still owned. Yes, they'd left the town, him on a promotion which had arrived surprisingly quickly, come to think of it, with the way the lesser guilds usually worked. But no one quite seemed to know where it was that they had gone. No one much cared, either—but it *had* been in the spring of year 86, which was soon after my mother and Grandmaster Harrat had died. And they had lost a baby a while before; little Frederick Stropcock's grave was up there in the shadow of St Wilfred's, although the tangles of nettles told us far more clearly than all the records in the world could ever have done that the Stropcocks, the Bowdly-Smarts, never visited Bracebridge.

'Someone like Stropcock would love to come back here and lord it over everyone,' I said after tea one evening as I stood at the sink and scrubbed the pans with a lump of old swarf. 'Did I tell you I saw him once when I went into Grandmaster Harrat's guildhouse? It was through a door on Christmas evening. He was eating at their table . . .'

From our kitchen window, there was a view across half the valley. The settling pans were glowing, and the lights of a train were just snaking out of the valley. Behind me in the cramped room, I could hear Anna moving about, the clink of the grate, the rumble of the clotheshorse as she put up the day's washing. The high guildswomen she'd known in London would have been appalled by this transformation. But we were happy playing at this life, or pretending that we were playing at it.

SHOOOOM *BOOM*. The sound of the aether engines had changed. I was sure of it now. The first beat was too slow, the second too quick, and the pause between each surge and strike was a moment too long. I studied the faces in the street, these busy people who had been here too long to care or notice and would happily remain forever frozen in this Age. I watched the whistling window cleaners, the street sweepers whom I was sure had never existed before, the men on ladders who scrubbed bricks and cleared gutters. The whole of Bracebridge was glancing at its shoulders,

removing stray speckles of engine ice like dandruff. Grandmaster Harrat's house on Ulmester Street had been replaced,
but the new house was swathed in scaffolding. Builders were
whistling out with barrows of glittering dust which looked
too beautiful merely to throw into a skip; perhaps it was
taken all the way to World's End. I'd imagined, when an
aether town such as Bracebridge came to its end, that the
process of its encrustation would be precise and gradual,
welling up like water. But this white sparkle had no reason to
obey logic; it was an effusion of magic.

I migrated from the public library to the Halls of the
Lesser Guilds, which the Toolmakers shared with the Ferrous Workers and the Pressmen. In many ways the building
was similar, except that the guildsmen who lounged here
were allowed to smoke and their chairs were old leather
and more comfortable. I was greeted by the custodian like
the prodigal Toolmakers' son I claimed to be. He was a lad
I'd known at school who now had five children and another
on the way. Of course, he'd telegraph the necessary forms
to confirm my membership—but everyone knew who I was
in Bracebridge, so why hurry? Clocks ticked. Men snored.
Dust fell and rose. All of it to the same cracked rhythm.
There were books of spells. Manuals for long-dead machinery. The old pages breathed up at me with a scent of
rusting staples.

Stropcock had started this new life in London, and he
had taken that chalcedony stone with him as some kind of
evidence, insurance—a talisman. And I was sure by now
that he was involved in something to do with the day the
engines stopped, something which was still going on in the
town of Bracebridge—some fraud or deception involving
the fading processes of aether. But what? And how? These
endless pages, I realised as I blinked awake over a list of
superseded regulations, were drugged. They were like the
guilds themselves, designed to draw you in and send you to
sleep with promises of small glories until you awoke, still
wondering, from life itself.

Beth invited me to the Board School one morning. She was
nothing like old Master Hinkton, and had got the wild idea

from somewhere that the purpose of her guild was education. It would be useful, she'd suggested, for the class to hear from someone who'd lived in some other part of England. It was early and the whole place steamed. Hands shot up. Had I been up Hallam Tower—could you touch the flame? Did the great guildhouses really float? From what substance were London's pavements really made? The atmosphere, under Beth's stern but indulgent gaze, was quite different from that which I remembered, even if the place smelled the same. I tried to talk about the Easterlies, the Westerlies, the ferries and the tramtracks—even World's End—but you could tell they didn't want to hear about the real city. They were almost like me at that age. London was still a dream, and the last thing they wanted was for some ordinary-looking man who'd been born on Coney Mound to explain it to them. So I mentioned Goldenwhite instead, and unicorns and wishfish and dragons—red dragons and green ones, flying around the fabled Kite Hills. And dances, yes, there were great, wondrous dances, in ballrooms which floated over the river and glowed like pearly shells. Beth regarded me from her desk, half amused and half disapproving. Behind her, I could see the scarred old box with the sprung clasp which she would use to demonstrate the power of aether.

'They seemed to enjoy that,' I said to her as we walked outside afterwards.

'I'll have to spend the next two terms telling them what London's really like!'

'But they need to dream a bit, don't they? You're a good teacher, Beth—you understand . . .'

She nodded. Mist had settled over lowtown this morning. Bluish, filled with a cold gleam and almost clean to breathe, it was quite different to the fogs of London.

'What's happened to Hinkton?'

'He's dead.'

'I suppose the trollman still comes?'

'Yes, but it's not Master Tatlow now, if that's what you're thinking.'

'He's gone as well, has he?'

'People do. If you stay in one place for long enough to see it happening.'

But her digs and asides were losing their sting. I'd heard gossip that Beth had a man-friend in Harmanthorpe. A fellow schoolmaster, he'd gone with her and Father to Skegness. They'd shared, by all accounts, the same hotel room. I was happy for her to think that she had someone, although a little sad that she couldn't bring herself to tell me.

'Have you heard about the day when the engines here stopped beating?'

'Yes, but I was too young to remember, Robert. What is there to know?'

'But you *do* know that was when Mother got that scar she had on her palm—you *do* know that was why she died?'

Beth's pace slowed. 'Accidents happen here. One of my pupil's fathers broke his leg only last shifterm. He'll probably never walk again. Why d'you need to dig up the rest?'

The fences by the settling pans exhaled a rainbowed glow into the mist, but there was a scum of algae on their lustrous surface, and the cuckoo-nettles no longer flourished beside the concrete wall at the back. 'Beth,' I said, 'I ask you these things simply because I'd like to know.'

She snorted. 'My children would come up with a better reason! And *please* don't keep prodding at Father about these things whenever you see him. He's never been the same since Mother died. But at least he's found an ... equilibrium.'

'It's made me realise, coming back here, that perhaps what I thought I was escaping wasn't quite so bad.' I'd intended the comment genuinely, but Beth gave me a *what-do-you-want-now* look. I plunged on. 'My mother had a friend, they were a couple—father must have known them as well even though he denies it. They were called Durry. He was the uppermaster on Central Floor. He was in control there and he died from his injuries on the day the engines stopped along with seven other people. And his wife—well, she died eventually as well. And Mother was hurt. You *must* know something about all of this, Beth.'

'What do you want me to say?'

'The truth would help.'

'The truth is, I think you should leave Bracebridge before the snows come.' Her gaze flickered up towards Rainharrow

which had briefly emerged gleaming above the roofs of
Mawdingly & Clawtson. 'And that girl, that woman—Anna.
She's not just from London, is she? And she's not from
Flinton, either. She seems a sweet enough thing and I've got
nothing in particular against her, but there's *something* odd.
And I'm sure she's not your wife. So don't come here talking about the truth, Robert Borrows.' She thought about saying more, but at that moment the town hall gave a muffled
chime. 'I've got a lesson. I must go . . .'

I watched my sister walk off into the mist, pacing to the
beat of the aether engines.

In these days of December, the nights came in slow and
early. The hills settled like smoke, grey on purple on grey.
The guild signs flapped and creaked. The lamplights battled the wind. Anna and I were out walking as we often
walked, but this time, in the long, safe, anonymous hour of
settling darkness when she and Mistress Summerton had
once come to this town, we had determined to go to the top
of Rainharrow.

Hello, Mistress Borrows! Anna raised a hand and smiled
through the gloom to a neighbour who was out collecting
her washing before it froze, a woman with three daughters
and no husband who worked at the eye-straining business
of putting the lace on fine ladies' vests. I'd come home today to the smell of sweet, delicious bread wafting down
Tuttsbury Rise—stuff which crumbled to the blade and had
scarcely finished steaming before most of it was eaten.
Anna was becoming famous for the quality of her baking.
She could make the yeast rise, I'd been told over the fence
that morning, like no one else on this side of Coney
Mound. I'd even met someone who swore they'd known
Anna in Flinton. The life of Anna, Mistress Borrows, was
blossoming beyond our control. I was coming to understand now how it must have been for her in London and St
Jude's. Even to me now, with each gust of the wind, she
was, wasn't, Mistress Borrows.

Anna walked ahead of me to the pulse of the night with
that slow, slightly stooped and loping gait of hers in a long
pleated tweed skirt she'd been given to replace—*Oh my*

sirs, you can't wear that—the flimsier stuff she'd brought
with her. Anna, Mistress Borrows, hummed to herself
when she was dressing, always seemed surprised when the
kettle started screaming, left a rime of tooth powder each
evening around the bowl in the scullery. She liked cheese
which was hard and waxy, and blew on her tea before she
drank it even when it was cold. I'd grown pleasantly used
to the sight of her underclothes hanging dripping in the
kitchen because here you didn't hang such things on your
back line, and I suppose she must have grown used to
mine, too. We did our own things, the quiet things, the em-
barrassing things, in the times and spaces which we quietly
conceded to each other, but the house was so small that we
often bumped backs, clashed elbows, even occasionally
grew impatient with each other. Her hair had that slightly
wheaty scent which came and went according to when
she'd washed it. That afternoon, as I'd sat in the Lesser
Guildhalls and tried to rehearse the spell which caused a
worn cog to keep its bite, I'd found one of her hairs just lying across my shoulder. I'd lifted it and held it there in a
beam of sunlight. I watched it shiver in my hand to the beat
of the engines.

I thought of our staying on here in Bracebridge through
the deep snows, and of my working at Mawdingly &
Clawtson just as my father had done. I'd study those manuals. I'd learn to chant the spells, and the haftmarks would
spread up my arms like ivy. I'd bring home a pay packet
each Tenshiftday to replenish our vanishing funds. And
slowly, slowly, term through term, month after month of
this winter, I'd find out the truth of what had happened
here . . . Beyond the yards, beyond that long line of aether
trucks which I was almost sure now were mostly empty, the
ground began to roughen and rise. A thin moon delineated
the scant track which few people followed up here in winter.
Anna went ahead, her breath huffing in clouds. Mistress
Borrows, Anna Winters, Annalise, Anna, who could be anything, who could do anything, live anywhere, who could
bake the bread which the angels ate in heaven and stop
a church tower from falling . . . George's trial had sunk
back through the pages of the *West Yorkshire Post*. He'd

been incarcerated at the pleasure of his guild, which meant a suite of rooms in some pretty country guildhall where he could get on with designing the perfect house for the perfect workman.

Ahead, amid the brambles of Rainharrow which my mother had once explored in search of flowers, the cold air gleamed. White fronds, beautiful in their complexity, embroidered the dead ferns. The sarsens glittered, frozen but not frozen in the moonlight. The whole crown of this hill gleamed like a beacon, not with snow, but with engine ice. Anna was gazing south across the dim hills of Brownheath. Scarside, Fareden and Hallowfell. Somewhere down there, hidden in the darkness, was the valley of Redhouse. Here now, as well, the aether really was fading. And I was sure that the chalcedony stone had been involved in an experiment to do with its production which had been supervised by Grandmaster Harrat. And beyond him lay some other cause, and a much more powerful presence amid the guilds. It was this, the power of this high, dark guildmaster, which Stropcock had tapped into, first through Harrat himself, and then, down in London, on his own . . .

I went to where Anna stood amid the white jaws of the stones. 'It explains so much,' I said to her as we breathed the darkness. 'Not just here and now, but that experiment with the stone—even then, the stuff was running out. They were *desperate* to get more aether . . . But I need to get inside Mawdingly & Clawtson to find the full truth. Everything else is just . . .'

But Anna seemed distracted. She flashed me, back through the moonlight, what I'd come to think of as one of her smiles. 'I was talking to Mistress Wartington this morning. She told me that Testing seems to be coming early. The trollman's been seen down in lowtown. He was asking questions about a woman from the south, although that person is much higher guilded than I am now, and she certainly isn't married.'

'It doesn't mean . . .'

But to Anna, at the moment, it certainly did. I could tell that she felt that all the things which had happened in London were happening here as well, only more quickly. The nudges, the questions. People had their doubts about me, but things had been said about Anna, too, marvellous though everyone agreed that she was. It was no use pretending. And I was standing here in this strange place, spouting about changing the world just as George had done.

'So,' I said. 'What do we do?'

'We still have a day or two.' More dimly up here, but somehow more deeply, the engines pounded. SHOOOOM *BOOM*. Huge and dark and glittering, Rainharrow seemed to exhale as well. 'There's a dance tomorrow night at Mawdingly & Clawtson. I think we should go, Robbie— it's even on East Floor . . .'

IV

The Tapsters' Ball took place in that cold pause before Christmas, and was often postponed because of heavy snows, which made years such as this, when it was held, all the more welcome. Father had often gone—was going—and so was Beth. Mother used to go as well. She'd come down to me in the kitchen one evening, pleased with herself, with long black hair plaited, wearing a blue dress I'd never seen before, nor after.

Guild sashes were to be worn, which was a problem to me, albeit a little one, as Anna soon spoke to a widow in the house behind ours. A few stitches, a little borrowed silk to get rid of the mothholes, and I had something better than new. And that crimson dress which Anna had brought, which was vast and low at the front and high on the arms, and thus wildly inappropriate, was transformed, with the addition of a borrowed belt and the sacrifice of a blouse, into a tighter and more modest outfit which would have made any Bracebridge guildmistress, and this particular guildsman who walked into lowtown beside her, entirely proud.

The entrance to East Floor lay tonight through the main gates of Mawdingly & Clawtson with their twin friezes of

Providence and Mercy. The other workshop floors were closed, or on skeleton duties, although as ever the work of the aether engines was powered from Engine Floor to Central Floor deep below. Hastily made signs directed those few who didn't know their way beneath the pipework arches. The machines on East Floor, those which would move, had been hauled back. Those which wouldn't had been decorated with ribbons, or chalked with cryptic messages. The band was already tuning up—fiddles, accordion and drums—and the people were dancing.

I felt Anna hesitate when the light and the sound struck her. Massed people—people uncontrolled and wild—was something she avoided. Touching her shoulder, I felt the rise and fall of her breath.

'I can't dance like this!'

People were leaping and turning and hooking arms, twirling around the machines. The whole great shed of East Floor was booming and shaking. I linked my arm into hers and steered her gently forwards. These tunes, I'd heard them all, wafting out from pubs and on the lips of guildmistresses as they lifted their washing.

'You can do *anything*, Anna,' I murmured close to her ear, breathing the scent of corn.

But for once, she needed my help. The half steps, the arches and processions, the hands you held on to and the hands you let go of; they all had a logic which came easily once you let the music take you. The dances in the Easterlies weren't so very different. An extra turn, a lost phrase or a repeated one. These tunes pervaded all of England, and tonight, SHOOOM *BOOM*, the aether engines marched to the same beat.

Unlike that night in the ballroom above the Thames, people in these dances were forever changing partners. Anna, moving warily at first to my promptings, gave a shriek as she was suddenly swept off into the throng. But the next time I saw her she was hitching her skirts and twirling elbow to elbow amid the crowd, her face bright and smiling. Here was the girl who'd sat in front of me at Board School, and Beth, and then my father, even, seeing as the sexes always got mixed up by the second verse of

Lovely on the Water. Not that anybody ever minded. In fact, colliding, getting lost—that was all part of the fun. Had I explained this to Anna as well? But when we next collided I felt laughter through the push of her bosom. Then she was gone, and then she was close to me again.

It was hard, thirsty, work. I wandered off towards the beer barrels which had been placed on a trestle not far from my father's old lathe. A guildsman was dancing with his familiar. Others were shouting, tapping their clogs and boots. Anna was still out there, her hair fanning. The fertile custodian wavered up to me as I watched her, the latest of what looked like several recent beers in his hand. 'Heard from London about you,' he shouted. 'Bugger of it is, I hadn't got around to telegraphing them. But they did anyway.'

'Oh.' I took a slow sip of my beer. 'What did they say?'

He shrugged. 'Basically wanted to know if you were here in Bracebridge. Robbie Borrow, they said. Missed off the s and didn't even call you a master. That's head office for you.'

'Have you replied?'

'Thought I'd talk to you first.'

'Perhaps if you could hold off for a couple more days, eh?'

He tapped his nose and sidled away. Given the choice, he'd still take my word over some jumped-up southerner's—but Anna was right; our time here in Bracebridge couldn't last. Even tonight, as I stood surrounded by all the swirling faces of my childhood, I could feel them dwindling back into memories. Yet here was Mistress Borrows, bright in the lanternlight, and the people were stomping and cheering. With a mock bow, she gestured to the accordion player to unshoulder his instrument. One by one the other musicians fell silent, the dancers stopped dancing. For the first time in hours, the only sound on East Floor was the earth's pounding. Anna studied the keys. She gave the instrument a squeeze. A discordant squawk came out. Puzzlement ruffled back through the crowd. What *was* she doing? Then her fingers danced a run of notes. The sounds spiralled, and she filled their echo with another. The best of

the fiddle players followed with a swooping glissando.
SHOOOOM *BOOM*. That rhythm never changed but
somehow Anna made it slow, then quicken. A flute player
began to follow the melody which she had picked out. People began to clap. Soon, they were whooping, dancing.
Anna's playing went on. The tune was happy and sad. It
was wild and it was filled with yearning. Then, with
scarcely a hesitation in the beat, Anna lifted the accordion
back into the arms of its owner, who, grinning, took up the
tune. Now, this would always be the Tapsters' Ball when a
new song was discovered. It would spread out across
Brownheath and the story of its making would be endlessly
embroidered.

Mistress Borrows—where is Mistress Borrows . . . ?

People were looking about for Anna. They needed her
as much as the high-guilded dancers had at Midsummer on
the river. But Anna had grabbed my hand and was pulling
me away from East Floor around the cold black machines.
This, in the little time we had left, was our best chance to
find out the truth about Mawdingly & Clawtson. But
where, and how? Along dark corridors, past empty lockers.
Through yards and up sets of stairs. Over to the west, Engine Floor was glowing, steaming. Work went on there
with or without the Tapsters' Ball, but it would have been
impossible for Anna and I to enter such a place and take
the gated lift to Central Floor. The guilds guarded their inner secrets even from each other, especially here, close to
their core. But there had to be somewhere . . . Then we entered a corridor. It was cheap and low and dark, but suddenly entirely familiar. *Insolent little bastard, aren't you?*
Stropcock's ghostly face, hanging over a clip of pens and a
brown overall, leered before me. I tried the first door. It
was a stationery cupboard. But the next—here was the office into which he'd dragged me. It had changed little in
the thin strips of moonlight, with the filing cabinets
jammed lopsidedly next to the cracked leather chair. And
behind it, still covered by what looked like the same oil-
stained sheet, was the haft which Stropcock had made me
touch.

This, sonny, is my eyes and ears.

I studied it, then looked at Anna, but already she was reaching towards it. As she did so, her fingers grasped my hand, and the room vanished.

Dark sheds and empty corridors. Frozen yards. Dancers on East Floor, then the great turning axle of Engine Floor, driving into the ground. I'd seen such scenes before—they were part of my life—but, deep below, Central Floor had changed. The triple pistons still drove back and forth, but the floors, the walls, the ceiling which surrounded them, even many of the instruments, were glittering. The place was a grotto of engine ice. The great iron plug of the fetter was now a gleaming brooch, and there was no shackle attached to the engines. No wonder the engines of Bracebridge beat differently now—they were working against no pressure at all. We floated away through the aetherless rock. The whole factory lay below us now, then the night-black town; a monument to empty endeavour. How many people here knew or guessed or cared? Then we were looking down across the flat expanse of Bracebridge sidings. Even tonight, the long carriages of an aether train were being prepared to beat the snows. The wind-whipped straw; the empty caskets, and the lie that Bracebridge still produced aether would be borne down towards London. And there . . . I saw those laddering lines of Stropcock's numberbeads. And the ships down at Tidesmeet, the hulk of the *Blessed Damozel;* empty, storm-hollowed for a ghost trade . . .

We stepped back. The tips of Anna's fingers still glowed. 'What . . . ?'

She shushed me with a swirl of light, and the creak of the desk as she leaned against it. 'Let's go now. I'm tired . . .'

It was snowing next morning and our route through low-town blurred in wind as, on the day which Anna and I had determined would be our last in Bracebridge, we headed down towards the station. Today was a Fourshiftday, and all the ordinary work of the town went on even in this bitter weather, but Bracebridge seemed to me now like a

scratched and faded photographic plate of itself; thin as
glass, and equally frail. Down past the high guildhouse
door from which Grandmaster Harrat had once emerged,
then Anna waited as I rummaged some coal to feed the pitbeasts in their yard. Tatton Halt wasn't a *station*, the stationmaster shouted to us through the slot of his glass arch
over the banging of the waiting room doors. Hadn't been
anything there for years unless you counted the quarry,
which was closed, and Redhouse, which was used up and
deserted.

Across the iron footbridge, we sat on the same bench,
and the track, the nearer sidings, grew and retreated through
the snow whilst Anna shivered and stared into nothing
from above her scarf. I was a jumble of emotions. Elated,
because my suspicions about the Bowdly-Smarts seemed
vindicated. Impatient, because I now wanted to get back to
London. Concerned, because of Anna's evident exhaus-
tion. And then a little afraid. The train came. It was white,
too, all steam and frosted iron, and we sat in the cold carriage as the guard shook his head in even greater wonder
than the stationmaster at the pointlessness of our desti-
nation. After a shorter journey than I remembered, we
stood on what little remained of Tatton Halt's platform,
beneath the weathered sign as the huffing engine rejoined
the snow.

The silent ground. The invisible mountains. Wind-
rattled holly and snagging bramble and browned grass beside a small, frozen river. We walked on through the shelter
of the deeper woods and followed the old wall to the ruined
gatehouse. Redhouse, beyond, had shrunk. Its roofs had
declined. Even its engine ice had crumbled and settled,
forming a glittering slurry which the wind threw into our
faces. The rains had driven in, and there was a sour woodland smell of rot and foxes as Anna wandered its corridors,
tugged by something like the same waves of recollection I
felt in Bracebridge. But this must have been much harder.
The place where she had lived and slept and played had
fallen into beams and rubble. Her wonderful piano was re-
duced to a skeleton of grinning keys. The great glass dome
of the library had collapsed, and the bookshelves had

spilled their contents in a morass of pages which the wind whipped around us like smoke.

There had been a fire in the wing which contained Mistress Summerton's old study, but, miraculously, a child's skipping rope still hung on the same single coatpeg where it had been on that warm day at the last edge of summer. Anna explained how she'd seen a girl skipping on one of her and Missy's furtive visits into the world of towns and houses—dancing with something which blurred around her, then became a strip of ordinary rope. She'd pestered Mistress Summerton to get her one, but, alone here in Redhouse and with only an elderly changeling for company, she'd never worked out the trick.

The fountain which we'd sat beside still rose in wild white plumes. I remembered a different Anna leaning back in starbursts of sunlight, the strap of her dress slipping from her shoulder. And the words! The fine and ancient words which she had learned from those sodden books in that ruined library; the spells of human love which we both, in our adult human lives, had failed in our different ways to recreate. Anna glanced back at me and tightened her scarf. We kept a wider distance as we clambered into the valley.

It was more sheltered down here and the cottages were slipping back to earth more easily than the big house, shrugging off their engine ice and taking on roots and moss. But the river was doubly frozen; it hissed and crackled like an arthritic snake, and the church's fallen spire still glittered amid the gravestones. This, as I'd guessed, was the place where Anna's mother was buried.

KATE DURRY 51–76.

Crudely carved. As I crouched to examine it with her, I didn't comment that this was the only stone in this abandoned plot which wasn't comprehensively covered in dead brambles and ferns.

Mistress Nutall came to our back door that evening. She blew in on an agitated gust of cold and smoke.

'*Here* you are at last!' She wiped the snowflakes from her face. 'I've been looking all day through your windows.'

Her gaze travelled into the parlour with its many cuttings, guildbooks and newspapers, and the blanket-strewn couch where I slept. 'I thought you might have—'

'Done a flit?' Anna suggested. Our rent, paid in arrears, was due tomorrow. 'We've only been out.'

'Out? In *this*?'

'But we *are* leaving tomorrow. And we're so very grateful for all your help, aren't we, Master Borrows?'

'Oh? Yes . . .' It still took a moment to realise that Anna meant me. Then, almost as quickly as she had come, Mistress Nutall had taken her disapproval, and our rentbook, and was gone.

'You should go and see you father and Beth,' Anna suggested after we'd got the fire going and had eaten what little was left in the larder.

'What about you?'

She gave an impenetrable smile.

The snow came in screaming flurries as I walked the short distance to Brickyard Row. Perhaps the rails would already be blocked by tomorrow morning, but—with my local's feel for the weather—I doubted it. Anna and I would get back to London—and from there . . . I was almost certain now that Stropcock's wealth came from processing—I supposed *laundering* would have been something like the technical word—the illusory wealth which came from Bracebridge. Even when Grandmaster Harrat had taken me around Central Floor, stalactites of engine ice had been dripping from it, and I would certainly not have been the first to notice. The knowledge went back at least some ten years earlier, when, following that failed experiment which Harrat had supervised, Anna's parents had died. So, eventually, had my mother. Stropcock had probably found out about all of this in the same way that we had, through that little haft, or simply by doing what he was best at, which was poking around. In any event, he'd used that knowledge to blackmail Harrat and get himself that Christmastime seat at his high-guilded table. Then, when Harrat died, that same knowledge must have been his springboard to far greater wealth and glory in London. But here, my vision blurred and faded. Stropcock must have made contact with someone—*something*—far more powerful than Grandmaster Harrat to have achieved the extraordinary leap of becoming Grandmaster Bowdly-Smart. It had to be the guilds themselves which sustained him—but that answer, as I reached the terraces of Brickyard Row where the birch trees flapped and mooed, still wasn't enough. I needed a single person—that dark guildsman whom Harrat had mentioned, for whose empty face I had searched every photograph I'd found in Bracebridge, for whose unknown name I had scanned the endless lists, and who sometimes seemed closer than my own breath, yet remained more distant than the moon.

The wind gave a harsher scream; raw metal scraped on metal. I turned back suddenly at my old gate, but there was only the Bracebridge night, that endless, empty pounding. I beat hard at the front door of my old house until my father's face emerged through a crack in the door.

'Oh, it's just *you* . . .'

Beth was out—with her teacher friend, I guessed, from the way he wouldn't say. He sat back in his chair in the fug and warmth of the kitchen with the wind buffeting the flames in the stove. He nodded, unsurprised, when I explained that Anna and I were leaving tomorrow. *Back to London, eh?* And the newspapers, the marches . . . My father sucked peevishly on a cigarette. No doubt he'd entertained his friends down at the Bacton Arms for years with stories of how well his son was doing down south, how I'd come back one day in guilded splendour. I was a disappointment to him and, much though I would have insisted that my standards and loyalties weren't his, it mattered to me. I stood up from my stool. I told my father to give Beth my love. There was a fruitcake on the side which she'd made for me. I put a hand on the old man's shoulders. Before he could get up from his chair and protest, I kissed the stubble of his cheek.

The wind was still screaming when I got back to Tuttsbury Rise with Beth's cake. It looked as if Anna had been trying to squeeze into her suitcase all the heavy and practical extra clothing she'd been given or acquired here to take back to London, and then had given up some time ago.

'There's not much more to be done, is there?' She sat down on her bed beside her open case. I was about to sit beside her when there came a knock at the front door below. I imagined it was Beth, or perhaps Mistress Nutall wanting her keys back early, but even when I forced the door open, my eyes were stung at first by nothing but dark and snow. Then I saw a dark, hulking figure, and my heart lurched.

'Who is it, Robbie?'

Anna had come down the stairs behind me with the lantern. In dark plays and glimmers, its slow light revealed who was standing there.

'Heard you were here,' he croaked.

We both stepped back wonderingly.

He smelled like Redhouse—rankly of rot and foxes, and a little of soot, and of human filth—and his skin had blistered and greyed and crimsoned and bled into something far worse than I remembered in the years since I had last seen him. He shuffled into our paper-strewn parlour and slumped into a chair, a spill of rags, steaming with frost. When he unbound the scarves and clots of bandage which covered his head and face, it was hard to look at what was revealed. One eye was seared and dead. The other glowed like the red star I had seen hanging above Bracebridge during my mother's final days.

'You know who I am?' His breath rasped and bubbled.

'I saw you when I was young. My mother, she used to . . .'
But I trailed off as the Potato Man raised his ragged arm, and pointed a seared finger towards Anna.

'I was your father,' he said.

The Potato Man grabbed the enamel mug of tea I gave him and noisily inhaled its steam. When it had cooled a little, he lapped at it as a dog laps at a bowl of milk. He had scarcely any lips.

'You're saying you're Edward Durry?'

'No—Durry's dead.'

'But if *you* were there,' I said, 'on the afternoon the engines stopped—'

'The past is dead as well,' he growled. 'You, girl . . .' He slopped down his mug and gestured. 'Come a little closer. I won't bite—can't you see I've no teeth . . . ?'

Anna got up from the edge of a chair. She didn't flinch when his fingers touched her cheek, shoving her face towards the light of the fire and then away from it. 'You've got a lot of Kate about you . . .' He let out a bubbling sign. 'And that other thing. What you are—one of the bloody fairy people . . .' He grabbed her wrist, twisting it around so quickly that I saw Anna wince. He peered at the scab of her stigmata, then clasped a hank of her hair and dragged her face close to his own, studying her green eyes with his solitary red one. 'But you hide it well, I'll grant you that.' His mouth contorted. 'But I suppose it was the right thing, leaving you with that old witch in that crazy white house. What kind of life would you have had amid these people?' Finally, he let go of Anna's hair. His red gaze travelled over me and around the small firelit room.

Anna blinked and rocked back on her knees in front of him. 'You sound very bitter.'

He took his cup and thrust it towards me. 'Bitter's this tea—you call this *sweet*?' I spooned in more sugar. 'Place like this, you must have some bloody *food* . . . ?'

There was scarcely anything left in our kitchen but lard and dry bread. Casting us wary and furtive glances from over hunched limbs, the Potato Man sucked and slobbered at it. The more the fire warmed him, the worse he stank. Anna sat quietly before him, watching, her hands folded into her lap. The Potato Man, we realised, had come here not out of any great urge to see the girl he claimed was his daughter, but because simply he'd hoped we might feed and warm him. That, far more than his terrible flesh, was the most horrifying thing.

'What was my mother like?' Anna asked eventually.

The Potato Man lifted clots of his clothing to lick up wet fragments of fallen crumb. 'She was like you.'

'But . . .' She shrugged and made a small gesture. 'You *must* remember . . .'

He continued picking at the remnants of the bread.

'It's the reason we're in Bracebridge,' I said slowly. 'To find out what happened here. To our families . . . If you can

help us . . .' I thought stupidly, desperately. 'We can give
you more food.'

He looked up. We could have offered him wealth and
favours and affection. But the Potato Man had lived for too
long buffeted by the cold winds of Brownheath. As the
night howled and the earth pounded and the whole of
Beth's heavy fruitcake, chunk by chunk, disappeared into
the maw of his mouth, he told us about the man he had
once been.

They were a proud lot, he muttered, were the aetherworkers of Central Floor. Much given to looking down on
those who worked above them, as the old, old joke went.
Fine English aether from Bracebridge, which was the best
in the world. Sure, the southerners had their windmills and
the Welsh had their grubby diggings, and the Frogs and the
Latins across the seas had their own stuff, or so they
claimed, but it travelled as badly as the reek of their cooking. So, for all intents and purposes, Bracebridge to the
aetherworkers who lived there was the centre of the world.
And Aethermaster Edward Durry—for no one would ever
think to call him *Ted*—he'd done well, to get as far as he
had, so young. That nice house on Park Road, and married
to a girl who still worked in the paintshop, it was true, but
who was generally conceded to be the prettiest of the
bunch. He fancied himself a highermaster, did Edward
Durry. And perhaps, even, for such things happened, at
least in his thoughts, if not ever in a place like Bracebridge,
a grandmaster after that. The Potato Man grunted a bitter
spray of currants and shook his head. Edward Durry was
always counting the next step, the next day, the next beat of
the engines he spent his life tending. Why, even when his
wife announced that she was pregnant, Durry was thinking
that Board School wouldn't be good enough for *his* lad.
There'd be private tutors and posh academies where the lad
would sleep away. Durry had moved from nightwork to do
a few of the days by now, and he was regular gang leader
on Halfshiftday afternoons. Some of his fellow aetherworkers thought that that was the graveyard of the whole
term, but Durry had come to love the feel of the engines
then, the almost-silence and the sense that, apart from the

ever-tended engines of Central Floor directly above them, all the tuppenny outer floors were empty. The purpose of the whole factory had a purity, stripped of all the rubbish and clatter, and he liked to think with mingled contempt and pity of the other lesser guildsmen getting on with their stupid, lesser lives up top. Oh, he was a proud man, was Durry, and he'd noticed, in the time he'd worked the engines and had got to know them better than his heartbeat, a slight extra pull, a tension, not a change in the rhythm itself, you understand, but a sense, like a slightly stiffened muscle, of almost pleasurable resistance.

Then, one day, one of the toffs from one of those oak-lined offices—Grandmaster Thomas Harrat if you please—came to see him. Durry was torn as he was always torn when he was with such people between wanting to suck up and telling them that they were no better than he was. But the two men were of a similar age, and they were both ambitious, and they knew their aether. Harrat was never as direct as to say that Bracebridge was running out of the stuff. That wasn't his way. But *extraction difficulties* were mentioned. As were *long-term production exigencies*. One evening after his shift was finished, Harrat took Durry to an iron gate, which he opened in some fancy way and led him down and along abandoned corridors to a room of leaking shelves. There, he showed him something special, something large, something bright and heavy. A chalcedony nestled amid the newspapers of a wooden casket—massive with magic. And the plan was to boost production, to make Bracebridge more than the plain little town it was. Harrat spoke easily of these things, but Durry simply stared at the stone. For the one overriding rule which was beaten into the mind of every apprentice was to Do Things In The Way They Have Always Been Done. For aether was magic. Aether was dangerous. But what, after all, Durry thought as he stared into the lovely light of that chalcedony, did the guilds know? Think of the Founder working against the laughter of his Painswick neighbours. And Christ himself— they laughed at him as well, didn't they? Not that these things were said, not that they needed to be. The matter was swiftly agreed. There would be an experiment, an innovation. And their so-called seniors and supervisors would not be told.

There was much work to be done. To introduce the spell within the chalcedony into the production process required that it be inserted into the shackle between the three huge pistons and the fetter which gripped the rock. The existing shackle was a marvel of engineering, a yard-long cat's-cradle of metal and the highest grade engine silk spun like the chrysalis of a butterfly, yet it could not accommodate the stone. So a new shackle had to be fashioned. The process, the secrecy, was fascinating, and Durry always sensed, that, in their secret heart, all the great guilds were looking down on their task with encouragement and approval. When a far higher guildsman than Harrat came up one day from London, and smiled and listened, and raised his hand from his dark cloak and laid it on Edward Durry's shoulder, why, that seemed right. And the planning was a mighty work. Even if this process, this *insertion,* was done openly, you couldn't just stop the pistons as if you were the steamaster of some poxy train. Even done gradually, with a lessening of pressure, the aether would at some point snap back all the way from the quickening pools. To get the pressure up again would be the work of several shifterms. So the insertion must take place between one beat of the engines and the next.

Organising the day itself, arranging the absence of the rest of his shiftgang, was all another part of the spell they were weaving. Durry's men were incurious, happy to spend their day up top with their families, and he enjoyed the way Central Floor emptied of its previous shift. The machine was his. He was on his own and relishing the task ahead when Harrat finally arrived by forgotten tunnels from that hidden room with a squeaky trolley on which the carried the newly made shackle with the chalcedony glowing within it. This was all as they'd arranged, but he'd brought others with him as well. Two women from the paintshop, and Aethermaster Edward Durry, were he still living, would have sworn on the creed of his guild that it was Harrat rather than he who had made that decision. To bring his wife *Kate* down here, and then that friend of hers Mary

Borrows as well, as if this was some parlour show. Even beyond his own highermaster, the last person Durry had thought of confiding in was Kate. Not that he didn't love her, but, if truth be told, he loved his engines far more, and often felt a little empty when he went up to the world of sunlight and cobbles and cooking, which seemed in comparison a waking dream. Paintwork needed to be done, as Durry was fully aware, so that the new shackle was freshly adorned with all the necessary spells before it was inserted. And such ornamentation would, it was true, normally be performed by the girls of the paintshop, but Durry hadn't doubted that he could do at least as good a job.

After the forced, surprised, *Why are you here?* greeting, an argument between the two men ensued. But their relationship had been tempered with, if not a liking, at least a mutual respect, and Durry came to see that Harrat had a point. After all, there were many other things to get done. And the girls were experienced in their work. Kate—at least—was one of the best in the paintshop, even with the distraction of that growing lump in her belly. They would do it quicker and better, and who else was Harrat to choose? As the two women stood in the pounding and oddly empty lower floor and exchanged puzzled glances, Durry came around to seeing that, just like everything else which had happened, it was all another part of the spell.

So the two women set to work, dipping their brushes in the aether pots Harrat had provided and wreathing the new shackle in a glowing tapestry which, Durry had to admit as he loosened the bolts and cotters which held the old shackle in place, was finer than anything he could have accomplished. The new device, beautiful to him already, became a thing of wonder, glowing within from the chalcedony, and without from the aethered scrolls made by the women's brushes. Their shadows danced as they worked, were strewn as soft comets across the ceiling of Central Floor. They were the stone's acolytes.

Harrat removed himself to the control room, which was a brick dome which the shiftworkers called the igloo. With its steel supports and portholes, it was by far the safest place to be at the moment of insertion, but Durry understood that it was necessary for someone to be in there to check the readings. He, on the other hand, was standing right between the fettered rockface and the driving pistons, holding the lanyard of rope which would release the new shackle from its temporary wooden cradle above the old one. The two women were beside him, still working. For the extraordinary thing was how quickly their spells faded; like ink into blotting paper, spit on a hot stone. That chalcedony, for all the power it contained, was sucking in more and more magic through its woven casing. Kate was on the far side of the mechanism, leaning over the swell of her belly in a way that gave Durry a brief pang, and Mary was on his side of it.

Durry studied his pocket watch as the second hand beat towards the hour of three. He glanced back along the pounding tubes towards the brick igloo and saw Harrat raise a thumb through one of the portholes. Durry's fingers tightened. Mary Borrows, sensing the coming moment, stepped back a little, tripping slightly as she did so. Kate continued working. SHOOM *BOOM* SHOOM. The moment was perfect, and he pulled the rope.

The new shackle dropped beautifully in the shuddering pause between the beats, falling and displacing the old one with precision and a certainty beyond the mere pull of gravity. The old device shattered on the stained concrete in a tumbling spray of steel and silk, whispering up in smoke. Fragments of its metal spun around them and Durry heard Mary Borrows give a small gasp. But the new shackle fitted instantly, wonderfully, into its cradle, and its chalcedony glowed. The whole moment was such a triumph and the stillness which followed seemed so right, that even Aethermaster Edward Durry's senses were momentarily bewitched. But the silence held. The engines, without a single moment of slowing or hesitation, had stopped beating.

Several things, then, happened at once. Those three perfect pistons, solidly aethered, could halt more easily from one moment to the next than the hands of his watch. But they were powered through the great axle from Engine Floor above. In stopping, their pistons drove that force back up. Durry heard, felt, the long, solid axle sheer and give, sheer and give, all the way up through the rock towards the surface. But those many fractures weren't enough. From up top, the silence was rent by a series of earthquake detonations.

But the other thing which happened was that the glow of the chalcedony, which was already searing, increased. Spires of light broke out through the shackle, solid as polished steel. Somehow, without moving, they revolved, focused, pulsed. The scene would have been beautiful were it not too quick and too terrible for his dazed senses to understand. Then, like a snake coiling, like the snap of a chain gone wild, the glow turned in on itself, burst in a silent thunderclap and regathered as a glowing sphere—some new, unrecorded state of aether—which drove upwards and out across Central Floor at the exact point where Kate was standing with such wyrebrightness that Durry was sure he saw the shine of her bones, the grin of her skull, the beat of her blood and the shape of her baby. Then it puffed out. And was gone.

But for the tick of astonished dials, lower floor was silent. The chalcedony had lost almost all of its glow. Kate was just standing there looking shocked whilst Mary Borrows was sucking at a cut on the heel of her palm. They all stepped away, still gazing at the stilled pistons as Harrat stumbled from the igloo. They moved first towards the lift, which had lost all power, then found the iron stairway of the emergency route.

All the people of Bracebridge stopped what they were doing at three o'clock on that July Halfshiftday in the 75th year of the Third Age. Dogs began barking. Babies cried. Slates slithered from roofs. The old Ropeworkers' tower and several other of the town's frailer buildings collapsed in pale sighs of dust. Black-white plumes poured up from the crackling ruin of Engine Floor as the whole town rushed towards those famous gates with their friezes of Providence and Mercy. Word, as Aethermaster Edward Durry's fellow gangsmen instinctively sought each other out, quickly spread that he'd been down there *alone*. But as the first figures of the steamworkers emerged bleeding, coughing from the smoking wreckage, Edward Durry shrugged off the questioning hands and drove into that spilling heat. Truly, that afternoon, he was a man possessed. He saved six, eight men. He lifted up one of the fallen main beams single-handed. He moved through the ruins with the strength of an automaton, although, as the heat beat against him, his flesh became as blistered and smoking as the men he'd rescued. He was almost a hero and the story was that they'd finally had to hold him, strap him to a stretcher, when they'd given up screaming at him that there was no one left to save.

But most of Edward Durry was already gone by then. He understood, in the instant after the one when the engines stopped beating, that he'd betrayed his guild in the grossest possible way, and that he was ruined. When he awoke to the smell of mop buckets and bleached laundry and the slippery stick of pain in the astonishing, engineless quiet of Bracebridge's Manor Hospital, he was already the Potato Man. He was in a ward with three other men. They took it in turns to scream. Oddly, for him, there was less pain, although the figure who was sitting beside him in a spill of summer moonlight seemed so dark and powerful that for a moment he almost cried out. But it was only Grandmaster Harrat.

Harrat was in tears, offering limp apologies. Just like Kate and Mary Borrows, he'd managed to become part of the crowd when they stumbled up through the escape hatch from Central Floor. He'd escaped, near enough, and soon he fell out of his tears. Guild business, after all, was guild business, and life was life, even if Durry's own seemed wasted. There was bound to be an enquiry. But Harrat had been to his office to obliterate certain records and he'd used—he'd had to use, seeing as the snivelling little man had somehow found things out—a certain uppermaster of the Toolmakers' Guild to go back down to Central Floor and destroy the new shackle and somehow get rid of that damn chalcedony. Whatever evidence there was now would be confusing at best, and Harrat still had his friend from the south, that dark guildsman who'd laid the warmth of his approving hand on Durry's shoulder. Even though he didn't quite know his name and full status and had had no success in his attempts to contact him, he still really hoped that that great guildsman would come to his aid. Still, it looked as if things could be smoothed over. But a price, as always, had to be paid. And at that point, Harrat, who'd never exactly been a pillar of strength in Edward Durry's estimation, started crying again. The Potato Man waited. Eventually, as the man subsided unattended into murmurs and moans, he began to understand the deal which Harrat had made.

After all, Durry's life was gone, ruined. He'd be thrust out of his guild. He'd become a mart and quite possibly become changed as well. But he'd also been a hero of sorts yesterday and people of this town, if they were given the choice, would much rather think that way of him. So what if he was to let Edward Durry die, and take all of the blame? There'd be a funeral, a decent tombstone, an oration. The enquiry would be quickly over and forgotten, and people wouldn't spit when they mentioned his name . . .

Harrat stood up from the bedside. He was running out of words and the tears were coming back again. Somewhere, a door was open. Across his ruined flesh and through the sight of one eye and the dark space which was left by the other, the Potato Man sensed its breeze. He climbed up from the pain of his bed. The whole hospital was oddly quite as he limped out from it into the bright silence of the summer's night beyond. Harrat was already gone, a mere silhouette hurrying back along Withybrook Road into town, to his life, his career, his guilt and his worries. But there was Mary Borrows with a bandage on her one hand, and his wife Kate, who seemed beautiful as ever as she stood beneath a tree beside the old postbox, even if her hair had somehow greyed. The Potato Man knew he must look terrible to them as he lumbered over, but their faces registered almost nothing. *Look,* he moaned in his changed voice. *This is our chance to escape* . . . But Kate half smiled and said nothing. The tree was a lace of shadow. Up there in the moonlight, Rainharrow gleamed like the moon herself. And Kate's eyes gleamed as well. *We can go* . . . But she only smiled that smile again. It was like talking to a ghost, and he'd known already that she couldn't possibly go with him into the life he planned to

lead. The Potato Man genuinely thought he'd already lost
every last vestige of his old self when he tried to touch
farewell to his wife's face. But something was wrong. Even
though she was standing in the shade of the moon, Kate
was glowing. And his hands, ruined and clumsy in their
burns and bandages, snagged in her hair, which crumbed
and broke in bright shards. Whatever it was—the spell
within that stone—had caught her and left her changed.
And it was then, rather than as he glanced back at the dark
stain on his bed inside the hospital, that Edward Durry really died . . .

The Potato Man wiped his mouth. The fruitcake was entirely eaten, and the tale, at least to judge by his silence,
was entirely told.

'So my mother took Kate to Redhouse?'

He grunted and picked a currant from the back of his
mouth.

'And you went with her?' Anna asked.

The Potato Man shook his head, gave a long, convulsive
snort, then buried his ruined face in his ruined hands. Anna
leaned forward and tried to put her arms around him, but
now, when he saw her face, bright in the firelight, he drew
away with a moan. He'd been dragged back into his lost
life and Anna's face, like the face of Kate Durry who had
frozen into engine ice and died in bearing her, was too
much for him. I realised as he sobbed and cowered that the
Potato Man was right; Edward Durry really had died. His
grave was up there in the churchyard of St Wilfred's for
anyone who cared to visit it.

We tried to make the Potato Man spend the night by the
warmth of our fire. We offered him clothes to replace the curdled rags he was wearing. We'd have given him more food
as well if we'd had any. But he was up and lumbering away
from us. And that bastard Harrat had died as well hadn't
he? he muttered. Only it had been slower—and who was
he to say which way was the worse? *You,* lad! He gestured. You were there at his *house,* weren't you? So keep
away, keep away! He gave a slobbering howl. The fireplace
gloomed and the room pulsed and pounded with his dull,

sad rage. Then the front door slammed open and my carefully collected lists and cuttings flew up in a storm. But there was still one thing which I wanted to know.

'Wait! Please wait . . .'

The Potato Man cocked his red eye and cowered.

'That man—that dark guildsman Harrat talked about. You said you *saw* him. You said he laid his hand on your shoulder . . .' I grabbed a wodge of the swirling papers and thrust them towards him. 'Would you recognise him if I showed you a picture? Could you tell me who he was?'

But the Potato Man was still backing away. Beyond the flapping front door the night screamed through the trees in a white howl. Looking desperately about for something to give him, I saw the sugarbowl. It glittered like a small pile of engine ice.

'Here. Take this . . .'

The Potato Man cradled the spilling bowl to his body, breathing heavily as he shuffled back through the chaos of papers, his clothes flapping like black flames. But what could I show him? Where was I to begin? It was useless. But then he snatched a recent copy of the *Guild Times,* which Anna and I had used to study the progress of George's trial.

'That's not . . .' I began, but the Potato Man was sniffing at the pages.

'Him . . .' The copperplate flurries of a dying regime. 'He's changed, but not much. People like that don't change . . .'

I prised the page from him. Deaths and Marriages—photographs as well, and the Potato Man's bloated finger stabbed at some ceremony to do with the final preparations for the marriage of Grandmistress Sarah Elizabeth Sophina York Passington, which was to be the event of the season down at Walcote House. Sadie was standing in an elaborate dress with her lips half framed as if to say something, and looking more formal than ever, and less herself. There was no sign of the groom-to-be. The only other presence was that of her father, who had laid a proud hand on her shoulder and was standing at her side as he smiled his faint, handsome smile.

'That's him,' the Potato Man said with a smudging

thrust of his thumb. 'He was the man who came to see Thomas Harrat.'

'You're *sure*?'

But already he was blundering away from me, out into the blowing hall and through the open door into the night.

The house was dark and empty. The lantern had guttered with the last of the oil and the coals had fallen through the parlour grate. Barring that one precious sheet of the *Guild Times,* I decided that Mistress Nutall could burn the rest of these scattered papers. But her gossip about the way we had lived, the words over fences, even the beat of the engines and the screech of the wind across Brownheath, seemed already remote. All that remained of the Potato Man was his dimming, rancid stench—and the looming answer, still too big for me to behold that night, to my question which he had finally brought me.

The house seemed a stranger to me now as we closed doors and swilled out the sink. It gazed down at us from the dark patches on its walls of the empty spaces of photographs we had never thought to fill.

'You know, Robbie, I still don't know what I am,' Anna said as she stood up from raking out the parlour fire. 'All these years, and I still haven't got the faintest idea . . .'

I opened my mouth to say something comforting, but as she turned back to me from the pale glitter of the grate, I could see that her eyes were brimming. She took my hand.

'Don't stay downstairs tonight. You understand what I'm saying? I just don't want to be alone.'

Gravely, soberly, we went upstairs and lifted Anna's case from the bed. She could lie on the left where she usually slept, and I on the right. I was reminded, as I stared at the worn candlewick bedspread and wet snowflakes settled and slid down the window, of those knights of far away and long ago in the Age of Kings, who had laid their swords between themselves and the maidens they were protecting in situations perhaps not so very unlike this.

Anna unbound her hair and blew her nose. She unbuttoned her dress and smoothed her hands down her sides and unpeeled her socks and stepped from her outer clothes and laid them over the chair beside the faintly moaning fireplace. Her skin seemed whiter than her petticoat and shift, which reminded me in their cut and the bareness of the summer dress I had first seen her wearing, back in the hope and sunlight of a quite different Redhouse to the one we had visited today. She laid back the sheets on her side and gave a shiver as she slipped into bed. Then there were the dull practicalities of my own outer clothing to be removed before I lay down on my side against the cold, slightly damp cotton, and realised that the curtains were still open.

'It doesn't matter,' Anna said as I made to get up. 'We need to wake up early in the morning anyway, if we're to get that train.'

She'd turned to me across the grey-white pillow. The faint light of the snowflakes shone across her face as they pattered and slid beyond the glass. I was shivering for every reason but the cold.

'I'm sorry, Anna. I don't know what to say . . .'

'Don't say anything. You're here. Didn't I tell Missy that I wanted to find out the truth?'

'I think we've found it.'

'I . . .'

'What?'

'Nothing.'

I lifted my hand, laid it over her wet cheek, and I felt her smile.

'Don't say anything more, Robbie. I'm just glad you're here.'

I leaned a little closer to her, and smelled her hair, and her tears, and thought of wet cornfields. The curve of her chin lay just beneath my palm. My fingers met the lobe of her ear. I could feel the movement when she closed her eyes, and the change of her breathing as she fell asleep.

V

'Can't you see?'

Northcentral, brighter than ever in the stormgleam of a late December Sevenshiftday, roared all around us.

'Can't you see?' I was shouting to Anna. 'Can't you *see* . . . !' And Anna was shaking her head.

Capital and industry, coal and aether, import and export, money and labour, rose up around us on these teeming streets. But I'd seen it all on that cold, quiet night in Bracebridge as the snow slipped down the window in melting trails and I had lain with my hand against her face. And I saw it now, here, in the bowler hats and the eddying masses of wealth and poverty. I saw it in the tut of Anna's tongue as she walked on from me once again. But I felt a new knowledge, a new tenderness, towards and over everything. And I was walking with Mistress Borrows, with Anna Winters, Annalise, through the continuing flood of Northcentral life, and I could smell the fog of London traffic and, still, the sweet, wet scent of her hair—and I wanted Anna to see it all as well. She was wearing her grey scarf, a red tam-o'-shanter, that herringbone coat, and she was walking with that slow, light-heavy lope of hers, and I was tumbling backwards through the crowds and not caring as I blundered into people as long as I could get her to see . . .

I wanted Anna to understand that the better world of which I'd long dreamed was suddenly close. It was a place I was sure I'd touched on that last night back in Bracebridge as the shadows of the snow slipped endlessly across her sleeping face. It was a world which in many outward ways resembled this one, but where everything was different underneath. More than merely just another Age or a set of puny demands, it was a place where wonder mixed with the sounds of traffic. No citizen starved, not in this New Age which was more than an Age. And the guilds would be more a tale than a memory, their statues remote as sarsens, their deeds more distant than England's kings.

But Anna shook her head again as we walked through the bustling Northcentral morning. The truth was precious, safe, dangerous, close and near. I knew that I would soon get her to see.

We'd been staying back in the Easterlies, far from Anna's old apartment in Kingsmeet, which I'd visited cautiously and alone on the morning of our return, and where I'd found a rubber-stamped notice from the Gatherers' Guild pinned to her door. Then I'd headed east towards Ashington, where I was cornered in a courtyard. The so-called citizen-helpers were thinking of using their nailed clubs when a voice mentioned Citizen Saul. So it was back, not just to the Easterlies, but to Caris Yard, that I was dragged, which had become a smoke-dimmed encampment of citizens of every kind. Clots of mud were thrown at me as I was blundered past the pump on which I'd first slaked myself on London water.

Caris Rookery was now a hive of revolution rather than a haven for criminality, but, for all that, it had scarcely changed, and Saul had set himself up in the same leaky top room where we had spent our first summer. Even the view across London, as I first glanced at it, looked the same. Hallam Tower flashed. The guildhouses still rose. He'd arranged himself a desk of sorts, employing the old door we'd once used to keep out the wind. There was a firework smell now to go with that of poverty and rotten herring. In the corner, laid casually beside the yellowed remains of

one of his old drawings, were several crude silver-grey
tubes.

'What the hell are you doing here, Robbie?'

I rubbed my arms as the blood tingled back. 'I could say
the same of you.'

He'd lost much of the weight he'd put on in the good
years. He looked like a sharper, more wizened version of
his younger self as he came to stand with me on the ledge
from which we had once merrily pissed. The drop was far
giddier than I remembered and Stepney Sidings were oddly
quiet for mid-afternoon. Just a few trains moved like toys,
gently huffing, whilst, almost directly below, some crows
were squabbling over what looked like an animal's remains.

'Where's Blissenhawk?

'He's over by Whitechapel . . .' Saul gestured. 'We've
had our disagreements. But he's still a citizen.'

'Aren't we all?'

Saul's jaw twitched. 'You can see what London's like.
Out there—' He waved towards Northcentral. '—lies an
enemy encampment. You've come on a train from somewhere north, haven't you? So you've seen the soldiers, the
cavalry. Perhaps they're waiting for us to come to them. Or
perhaps they'll come to us first. Either way—'

'—but—'

He raised a patient hand. The crows bickered and
cawed. 'And now you come wandering back into the Easterlies as if nothing has changed. Physical or moral force,
eh? And bloody Goldenwhite.' His face creased as he
smiled. 'And you—you mix with people who can only ever
be our enemies. That blonde girl. And that old troll over in
those ruins in World's End. And Highermaster George—
but at least he's proved to have his uses . . .'

I nodded. One of the most amazing sights in this
changed city was to see George's name scrawled across the
tidemarks of graffiti.

But Saul hadn't finished. 'And even that bloody grandmistress who's supposed to be getting *married,* for Christ's
sake! You know *her,* don't you? And then you go up north
on some stupid trip, and you return with that blonde girl—
what *is* her name?'

'Anna . . .' I hesitated.

'There have been some pretty unsavoury types asking after you as well. They have an idea that there's something you're after. And now you're standing here again as if nothing's ever changed. So what do you expect me think?'

'Look, Saul . . .' But I trailed off—there was so much I knew now, so much I had to tell. But where to begin? 'Can't you *see*—don't you still believe in the dream?'

Saul sighed, and nodded his dismissal to the citizens behind him, who looked disappointed as they lumbered down the stairs. But there was still puzzlement on his face when he turned back to me. 'What are you talking about, Robbie? *What* dream?'

And now I was with Anna, walking backwards along the impossibly bright pavements of Threadneedle Street, and trying to explain. It was all so clear to me now. It wasn't just about the past, or even this present moment as I tried to make her see the truth in the glint of those green and lovely eyes. Look, up here ahead, see the triumphal arch of Goldsmiths' Hall, a rainbow of stone so big that the nearby spire of St Peter's could fit underneath it? Gilt and glass, Anna, guild piled upon guild. And the subterranean safes of England's monetary wealth lie below. Can you imagine anything more solid? But see that keystone, far up there in the blurring winter light? You could pluck that stone out and bring that whole building down, Anna. *You* could, Anna, far better than anyone. Far better than I . . .

In the face of Saul's evident disbelief, which by now had changed to something resembling amused encouragement, I'd found the yearly accounts for Mawdingly & Clawtson, which were freely accessible in the domed and echoing cavern of the Public Reading Rooms. Books the size and weight of boulders confirmed that their sole operating business was the factory in Bracebridge, and that every month the same amount of aether was supposedly delivered to Stepney Sidings. No wonder Grandmaster Bowdly-Smart was doing so well. I'd given a loud sneeze as I tore out the pages. I glanced behind me through the pillars of dust and light. No one was there but I'd taken to varying my routes when I made my forays into Northcentral. I felt safer now, oddly enough, in Caris Yard. But today—today, I just *had* to make Anna see. I needed to make her understand. The truth was so obvious, in fact, that we needn't even have gone to Bracebridge to find it and I no longer cared who saw us I waved my arms and nearly tripped over a bollard.

A passing officer of the Guild Cavalry, who had become a common sight and no longer wore plumes on their helmets, gazed down at us from his horse. He was about to rein up and ask us what we thought we were doing when the chestnut seller just ahead of us spilled her tray. His mount reared as smoking nuts scattered across the paving and Anna and I slipped into the shadows beneath the gleaming arch of Goldsmiths' Hall.

Anna was also living in Caris Yard in a place not far from, and in many ways similar to, Maud's old nursery. Nappies dripped, babies squalled and toddlers stumbled whilst displaced guildswomen cried and argued and lived from one day to the next. I had to share a separate shed with a farting, coughing assortment of male citizens. The elected committees were surprisingly strict about segregating the sexes. Of course, the women loved Anna, and she seemed the same to me now as ever, but I realised as we moved with the crowds beneath that arch and the light softened the shadow of her jaw which my hand had cradled that night in Bracebridge that, to the ignorant gaze of these investors, speculators, messenger boys and company secretaries who hurried past us in their fine suits and cravats, she was starting to look more and more like some lesser guildmistress—perhaps even a mart—of the Easterlies. And I looked all the more so, although I'd learned how a rub of oil and soot and a scrap of white card could make my trousers and shirt shine enough to spend my hours in the Public Reading Rooms. But I had it all now—or almost all. The final thing I needed, as we passed back into winter sun along Threadneedle Street, was to make Anna understand . . .

We'd called on Mistress Summerton since our return. The Thames was almost fully frozen now. A few more days, the coming of a Christmas which the holly sellers and the shops along Oxford Road still hawked as if it would be like

any other, and we'd have been able to walk, but for now
we'd had to spend money we scarcely had for tickets on the
aether-braziered ferry. Hoar frost and engine ice. Those
white hills, empty as the Ice Cradle. And the ruined gardens
beside the great, shattered domes where the roses were
blooming wildly and out of season, curving in blood-red
plumes and thorns like the guardians of some ancient curse.
We banged worryingly long and hard on the door of her
cottage before her head extended like a tortoise's from its
shell. Her gaze had dimmed since the last time I had seen
her and her fire was scarcely lit. She claimed she'd been
asleep, even on this cold midday, as she bumbled about for
her tea and tobacco and managed to spill both. She even
had that same sour-sweet smell I'd noticed with old women,
although it was bound up with many scents and herbs. Her
hands lay still upon her lap and moved, lay still and moved,
as we told her about Bracebridge, the aether engines,
Grandmaster Harrat, the Potato Man.

'You must have always *known,* Missy. But you never
told me—you just left me to find out.'

'Edward Durry died long ago, Anna. Didn't he tell you
that himself?'

'Yes, but . . .'

Mistress Summerton could, as she gazed at us, have
been looking long into the empty future, far into the lost
past. 'Did you see those roses? They're quite out of my
control. But I don't know why I ever imagined they were
mine . . .' She gave a slow, sad chuckle like water trickling
through a grate. 'But who am I to think I ever controlled
anything? And it *has* been a hundred years, after all, give
or take a season, since this place was young. I'm almost the
same. The two of us are fading together . . .' Her eyes travelled down to Anna's boots, which were muddied and almost worn through, then across her socks, which we joked
were more hole than wool, to the tear in her moleskin skirt
and the fraying hem of her once good herringbone coat.
Then her eyes flickered towards me. *This,* she sighed in a
fluttering pulse, *is what you've done to my Annalise . . .*
The unspoken words trailed off into the wind hissing outside through the thorns.

'I have no money now,' she said eventually as she poured us cool, half-stewed tea. 'Or at least not unless I sell my car.'

'We're not here for your *money*, Missy!'

'I suppose you're not. But don't expect me to continue the tale of your poor father, either. Or that of your mother. She lived long enough to give birth to you after that terrible accident, and for that we must all rejoice. And your father's dead—as good as. But these are things you've always known. You didn't have to go to Bracebridge for them. Isn't that enough? I once hoped . . .'

But Mistress Summerton never did quite say what she'd once hoped, other than that it was plainly something other than for Anna and I to be sitting here in winter with the smell of the Easterlies upon us. I could have told her about many things, about the real truth of how I could change this Age, but she was old and cold, her hands were like a frail bird's, and the best it seemed we could do was sort out some blankets for her, and feed her fire, and commiserate with her about her madly blooming roses, which tore at our clothing as we walked back towards our ferry and the greying lights of a city which was preparing for war.

Butterfly Day was a fantasy of summer. This time, the workshops of the Easterlies were pounding to a rhythm set by no guild. Swords from ploughshares, or at least sharpened spikes from railings, and bombs from paraffin and sugar. Even guns of a sort—crude and aetherless things at least as likely to blow your own hands off as to stop a charging cavalryman, but guns nevertheless, which, like Grandmaster Harrat's electricity, were a technology which the guilds had long known about but, apart from the boom of ceremonial cannons, repressed. Saul had a touching faith in his guns, but he wasn't walking here in North-central. He'd forgotten about the power and pull of these buildings, or he'd never really known. He failed to understand what he was really fighting, which was aether and money—the true might of the guilds, which roared unabated in these streets and shone in the purring, wyreblack mass of the telegraphs which scribbled the sky, SHOOM *BOOM*—for money was magic as well. How, otherwise, could the aether engines of Bracebridge still pound the earth when they produced nothing? Anna had shown it to me through Stropcock's old haft, so surely she of all people could understand. Mawdingly & Clawtson, by the public records, produced a little under a quarter and slightly more than a fifth of all the aether extracted in England. The French and the Saxons, they tended their own industries and mysteries and guilds, whilst aether from the wildernesses of Thule, Africa and the Antipodes was like the people of those regions; strange and wild and notoriously difficult to tame.

I'm no expert on company affairs, Anna, but I do know that all companies are owned by shareholders—and that those shareholders are mostly the guilds. And Mawdingly & Clawtson is majority-owned by the Telegraphers' Guild. It's a major part of their wealth, Anna! Stropcock, Bowdly-Smart, he's just a henchman who goes through the motions of spending the income they pretend they have on imaginary cargoes and the contents of empty warehouses. But the Chairman of the Board, Anna—it's down in black and white, and I've still got the page in my pocket if you don't believe me—is Greatgrandmaster Anthony Charles Liddard Seed Passington!

All these years, almost all my life, there's been this creature, this figure. It used to be Owd Jack who betrayed Goldenwhite. Then it was the trollman, or Grandmaster Harrat's dark guildmaster. Up here in London, it was poverty and money, and places like this street where the guildmistresses wear white gloves to show that they never have to touch anything dirty. I've even *seen* him sometimes, Anna, or I've thought I have. He's come out of the stuff of shadows and bad corners of my dreams. But he was none of those things—and he was every one of them. The dark guildmaster was the real, living man who went up to Bracebridge more than twenty years ago with that chalcedony in a wooden casket, and he used Grandmaster Harrat in that experiment, and he used my mother as well—and your mother and father—and many people died and suffered as a result. It's *him*, Anna. There are records of speeches he made in neighbouring towns. He came and gave his orders and went away and took none of the blame. Even Grandmaster Harrat didn't know who he was. But for all that, he's just a *man*, Anna, which to be honest is almost a disappointment. But we can bring him *down*. You've got to understand. You've got to help me . . .

We found a small, quiet park with pale winter-bare sallow trees through which the honeyed stone of Northcentral glowed like firelight through a tapestry. In the cold shadow of its walls we walked the spotted marble paving and sat on a bench. Anna shoved her hands into her tattered pockets. The sounds of London had receded. A russet squirrel ran along a branch.

'You're just saying that we could ruin yet more lives.'

'It's *Anthony Passington,* Anna! He's the man who destroyed our parents.'

'But I know him. I've accepted his hospitality, and he's always been decent to me. He doesn't seem . . .'

'How do you expect such people to seem?'

She shrugged and shivered. Her lips looked chafed. She had a smear of soot on the end of her nose. 'He's Sadie's father, Robbie. Despite all that's happened, I'd still like to think that she and I are friends. And it's *her* guild, too.'

'Why do you think she's being forced to marry Greatmaster Porrett? The Distemperers' Guild is one of the few which doesn't have shares in Mawdingly & Clawtson. The Telegraphers need their wealth to keep going. That's exactly why they're being sucked in . . .'

Anna smiled. She gave her knees a jiggle. 'And Sadie always said it was just about paint.'

'Can't you see it's all part of the same thing? It's not these buildings around us which make the guilds what they are, Anna. It's money, and money's all about belief. England's already in a mess, so can you imagine what would happen if everyone knew that one of its major sources of aether has failed, and that the Telegraphers' Guild is bankrupt?'

She blew out a grey plume of air. 'It would be a catastrophe.'

'It would bring the Telegraphers down, Anna. And most of the other guilds, or near enough. Can't you see?'

'And that would be good, would it?'

'You made that banner back in the summer. I thought you believed in a New Age.'

'That was before a lot of things.'

'You've seen what it's like in the Easterlies. The citizens are just waiting for a signal to march towards North-central. This time they won't be carrying banners. But the guilds have their spells and their soldiers and their bale-hounds and their cavalry. They'll be prepared—why else do you think they're waiting? And why do you think all the so-called great and good are heading out of London for Sadie's wedding? By the time they get back in the New Year, all the blood will have been washed away. Saul and all the other citizens will have been killed or imprisoned, and the Telegraphers will be flush with new money. Everyone will continue just as it was, only it will get worse.'

'You make it sound terrible, Robbie.'

'But it doesn't have to be that way. We're the ones who can make sure it isn't.' I swallowed. The words in my head were simple now, but I needed her beside me to make them feel true. 'Between us, Anna, we can change this Age.'

But there was still doubt and horror in her eyes as she dragged back her hair, and she'd stood up before I could touch, as I'd been longing to do all morning, the downy space at the turn of her jaw.

'What else can I show you, Anna?'

I'd almost given up pleading.

Anna stopped in her tracks when she saw two weather-cocks prickling above the winter chimneys. But her whole life had been a battle against places such as St Blate's. As she tightened her scarf around her neck and started walking again, I think she understood that no one, now, could simply be ordinary. I pulled the bellchain. I hadn't noticed before how covered the long high walls were in graffiti. *Freedom from rest. Out demons. Lady* (something) *is an ugly monster.* Perhaps even the trollmen were feeling the pinch now and had given up scrubbing it off. The small door within the larger gate screeched open.

They didn't get many visitors, this close to Christmas

and this late in this Age, and Warderess Northover even remembered me from my visit to Master Mather. Of course I
could see him. In fact, he'd just got back from working for
his old guild a few minutes before. We were led into the
gravelled yard where the sea-voices washed through the
blue dusk from the main wing, and an anonymous green
box-carriage stood, lamps hissing and dray steaming. The
driver leapt down, flat cap and smile askew.

He hoiked a thumb. 'Just been back to the place he used
to work—Brandywood, Price and wotsit . . . Solid gold
thread curtains some dog had pissed on. Job for Master
Mather here if ever there was one . . .' The trollman took a
half-cigarette from behind his ear and walked beside his
wagon, absently banging on its side. He unbolted the rear
doors and slid down a wooden ramp.

'Come on, me dear . . .' He clicked his tongue and whistled. He found a chain in the shadows and gave it a tug.
'We're home. Even got some nice visitors for you . . .'

Master Mather emerged in a trickle of chains and a
huge, soft tumble of white flesh like a pile of dropped new
sheets. He'd put on weight since I'd seen him, or some kind
of substance. His skin had puffed up, was blister-smooth,
and the features of his face had entirely vanished. Only his
hands, suddenly narrowing at the wrists like a baby's or as
if an elastic band had been twisted around them, were still
recognisably human in their shape, although their flesh was
impossibly pale. He squealed and slithered like a huge bal-
loon filled with warm, swishing milk. And he smelled sear-
ingly of solvents, soaps and bleaches. A cross and C, I
noticed, had been branded on the taut white cushions of his
flesh, although it was nothing like the size of Mistress Summerton's, or even Mister Snaith's; things, just as Warderess
Northover kept saying, had improved.

'You recognise your old friend, don't you . . . ?' The
trollman crooned. But then, lunging on the cotton slippers
which encased the paddles of his feet, Master Mather made
a quick movement towards Anna, catching the sleeve of
her coat. A brief, odd tussle ensued before Anna snatched
her arm back and Master Mather gave a loud squeal as he
tried to scuttle back into the safe darkness of his van. The

moans and howls of those enclosed in the main wing rose in pitch and agitation. Even in this light, the left sleeve of Anna's herringbone coat was suddenly cleaner. The groom yanked hard on the chain. Master Mather whimpered.

'Does that sometimes. But we'll make sure he knows he *shouldn't*—believe me . . .'

'Please,' Anna said. *'Don't.'*

The trollman pushed back his cap and nodded. There was something about the tone of her voice.

We left St Blate's without entering the main wing and with the visitors' book, much to Warderess Northover's grief, still unsigned. It was fully dark now, the depths of the year. Cyclists whooshed by us on the dark streets of Clerkenwell like so many black birds.

'And there are other such places, Robbie?'

'Several, at least.'

'Then yes. I'll do it.'

Just like all the citizens in the vast army which filled Caris Yard, Citizen Simpson had a tale to tell. He'd been an upperaccountant, but his wife had been tubercular. There had been a need for money. And then . . . His eyes drooped as he crouched like a gargoyle on his freezing stretch of roof above the night-time mass of light and noise and stench in the yard below.

'Well?' Saul asked. 'Can you do it, citizen . . . ?' He took out a screw of paper and unwrapped it to reveal the small and faintly sparking stone hoop of the fresh numberbead he'd got hold of from somewhere. Citizen Simpson almost snatched the object from him, and muttered something which turned its light faintly blue. A half-recognisable song started up down below near the wall where Saul and I had once sat with Maud. I took out the papers, and Saul chuckled as he studied them, then passed them to Citizen Simpson, who smoothed them on the slates and began to mutter to himself as he clutched the numberbead.

'So,' I said. 'How many days do we have?'

Saul considered this for a moment. A solid darkness had filled the sky. You could almost see buildings up there,

whilst the blue smog and bonfire lights were like the glimmers of stars in the yard below.

'So you're really going to that big house?'

'How many people do you need here? What difference
would Anna and I make? All I need to know is the day you
march, Saul. That, and for you to let me go . . .'

Citizen Simpson's voice made a soft song and the little
stone glowed in his palm, warmly gold with all the loveli-
ness of aether. Then, as his phlegmy voice rose towards a
final flourish, a swirl of new light gathered around us and
spilled down across the square, shifting and glittering.

Saul gave a laugh and spread his arms.

'Hey, look, Robbie! It's snowing!'

VI

Twin lights came out of the snow, tunnelling our shadows as Anna and I trudged along Marine Drive. We'd taken what seemed like the last train ever out of London early in the afternoon of this Christmas Eve. Now we were finally here at Saltfleetby and dragging our old suitcases towards Walcote House. The great houses, even the walls beside them, had vanished. All that was left was this clifftop road and the dancing, battering snow. The lights grew wider in a grin of chrome. The machine was long and black and low. It gave off gusts of bitter-salty smoke. A blade was twitching across its front window.

Sadie's voice came and went, and the driver, in a shiny peaked cap and gloves and boots, emerged to open a rear door for us. Big though it was, the machine's cabin was far more cramped and low than any decent carriage's. Sadie was wearing her silver-dark coat, and a hat and a scarf which matched. Her lips, when she gave us a composed smile, were astonishingly red, her hair had acquired a coppery sheen, and there was a huge greenstone ring on her left hand. It was as if she was making up for all those grey and white newspaper photographs.

'So you decided to come after all,' she said after Anna

and I had borne in drifts of melting snow. 'I'd still have invited you, Anna, if you hadn't moved from Stoneleigh Road in such a hurry. You as well, Robbie—but you both vanished in the most extraordinary way . . . Do you like this new toy of mine, by the way? It's my main wedding present—or it is so far. I get the driver as well, although he and it's only any good on a decent road . . .'

'It's not that we haven't thought about you,' Anna said. 'It's just that—well, you saw what happened at that church with George. And I'm sorry if I've lied to you about who I am. But I hope you can at least understand why.'

Sadie studied us as we sat in our sodden clothes on these burnished leather seats. Anna had changed even more than I had. Her hair hung lank, her lips looked bruised, and there were tidemarks of dirt around her neck. And the Mark of her stigmata, towards which I couldn't help notice Sadie's eyes were travelling, was scarcely a scab.

'There's a lot,' I said, 'that we need to explain.'

'But somehow,' Sadie worked down the window, 'I don't think you're going to.' White specks had settled on her eyelashes when she looked back at us. 'You don't happen to have a cigarette, do you, by the way . . . ?'

The gates to Walcote House, which had been open in summer, were now closed, and the driver had to parp his horn. Then four huge balehounds came dragging their uniformed keepers. Sadie pushed her window back up just as one leapt at the glass. There was a clash of fangs, a spill of drool. A lantern was tilted towards Anna and I.

'For God's sake,' Sadie shouted. 'Can't they see who I *am*? I'm entitled to guests, aren't I?'

The huge wrought-iron gates, which were now topped with barbed wire, shuddered back. The car moved on through the lacing white. There were more sounds of barking, the fires and structures of some sort of encampment, but it was hard to tell as the smooth white road spread and glimmered until the lights of the great house finally loomed. So much had changed here, and yet so much hadn't. Just as in the summer, last minute arrivals were to be expected, and the servants scarcely raised their eyebrows as we were presented to them in the clamorous candlelight of the great hall, which was scented and filled to its mighty roof by a huge fir tree. It glittered and twinkled with ornaments, and the coloured flutterings of birds.

'Oh, we always have a little *flock*,' Sadie said, almost back to her old dismissive self as a golden parakeet cocked its eye to study us from its perch atop a landscape painting. 'How boring to have just *dead* ornaments on your tree, eh? I mean, you do have *trees* up in the north, don't you, Anna, Robbie? Or is that something else, like soap and education and being truthful about who you are, that you haven't quite discovered yet?'

'You two can share a room if that's what you'd like,' Sadie added as she was helped from her hat and coat, and the crimson dress contained within it puffed out like a flower from its bud. She gave us a frank, appraising stare. 'Or perhaps not.'

We were up on the third floor of the east wing this time, overlooking the front. I was the fourth door down on the right, and Anna was the sixth. We passed wafts of cigar smoke from half-open doors, and children somewhere were singing carols, but the atmosphere in Walcote House tonight was essentially quiet. After all, tomorrow would be Christmas Day, and the day after that, Grandmistress Sadie Passington was getting married and two guilds would be united in their pomp and joy. I glanced at Anna along the corridor as servants hefted what was left of our dripping cases into our separate rooms. Then I closed my door. My room was sky blue and burnished walnut. Swallows almost as livid and living as the parakeets in the hall chased silk clouds across the walls. I kicked off my sodden boots and sat down on the side of my bed, massaging my frozen toes. A log crackled in the big grate. Apart from my feet and my wet clothes, the air smelled chiefly of sallow smoke and antique wood. I touched the fresh sheets. From Bracebridge, to London, to here, where—the feeling welled up within me softly and easily as this cool, dry warmth—I finally felt as if I was home. This kind of life was so seductive. Yet outside, beyond the snow which feathered against my windows, people were starving and a day of bloody revolution was being prepared. Still, it had been a long time since I had felt as warm as this, or had enjoyed the pleasure of peeling off all my clothes. I spun the knobs of the taps in the bathroom, then tilted in vials of oil and perfume. Foam, whiter than engine ice, whiter than snow, billowed up. I let out a long, blissful sigh as I slipped into it, then fell, almost instantly, asleep.

I awoke coughing in cold slippery water, conscious that I should be up somewhere, doing something—but it was still Christmas Eve here in Walcote House. I dropped armfuls of towels as I went to dry myself in front of my fire. For some inexplicable reason, a large single boot had been placed as if to warm beside the firegrate. The thing felt warm and light and weathered, was little-used, but ancient. Plainly, a servant had been in; as well as that odd boot, pyjamas which matched the blue of the room had been laid out, along with a tray with wine and crustless sandwiches. With a sudden shock, I remembered my case. I found it on top of the wardrobe, and flung it open on the floor. But, if the servants had looked inside, they hadn't known what to do with its dripping contents, and my fingers closed almost instantly on the scrunch of greaseproof paper. I sighed and sat back, my heart still hammering. How easy it was, once you were here, to fall, literally and figuratively, asleep. I peeled back the paper and touched the numberbead. Cool figures snowed inside my head. I *knew*—I could *see*—but would anybody else? I balled the paper up again and stuffed the numberbead beneath my pillows. I devoured the sandwiches, and drank a little of the wine. Inside my wardrobe, there were black suits and white shirts. Nests of wing collars. Waterfalls of tie and cravat. I dressed in my pyjamas, put out the lanterns and lay down.

Silence. The tick of the settling log. The faint voice of the wind. This bed was so big, so white and empty, so warm and so cool; you could get lost forever just lying in it. I turned over. The ghost of Anna smiled at me from across the pillow and I cupped my hand across her cheek, but tonight her image wasn't enough. I'd fallen asleep easily enough in the bath but the slick feel of my pyjamas, the glide of the sheets, were all too much. SHOOM *BOOM*. My heart thudded against the mattress. The swallows in the room were dark as bats. The warm, one-legged boot waited. Sleeplessness was a luxury I'd scarcely experienced, and it was especially ridiculous, after the day I'd had, and with what lay ahead . . .

Trains shooting by in the darkness. Voices coming up from the kitchen and through the walls. *Are you still awake, Robert . . . ?* The fire gave a chatter of sparks. The wind, the night, sang in my head. When I heard the turning of the door's handle, the part of me which was still in Walcote House was slow to react. But it was Anna. It had to be. A shadow shifted. A shaft of light from the corridor set the swallows wheeling. I rolled over and the spin of the sheets made me feel dizzy as shadows drifted across a forest of turned and polished wood.

'Is that you, Anna . . . ?' I murmured.

The sigh of something heavy being dragged across the carpet. Then the smell of woodland and cologne. I could have got up but I was frozen, and oddly enchanted, by the scene which was playing before me. A man, dressed in a softly crackling suit of dry leaves, and oddly masked, was crouching, emberlit, before my fire and fiddling with that boot. There was an almost birdlike edginess to his movements, and his eyes, as he stood up and they flickered towards me through dark knotholes in bark, were wary. *Is that . . . ?* But the questions were beyond asking as this strangely attired creature and I briefly regarded each other. Then he rustled back across the carpet and closed my door with a *click* of wood on wood which sent me tumbling towards sleep as if falling through giant boughs into a twilit forest.

The corridors of Walcote House filled with surprised laughter on Christmas morning. *Has he been? Did you see him?* My boot had a full and luxurious feel as I tumbled its contents onto my bed. A silver-spined notebook. A boxed fountain pen. Chocolates. The children, who had been up for so long that they were on their second shift of nannies, charged about, the boys with bronze breastplates, the girls in silver tiaras. The hooved and masked Lord of Misrule who came down from the moon of Christmas Eve with his

cloak of leaves and his gifts of apples and nuts was a rarely
heard myth on Brownheath and in the Easterlies, but at
Walcote House he was legend made real. Many had found
forest litter across their rugs, had smelled woodsmoke, or
had glimpsed his whispering grey form. And outside, right
up on the highest roofs, there were crescent prints where he
had strode the pristine snow. I guessed, looking from my
own window, that some servant must have risked his life to
put those marks there, but here at Walcote House it was always hard to tell. The guests smiled to see the puzzled face
of a stranger as, still in a half-daze, I wandered in, shaved
and dressed in my crisp new clothes. Yes, *he* had visited
them as well—the Lord of the Lost Seasons the children
knew, and whom the adults understood to be none other
than the greatgrandmaster himself—had come to them out
of their dreams even in this of all years, and with so much
else on his mind. But the nuts were gold. The apples were
silver pomanders. And perfumes for the women, and
bracelets studded with their names in tiny jewels. Cigars
for the men. Hairbrushes as well, discreetly embossed, but
only for those who weren't noticeably bald. I remembered
the glitter of those eyes, gazing at me through a mask of
old wood. There was a precision and a thoughtfulness to
these gifts, even down to my own pen and notepad, which I
found both pleasing and chilling.

'You could have warned me,' I said to Anna when she finally emerged from her room in a crisp blue outfit as new
as my own. She'd washed her hair, tying it up with studded
ebony pins which I guessed had been her own stocking
presents.

'Walcote's supposed to be about surprises. Besides,' she
glanced both ways, 'I know you're not so stupid as to leave
anything lying about, are you, Robbie?'

The tide was against us as the guests hurried towards the
smells of bacon and subtle spices, the delicate sound of
sizzling, and we headed up through the house.

'Has Sadie shown you this as well?'

We were alone at the end of an upper corridor on the
central wing, staring at a blank willow-green wall.

Anna nodded. 'She took me up when I first came here

from St Jude's. I think she does it to most people she wants
to impress . . .'

I stroked the smooth surface.

'I was *sure* this was the right place . . .'

'Oh, it is.' She crouched down to inspect the unbroken
wainscot. With her hair up like this, the silvery down at the
back of her neck was revealed against the white collar of
her dress. And she smelled differently, too—fresh-washed,
as I leaned beside her and wondered how I could ever have
been so stupid as to imagine that the Easterlies hadn't
changed her. Then she muttered something. It could have
been a clock-chime, a bell, and, like a shadow cast by the
snow's light, there came the shape of a door. I reached for
its outline, but then it was gone. Anna said the same thing
again, and added something else. The door came more
strongly this time, but it went again. There was a sensation,
not so much a feel as a sound, of something grinding shut.

Anna stood up and leaned her hand against the wall. I
though that she was about to try something else, but she
seemed merely to be resting against it.

'Can you do it?'

'I don't know.' She took a breath. 'Walcote isn't just
some ordinary house. This door guards the access point to
one of the mysteries of a great guild. And I'm hungry.
Let's get something to eat, shall we?'

Food was served in the same breakfast room as it had been
that summer. The guests mingled, waving forks as they
conversed, smiled and dabbed the juice from their faces
with white napkins the size of sheets as light poured in
from the snow-clad gardens. Some of the Christmas tree
birds had found their way into here. Their feathers and
chirps added to the clamour as they fluttered in search of
scraps.

One of Sadies discoveries. Not that the phrase was mentioned as I addressed myself to filling my plate with a
sausage-stuck mountain of mushrooms and scrambled egg,
but the glances still said the same thing. My day in the
summer, after all, was supposed to have been *It.* You were
invited, patronised, parodied, paraded. Then you were sent

away again. It was all *too* charmingly scandalous of dear
Sadie—to invite one of her minor beaux back to her own
wedding.

Many of the younger guests had been, or were how
claiming to have been, outside the Advocates' Chapel on
the night Highermaster George sung it down. *Of course,
you knew him, didn't you? And wasn't he always so . . .* To
these people, instead of residing imprisoned in that guildhouse as a watchword amongst the dispossessed of England, Highermaster George Swalecliffe, as they sipped
their coffee and chuckled wisely over last night's visit from
the Lord of Misrule, was as good as dead. Then they turned
their gaze, if it had ever been away from her, towards Anna
Winters. How much did they guess? How much did they
know? Something even odder than mere destruction had
certainly happened in the Advocates' Chapel, and it didn't
really sound like Sadie not to have dropped hints. But here
she was, Anna Winters, resurrected at the very moment before her friend's wedding like something from a tale.
Slowly but inexorably, they were drawn back towards her
just as they had always been. Mistress Summerton was
right, I thought, as hands touched her and smiles were
flourished. Despite everything, Anna could have carried on
with this life. The only thing, perhaps, which didn't seem
quite so right on this blissful Christmas morning was
Anna Winters herself. Yes, she had and hadn't changed.
Yes, she was and she wasn't different. The Anna I saw now,
backlit against a blazing window, seemed frailer, more
shadowy. In a situation such as this, the attention she
brought to being the person she thought people wanted her
to be had always been absolute. But I sensed now that she
was wavering.

Drawn by the toot of Christmassy tunes, the guests
started to move out from the breakfast room, and servants
began stacking and wastefully heaping together steaming
piles of syrup and kippers, cream and bacon, which, even
in their mingled state, would have been fallen upon by the
residents of Caris Yard.

'Hey, just leave all that will you!'

I didn't need to turn to know who had made a belated

entrance. I'd expected to see the Bowdly-Smarts here at Walcote House. After all, little incidents such as the one which had taken place that night in Fredericksville were easily forgotten, and the greatgrandmaster himself, as I now knew, had reasons to feel obliged towards them. Pretending a fresh hunger I certainly didn't feel, I picked up another plate and moved deliberately beside Grandmaster Bowdly-Smart along the remaining displays of food. He began a thin smile as he glanced my way. Then he realised. At that moment, his wife also appeared in robes and gleaming rubies, although the confused look on her face suggested that her husband hadn't confided with her about me, any more than he seemed to have confided in Greatgrandmaster Passington. The silence as the three of us served ourselves food was punctuated only by the tink of ladles. This, I thought, is the moment when he could shout out that I was an impostor, a dangerous charlatan. But, for all that Grandmaster Bowdly-Smart knew much about me, there was so much more that I knew about him. He and his henchmen might have been searching for me these last few shifterms, but that didn't mean he wanted to find me here at Walcote House. This, anyway, was what I'd been hoping, although, oddly enough, I felt something like a sense of mutual recognition as I worked my way along the breakfast displays beside him. After all, Stropcock and I had both come here from Bracebridge by dangerous and tenuous routes, and he was now behaving exactly as I would have done in his situation, which was to do nothing, and to wait. I handed my freshly loaded plate to a servant and walked off, my head singing.

The seamless blue sky was reflected in the snow and the whole wyrelit world was punctuated by the black hafts of moving figures and the shimmering, semi-transparency of the trees. A path had been flattened and set with flaming braziers. In another direction, many of the younger set were heading off towards the great frozen lake to skate. Ahead of me, the trunks of the perilinden trees were like huge upward brushstrokes. The snow was so clean it squealed like sap beneath my new boots.

The stables were a jumble of eye-stinging cerulean shadows, within and around which a hundred or so guests had gathered. There were many half-familiar faces, but no one I quite recognised, and there was no sign of Anna. Then, from off between the trees, came an angry buzzing. Already, people were smiling, for this sleigh was magical; it pulled itself. There was Sadie in her furs, and Greatmaster Porrett seated beside her, manoeuvring the smoking machine between the trees. It stopped with a clatter. They climbed out, and Greatmaster Porrett, in the lurid red fox fur of his huge coat, gave a bow whilst Sadie just stood there to accept the applause. Then he emerged, Great-grandmaster Passington himself, and the freezing air stilled until the only sound was the sigh of snow from a branch, the distant shouts and calls of the skaters. He was dressed in a plain black cloak. His head was bare and his hair was as dark as ever. He was a tall man, I thought, and made for this role, and his people loved him. Of course, he looked somewhat tired and pale this morning, with shadows pooled beneath his eyes after his visitations of last night, but that only added to his sense of gravity and caring. And the smiles which played across the lips of these women, the grave adoration of the men; I'd only ever seen anything similar when people were around Anna, and this veneration was far more shameless. He both was and he wasn't simply a man. For he was the pinnacle of his guild, and I could kill him now, run forward screaming with a knife I didn't have. Like George, I could have my small, useless moment and there would be blood on the snow. Then I would be taken away and this Age would carry on unchanged. Someone else would clamber to the top of this great earthly pyramid. To truly destroy him, death alone wasn't enough. I needed to bring him *down*.

A guildmaster came to see me here. Grandmaster Harrat's voice billowed back to me. *He was waiting inside this house one night, standing in the hall even though the maids denied letting him in. So I knew instantly he had power. And he had a face I can barely remember, even though he was standing close to me and I could smell the rain on his cloak . . .*

I slipped my hand into my new pocket and curled my fingers around the numberbead as we all trooped to a court-yard inside the stables where the swept bright-red bricks steamed in the morning sun, wreathing Sadie in mist as she took a pair of giant scissors and cut the pink ribbon looped across one of the stable doors. Greatmaster Porrett did his best to mime surprise as a russet unicorn, big and broad as a carthorse, nervous as a yearling, was led out. Starlight, Sadie's own black and silvered mount, followed, and the two creatures whinnied and reared like beautiful statues as we all gathered before them for the smoking flash of a photograph.

Sadie came over as we were ushered on across the snowlit space beyond. Flowers grew here, and their shapes and colours were beautiful. Touch their frozen petals, though, and they shattered.

'Poor Star,' she said. 'I'll have to ride him straight after all this is finished just to soothe him down. But I doubt if Isumbard'll ever ride that other creature—he prefers ma-chines.' She took off her gloves, fished in her pockets, sighed. 'Things have changed a lot since you and I were last around here.'

'You did say you wanted me to come in winter.'

'Did I? Well—and here you are. But where's Anna?'

'I'd guess she's off skating.'

'Yes, she's good at that . . . And we really need to talk, don't we—about why you're both here, for a start.'

'It's not—'

'I'm a big girl now, Robert. And I've got a lot better at seeing through things recently. So please don't bullshit me. But this—' She nodded ahead through the trees, where the intricate metal dome of what looked at first like a medium-sized church was rearing. '—is something I'd like you to see. It was the one thing I insisted on after tomorrow's wedding. I didn't lose all our family traditions.'

The dome was wrought iron, and it resembled a huge birdcage. Disturbed by our approach, the creature within was cawing and fluttering from trunk-sized perch to perch. There was much talk, as the more knowledgeable gathered closer and the more sensitive hung back, of how, this year, the Guild of Beastmasters had once again excelled itself. The dragon was even bigger than the unicorns, but, as it stretched its pinions and screeched, it stirred up the same ammoniac gusts from the slurry pooled at the bottom of its cage that I remembered from the Tenshiftday when my mother and I had stood before that rabbit hutch on the rivermeads. The dragon-hunt, I gathered, was a big event of Christmas at Walcote House, and Sadie and her father were amongst its keenest exponents. In an ideal world, their unicorns would spear their quarry with their horns, but in reality, long, light spears were carried. The creature could fly but it would have its wings trimmed before it was released, and I was disappointed to learn that it couldn't actually breathe fire. The dragon bared its serrated teeth to emit an ear-splitting scream. Splatters of blood broke from its wingtips as they beat against the bars. People scurried back until only Sadie and I, and then just the greatgrandmaster, remained. He looked up as the dragon thrashed its tail and paused in its screeching to stare back down at him. An odd silence fell over the crowd. In the distance, still, came the cries of the skaters, and beyond that the baying of balehounds. And beyond that—but the grandmaster turned and gestured us back towards the celebrations in the great house. After all, this was Christmas Day.

Hot chocolate was being served in the sunlit hallways. It looked like mud but tasted like heaven, and I was on my third or fourth cup by the time I found Anna sitting on one of the large sofas at a turn on the east stairs. She had her skates around her neck. Bits of her hair had come loose from those ebony pins. But for two small bright lozenges on her cheeks, her face was pale.

'Have you seen Sadie yet?' I asked.

'She's off riding Star. But I've had a message from her. She says she still wants me to be head bridesmaid. Can you believe that?'

'I'm not sure that even *she* does,' I knocked back the rest of my steaming silver cup. 'The way she's just been talking to me.'

'But we're planning to betray her!'

'You're having doubts? I thought—'

'What do you *expect* me to have!' We waited as a couple drifted by. 'This is the last day of my life I'll spend like this,' she continued more quietly. 'Whatever happens tonight, nothing will ever be the same. Why d'you think I'm sitting here? Why do you think I went skating?'

'I'm sorry,' I sighed, and gestured to a passing servant for more chocolate. 'I'm always—ow!' My finger was twisted as my empty cup was snatched from me. The servant stalked off. 'What was *that* about?'

'You should know, Robbie. Most of the workers here come from fishing families in Folkestone and Saltfleetby, and there's been a lockout at the smokehouses, some kind of trouble with the guilds. Things are bad down here as well. At the end of the day, though, he was probably just upset because servants like the odd *please* and *thank you* like everyone else—or hadn't you noticed?'

The Christmas banquet began in the great hall at noon and was to be followed at six by a service in the chapel, which in turn would give way at about midnight to the evening ball. Six hours seemed like a ridiculously long time to set aside for a meal, but, as always, I hadn't allowed for the bloated wondrousness of Walcote House. The guests fanned in beneath slim white pillars entwined with holly and were presented with what the untutored might have assumed to be the entire meal. Sweetmeats and delights; nuts and berries; amber, ruby, pink and russet varieties of wine. At least I was sitting directly beside Anna this time, and there were no big displays of flowers immediately in front of me. We were far from the main tables amid the last minute additions, all of whom seemed to have a long story to explain how they had got here . . .

'And what about you—Master, Mistress?'

'Oh,' Anna gave me a glance. 'We're old friends from Yorkshire.'

The conversation crawled on and a servant delivered soup into the bowl he'd placed in front of me. I selected the correct spoon from the outer edge of my place setting, dipping it away from me. I didn't even blow on the surface, or pull a face when the green fluid turned out to be cold. Despite my many other concerns, I'd found time to study a book on etiquette whilst I was in the Public Reading Rooms. I glanced at Anna, and raised the correct glass in whispered tribute to the kindness of Highermaster George.

There was poached turbot and salmon mayonnaise. The main courses began with snipe followed by ortolan, then grouse, then pheasant, then duck, then woodcock, then a goose, all of which were punctuated by sorbets, salads, jellies and truffles. But most of the hot food was cold by the time it reached us, and most of the cold was lukewarm. Perhaps it wasn't so much fun to be rich after all, I thought, gazing though the maze of bored, masticating faces towards the top table. Greatmaster Porrett's brown, bald head bobbed as he addressed himself to the cream-sautéed fillet of leveret and cast occasional and almost equally hungry glances towards Sadie although the greatgrandmaster beside him was scarcely eating, and his wife looked more withered than ever. By now, sunset was flaring across the room and the children had long been released to run about the house. I was sitting envying them when a servant came to tap Anna's and my shoulders and beckon us away.

The so-called chapel to which he led us was in fact a huge church. Here, all the deeds of the Passington family were celebrated in their many guises, deeds, alliances. From up on that balcony, the third greatgrandmaster's wife had fallen to her death, and this very patch of paving bore the stain of her blood which no amount of scrubbing can remove. Canon Vilbert was in fine and tipsy mood as he showed Anna and I around this vast, sweet-smelling mansion of God, which members of the Plantmasters' Guild were busily decorating for tonight's service with swathes of holly, red berries and lanternflowers which gave off a fiery glow.

'Of course, all this will be removed in time for tomorrow's wedding, when there will be—ah, but here she is . . .'

Sadie, dressed in what looked like her riding clothes, and with bridesmaids, pageboys and servants scurrying in her wake, charged up the aisle.

'Of course, you'll have to walk a lot slower than that

tomorrow morning, if I may venture, grandmistress. But that's exactly why we're here . . .' He clapped his hands, gestured, pointed. The bridal procession, in today's odd mixture of clothes, was arranged in a diminishing line. 'Now, if you'll stand *here*.' He grabbed a valet. 'And if you could stand exactly *here*.'

I resisted. 'Shouldn't we wait for the greatgrandmaster, and the groom?'

Canon Vilbert sighed. 'That's why *you're* here, isn't it?'

After all, I thought as Sadie and Anna and their entourage trooped all the way out of the chapel so they could troop back in again, Porrett's done this three times before. And the greatgrandmaster of one of the highest and most powerful guilds was hardly likely to be troubled by something as simple as a mere, albeit extremely grand, wedding.

'Where's the organist? He should be here by now. You over there—go check the billiard rooms . . .'

I almost wished that I was back at the banquet, stuffing myself with out-of-season pears, grapes and nectarines. But it was certainly an odd sensation, to be standing in place of the greatgrandmaster himself, and waiting for my daughter Sadie, who would appear and disappear occasionally amid Canon Vilbert's moaning instructions. *Here* not *there*. Not *that* but *this*. Sadie finally linked arms with me, then with the valet, muttering something which caused him to smile and blush. A dummy ring had to be found; a huge thing the size and weight of a doorknob which the canon provided from his own fat fingers. Tomorrow, out beyond these walls, the normal calendar of guilded work was supposed to resume. But here, it was the feastday of St Stephen. Even without Sadie's wedding, the Christmas celebrations at Walcote House would continue, if things went as planned, all the way past New Year until something called Epiphany.

Finally—step and *pause,* step and *pause,* my dear—the canon succeeded in getting Sadie to walk sufficiently slowly up the aisle, then she and the valet exchanged vows. The canon turned to the altar. He opened a silver cupboard, extracted a chalice, genuflected, and poured himself a slosh of hymnal wine.

'Why not the rest of us, eh?' Sadie asked.

The canon, smiling as ever, was about to explain, but Sadie grabbed the chalice from him, drank back its contents and stomped off down the chapel.

Baths were being run. Flesh was being squeezed into outfits and appraised before mirrors in preparation for the evening's ball.

'What would be worse, I wonder?' Anna murmured. 'That we leave here and nothing has changed, or . . .' She ran her hand across the willow-green wall. 'Can't you remember anything of what Sadie said?'

'Can you?'

'It was years ago for me, Robbie. Do you think I remember every spell?'

I watched and waited, glancing back along the quiet corridor. Anna said something. Nothing happened. She bit her lip.

'Perhaps,' I suggested, 'I should find a pickaxe.'

'This wall and the tower beyond it would be standing after you'd demolished every other stone in this building . . .'

Anna leaned to the wall, pressing her ear to it. She nodded and stepped back, rubbing at her shoulder, wincing slightly. Then, in a cracked voice quite unlike her own, she spoke a long phrase. There was a pause. The house seemed to hold its breath. Then it gave a shudder and Anna staggered back as, in a hail of plaster dust, a long crack snaked across the ceiling. But the wall still held. The door remained invisible.

'It knows we're here now. That's why it's resisting.'

'We can't just . . .' I stopped. Whispering, squealing, something huge and white was rushing towards us along the corridor. It was Sadie in her wedding dress. Several seamstresses with pins in their mouths came in her wake, nipping and tucking around her.

'What exactly are you two doing here? This is my private wing.'

Anna and I exchanged glances as Sadie took us in—and the crack across the ceiling.

'I think we'd better have that talk. And *you* lot—' Sadie

shooed the clustered seamstresses. '—just leave me *alone*!
You've still got the whole night to get this damn thing
sorted.'

She took us to her nearby suite, where there was a chaos
of clothes and presents.

'I think the ones over there are for the wedding,' she
said airily. 'And these here are for Christmas. Grab some if
you want.' Squeezing her dress between the gleaming furniture, she worked open the top drawer of a cabinet. 'Ah,
thank God for that!' She flourished a packet of cigarettes.
'Would you light one of these for me, Robert? I can't go
anywhere near that fire in this—I'm told I'd combust.'

She eased herself down on a huge sofa beside a glittering tree and her dress, in sighs and flurries of light, slowly
settled itself around her. The dazzling snow of this morning had found its way into the fabric, along, as Sadie wearily
pointed out to us—here on the braiding, and up here as
well—with the entwined spells of Telegraphers' and the
Distemperers' guilds. Huge and impressive, hooped and
arched and aethered and boned, it was much more than a
dress, and Sadie, as it sparked and whispered and writhed,
seemed lost within its folds as she drew on her cigarette
and absently flicked ash from her bosom.

'Have you heard—there's been some big demonstration
in Dudley? Twenty dead, a hundred casualties. The main
telegraph route north has been severed.'

'Does that mean messages can't be sent?'

'So sweet of you, Robert, to be concerned about the
workings of my guild. Messages don't cease to flow because one measly pylon's been brought down. But all this
pointless destruction! It's about this *Age,* isn't it? Just because it's year ninety-nine, every mart and lesser guildsman seems to think there's some great need for change.
People expecting something different every hundred years!'
She gave a laugh. 'Can you *imagine*?'

Anna and I sat and waited. Now, I thought, she'll challenge us. Now, she'll throw us out. But instead, Sadie lit another cigarette from the nub of her first and began to talk
about Greatmaster Porrett. Two of his wives, it seemed,
had died in stillborn childbirth, and a third was still alive

but not quite herself. He'd had a sad personal life but he was still surprisingly young in his attitudes, once you got past the bald head and the tremor in his hands. He even claimed to be fertile. It was part of the contract between their two guilds, in any event, that she would have his children. And if that didn't happen—she shrugged and squinted through clouds of smoke—there was bound to be some way around it. There always was. He'd told her over their first private meal that he enjoyed painting, and Sadie had been pleased to imagine an unsuspected familiarity with the arts. But he really did mean *painting*—the sort his guildsmen did with their brushes up and down railings. The one holiday they'd had together had been spent renovating the mildewed walls of one of his ugly mansions. Sadie now knew the spell which would retard permeation and blistering on a cuprous oxide mix applied to whitecast iron, and had—look, see—she held out a hand across the foam of her dress, indelible blue half moons of cobalt under her fingernails.

'And now *you're* both back here,' she said finally, 'and looking almost like a couple. But *that's* not quite your style, is it, Robbie? Nor yours, Anna. And George's imprisoned and London's a mess and I'm getting married, and I somehow doubt that you've just come here to celebrate. I tried, or I attempted to try, to find out a little bit about what you are and where you really come from, Anna. But why spoil the mystery, eh?' She lit another cigarette and ground out the old one in the crystal ashtray she was nursing in the folds of her lap. A few sparks flew out, glinting with her whisperjewels. 'But what do you want? I mean, *really* . . .'

'There's no mystery, Sadie,' I began. 'We're simply here because—'

'No!' Anna's voice was harsh. Sadie's dress gave a louder rustle. 'No.' Anna looked at us both. But for those twin red patches on her cheeks and a bluish tinge to her lips, her face was entirely white. 'I'm tired of all these lies. We owe you the truth, Sadie. Then you can decide what you do with it . . .'

Sadie puffed her way through the rest of her cigarettes as Anna told her about her childhood with Mistress

Summerton, and learning the small deceits which she eventually became so good at. Then there was her life at St Jude's and being Anna Winters, which became something she believed in as much as everyone else. But the past had hunted her down. That was why she was here, that was— and then I, all caution gone, I began to share my own tale from my first visit to Redhouse, and meeting Anna, who was then Annalise, and how our stories broke and entwined from here to London to Bracebridge. Our fates were joined even now as we sat here in the firelit room, until we came, at last, to the experiment with the chalcedony, the death of our mothers, to Grandmaster Harrat and the man who was once Edward Durry, and to the Bowdly-Smarts, and Bracebridge's emptily beating engines, and the loss of aether, and finally to the pivotal role which her father had played in all of these things.

The firelight pulsed. Sadie looked at us. 'How much of this can you prove?'

Anna thought for a moment. 'Most of it.'

'My getting married—no wonder it's so important if our guild really is bankrupt! And you know what would happen if this came out—but that's why you're here, isn't it? That's why you were trying to get into the Turning Tower . . .'

'We're trying to make a better Age, Sadie.'

'Or to destroy my guild—wouldn't that be another way of looking at it, Robbie?'

But there was nothing more to say. Sadie had the truth. Now, as Anna had said, she had to decide what she did with it.

'My father, you know,' Sadie said eventually. 'He's not a *bad* man. If he did something wrong, if people got hurt, he'd have had his reasons. They would be good ones, too, and it was all so long ago. You yourself said the experiment with the chalcedony failed, which means that no one meant what happened to happen. The way you talk about my father, Robbie, he's the devil personified. That's not him. And the false accounting of that factory—is it really such a crime, to keep the people in your hometown well and happy? You make it all sound so simple, the way only someone who's lived their life outside the guilds could ever possibly do. I mean, where did the spell in that chalcedony come from? You really think that by pointing your finger at Daddy, you've got to the end of the trail?'

I said nothing. All my life—or what now seemed like most of it—I'd been searching for my darkmaster. And I wasn't going to let Sadie's equivocating words take him away from me.

'And do you imagine you'd end up with those monsters in St Blate's, Anna, someone as lovely and beautiful as you? What would happen if I tried to pull that bellrope over there and called for the house yeomen?' Sadie shook her head, inspected the empty contents of her cigarette packet and threw it towards the fire. 'What would you do, Anna? And just how hard would you try to stop me, Robert? Have you really got it in you to kill someone?' Slowly, with a rustling effort, she stood up. She had her hand laid across the whisperjewels at her throat. 'Just how badly do you want this thing, Robert—whatever it is that you really want? For it isn't you, Anna, and it certainly isn't *me,* or anything or anybody in this house, or back in London, either . . .' Slowly, she was moving towards the tasselled bellpull, when, with an angry twist of her mouth, she jerked her hand and the chain of whisperjewels parted from around her neck. One of them twinkled in her palm, then it clattered onto a low table.

'Sadie, I—'

'Don't *thank* me, Master Robert. Don't say *anything.* I'm not doing this for any reasons I'm proud of, or because of your fucking citizens—I'm doing it because I'm Grandmistress Sarah Passington, and I'm entirely bloody selfish . . .'

In a swoosh of white, she left the room.

It's a trick that many guildsmen have. On the edges of some building site or outside the summer-hot doors of a foundry, we Coney Mound children would gather around a plasterer or ironsmith who'd grown bored enough to entertain us for a few minutes while the foreman wasn't looking. He'd take a few scrapings from a jar or chalice, and then half a handful of dry earth, which he'd spit on, shape, make into something small and neat and hard in his big, quick, hands, muttering as he did so. Then, flourishing it— look, lads; a little dog, a flower, more daringly, a lady's bare torso. Sometimes, they even let us touch the things, which felt light and hot and scratchy. Often as not, you'd have had to be told what they were, but to me they were fascinating, and the most interesting part of the performance came at the very end, when the guildsman took the little object back from us and cupped his hands around it again and blew softly as if it were an ember on a fire. Puff! He'd spread his palms and laugh as we children spluttered in a cloud of empty dust.

From something, to nothing. A puff of air, the breath of a spell—then dissolution, unmaking. That was what that numberbead and the guilds of England were to me, that Christmas night in Walcote House. Back in London, and in many other cities and towns, the signal would soon be given for the people to stir themselves and advance. Neither secrecy nor openness really mattered now. This was winter instead of Midsummer, and it would be to the back and underbelly of Northcentral and the tinder of factories and the gates of sidings and the doors of engine houses towards which these citizens would now march. Those guns of Saul's, perhaps, would make the difference. That, or a willingness to violence which the guards and police, guildsmen themselves who had also suffered, might be slow to counter. But nobody knew. And meanwhile, those who had given their orders were preparing themselves for midnight and the Christmas Ball, which would continue, just like the bloodshed, long beyond the dawn.

The corridors were bustling when Anna and I left Sadie's suite. It wouldn't have been safe to open the door to the Turning Tower yet, even now we had Sadie's whisperjewel—and it was still before the time I'd promised Saul. So there was little for Anna and I to do other than to return to our rooms, and pretend to prepare for the ball. A suit sprawled on my bedspread like a beautiful corpse. I sat down. I stood up. I gazed from my window at the snowlit parkland. I decided against running myself another bath. I touched the swallows on the walls. All of this, one way or another, would be taken from me in the morning. A hotel, a hostel, a citizen's university, a roofless and ivied ruin— Walcote House might become any of those things in the coming Age, but in its heart, and in mine, it would remain the place I remembered tonight. The people who bustled towards the ball along the passageways outside could be as graceless and disappointing as the worst inhabitants of the boroughs of the Easterlies but there was a beauty to this building, and the entrapments of wealth, which I told myself I would be sad to lose.

Fully dressed in white tie and tails, I held Sadie's whisperjewel, and the breath of Walcote House sighed out to me in whispers of holly and dark. I thought of the springs here which I would never see, and of firelit autumns, and endless days and nights of dream. Even now, the place was stirring with light and colour in the ballroom as the Master of Ceremonies began the call of names. Bows and smiles, the beckoning music, rustles of taffeta in crimson and green . . .

There was a brisk knocking. 'Robbie? Are you in there?'

Anna had also dressed for the ball. I blinked and swallowed as I gazed at her, in a red gown, her shoulders bare . . . 'You look—'

'Let's just get this thing *done* shall we—before someone finds out or we both change our minds.'

But no one would have suspected us, not the couple I glimpsed in mirrors as we swept along the empty hallways, who were sleek and handsome and proud.

It was almost a surprise to find that the ceiling above the willow-green wall still bore a crack in it.

'You've got the numberbead, Sadie's whisperjewel?'

Anna took them from me as I glanced back along the empty corridor, sure now, somehow almost willing, that someone, something, would come—but her manner was brisk as she clasped the whisperjewel and began speaking. The door had formed itself and was beginning to open even before she'd finished the spell. Then we ducked in, and it slammed shut, and we were scurrying up the stone spiral stairs. For a moment, with Anna bustling ahead of me, it was almost like being back in that hotel on Midsummer, the two of us searching for nothing more than a decent set of clothes, but then we reached the summit of Walcote House.

There were no clouds and the moon was high and its light flowed over the grounds, etching every shadow. The frozen lake shone and the dark, breathing mass of the sea loomed to the stars beyond the southern walls. Over there, sullying the snow, were the encampments of the guards with their balehounds and there, along Marine Drive, was the glitter of Saltfleetby, so sharp tonight that you could count the slates of the rooftops, the spars of the ships moored in the little harbour. Beyond that, Folkestone was a larger, twinkling, sprawl. Inland, too, far beyond the gardens' huge and intricate whorls, you could see villages and farmhouses and lives stretching all the way to a grey, glowing mass like the last settlings of a fire which was surely London . . .

I looked at Anna and she looked at me. Our breath clouded and hung. Already we were shivering. Below us in the ballroom, the music surged, and the lights from its windows steepled far out across the snow-sweep of the gardens. The clocks chimed midnight. The new Threeshiftday had started. If things went as Saul was hoping, there would be decoys and disruptions as the massed citizens commenced their march. But I knew more than he did about the power of the guilds. In London, the main watch of telegraphers would be replacing the skeleton one which had nursed England through the dream of Christmas. Already, they would have ascended Dockland Exchange and a thousand lesser transmission houses. By now, they would have set aside their kitbags and jokes and would be placing their hands against their hafts. Whilst down along Threadneedle Street, the messenger boys would be sharing cigarettes around braziers outside the great trading houses.

The haft of the Turning Tower was sheer black in the moonlight. Shoulders gleaming, her dress rustling, Anna walked around the frozen parapet to study it. It cast no shadow.

'I'd like you to help me.'

'To do what?'

'I don't know.' She held out the numberbead. Our fingers clasped around it, and I felt once again the pages which Master Simpson had sung. No wonder Saul had smiled. They were so simple, so obvious. After our long journey, after all that I thought I knew, it boiled down to two documents which any mart could have obtained. One was the weather report for Bracebridge over the last ten winters, listing the many terms when the tracks south around Rainharrow were blocked by snow. The other, covering the same period, was the page from Mawdingly & Clawtson's Shareholders' Report which detailed the receipt of aether at Stepney Sidings. The two didn't match; aether was received when none could possibly have been sent. It had been Anna herself who'd insisted on this simplicity when I'd wanted to say everything. People, she said, could only absorb so much. And they weren't stupid—they could draw their conclusions, make their own enquiries, far better than we could. But it seemed scarcely anything now; a couple of obscure pages and a small contradiction, even if we would be transmitting it with the highest priority from a prime haft bearing the seal and spell of the Telegraphers' Guild and Walcote House.

We stepped together towards the haft, and Anna reached out her hand. I'd expected something powerful, terrible, dizzying, but instead I was instantly immersed in a warm song. There were no barriers here, no blockages. We were *known,* we were *expected* . . . How, as my sense of being teemed out and was joined by a thousand others, could it ever have been otherwise? For the telegraphs knew, the telegraphs understood, the telegraphs sang. This was all of England, the hovels and the palaces, the guildsmen and the mistresses—even the marts—and it was beautiful and filled with a simplicity of purpose which I had never imagined. There were no guilds, or rather there was one great guild, and we were all its acolytes. We sang aether's praises even as we swam in our mothers' wombs; our last breath was its spell. The ballroom dancers below us, yes, they were also part of it, but so were the sleeping farmers and the cold and angry men gathering their weapons in Caris Yard—so, too, were the telegraphers and the iron-masters and the captains on their ships in iceberg waters. In other countries, in other latitudes and languages and lives, amid bondsmen and savages and lives yet to be made, it was always, always the same beautiful, innocent song . . .

Robbie! You've got to help me . . .

The haft was Anna as well. Simply and seemingly ef-fortlessly, we tunnelled down through gates and sluices and along the pylons which strode across the frozen country-side into London and the web of Northcentral which, even now, still roared. I could feel our numberbead as something small and hard and neat. We passed through the stone walls of guildhalls, through glass and plaster, paper and ink. Messages for the traders and bankers and investors were swirled into the heavy aethered millstones of telegraph of-fices. Here and there, a guildsman looked up, briefly star-tled, as we passed by them in an invisible wind, but for Anna and I it was simply a matter of leaving the contents of the numberbead *here* and *here* and *here* . . . Goldsmiths' Hall, the vaults and the trading rooms, wave upon golden wave of wealth, surged through us, and already the words and numbers were trickling out, as tickertape and short-hand, pinned through carbons or beneath the clacking keys of stenographers who worked too quickly to read their words, for they, too, were all just part of the same mecha-nism, the same song, which our message as it multiplied, copy on copy, pinned and licked and enveloped and posted, became part of . . .

The snowy roofs of Walcote House fizzed into view. Anna was no longer touching the haft. The music was still playing below. It was colder than ever. The moon shone across the grounds.

'Did we do it?'

She shook her head. 'I don't know.'

'Where's the numberbead?'

'It's here.' She held out a cindered lump.

'It seemed too . . .' Easy? But Anna's teeth were chatter-ing as she brushed the ash from her hands into the snow.

'Let's just get down from here, eh?'

The house was quiet, but the band was playing in the blaze of the ballroom, and the people were turning. A servant floated past, silver tray aloft. Anna grabbed two glasses, and then another, and drank them down, their facets flashing on her throat.

'Are you sure we should be here?'

'What have we got to lose now?' She suppressed a most un-Anna-like burp. Her face was pale. Her eyes were blazing. 'Let's dance!'

The ceiling spun, the chandeliers turned, faces and dresses loomed and fell away from me, and it was the lancers, then the quadrille. Mad gallops and slow turns, legs and arms and feet, the push and the lunge, but of course I could do everything when I was with Anna. The fever-heat of her flesh and her hot wheaty scent poured out through the fabric of her dress. She was white, her face was shining, and her shoulders were marbled with sweat. *Come on, Robbie. This is what you always wanted, isn't it?* But this was like some mad fairground ride, with the rainbowed light of the chandeliers flooding overhead. Finally, I fell back, but Anna was still determined. She grabbed the arm of one of the old gang, one of the faces from the pier, and drew him to her before he could shake his head. I staggered towards the wall, my lungs rasping. Nothing had changed here. Nothing ever would. The only thing I noticed, and this was hard to tell at first through my sweat-damp clothing, was that the air seemed colder; it was as if a window had been opened somewhere.

There was a pause in the dancing. The band was replaced by a string quartet and the guests drifted towards the clawfoot tables around the edges of the ballroom as supper was served. I looked up at a cherub clock. Their wings were already pointing past two thirty. Anna had found a plate and another glass of wine. I followed her and watched in disbelief as she heaped herself cutlets and peas. Tonight, her arms were entirely bare. She had seemed so complete to me before that I hadn't noticed that the Mark on her left wrist had entirely vanished. I leaned towards her. 'Shouldn't you . . . ?'

'Oh, *that*.' She knew instantly what I meant. But she was

speaking loudly enough for the people on either side of us to glance at us. 'What difference does a little thing like that make now?' She waved the serving spoon to emphasise her point. Gravy splattered the front of my shirt. 'Oh, dear.' She giggled and grabbed a serviette. 'Now, spit . . .'

I shook my head, breathless.

'Well, *don't* then.' People watched as she pressed the cloth to my chest. The stain vanished. 'There you are.' She looked at them. 'And what on earth are you all staring at?' There was a muttering. Word was fanning out. After all, there *had* been rumours about Anna Winters since that night at the Advocates' Chapel. The things, *dreadful things,* which had been shouted at her by poor, mad Highermaster George. And *now* she—but at that moment the Master of Ceremonies announced that the greatgrandmaster and his daughter the grandmistress would lead the next dance. For now, at least, the faces turned away from us, towards the man and the woman who were emerging from opposite sides of the shining and empty dancefloor.

Sadie was slimly and somewhat sombrely dressed in stormy greys and blues. She'd done little to her hair and her face since we'd last seen her, but she made a fine sight compared to the overdone herbaceous borders of rustling gown which surrounded her, and her father did, too. Perhaps, I thought, these people really are special—after all, isn't that what we're supposed to think? Then the violin sighed its first note, playing with the melody as, graceful as the music itself, the tall and elegant couple began to turn. I doubt if I was the only person who glanced then towards Greatmaster Porrett, and it would have been hard not to think that he was the wrong partner for her. This man—this darkmaster—and Sadie, they plainly belonged to each other. The way he held her, the way his arms clasped her back and his face lay close to her hair, would have been almost scandalous for a father and daughter were they not the people they were, and for the rightness of how they seemed together. No wonder, I thought, he persuaded Grandmaster Harrat and Edward Durry to take the risks they took. No wonder, even now, that he seems to float above his slim reflection as he swirls with Sadie across the dancefloor.

It really was getting colder now. Some of the women were pulling on their stoles, and you could see the great-grandmaster's breath hanging amid Sadie's hair as his hand touched the whisperjewels at her neck, fingers drifting along them like some sensual rosary. Then the flow of the music changed. It was the point in the melody where its ache was the strongest. The darkmaster's fingers paused amid the whisperjewels as he caressed his daughter's neck and I saw his eyes widen slightly as his knuckles clenched and loosened on that missing space. The dance moved on and he murmured something, a question, an endearment, a spell, into Sadie's ear, and she replied, and said something more, and their whispers mingled as the slow, stately dance continued. No one but Anna and I would have known that they were exchanging anything more than loving words. Still, there was something strange and shocking about the conclusion of their dance. The music stilled and the two dancers drew apart. One or two guests started clapping, but the sound only added to the empty clip of the great-grandmaster's heels as he turned and walked across the dancefloor and left the ballroom.

There was a pause. Streams of condensation froze on the windows. Sadie stood alone. Then, with a clatter of silverware, a guildmistress started screaming. She was by the serving tables, and from the commotion around her an odd sight emerged; the lid of the big silver tureen seemingly moving by itself, leaving a brown trail in its wake. Finally, someone leapt forward and picked the thing up. Beneath, coated in gravy but otherwise unmistakable, was a huge dragonlouse. The brave guildsman stamped on it until it was dead, then, in the absence of any nearby servants, managed to scoop it up using the tureen whilst several guests retired to be more or less ostentatiously sick.

The music struck up again. It was getting damnably cold now, so what else was there to do but dance? And the candles, too, were guttering. I wandered at the edge of things, watching Anna as she whirled, clapped, turned. It had been a while now since I had seen a servant, although the drink trays were still plentiful and she was one of many

who, on the night of the last dance of the Age, made the
most of them. It was hard to tell when the difference between a disappointing ball and something more became
obvious. Many of the older guildsmen, I noticed, had gathered in groups and were talking agitatedly, and there was
no sign now of any of the Passingtons, or of Greatmaster
Porrett. But the music went on; every time the band tried to
stop, they were shouted at to continue. Dance after dance
beat down through the hours as the wings of the cherubs
turned and the music grew shriller and more irregular and
the lights gloomed and vanished until the ballroom was
only illuminated by the snowlight of the settling moon.
There were few people left now in the middle of the dancefloor. In the pauses between numbers, when the band
pleaded to be allowed to rest, the unmistakable moan and
yelp of the balehounds could now be heard. But Anna was
still dancing. Anna would never stop.

'Robbie!' She grabbed me again. Her eyes were sunken
and blazing, and her forehead was bone-white. 'And the
rest of you! Come *on*!'

Somebody turned and muttered something. Anna, her
hand digging sharply into mine, tilted her head. '*What* was
that?'

'I only—' But the man was jerked back and fell coughing to the floor.

'Come on! All the rest of you . . .' Grudgingly, a little
afraid, a few other couples began to move. But the whispers were louder now, and people, at some point, had begun to notice the absolute bareness of Anna's left arm.
Annasachangeling . . . Annasatroll . . . But she swept me
on, and shouted and beckoned, and the exhausted band no
longer mattered, because the house itself, in slow creaks
and booms, seemed to be lumbering out its own sad music.
The cherub clock had stilled. Bits of plaster and gilt crackled from the ceiling.

'What are you all afraid of?'

Anna swirled her red dress. But by now, we were all
afraid. Windows around the house really were open now, or
had burst, and freezing air swept in. Oriental tapestries

took flight. A chandelier creaked from its rosette and exploded across the dancefloor, spraying blood and glass.
Out in the main hall, the untended candles had set the great
tree alight until a few enterprising guests used the foaming
jets from shaken wine bottles to put it out. The tree became
a corpse, dripping, smoking and stinking. The parakeets had
fled from it, and were circling the ballroom when the world
outside suddenly began to pale and brighten.

'What is it!'

But even Anna stopped and looked about her now as
the shadows changed. This, stalking huge and white across
the glittering lawns, spearing the wrecked ballroom, was the
dawn of a New Age. It flared through the trees and Walcote
House groaned as a turning spear of light struck the ballroom's windows as the edge of the sun rose, and, right to
left, and one by one, the panes burst in sighing, glittering
plumes.

There was a long pause, sounds of weeping and coughing, the drip of wreckage. Glances were cast again towards
Anna. *Troll . . . Witch . . .* But she looked small now, flecked
with plaster and glass; harmless and helpless and withered.
I steadied her and helped her to stand. Her eyes were dark
tunnels, and her breath was fierce and sour. She felt impossible hot and light. How could they blame her for *this*? But
people were turning, moving slowly towards us with hate
on their lips and the need for someone, something, to ac-
cuse. *Troll . . . Witch . . .* I dragged her back between the
tables, but we were being cornered when shouts wafted
through the broken windows. It was something about *The
stables! The greatgrandmaster!* and the strange, sleepwalking figures blinked and turned and walked off that way as
well, slowly at first, drifting out through the shattered glass
and across the snow which was littered with the bright bodies of the parakeets.

Anna and I followed. People were running and the
freezing air filled with the distant bark of balehounds, the
smell of smoke. Walcote House, when I glanced back at it,
still looked white and entire, but its windows were deep
and dark; the sunken sockets of a skull. I stumbled on with

Anna slowing behind me until she stopped in the dragging snow with her hands pressed against a tree, her hair dangling lank.

'Are you all right?'

She coughed and shook her head, then nodded. 'You go on.'

I hesitated, but the commotion ahead through the woods was growing. Guests were milling down by the stables. There came a whooshing of air. A shadow passed over me. A branchful of snow deluged over my neck. Women were screaming, people were pointing upwards from where I stood. The shadow beat again, shaping itself into giant wings. Green and heraldic, the dragon was perched on top of the steeple of a perilinden tree which shivered and swayed under its weight. The beast split its mouth and cawed, then flapped its wings and half rose and then settled again. It seemed at first to be the entire focus of all the shouting, but as I backed off, I sensed that an even more agitated crowd had gathered around its empty cage.

The door hung open. But someone was inside, kneeling in the floor's sulphurous mess. It was Sadie, and her head was bowed as she cradled what I took at first to be a long lump of meat. People were murmuring, making signs as they pressed against the bars. Many of the men were weeping. No one seemed to know what to do as I stepped into the cage and stumbled towards her. Then I saw that thing which stretched from her lap had had a face. Even now, it was breathing.

'Can't you help me, Robert?' I looked down as Sadie stroked the pelt of the greatgrandmaster's black hair, which hung from his bared skull. 'I did this, you know.'

'You didn't. It was my fault.'

Her fingers strayed over what was left of his eyes and nose. She kissed his torn lips. 'I'm so sorry, Daddy,' she murmured. 'I was stupid and selfish. And all about some silly wedding. And now it's too, too late . . .'

I crouched beside her. I tried to look into the greatgrandmaster's eyes. But there was nothing to see in them, and then, with a spray of blood, a wet spasm of bones, he died.

I laid my hand on Sadie's shoulder, but she shrugged me off and stood up. She looked, as many would remark later, composed and impressive as she stood inside the dragon's cage beside her father's body in her bloodied clothes.

'Well . . .' She wiped her hands on her frock. 'He's dead. You should all go back to the house.'

The guests, now entirely silent, began to drift away.

'Where's Anna?' she asked me.

'She's back there—between the trees. People—'

'I *know* what people were saying, Robbie. She can't stay here now, can she? And neither can you. Are you sure she's all right?'

We found Anna crouched against the same tree with her hands on her knees. 'Look . . .' She smiled and pointed. We watched as the dragon, with a stronger beat of its wings, lifted itself from the perilinden tree and turned and rose and diminished, flying north.

I crouched towards Anna, half lifting her up. She neither cooperated nor resisted.

'I'd let you have that stupid car,' Sadie said, 'only it wouldn't get you anywhere.'

'We could walk.'

She shook her head.

The stables were entirely empty and peaceful as Sadie led us into the yard where, yesterday and in another Age, we had stood to be photographed. She unbolted the door which held Starlight. Big and beautiful, a sigh of light and muscle, the unicorn emerged. She embraced his huge neck.

'I haven't got any tackle for him. I ride him bareback, but he knows you, Anna. D'you think you'll be all right?'

Anna, who could once have done anything, been anyone, just stood there.

'You can't do this,' I said.

'Why not?' Sadie fanned her fingers up through the creature's dense black mane. He nudged his nose against her. 'Can't you hear those balehounds? How long do you imagine Star can last here? I'd rather he just went—and took my Anna with him—before I change my mind.'

She opened the adjoining stable and the russet unicorn

which had been her gift to Greatmaster Porrett whinnied
and clopped out.

'He seems like a good beast. And he'd be wasted here—
always would have been, even if I had got married. So you
might as well take him, Robbie.' Walking between the two
great unicorns, Sadie led them towards a stone mounting
block. 'Come on . . .'

I held the creature's mane, and Sadie paused and gave
Anna a wordless hug, then helped her up. Then it was my
turn. It seemed ridiculously high up there, but at least the
unicorn's back was broad. Sadie looked up at us—or
rather, she gazed at Anna.

'Where will you go?'

Anna shook her head. 'I don't know.'

'We need to get back to London,' I said, swaying and
gripping the unicorn's mane. 'And I doubt if there'll be
trains. What about you, Sadie?'

'What do you expect me to do? I'll stay here. I owe it to
this house, my father and my poor mother, to my guild . . .'

'It won't be like that now.'

Sadie didn't bother to answer. 'These creatures, they'll
go faster if you heel them, slower if you pull on their
manes. Left and right's the same—but not as hard as you're
doing, Robbie—so treat them with respect, and, above all,
take care of Anna. Otherwise, I'll come after you. And
have this . . .' She pressed several balled-up notes into my
hand. 'You'll need money, if it's still worth anything.'

I looked at Anna. 'Are you ready?'

She nodded.

I was about to get my creature moving when Sadie
tugged it back.

'My whisperjewel,' she said. 'I need it back to protect
this house . . .'

In my pocket, I felt a surge of light, the lost music of all
those endless dances. With an effort, I tossed it down to
her, gleaming wyreblack. Sadie caught it. She slapped the
creatures' rears and we trotted from the stables.

'Go for the main gates! Take Marine Drive!'

But when I looked back she had already gone from
sight. And she was right about these marvellous creatures;

they were far from stupid. Sensing my inexperience and
Anna's weariness, they slowed to a smooth walk across the
snowy morning gardens, their horned heads nodding, their
warm scent and breath wafting back over us, their heavy
hooves crashing through the crusted snow.

VII

Marine Drive was empty and the loudest sound in the town of Saltfleetby came from the tide sluicing in under the pillars of the pier. The shops on the main street, which in the summer would have spilled out in carousels selling rock, postcards, novelties, buckets and spades, were shut and boarded. But, here in winter, they were probably always that way. Had the world changed? Was this the New Age? But I was cold, and Anna's lips were blue and she was shivering, and we needed warmer clothes. I found a shop with the golden scissors of the Outfitters' Guild dangling above it, clumsily dismounted and banged hard on the door until a man's face, sleepy and wary, finally peered at us through the glass.

'Do you know what time this is?' He asked reassuringly simple questions as he pulled back the bolts. He glanced up at Anna and our mounts. 'I wouldn't stay long around here if I were you—you know what things are like.'

'What are they like?'

But already he was lumbering back into the rails of his shop. He found us cloaks and warm tops, riding trousers for Anna and boots for us both. He studied one of Sadie's twenty pound notes. 'Don't you have anything else?'

'Don't worry about the change.'

'No . . . ?' He laughed. 'But I'll take it. Maybe I can frame the bloody thing, show it to the kids . . .'

The telegraphs, I noticed, as we rode on out of the town, were black, but not wyreblack; they were simply dead.

The sun vanished. Dense white mist set in. The unicorns were slow, awkward mounts; they'd been designed for the brief speed of the chase. My legs were chafed, my back and buttocks ached, and Anna took to leaning across Starlight's neck.

A boy ran up to us through the dim hedges. The unicorns started, but were too tired to rear.

'Did you see it? Did you *see* it?'

'What?'

'The dragon! It was over there in that field.' He pointed, his eyes alight with wonder. But all I could see was mist.

We stopped at a stables and farrier above the North Downs on the first night of our journey towards London. The stableman shook his head at the state of our mounts. What we needed were *saddles*. Just had to widen the girth. And no, he didn't want our *money*—that stuff was for wiping your arse now. And we could sleep for free in the roofspace above the straw. That night, less asleep than unconscious from weariness, I was sure I smelled smoke, and heard shouts and screams. And the unicorns, and the other beasts in the stable below us, seemed restless. I moved closer towards Anna, but she was light and still, scarcely there. And then I was gone, too, drawn back into the blackness, although I could still hear the beasts below whinnying, snickering, an agitated panting, then the churn of a saw, until I woke up to find myself and Anna covered in dust and frost.

Down in the muddy yard, our mounts were already saddled. Starlight was trying to bite the hand of the stablelad who held him and there were wheals across his flanks. They'd tried a bridle, apparently, which the beasts wouldn't take. Greatmaster Porrett's russet gift was shivering and steaming as if he'd already been ridden a dozen hard miles. His forehead was a bleeding stump.

'They're just *horses,* you know.' The stableman was as bland and casual as he had been yesterday. 'The damn things fall off.' He fixed us with a smile and a glare.

The mist was thicker still on the second day of our journey, laden with the smell of burning, and we caught glimpses of flames and wreckage. Still, no one knew quite what was happening up in London, other than that the trains weren't running and the telegraphs were dead. The saddles were some help in keeping upright, but my mount's shivering increased as the morning progressed and blood wouldn't stop flowing from the stub on his forehead. It dripped in the mud and splashed back across me. The unicorn was in pain, half-blinded. I tried getting off and leading him, but in the late afternoon the creature stopped in his tracks, belched a torrent of bile, then keeled over and died. We had to leave him where he fell; it wasn't the first carcass we'd seen at the roadside.

I walked. Anna rode. We camped out for our second night in the darkness at the edge of a field. There were no lights, and the only sound came from the snow's dripping. Finally succeeding in undoing the complex fittings of Starlight's saddle, I left the beast to rummage. Then I found some sticks and made a drier patch of stones, and tried to light it with a flintbox.

'Let me.' Anna leaned from the huddle of her cloak. She said something, then something else again. The cheap little box, scarcely even aethered, still ticked uselessly. After half an hour of muttering, breathing, she caused the fire to burn, but it hollowed her face terribly, gave off little heat, and the flames danced madly through the branches, telling the whole world exactly where we were. I was almost grateful when it went out.

I leaned against Anna as she lay under a tree. We were both wet. I could feel the shivering grind of her teeth.

'Do you really think this is the New Age?'

'We've got to get to London.'

She chuckled, then coughed. 'Why will London be any different?'

A last ember flickered across a twig.

'Can't you get a bit closer?' I asked. 'A bit warmer?'

'I *am* close.'

But she wasn't.

The night poured around us as the snow ticked and melted, and somewhere, clear but distant, like the passing of a train beyond the horizon, I was sure I heard the beating of giant wings.

What is it that you really want, Robbie? Sadie was right when she said it wasn't me . . .

But that night in Bracebridge, Anna, when you let me lie with my hand against your cheek.

I was asleep. I don't even remember. And what now?

I still don't know.

There was mist again in the morning. But it was thinner, and the ice hanging from the branches had refrozen into beautiful jewels. The huge black shape of the unicorn came edging through the sparkling trails, its horn glistening. Anna was still asleep, her face cupped in her hands, seemingly tranquil . . .

What is it that you really want, Robbie?

I could still hear her voice, edging in through my dreams. For a long time, as the world sparkled the unicorn stood as her guardian, I left Anna sleeping.

Another morning. A gathering smell of rot and smoke.

The Thames was still frozen. Blurred by hunger and tiredness, we'd gone too far east, scarcely brushing London's southern outskirts. Had children really scampered beside us chanting that Anna was Goldenwhite, that she'd come again riding a unicorn to rescue the city? I didn't know. Starlight was suffering, and the straps of the girth—although I doubted if Anna could have ridden this far without a saddle—had bitten into his flesh. I helped her down. There was the steep slope to the river. The ice looked solid enough, but it had a watery sheen. It might take us, but it probably wouldn't accept the unicorn's huge weight. I hacked off the buckles and shooed Starlight into the fog.

VIII

London, London, city of all my hopes, was more dangerous than ever at the start of this New Age. As Anna and I
entered the smoke edges of the Easterlies, the sights we
had seen on the way were soon dimmed. True, and as far I
as could get the story, the great advance towards Northcentral on Christmas night had succeeded, or at least it hadn't
failed. Yes, citizen, all the guildgates are open and the
houses of the filthy rich are there for the plundering if
that's your fancy—those, that is, which haven't burned to
the ground. Children were parading with top hats and silk-
lined coats, and a wild, chattering chorus of familiars had
been released around Caris Yard, much to the irritation of
the few citizens who still inhabited it. Flock curtains and
fine enamel snuffboxes and great golden sea-beasts of pillaged furniture could be yours for two-a-penny, except that
nobody would have wanted your penny in the first place,
but food—water, even, now that the pumping houses had
stopped working and half-frozen sewage was backing up
through the grids of the drains—was in short supply.

Anna and I wandered slowly through the mist beside the
dead tramtracks along the middle of Doxy Street. Bodies
hung from lampposts and there were grey scraps of carrion

in the gutters over which the kingrats, grown bigger and
bolder than ever, were squealing. Doors hung open, shattered windows spilled their contents. Everywhere, too
common to be noticed, was the reek of smoke and shit, and
the sound of people weeping. Here, a telegraph was still
glowing, although its line was broken, and a boy of apprentice age was standing barefoot in the frost and gripping it
as it writhed and glowed, chanting the lost messages of his
guild. Horses and drays ran wild, hungry as the citizens
who were trying to capture them. I was glad we'd released
Starlight on the far side of the Thames. Along with the familiars of Caris Yard, many stranger creatures had escaped
into the city. The western flow of Doxy Street was interrupted by a great steaming pit and the crowd who were
standing around it. Down below, burying its way in or out
of the earth, was a saw-toothed pitbeast far bigger than I
had ever seen. And St Blate's had been opened—have you
tried riding a troll, citizen? But they were all gone now,
cast and scattered, lost for many days . . .

There was much sport and there was much madness at
the start of this unnamed Age. Dragonlice in the churches.
Cuckoo-weed growing from the untended factories. Some
children invading Thripp Sidings had managed to get one
of the big locomotives going. But they didn't have the right
spells and the engine had exploded, killing and maiming
dozens in a giant blast of superheated steam. So many
sights, so many stories.

I could guess even then that the histories would tell of
these days quite differently. And there *were* gatherings and
debates in the lesser guildhouses. There *was* talk of liberty.
Many people striving to get the city going. A guild training
might still be acknowledged as a skill, as long as you were
prepared to work like everyone else and not flaunt it. And
wealth—wealth was like poverty, really; a burden to be
cast off in exchange for the common rights of citizenship.
And the shiftdays—they might still be changed. I was
amused to hear such talk wafting out from a needle factory
in Houndsfleet. And there was kindness as well, amid the
madness, in those first days. But it was the madness which

predominated. Armies of the citizen-helpers were still roving the streets with their clubs and guns.

I was wary of mentioning Saul's name, or Blissenhawk's. London was plainly at war with itself and I had no desire to draw attention to myself and Anna. Many of the major streets were blocked by barricades and the lads—ne'er-do-wells of the sort Saul and I had both been when I first arrived in this city—had set themselves up as guardians. They had no use for what was left of Sadie's money, but still required payment before they let you pass.

'What guild were you in?' I was asked after I'd handed over my cloak.

'Does that matter now?' I didn't like the way he was looking at Anna. Even with her hood up, she looked odd and frail.

'Just asking. You don't look like a mart. And neither does she.'

'Well, we both were. And we're all citizens now, aren't we?'

An unpillaged pub cellar, probably the only one left now in all of London, had been discovered just across the way and the first barrel was being hoisted out. Then the ropes broke and the thing shattered into staves, spewing beer across the pavement. One of the lads was suddenly weeping, holding his arm the wrong way.

'I heard Citizen Saul was up this way . . .' I muttered, nodding towards Northcentral.

'Oh, *him*.' Our young citizen was distracted, unimpressed. 'It's the opposite way entirely. You'll need to go up Tidesmeet . . .'

We were lucky that one of the men who picked up Anna and I at the docklands gates had once been a fellow seller of the *New Dawn*. Two of the citizens he was with were struggling to control a captured balehound with a tangle of chains. Another was carrying one of Saul's guns, and was missing a hand. They looked comical and dangerous, although I knew not to smile, and they chatted with me and Anna in a weary, disconnected way as they led us towards the looming bulk of Dockland Exchange. *Saltfleetby,* eh? Why, Stan here has a brother who's been that way . . . No story you could tell at that time would have been too mundane, or too bizarre, not to be believed.

The fog, thickened by the smoke and the nearness of the river, hung heavier here. The silent buildings Saul and I had once scampered between through the bustle of my first summer, that tea-scented warehouse, came and went in the murk. There were the same bad smells here as everywhere, but they grew more intense as we finally reached the thick circular base of the great Exchange. The balehound, and others jammed nearby in makeshift pens, roared and howled. There was a charnel house reek, and a grey mass of gulls seethed beneath the building, screaming and flapping. My feet slipped and crackled through bones and slurry. Then there were endless stairs curving upwards because no one had yet got the machines which drove the lifts working. My legs were aching, and Anna was wearying. There were glimpses of deserted offices, unattended hafts, the stilled insect mouths of typewriters; all the lost bustle of a great guild.

Finally, we reached the upper levels, which the architect, unable to resist some last flurry of his skills, had broadened out and filled with glass so that the building swarmed with grey wintry light. A final run of stairs and we were amid wood panelling and smooth grey carpets which extended from the windows like tendrils of fog. Then to the room, the office, which Saul now inhabited. The doors to a balcony were open and he was standing out on it. The air was hazed. He turned when we were announced.

'You're back!'

I was relieved to discover that he seemed pleased to see me and Anna. And his manner of dress, the fact that he'd found a decent suit, and beneath it a waistcoat even brighter than any of his usual outfits, was reassuring as well. He almost seemed like the same old Saul.

'You both look exhausted. Sit down . . .'

We did, although the leather chairs were slippery with condensation from the fog. The whole room, in fact, as

Saul congratulated us on getting here and doing whatever the hell it was that we'd done—as he put it—at Walcote House, had a cold, wet sheen. It seemed to grow and subside within the mist which plumed in from the balcony as Saul told us about Christmas night in London, shaking his head as he did so like an old man amazed at some distant memory. There had been many casualties and things were still difficult now, but it really had gone as well as anyone could have expected. There had been resistance, yes, but the guns had worked, and many of the troops and guards had changed sides, become citizens, vanished. Northcentral's key points and great guildhalls had collapsed with surprisingly little struggle. Like pushing at an open door. Some rich bankers along Threadneedle Street had even committed suicide before the citizens got near them.

'It really was quite a sight. Have you been up Northcentral yet?'

I shook my head.

'Well, you should. And Goldsmiths' Hall—didn't you say something about bringing down the building without damaging a single stone? Well, fact is, one whole side of it's caved in—happened at about noon on the first morning. You really *must* go and see, Robbie—Anna as well, of course . . .'

Saul had taken possession of the room's wide cedarstone desk in the sense that he'd laid a few pens on it and done some doodles of what looked like trees on a notepad, but, as he eased himself behind it and swivelled on the chair and continued talking of what an ideal base this was, necessary for command and easily defensible, the impression was of a schoolboy holding court behind teacher's desk. I found myself glancing towards the double doors as if Greatgrandmaster Passington might still drift through them at any moment like a darker, more certain gathering of the fog. I picked up a brass frame and ran my hand across the glass to clear the dew. Sadie looked amazingly young and happy and glamorous in the posed photographic print. The dress could have been the one she wore on that distant Midsummer.

'Strange isn't it, to be here of all places?' Saul nodded

towards the oil portraits. 'And *you* must have seen Passington. Killed himself, the bastard, didn't he? And good fucking riddance to all of his kind . . .'

I put the frame down and glanced at Anna, with her hair
lank, her shoulders thin, her eyes focused on nothing. I
thought of our long journey, and quite why it was that I'd
dragged her here. And why did I feel this stupid sense of
loss? Hadn't I wanted my darkmaster dead and destroyed
above all else? But after all, as Sadie had said, he'd only
been a man, and he'd done things which were no better and
no worse than many others. That last night, as Sadie and he
danced, his gaze had passed over me without the slightest
recognition. The real darkmaster, the real truth, somehow
still evaded me—even now, as I stood up and lifted a cloak
from a hatstand and breathed the waft of its cologne as I
put it about my shoulders.

'So,' I said, feeling it pull and lighten and settle about
me. 'What do you plan to do now?'

Saul gave his chair another spin. 'There's this city to get
going, for a start, and we need to make proper contact with
the rest of England. At the moment, its just rumours. But
Preston's definitely citizens' republic. So's Bristol and
most of the west. There's word of a battle going on between some recidivists down on the south coast just by
where you were, and we're still not sure about the bloody
French, although the word is that there have been riots and
upheavals across most of Europe. But nothing *works* at the
moment. We need to get the trains, the trams, going. Even
these telegraphs . . .' He gestured. 'Up on the final floor,
there's this giant black haft. Unlike all the others, it still
seems to be functioning. Got one of my lads who claimed
he knew about such things to try it—he's a gibbering
wreck now. So I suppose we'll need to capture a few proper
telegraphers, get them up here to tell us the basic spells.
But everything's in such short supply. I can't even get any
cheroots. And *aether*—I thought the stuff was supposed to
be stockpiled. But it isn't.'

'That was the whole *point,* Saul, of what Anna and I did.'

'Was it? And I thought it was all about money. That
place of yours, by the way, the town you went up north

to—what is it, *Broombridge*?—I've also heard that the factory there has stopped working.'

'It never did work. It hasn't for years.'

'Well, that's the old regime for you. Lies and illusions. *This* is the new.'

Beyond the open doors, the telegraphs drooped dimly into the swarming mist. The rest of London, for all that we could see and smell and hear of it, might have vanished.

'You will stay, won't you?' Saul said. 'Now that you're here. You, and Anna. I could do with some trustworthy citizens to make up for the useless rabble we've got here at the moment.' He'd finished swivelling in his chair, and was looking at Anna. Without moving, without speaking, she seemed to be receding. Saul's gaze grew puzzled. A question started to form on his lips.

'Where's Blissenhawk?' I asked.

'Oh, he's up in Northcentral. He's trying to find the right spells to get the presses for the *Guild Times* working. Not that we'll call it that now. By the way, didn't you say you travelled through Kent?' He inspected a wet paperweight. 'Didn't happen to see Maud by any chance?'

'I'm sorry, Saul. Kent's bigger than London. It's a whole county.'

'It was just a question. Anyway . . .' Carefully, he placed the paperweight back down on the polished cedarstone. 'There's so *much* to be done. Two days' time and it'll be New Year, and you'd be surprised how many citizens are debating whether the Age should start officially then. But that would mean we're still in the old Age now, wouldn't it? Some even say we should begin with Butterfly Day. Frankly, it's all just numbers.'

'I'm sure it is.'

'Still, it's odd when you think about it. All that talk about Ages, and the people who went on about dates were mostly right. One hundred years ago almost to the day as if some greater force has been guiding us. I'd say it was fate if I believed in such things.'

'But you don't . . .'

'Why should I? I'm a man of this New Age, Robbie, whenever it officially starts and whatever it's called. But there's a lot of superstition about. All kinds of things. There's talk of a dragon—not some little fairground freak, but a huge thing you could ride on—circling Hallam Tower.' He chuckled. 'And then there's World's End. A lot of the citizens are planning on gathering over there this afternoon. After all, that's where the old Age started . . .'

Look at me now, and look at Citizen Anna, as we tumble from Dockland Exchange and head west and south in the muffled light of that last afternoon, when the sun, smaller and paler and colder than the moon, is breaking through for the first time in days. Down by the embankment, there is a holiday air. The ferries have burnt out and are keeled sideways through the shattered ice. Funnels like sarsens, masts like fallen steeples. The wreckage of recent days rises from the frozen river. A beautiful brass bedstead gleams, its coloured covers swarming beautiful wings. Everywhere, tiny and intricate, figures scurry. Children play football and race toboggans, but the main tide is across the ice, which is puddled and treacherous, and towards World's End. There are trays for sliding down the white hills and baskets for picnics, although the latter seem suspiciously light. These could be—and probably are—the same families I saw taking the drowned ferry in the spring.

Anna and I crossed the river just ahead of the crowds. We had a purpose and we knew the way. Whilst people were still dragging benches up from the ice or merrily clacking through the turnstiles past the open fencing, we were fighting the roses and tin cans towards the little house amid World's End's far ruins. The door still bore a permissory order from the Gatherers' Guild. I tore the thing off as we banged on it, but that still left a darker rectangle on the wood, and the damning rustmarks of the nails.

'Well,' she said once she'd finally emerged. 'At least you're still both alive.'

'We need to leave here, Missy,' Anna said.

'You're right.' The whole cottage seemed to creak and exhale. 'I should have gone from this place Ages ago.' She turned back inside and we had little choice but to follow her. Now, there wasn't even a fire going.

'You both look tired. Can I get you tea?'

'Missy . . .'

But there was a slow certainty about her movements as she made us sit down and wait whilst she pumped the spirit stove and filled the kettle. From outside, I could hear shouts and the crackle of glass, but this seemed to be Mistress Summerton's moment, and Anna and I were trapped inside it.

'So London's changed, has it? Is it the place you'd hoped for, eh? Are all the bad guildsmen gone, or turned into good ones?' Her vanilla pod thumb hooked around the saucer as she handed me a cup. Perhaps she doesn't need the fire, I thought, as she eased herself down in her low chair beside the dark, dead grate, for she radiated heat as much as Anna now seemed to exhale cold. White winter sunlight streamed in through the window, tumbling with dust and frost to catch on the old tins lined along the shelves above her. In the changing light, this place could almost have been the room in Redhouse to which she had first led me and my mother. *And you must be Robert . . . Annalise will be here at any moment . . .*

Mistress Summerton lit her pipe and exhaled two jets of smoke. 'Passington's dead, isn't he? Such a pity, really, although I suppose the time to go comes to us all. Did he tell you much?' The smoke settled in layers. Outside, there was a tearing crash. The little house shook faintly. The dottle glowed as she sucked again on her pipe.

'Missy?' Anna leaned forward. The light blazed on her face. 'What are you saying?'

'The whole of England's running out of aether—you still haven't quite grasped that simple fact, have you, Robert? The guilds have sucked it all out of the ground. It was vanishing even when I was born. But yes, I had my dreams in that sour prison in Oxford which you two chose to visit. I dreamed of a world beyond power and wisdom . . .' The room shimmered and darkened. The sun had set a little lower. 'But instead I have lived this life of *duty.* This life of *labour.* It was aether which had made me this way, and it was aether which destroyed me, not because it existed, but because there wasn't *enough.* Plans and blueprints for

machines that wove hosiery which I had to waste my life
fixing. Implements that scarcely work. Pointless trophy
plants. Clumsy guilded spells. *That* was the legacy of
aether. *This* was the life I had. And then, when I was
wearying of it and feeling myself strained and stretched
out, I was taken at last to Redhouse, where a clacking, dying, engine was extracting the stuff. Of course, the people
there were as stupid as they are everywhere, but they were
also uncommonly trusting. You—Robert—you know what
aetherworkers are like. I mean, look at Anna's own father.
So when the engines began to fail and strain, when output
declined—well, they must have tried many things . . .' She
paused. 'But they were wildly optimistic in what they
asked me. Their engines were running down, but how
could I turn back the draining of aether? But, to be honest,
I lied to them because I was happy fiddling with their machines to make my spells. And the village was a pretty
place, with a fine big house which was already wanting
roofwork and the cottages down by the river, even if the
engines did clack and creak. And I was nearly treated with
respect. They were almost kind to me, were these people,
which is the best that most can manage for my kind. Of
course, they still called me a troll . . .'

The chair creaked. Her pipe bubbled. The lowering light
of the winter sun had thrust her into a deep pall.

'You always told me never to use that word, Missy.'

'What other word is there? Changeling—elf, goblin,
fairy or witch? But you've led a lucky life, haven't you, my
proud, expensive Annalise? So perhaps you haven't heard
these words, or at least only in jokes. You haven't been spat
at through the bars of cages, you haven't heard the whispers behind the walls or the curses along the aisles of factories as you're led like a tame ape. I hate the word only
because it's used up and useless and filled with spite. But
it's what we *are*—that's the most terrible thing. We're
freaks, all of us, from the most bloated monstrosity at St
Blate's to you, Annalise. The world of love and life and
happiness is taken from us even before we're given the
chance to grasp it. This isn't *our* Age, Anna, and the next
one won't be either. Look outside. And listen. All I've

smelled these last days coming across the river from London is shit and smoke . . .' *Shit and smoke* . . . There was an echo now, a weight, to Mistress Summerton's voice. 'Things change, but they get worse instead of better. *There*—that's the wisdom of Ages for you, Robert, my Anna. It's something I should have realised long ago. Perhaps then I would never have bothered with making and casting that spell.'

'What are you talking about, Missy? *What* spell . . . ?'

But I knew. 'The chalcedony.'

'Bravo, Robert! Perhaps, after all, you do have some abilities. Yes, there was a chalcedony at Redhouse, which the guildsmen had bought with the last of their profits. And they trusted me to use it because they thought I could rescue them from the death of their village even as their steeple whitened and the sheets on their beds froze. Not that I ever could, but I made and shaped that stone with the very last shudders of those dying engines, and I knew I was making something perfect—something that, although this village would die, could change this rotten world . . .'

Anna said nothing now, but her face was glistening as the sun's last rays poured in from outside, tangling with her tears and the shadows of the roses outside.

'And *he* came to me there at Redhouse. He came slowly as the swirl of the weir and the turn of the seasons. He was like a feeling, a messenger. Sometimes, he even stood beside me and whispered instructions, so solid did his presence become. He guided me with that spell, even though I didn't know what he or it was, other than that it lay beyond these stupid villagers' imaginings. It glowed out at me. Sometimes, as I gazed into my stone, it seemed the very essence of everything which had been stolen from me in that prison-house . . .'

Mistress Summerton gave a bitter chuckle. 'Somehow, when the waterwheel finally stopped turning, I didn't mind that the greater guilds took my chalcedony from me. In many ways, as Redhouse emptied and died and whitened, I still felt its presence, even though I knew that it had been stored and labelled in a casket in some remote warehouse. And I was left and forgotten—at last, the trollmen overlooked me, and that, too, was part of the spell. The stone still spoke to me, and I knew it would speak to others when its time came. And the little things which happened to me through those long and empty years of waiting—the visits from your mother, Robert, when she was a young girl—were all part of the same vast but inexplicable spell.

'So when I heard that a high guildsman named Passington had come to Bracebridge, when the very air whispered to me that the stone itself had returned, I knew that something strange, magical, was about to happen. I took to lurking at the edges of the town. I even saw the young greatgrandmaster once, standing at twilight out by the sarsens in a fine black cloak much like the one you're wearing, Robert. I even thought that it was *him,* the presence which had come to guide me before, but when I got closer, I realised he was just an ordinary man, and that he was the stone's servant just as I was. And I felt the moment of the seizure of those engines like the stopping of my own heart. And I expected—well, I was too old to imagine that the trees would instantly brighten, that the sun would dance, that the clouds would uncurl. But it would be something, *something*—and I waited through the long day after until I saw two figures stumbling up the path towards my ruined house. It was your dying mother, Anna. The chalcedony had blasted its spell through her and she was turning into a frosted statue even as she walked, and your mother was with her, Robert— although your father, Anna, was already ruined and gone. But Kate Durry was with child. And I knew even then as we talked pointlessly of tending her that *you,* and not her, were the spell's gift . . .

'You came, Anna, just a term or so later as your mother died. But at last, in your eyes, Anna, in your thoughts, I saw the spell made flesh. A perfect human, but also a changeling, just as in the oldest of tales. Aether, in its fading, had conspired through me and its many other servants to bring you about. And you were wonderful, Annalise! You truly were. And I loved you then just as I love you now. I would have given you anything, done anything, just to let you live the life I'd never had. So I tended you, Anna. I raised you and I gave you love and I lavished . . . I lavished *everything,* my

Annalise, although I'm not sure you ever entirely noticed. And I hoped that, in return, you would repay my faith and hope.'

'Hope! Love! You make it sound like a contract, Missy.'

'Haven't I let you live the life you wanted? Haven't I trusted the spell to work itself out? I spent my money on that life of yours—I even came back to this awful city and back into the clutches of the trollmen for *your* sake, Annalise. So don't talk to me about hope and contracts and duty and love. I've done everything I ever could for you— and more. But perhaps I was wrong. Look where it's got us, eh? Listen to those shouts. Even though this place is ruined, they still want to destroy it. And I look at you now, Annalise. You're like that stone, you're like your poor mother—you're worn out. And what's it all been for, eh? Just for politics, for the change of an Age?'

Anna sat back from the light and covered her face with her hands. Silently, she was crying.

'I *loved* you, Missy.'

In a glitter of sparks, Mistress Summerton tapped out her pipe. The voices were louder now. Tearing. Pulling. Chanting. Something crashed against the roof.

I said, 'We can't stay here—'

'No! Not after all the havoc you've wreaked!' Mistress Summerton stood up and the sinking light of the room was sucked into her. 'There's my car . . .'

The last of the sun was blazing through the clouds, stretching enormous shadows. The river was a deep trough, and the city beyond it was tipped with fire. Hallam Tower, through some trick of the light, blazed once again, but then so did Dockland Exchange and the spires of all the churches and the cranes of Tidesmeet and the brassy domes of the guildhouses. London was coated in gold. Then, as if in celebration, its bells began to ring in a rising, joyous and incessant surge as we followed Mistress Summerton through a thorny maze between the dazzling roses. I could hear children shouting, sighs and shudders as things collapsed. But we were lucky—we were seen by no one as we hurried past the dried-up boating lake and the fallen swings and the signs towards the Tropic Wing.

'It's here.'

We ran from the trees, then stopped. Children were clambering over the car beneath the open corrugated shed. Two women were preening and laughing in floral hats as they pretended to drive it. Many of its panels had already been cast off. Even if we could get these people—who were too absorbed in their gleeful destruction to notice us—away, I doubted if the machine would still work. I caught Anna's arm and was turning back through the trees, but Mistress Summerton strode forward.

'This is *mine,* you wretches!' Her voice was an eerie screech. 'Leave it alone!'

There was a pause. The springs of the car creaked. Faces turned towards her. Distantly, London's bells still clamoured.

'Leave here *now* . . .' An emanation of the deepening twilight, she strode across the space of winter grass.

The women exchanged glances and climbed out, whilst a lad who'd been jockeying astride the car's dented bonnet began to slide down, but, as he did so, his boot pressed on the horn's rubber bulb. The thing gave a prolonged *parp.* People started laughing. When they turned their attention back towards Mistress Summerton, there was a different look in their eyes.

'So? This is *yours* is it?'

'And who exactly says *that*?'

Taunts about the wrongness of ownership and possession came easily now.

'Just who do you think you *are,* anyway?'

The horn gave another squawk. Laughter came and went in a quick surge. More citizens were being drawn towards this spot by the voices and the sound of the car's horn. After all, there were rumours about who or what lived at World's End. And those damn roses, these bloody tins! And hadn't there been a sign, somewhere, from the trollmen? But in truth, these people needed to be reminded of none of those things, for Mistress Summerton, as she stood and cursed them, with her head bared and bald and her withered face exposed, her hands like the claws of bare winter trees, looked exactly what she was.

Witch . . .
Troll . . .
Changeling . . .
I still stood with Annalise beside the trees, fully expecting Mistress Summerton to flee the hissing, chanting, gathering crowd. Instead, she moved towards them and I grabbed Anna's arm before she could do the same. *Witch. Parp. Troll. Parp.* The lad had ripped the horn from the car's body and was squeezing it to the rhythm of the voices. In the distance, London's bells still clamoured, and the sun's dwindling rays spiralled across the sky like an explosion of stained glass. *Get it, someone! Get it, before it escapes!* The first of the children jumped at Mistress Summerton with a wild yell. She threw him far back through the air. He landed squealing, clutching his ribs. The power of the shadows poured into her as the sky deepened, and the second of her assailants was thrown back just as easily as the first. *Witch. Parp. Troll. Parp.* She grew stronger with every fresh taunt. But the people were circling, chanting, and their numbers were growing. Bodies and elbows began to push around Anna and I as she tried to pull herself away from me. *Witch. Parp. Witch. Parp.* Surge by hopeless surge, we were swallowed by the crowd. Somewhere, far ahead of us now, a wave of citizens grabbed Mistress Summerton. She was lifted; a writhing bundle of rags. She was dropped, then lifted again. Still, the chanting and the sound of that car horn went on. Anna fought against me, but, for once, I was stronger than her. But we were both helpless now, driven by the will of the crowd.

Mistress Summerton's body was borne up. Higher this time. *Witch. Parp. Witch. Parp.* But what to do with such a prize? There was only one answer. After all, there was so much kindling around this place. And these fucking roses—they needed getting rid of as well. Even without the incentive of a witch to burn, flames would have flickered across World's End that evening. But now there was an exultant purpose such as sometimes seizes a crowd. I'd seen and felt it before, and the most terrible thing was that Anna and I seemed to be part of it as we were dragged onwards by the press of bodies and our own horrified need.

Past the signs and displays. Past the twilit and glittering mountains of glass. Like an army of ants, the crowd was carrying beams and panels and great snagging heaps of the thorny roses over their heads. The sky was fading, the ruins were sinking back. I looked down, almost losing Anna as I stumbled, and saw that we were trudging upwards now across the great hills of engine ice. Ahead of us, rising up across these waves of white, was the darkly breaking edge of the crowd. Mistress Summerton was no longer visible, but I could tell where she was from the deeper sense of purpose which clustered around her. Dimly then, came the smell of smoke, and a vast and terrible *aaaaah!* swept back. We pushed on. These, as light flickered over them in all their teeming variety, were the faces I'd seen all my life. Straddle-legged women who humped tubs of washing down their back steps. Men who smoked and read newspapers as they queued for work outside the houses of their lesser guilds. Children I'd shared my long desk with at Board School. Old men who shoved dominoes in the noonday gloom of pubs. They were all here, and they were laughing and they were pushing against Anna and I as we drove through them towards the thickening smell of the smoke and the cackle of flames.

Somehow, we were near the front, and the scene really was like something from a woodcut. Mistress Summerton had been bound in roses to the wooden mast of an uprooted sign which still pointed lopsidedly towards the Tropic Wing, then hoisted amid all the wreckage which had been borne here. The air shimmered. The fire danced and licked, glowing in towards its core. Gleefully, the wind rose in twirls of sparks with the *whoosh* and *ahhh* of the crowd. Already, it was too late. If Mistress Summerton had struggled before, there now seemed an inevitability about the way the flames closed in on her. Apart from the roses, which writhed and spat, the fuel was tinder-dry, and I told myself as I held Anna and the heat surged against us that she had probably already stopped breathing, that the air had been sucked from the fire's core . . .

The wind rose. It urged on the flames and set the engine ice hissing around our feet. It drew upwards as the pyre plumed and glimmered as far as the sky. Mistress Summerton was now a twisting, blackened thing within the flames. I imagined that this movement was an effect of the heat and this strange wind, but then she began to scream. The sound went on and on. People covered their ears. No one who was there and survived will ever be able to describe it, and no one who was not will ever understand. It was in our heads. It burrowed beneath our flesh. It made us part of her pain. And the searing wind was still rising, shrieking with it, tearing at the loose engine ice until that, too, tumbled into the flames and there was nothing but bitter heat, and one last, terrible scream.

The wind was so powerful now that the earth itself seemed to fade, glittering and blurring as the hill we stood on was sucked from beneath us in swooshing waves. People were cowering and trying to turn their backs, to somehow cover their eyes as well as their ears. But the screaming was still rising, twisting beyond all sense and into one great sensation which the flames had torn from the sky. From those further back, perhaps, or the thousands who were gathering on the far bank of the Thames to witness the scene, it might perhaps have looked beautiful, a swirling combination of the Biblical pillars of smoke and fire, but for those of us who were close, it was terrible. People, blinded and helpless, were stumbling and shrieking as they tried to escape the spreading chaos of wind and fire.

Then, as suddenly as it had started, the wind subsided. And the screaming stopped with it, and the flames diminished into the ordinary realms of light and heat. The citizens, coughing and glittering, looked at each other. Almost, they began to smile and stumble back towards their lives. From the still air, as they sought out their friends, there still came a gentle hissing as a fine prismatic snow of soot and engine ice resettled about them. It *did* seem lighter. But the flames were still sparking and the ruined thing at their centre was spitting and glowing. The realisation that the earth itself, the hill of engine ice on which we all still stood, was continuing to subside, came slowly, and for many it was already too late.

Saul, who had been watching the scene from the top of

Dockland Exchange, was one of the quickest to arrive, and he brought many citizen-helpers with their clubs and guns. Even before this outburst of madness, he and many others understood that the city would still need to be tamed before it could be governed. But I think that he was one of the first to appreciate what was happening, if not yet, perhaps, its full import. After all, and despite the proudly guildless heritage of which he had come to boast, he was his mother's son. In Marm's dreamhouse, he must often have seen the gleam of vials far more powerful than the dull oils and catalysts upon which it was most guildsmen's lot to gaze. Better than many, he knew the wyreglow of aether, and he saw it now—even if it came from the white hills of World's End, where everything but its ashes had long expired.

'Robbie! Robbie!'

He found me. People, not just children, but adults who should have known better were playing in the fiercely glowing ribbons which threaded between their feet. They were crouching in spreading pools of the stuff, cupping it in their hands and spilling it through their fingers, laughing wildly as the gas of visions poured around them even as their flesh suppurated and bled.

'Look . . .' Saul grabbed and shook me. 'We've got to get some sort of *cordon* around this place. We've got to get these people *away*.' Then a pause. Momentarily, pouring up from the earth all around us, the wyrelight was in his eyes as well. 'But do you realise what this *means,* Robbie! D'you realise what this gives us?'

For aether is power even more than it is magic, and those who were swarming across the thawing river—those who did not drown—were awe-struck as they saw the white hills of World's End begin to blaze. Thousands fell to their knees. Millions took it as a sign. All of us, and all who heard the news as it spread across England and then the world, knew that this, finally, was the moment when this new Age of Light began.

I stumbled back from Saul, away from the glowing smoke and the wreckage as more of the hill hissed and subsided and the thing within the pyre, the burnt-out matchstick which still somehow resembled Mistress Summerton, finally sank into the glowing ash. My head was buzzing and empty. In my stupid absorption, and amid the distraction of Saul's arrival, whole minutes had fled. But when I looked around, I still imagined that I would find Anna beside me.

PART SIX
CHILDREN OF THE AGE

I

Niana uncurls herself. It has long been dark up here on the ruined bridge, although the sky above and the river beneath her eyrie still have that steely gleam which, in London, they never lose. And there are lights—always, now, there are many lights in the distance.

'Yes,' she hisses as the water hisses endlessly below. 'I *remember* that night, grandmaster. The flames, the crowds—although I'd thought the screaming was my own. Of course, I was merely a child, and for me it had simply been an outing across the frozen river to escape the wreckage of the town in those terrible days. But I remember my old tin tray for sliding down the hills, and the blanket for sitting on, and the slippery river. I even remember the smell of rot and smoke, and the toot of that car horn, although I'd imagined it was a trumpet. But how *old* could I have been, to have been there at all, and then to remember? And my parents, my family—I wonder what became of them?'

'Perhaps they suffered the same fate as you.'

'*Fate*? Must you call it that? And must you still describe us all as trolls and changelings, grandmaster, when you know there's a much better word.'

'Words are just spells.'

'And spells are for casting.' She's colder and greyer before me now than the night-breath of the river. 'And that sad old creature—the one you kept talking about whom we citizens finally burned—I'd never realised that she was both so innocent and yet so much to blame for it all. But, whatever *she* was, please think of me, grandmaster, if you think of me at all, as a Child of this Age. That's what we all are, even the likes of you who returned from those shining hills superficially unchanged, as well as the many of us who did not . . .'

Children of the Age; such a sweet, innocent phrase. Yet she's right. It fits Niana and those of her kind who were changed in the first wild effusion of new aether that night in a way which it would never have fitted Mistress Summerton— or even Annalise. And I realise in an odd, strange rush how much younger than me this creature is. *I must be getting old,* the thought quickly follows, *when even the tr*—the word I cannot think or mention, in this enlightened Age— *seem young.* And there is a much greater tolerance now. So many of them came into being that first night and, with so much new aether, there have been so many since. They seem different, as well. Fairer and more fey, stranger and paler; far harder to reach and understand. They truly belong to this new Age.

But what of the days which have followed, Niana, which we still count, despite all the talk, in the same twelve shifts? The discovery, once the first catalysation of engine ice had begun, of vast new supplies of aether almost at the heart of this city, and then in every other place where the stuff was to be found, was also the catalyst for the new regime. Citizen-helpers were needed to control this surprising new wealth, as well as citizens with the arcane skills required to retard the work of aether. And citizens to marshal the pit-beasts which would make the trenches, and citizens who worked in wood and citizens who worked in iron, and citizens to control engines, and of course citizens to guard the fences which were necessarily erected to keep all the other citizens out. Then there were the telegraphs to get working, and the trains and the trams.

They called these workers *servants of the nation* at first.

Do you remember that, Niana? How the ex-guildsmen were re-recruited and given the privilege of extra food which was only necessary if they were to perform their vital work? And the organisations, the loose agglomerations of old rivalries and new loyalties which were formed in bars and in kitchens and ransacked guildhalls, we called those *unions*. I remember that as well. But somehow, as the thin skeleton of the old London began to smoke and clatter just as it always had, the word *guilds* crept back in. They were *new guilds* at first, or they were *non-guilds*, and their members were *citizen guildsmen*, and that term, as it was shouted out on the first mornings of the new spring, was probably intended at first as nothing more than a jokey reference to the bad old times. But words are spells, Niana. Of course, you still sometimes see the word *new* or *re-amalgamated* on a letter heading or guildsign. And technically, I know, we are still all citizens, even the hopeless marts, for this has been legally established by the grand-judges in Newgate on a day when the corpses didn't swing.

For things have changed and things have remained the same, and I realise now that this is the pattern which life always makes for itself. The rebellious children who curse their parent's lives soon end up whistling as they head towards the same factory, and the new tenements which were erected on the old slums of Ashington and Whitechapel have become slums again. There is a spell in our heads, in the earth, in the air and in the aether, and it is one that we can never unbind. Look at Bracebridge. In the days after the engines stopped and the long-standing fraud of the directors of Mawdingly & Clawtson was made public, you would have thought that that was the end of the town. But if you were to go there now, Niana, you would find that the place is as busy and ugly as ever. The settling pans still glow, and the long straw-bedded lines of aether trucks clack beneath the same iron bridge—probably watched by some confused and half-angry lad. The biggest change you'd notice about Bracebridge is Rainharrow. That hill is a bustling crater now, threaded in grey dust and the workings of machinery as the engine ice infused in its rock is extracted. And once every quarter hour, day and night, the ground shakes, *BOOM,* to a fresh explosion as more open-cast is revealed. The workings are even administered from offices beyond an archway set with the twin friezes of Providence and Mercy. So the rhythm of life goes on, and my father smiles or scowls into his beer as he helps out at the Bacton Arms, and Beth scolds her pupils and stirs her ink and smiles to herself with thoughts of the shiftend and her colleague from Harmanthorpe.

Redhouse has changed more. In this Age when guild-mistresses collect precious thimblefuls of glittering leavings from the seams of their husband's workclothes to give to the local redeemer, when the very dust of the air of larger workplaces is distilled, such a prize could hardly go unclaimed. Go there now, and you'll find that the old house and those cottages have all been ground to rubble for their engine ice by big machines, although, oddly enough, in a small square beyond the major workings, the statue beside which Annalise and I once sat remains. But the sound which fills the air there now is of chipping and hammering. It drowns out the hiss of the river, which in any case is polluted and changed.

So perhaps I'm wrong about things staying the same, Niana. And you must excuse me if I wander from my subject and seem to change my mind. Such behaviour, as I was saying only recently to Grandmaster Bowdly-Smart, is a prerogative of privilege, and that other kind of age. From his humble beginnings, from his struggle to become an uppermaster and his realisation after the loss of his child that mere hard work is wasted, from his blackmailing of Grandmaster Harrat to his handling of the Telegraphers' Guild's imaginary money, Ronald is, as he will readily admit, a parable of all that was right and wrong with the old Age. He lives a worthy life now, semi-retired and dabbling in this and that investment as people must if new wealth is to be created, and his wife thrives better than ever in what she calls *the social whirl.* For every invitation she accepts, she must turn down a dozen others, and Grandmaster Bowdly-Smart and I both laughed over our whisky as we wondered which it was she enjoyed the most, whilst outside the adopted child they call Frankie shouts to his nanny in coarse tones as he plays. For the one small change we have both noticed is that a rougher accent is now socially acceptable. Indeed, on a recent visit to Walcote House, many of the bright young things were affecting such voices. Unlike the rest of the world, they sometimes even actually call each other *citizen,* although they only mean it as a joke.

Still, I have to admit that I sometimes feel a slight queasiness at the thought of my friendship with Grandmaster Bowdly-Smart as I gaze across his grounds from the windows of my sparkling new car and head on through the streaming lights of this city with its colours and great new buildings and the flashing trains and trams. I wouldn't call it an *unease,* Niana, because I always feel that in disowning Uppermaster—I mean *Grandmaster*—Bowdly-Smart, I would be disowning part of myself. It is more the slight but vertiginous loss of balance I would probably feel if I were to live long enough to stand at the top of that new ziggurat they're building in the centre of Westminster Great Park, which will dwarf Hallam Tower, so I'm told, in height, and would swallow even the largest of the guildhalls in breadth and depth. Feeling at a loss in the Age you're in is, after all, a rich old man's luxury; something to nourish and cherish when all others pall.

You might find it strange, Niana, in view of his exalted position, but the person I feel most comfortable with nowadays is the Greatgrandmaster of the Reformed Guild of Telegraphers, Architects and Allied Trades. He, more than anyone, and when he can find the time to muse on such abstract matters, will concede that this isn't the Age he intended. Sometimes, he'll say, he still awakes with a start and finds himself lost and dwarfed by his huge rooms and the extraordinary circumstances of his life. But the people still love him almost as much as they did on that day in January when he was liberated from his comfortable prison-house and borne through the streets of the Easterlies. The citizens were so happy to see him. Here, at last, was a symbol both of this new Age's innocence, and yet also of the old. *Not going to sing down any more churches, are you?* they asked. Of course, George being George, he smiled

and looked uncomfortable, just as he still would now if
anyone had the courage to say such a thing to him. Compared to me, compared to Saul—compared, yes, even to
Uppermaster Stropcock—his rise has easily been the most
vertiginous. But then, he was the highest placed at the start.
And marrying Sadie—well, they were already friends, they
were at ease in each other's company, and it was entirely
necessary for the union of their reformed guilds. And Sadie
was a respected figure herself after the fine show she had
put up in defending Walcote House against what it was
once again becoming acceptable to term as a *mob*.

I even think they were happy as a couple. Only last
shifterm, I stood with the greatgrandmaster at her grave
near the stables where her beloved Starlight is also buried.
What? Oh, yes, Niana, her unicorn made it back to Walcote
House, although he was never fit to be ridden again. But
Sadie's greatest joy for the remaining years of her life was
to ride. It was how she died. Tragically early, of course, but
then George and I agreed as the perilinden trees hissed in the
breeze that growing old gracefully would never have been
one of her strengths. The private truth of their marriage,
beyond the fact that they were genuinely dedicated to each
other, is something across which he continues to draw a veil.
I'm sure Sadie had lovers, new discoveries, but I'm also
sure that none of them supplanted her feelings towards her
husband, and towards Anna Winters.

Bald and red-faced, no longer the tall young man of
twenty five years ago, the greatgrandmaster now somewhat
resembles a more portly version of Greatmaster Porrett.
But, inwardly, I think he remains the same Highermaster
George. The pain and suffering of the disadvantaged still
cause him grief. Above all, he still *hopes*. I often think that
is why his people tolerate so much in this new Age, and
why, despite that failed bomb attack of last winter, they
still mostly love him. I'm not sure that I ever did *hope,* Niana, in the way that he did, but I think that he still trusts
me enough to let me warn him that his revels will soon become more common knowledge than they already are.
People have a clear vision of their greatgrandmaster, and it
doesn't extend to his being the ringmaster at male orgies.

But Blissenhawk may already be publishing this news. Oddly, seeing as he started his career as a guildsman and never really diverted from plying his printer's trade, he remains truest to the rebellious spirit of the late last Age. Believe it or not, Niana, people now actually *collect* old editions of the *New Dawn*, smudged and browned though they are, and filled with my rambling, semi-literate rants. I've seen them laid in glass cases. People claim that they are invaluable historical documents, and fine investments, although, in truth, Blissenhawk's latest publications are little different. I came across an edition recently, and found it both sexually and politically offensive. It's banned, of course, but I'm sure he would have it no other way.

Saul, of us all, has led the wisest life. In the darkest days of the old Age's last winter, he did the many things which were probably necessary. But, as the years progressed and the disputes between rival groups of citizens became re-entrenched in the monumentalities of wealth, he was able to withdraw. In his renewed courtship of Maud, he was as patient and determined as he had been in planning the Christmas Night Revolt. But I was still surprised when he announced that they really were moving to the country. I visited them often to begin with. I was guildsfather to their first child, who must now be of an age to have children of his own. We still exchange those cards which have now become the fashion at Christmas and Butterfly Day, ornamented with brief expressions of how we really must meet in the coming year. But I'm happy to know that he's still with Maud, with their horses and their debts and their problems with the harvest and the arthritis which I believe is coming to affect his back and hands. He no longer draws, but then, who does find the time, in this Age, to do such things?

As for me, Niana, I suppose I've coped well enough with this New Age. I'm wealthy, as you see, although I find it easier these days to count my numberbeads than I do my blessings, or to get good service in a restaurant. Too often, I'm drawn back into the past. Anthony Passington, for example, still often visits me in my dreams. He glides along the corridor of an impossibly vast mansion to lay a hand on my shoulder, but he's a dark wraith; he never speaks. When I awake, the emotion which most fills me is grey disappointment that I was never able to know him. After all, he did the decent thing when he realised that the illusion of his guild's wealth was collapsing. Even back in his youth, when he came upon that chalcedony which Mistress Summerton had forged, he already understood that aether was running out. And how could he have known that the experiment he organised to reverse that process would go so badly? What would have been gained, if he had shouldered the blame? So he carried on living instead, and the engines slowly failed, and with their failure came the lie, which he must surely have known in his secret heart would eventually be his undoing.

So in a way I miss the old greatgrandmaster who hardly spoke more than a few brief words to me, and who never was the monster I wanted him to be. The true darkmaster never was as simple as a mere human being. I know that now, although I'm sure there was a little of him in Anthony Passington, just as there was in Grandmaster Harrat, and Edward Durry and in my mother and Mistress Summerton and perhaps even Anna—and most certainly in me. *He* still comes to me as well. I see my darkmaster in the reflections I catch mirrored at the edge of my failing sight in the shops along Oxford Road, and in the sunken mask which gazes back at me from my many windows in the long, electric night. And I see him in you as well, Niana, and I see him in the deeds of the guilds and in all the workings of this new Light Age. For the darkmaster was aether, and it was aether which conspired, through the chain of our lives, to remake itself and become fully powerful once again. A spell to make many spells. What, at the end of the day, could be more natural?

The dark-white wyreglow of aether stalks everywhere, Niana. I see it in the dazzle of noonday and I see it in the darkest corners of the night. It prowls my memories, and the shape it most often assumes is Mistress Summerton, and I love her and I hate her for all that she was and wasn't, just as I must love and hate you for being and not being the same.

Dimly, the wind bites through me, although I find I cannot shiver now, not even when Niana lays an impossibly cool hand across my face. Shadows swirl. My sight amazes.

'But what happened,' she asks, 'to poor Mister Snaith?'

I shrug. 'I really don't know. When I last looked for him, he'd already left that warehouse. Some people just fall through the cracks of life . . .'

'Ahhh . . .' Through my skull, her fingers, the breath of the wind. 'You're calling him a person, now . . .'

'Isn't he?'

'Well yes and no and perhaps. I thought he might have turned up later in the tale, in the part that you and I are still living. I thought that he might have made it to that fabled place—to Einfell.'

Einfell. The word sounds different from her. It's still a breath, a spell.

Her fingers draw back, then caress my eyes. 'So. This *is* one last thing you still believe in?'

'Of *course* I do,' I say. 'I took the train there only last Fourshiftday . . .'

II

Einfell.

There it was, the word I'd dreamed of spelled out on the sign of a station in Somerset, and painted on the firebuckets and picked out in white flowers in the little bed beneath. Einfell. But I still half-expected the wooden platform to dissolve. And it was a warm day, Niana; a sunny day quite unlike this one. And there were stoneclad houses along a tufted road, and dust on the hedges, and the sounds and the smells of cattle. Einfell. The birds were singing.

To a signpost, and then another. Of the few other people who had got off the train, one, I realised with the odd awkwardness that comes on such occasions, was heading in exactly the same direction. She was just ahead of me, and seemed oddly familiar in the waddle of her walk, the scarf she'd tied around her grey hair, the stretched and faded polka dots of her dress. A plump body in a sunlit lane, with a face, warmed and reddened, which finally smiled back to me.

'You're going there as well?'

We walked the rest of the way together, talking absently at first about our journey here. She had a large wicker basket propped against her hip which was covered in a gingham

teatowel, and I imagined that it contained food, until the
towel caught on a bramble. Underneath, there were jars and
packages of various proprietary soaps and cleaning fluids.

'What's you name? I hope you don't mind me asking . . .'

'Not at all. I'm Mistress Mather. My husband—well,
he's in there . . .'

As we walked to the gates of Einfell, Mistress Mather
told me of how she and Master Mather had *fallen out,* as
she put it, over her husband's long hours at Brandywood,
Price and Harper, and his obsession with his work. Stupid,
really, but then that's how it is when you're young. She'd
gone to live with her sister in Dudley, and she'd fully expected he'd come for her in a few days, or at least send a
telegraph. But he was a shy man, and he'd thought she'd
meant far more in her leaving than she really had. And
she'd found work, and she became worried after a shifterm
or two about what, if she did go back, the neighbours
would say. Such are the burdens we make, eh? And then,
years after, she heard about St Blate's. But here—well *this*
is different, isn't it . . . ?

'You come to Einfell often?' The phrase still sounded
strange on my lips.

'Often as I can.' We'd reached the gates, and she knew
where the bell was to ring for the porter. 'Me and my sister,
we've moved to Bristol so I can be near him. Not that
things are the way they used to be between me and him, but
life's life and you have to get on with it, don't you?'

I could only agree that you did. Then the gate was
opened, and I was detained whilst Mistress Mather was allowed to waddle up the rhododendron path towards the
sunlit, flatroofed buildings.

'We don't permit anything containing aether in it here,
sir,' I was told, and I assured the porter that I'd brought
nothing that would fit such a description until I read
through the dog-eared cardboard list.

'What about all that cleaning stuff?'

'Mistress Mather knows to read the contents on the
packet.'

Divested of my tieclip, my fountain pen, my pocket
knife and my collar studs, and probably lucky to keep my

shoes and jacket and still to be wearing my cologne, I finally made my way towards the main entrance. There were
trees and parkland. There was a smell of clipped grass. Figures, too distant for me to see in this bright sunlight
whether they were Children of the Age, were wandering.
Through swing doors, I introduced myself to the nurse at
reception and found that I really was expected. There were
many windows along the corridors. The atmosphere was
sunny. The place smelled like an exceptionally clean hotel.

We finally came to a door numbered like all the rest,
and the nurse turned to me.

'You knew her, didn't you?'

I shrugged. 'I used to.'

'I mean in the *past*,' she said in that half-disgusted way
in which people often refer to the last Age nowadays. 'I
wouldn't spend too much time dwelling on it if I were you.
She's not like that. She's a saint, but she gets impatient.
She only likes to look ahead.' The nurse strode off down
the shining corridor, heels clipping.

Breathless and lost, with my heart already pounding, I
thought briefly about knocking, then simply opened the door.

'Ah, Robbie . . .' The sunlight was behind her as she
moved around the desk. She was offering me her hand, and
she was dressed in the same uniform as that nurse. There
were filing cabinets, a calendar, nothing in her office that
wasn't practical. Not even a single pot plant. 'You're
slightly earlier than I'd expected. Otherwise, I'd have . . .'

She was still holding out her hand. It felt rough, warm,
detached. 'This is an impressive place.'

'That's what everyone says.' With the light behind her
from the window, I couldn't see if she was smiling, or quite
how it was that she now did her hair. 'Sit down.' She moved
back to her desk. 'It's a fair journey from London. Can I
get you tea? I think we can manage something to eat.'

'That's all right, thank you. The, ah, station name—it
came as a shock . . .'

'Stupid, isn't it? But it costs a lot of money to run a
place like this. We have an official title, but the local people
don't seem to mind the name, and you sometimes have to
play to people's preconceptions before you can change

them. The art of compromise—it's not something I'm good at, but I've had to get used to it. Did Nurse Walters give you a tour?'

'She brought me straight to see you.'

'Oh? Well, perhaps later.' Anna almost sounded surprised. Was this the first chink in her armour—the sense her employees had gained that I was different from her run-of-the-mill visitors?

'To be honest, I came to see you, Anna. I met this woman on my walk from the station. It's really quite the most extraordinary coincidence—'

'You mean Mistress Mather? You forget, Robbie. It was you who took me to St Blate's'. I made some efforts to put them back in touch. It's worked very well.'

'What does he do here?'

'Just the ordinary things of life—just like all of us. As best he can.'

Nurse Walters had been right about Anna. All my plans, all the things I was going to say and do . . . I reached slowly into my inside pocket and extracted the strip of paper which I had made out yesterday in one of the great banks which inhabit the rebuilt edifice of Goldsmiths' Hall. My hand shook as I placed it on the desk, halfway towards Anna. There was a pause. My eyes had adjusted somewhat to the light which poured in behind her from the grounds and I could now see that she hadn't cut her hair short as I had first imagined. Rather, she'd plaited it up and wound it around in a tight, impatient bun. Strands hung loose. They glimmered silver, and her face reminded me now of her mother's as I had glimpsed it long ago, although Anna was far older now than Kate Durry had been when she died; a vision of how she might have been, if her life had continued, if Anna had been born ordinary, and if she had lived with her parents in that house on Park Road. But her father was an aetherworker and mine was only a toolmaker. By the standards of Bracebridge, there would still have been an impossible distance between us.

'This is . . .' Anna took the cheque and held it close to her eyes, studying the amount. 'Entirely unexpected. And incredibly generous . . .'

I knew that Anna had money of her own, a sort of wealth, even if she'd probably hate the phrase. It came from Mistress Summerton's long occupancy of Redhouse, and her acquisition of rights over that land which, in a landmark legal case which I knew George and Sadie had a large role in swaying, passed on in her estate. Children of the Age are now permitted to own property. And, Anna, officially, had never been anything more than entirely normal in any case. She must have been back to Redhouse, although she had sold every acre, and I wondered as she studied my cheque if I should mention the survival of our fountain. But that was in the past. Anna had a watch pinned to her blouse. Tick. *Tick.* Tick. *Tick* went the sound of its mechanism.

'I thought,' I said, 'that you could do something more useful with it than I could.'

Slowly, Anna laid the cheque back down on the desk. Her hands had that scoured look which comes from being plunged for too long and too often into tubs of washing. 'Perhaps we could. And we're always seeking donations. But this is such a large amount. It's just that . . .' Tick. *Tick.* Tick. *Tick.* 'In my experience, unsolicited gifts always come with strings of some sort attached.'

'It's most of what I have.'

'It's certainly most incredibly generous. Although I rather expect your accounts are re-filling as we speak.'

She was right, but that was hardly the point; I'd give her all of that, as well. I'd give her everything. And outside, the glorious late spring light was sparkling over the trees and across the lawns. These grounds must go on for miles, and there were places in the distance where the copses gathered into deeper pools of forest. It required no imagination, no imagination at all, for me to see Anna moving through them at twilight, and along these corridors, carrying a lamp, trailed by strange and beautiful creatures amid wings of light.

I cleared my throat. 'You know, Anna, Goldenwhite was never really a historical figure. I've paid skilled people to investigate all the records. There certainly were rebellions and outbreaks of war across the first Age, but there was no one figure, there was no one march. The burnt patch of stone in that square in Clerkenwell can only have been there for the last two hundred years. And there's no tomb, and she never gathered her forces before they descended into London from the Kite Hills.'

'Why are you telling me this?' She glanced down at the cheque, her eyes an emerald mist, lined by a life of frowns or smiles and perhaps even a little laughter as well. Perhaps fearing that I might mistake her gesture in leaving it there, her left hand moved back towards it.

Just as she laid her fingers on it, I grabbed her arm.

'I love you, Anna!'

The air fell silent between us. I was still holding her arm. Tick. *Tick.* Tick. *Tick.* My fingers dug against the warm, soft skin, and I waited for something to happen, for her to repulse me or come forward—for the world to change.

'Do I need to call for someone to help me?' she finally asked.

'No.' I let go, sat back. My heart was hammering. Against my fingers, I could still feel the shape of her bones.

She sighed and rubbed her arm. 'I thought perhaps it might come to this.'

I looked at her. *I love you.* I was still thinking it, screaming it out from my head.

'I'm not what I was, Robbie. Look . . .' Again, but more cautiously this time, she held out her left arm. It was still reddened by the marks of my fingers, but beneath, on her wrist, there was the stigmata, the scab, the Mark. 'I don't have to make this happen now. This is how I am—the thing just won't go away. I'm ordinary. I would say I'm like you, Robbie, but I don't think that ordinary's what you ever were. It must have been that last night at Walcote House, touching that haft and sending out the message. It used up most of whatever was in me . . . And the rest has been going ever since. And to be frank, I'm glad. Who wouldn't be?'

'But that means—'

'It doesn't *mean* anything other than what you see here. It doesn't mean that I can love. The only person I ever loved was Missy, and that's all gone. Of course, I sometimes

watch the couples who come to our station and walk these
lanes on Noshiftday—they think it's romantic because of
that damn name. But that wasn't me. That never was. Or is.
I'm sorry if I can't make this any plainer. Of course, and
contrary to what Nurse Walters might have told you, I do
think about the past. But I try not to make a meal of it.'

Make a meal of it. Would the Anna of old have said
something so mundane? But I didn't know. I never really
did know. 'The children of the Easterlies chant about
Missy when they're skipping,' I said instead. 'Although it's
something about her being *here* and *near* and wanting to
suck their bones. D'you think she'd mind?'

I could see her clearly now, my Anna, Annalise, with the
sunlight all around her. *I love you, Anna.* But she didn't
hear. She simply smiled. 'Not that much. And it's not such
a bad thing is it, to be in the minds of children?'

I smiled back at her.

*And I've thought what I might do, Anna. I've planned it
for so long, far better and more thoroughly than this foolish
gesture of giving you my wealth. I've opened an aether vial
and poured it into a silver cup and stared at it through all
the night's long hours and willed myself . . . I love you,
Anna. I love you as much as I could ever love anything or
anyone. But perhaps that's not enough . . .*

'Things aren't so bad,' I heard her saying. 'I mean, look
at you. Look at this Age. And here, at what's happened to
me. This loss of what I was, it's a beacon to the future. It
means that a lot of the physical processes which cause people to change can perhaps be reversed. It's something we're
studying. That's why we have that total ban on aether.'

*They'll make a statue of you when you die, Anna, for
what you've done here at Einfell, and for what you did to
create this Age. And you'll hate it.*

'Don't the new guilds sometimes ask . . . ?'

'We always refuse. No more of those dreadful dark
green vans, eh? Oh, I know there are still wraiths and wan-
derers out there. There probably always will be.'

'There's a Child of this Age lives on that bridge they
never finished down on Ropewalk Reach past the wastetips
in the Easterlies.'

'She'll be scavenging for aether, which is the worst possible thing. Or people like you will bring her the stuff for the few tricks she can probably play.'

'Or money.'

'Well, that's almost as bad. But we're an open house here at Einfell. You should tell Niana that, next time you see her. We'll accept anyone, and we let them leave again if that's what they wish. Like the—' Only the slightest of hesitations. 'Edward Durry. He sometimes comes and goes.'

'You called her *Niana,* Anna. You must have—'

'I've *heard* of her, that's all, Robbie. I don't need to read your mind to know what you're thinking. I never have. It's always been there on your face. And there are tales and rumours, just as always, in this Age of Light. I simply make it my business to listen to them, distasteful though they often are, and to winnow out the truth.'

Winnow. The thought sends me tumbling back. The scent of cornfields. Snowlight streaking across a window. My hand cupping Anna's cheek. Einfell. I know now. It was then, it was there.

She stood up. 'And I'm sorry. I truly am . . .' This time, she didn't hold out her hand. I stood up as well. Sere and plainer and more beautiful than any magic, daylight flowered around her.

'Well . . . Goodbye.'

And the door was in front of me. Almost, it seemed to open of its own accord.

'Oh, Robbie?'

Quickly, I turned. 'Yes?'

'This cheque—I assume it's still all right for us to keep it? I mean, we do need the money.'

'Of course. Keep it all.'

And I was in the corridor. The door had closed.

III

Niana is more remote from me now.

'So,' she preens, minces, curls, snarls, becoming more and more of the thing she thinks I want her to be. 'The famous Anna Winters has heard of me and disapproves. She'd have me in sickroom cell learning my vowels and clauses and how not to scare people.'

'She's not like that, Niana.'

The night of this ruined bridge presses down on us. For once, Niana has no reply.

'People can be so uncaring, can't they?' she mutters eventually.

'Yes. And they can be so kind.'

'And there's the greatest mystery of all.'

We fall silent again, shocked by how much we suddenly have in common.

'Well, grandmaster. You can't stay forever.'

'No . . .' My bones ache as I stand up, and the boards of this rough nest sway and sparkle as they slope away from me. But I still don't want to go home, even if I could ever find such a place.

'Tell you what, grandmaster.' Once more, Niana sweeps down to rummage in one of her teachests. 'Let me give you this. Oh—don't say no. Just a little. I think you of all people know what to do with it.'

Money. Real money. Several notes which would probably buy an aether vial.

'But not that.' She almost takes it back from me.

And I'm moving out across the stanchions and walkways which have grown oily with London mist. The foetid river. Then the wastetips, their buried stink clouding the night. Soon, I reach the dim lights of the Easterlies. The sounds of dogs and babies. The reek of herring. Caris Yard is empty, and the old pump now bears a warning sign about its potability, although I bury my face in its musty gush and drink and drink from it, and then look around. But there's nothing, nobody. Just the same old buildings, dense as ever with hope and hopelessness. I walk on. Through Ashington, and the tall flesh-coloured buildings which the new great grandmaster's dreams once created, which are graffitied now, and reek of refuse and piss. Doxy Street is brighter, busier, but then it always was. Along Cheapside, past Clerkenwell, the grinding tramtracks dissolve. A new tram flashes by, an incandescent dream trailing sparks from the antennae on its roof. The gaslights have gone here as well. The air has a sharper, different feel, and I stop and my breath halts in my throat when I see a shadow stretch before me, sharp and sweet as the ache of a pulled knife. But it's only my own image cast down across these pavements by these new lampposts with their flaring lights. *Electricity, Robert! It's the way of the future!* And he was right. It is. But all I see are ghosts.

Then the final turn which leads me to the place to which it seems I've always been heading. To the house at the end of the cul-de-sac with its dark clouds of privet still in the same need of trimming as they were all those years ago. There are a couple of carriages and a car parked outside, but the place seems scarcely lit. My shadow sweeps over the door and I bang long and hard until I get a reply.

'We're closed. It's . . .' A young face peers through the crack in the chained door. But she takes in who and what I am, and cranks back the bolts. Yawning in a sliding dressing gown, she leads me up far more stairs than there ever used to be to the final room on the top floor.

'Master Robert...' By slow increments, Marm gets
herself up from the divan by the window and stoops towards me. From her, the loss of the *grand* part of my title
is a blessed relief. It takes me back, and I love the sour buttery scent of her old woman's flesh as she leans against me,
and the bitter tang of smoke which lies beyond. She's taken
to wearing a curly wig now, over what remains of her hair,
and her hands, as I ease myself from her and settle into my
accustomed chair, are even more bulged and arthritic than
those of the son who never visits her. Yet still she manages
to maintain a semblance of a guildswoman's grace as she
shambles across the rucked carpet and flicks open the
catches of her marquetry cabinet with her brown nails and
extracts the seeds and boxes. She and I, we're like two elderly actors reprising the characters which we once did so
much better in another Age. But they're the only roles we
have left to play.

'It's been such a long time since I've seen you. Why
downstairs, they've almost forgotten your name...'

I settle back into the straps and cushions as the small
pot bubbles and the blue flame glows, soothed as I always
am by her croaky patter, which never changes, and is designed to make me imagine I come here far less often than
I do, or should. Then the glow of aether and the hatpin's
swirl. I could do all this myself, but I never would. I love
being here too much, and her presence, and the flood of an-
ticipatory saliva and the thickening of my tongue which
comes with that first glowing waft of smoke. Her guild, at
least, hasn't changed. It never will. Ages might crumble,
heroes die, the greatest love might fade, and we could remain forever in this room. But then, even as she wrinkles
her mouth around the long pipe, there's the final and most
important exchange. I reach into my pockets. I give her the
money, Niana. All of it. Marm lifts it to her face and inhales the crumpled flower of notes before she stuffs it into
her special jar. And she smiles.

'You're most generous tonight, Master Robert. We'll
have to see what we can do. Where we can take you to
that's special...'

'But you already know.'

'Yes.' She studies me, her face quivering, her eyes dulled and alight. 'I suppose I do.'

Then, finally, finally, she puts the pipe back to her lips and inhales the glowing spell, and then leans forward, one arm trembling to support the weight of the other until she can place her dry lips against mine. She kisses me. And I kiss her. I breathe in. And I'm flying. Floating.

The Ages drop away until the time and the place which will always be more real to me than any other swarms back into view. I'm sitting on a small train heading on a single track line out of Bracebridge on a day at the last edge of summer, and my mother smiles back at me as the great hills slide by beyond the rippled glass and we rock to and fro. Rainharrow, then Scarside, Fareden and Hallowfell. I know we only have tickets for some obscure local station, but in my mind we're leaving Bracebridge forever, heading together into incredible adventures which will take us to the deeper truth on which I have always felt my life to be teetering.

I still don't know what that truth is, but I'm sure that, when I find it, it will be marvellous.